LOVE

OVER

BOARD

by Kandi Steiner

Arndell

Also by Kandi Steiner

A Love Letter to Whiskey

Love of the Game Series
The Wrong Game
The Right Player

LOVE OVERBOARD

KANDI STEINER

Arndell

LOVE OVERBOARD

Copyright © Kandi Steiner

Published by Arndell, an imprint of Keeperton 2025

Dharawal Country, 1 / 18 Manning Street, Kiama, NSW, Australia, 2533

10 9 8 7 6 5 4 3 2 1

ISBN: 978-1-923232-10-5 Paperback

The moral right of the author has been asserted

Edited by Elaine York / Allusion Publishing

Formatted by Books and Moods

Cover Design by Bailey McGinn

Printed and bound by CPI Group (UK) Ltd, Croydon, CR0 4YY

Sydney | Washington D.C. | London

www.keeperton.com

I dedicate this book to the angst lovers,
the ones who understand that love doesn't always play by the rules,
who cherish the feeling of a knot in the throat and twist in the gut,
who trust me to take them on a bit of a painful journey
knowing I'll always put their shattered hearts back together.
You are the reason I'm here and able to write what I love to write.
Thank you.

Prologue

He loved lying with me almost as much as he loved lying to me.

It was a harsh truth, one that pierced like a knife between the ribs as I walked the empty shoreline of Kontokali Beach, a half-empty bottle of white wine in hand and mascara-stained tears drying on my cheeks.

Less than twenty-four hours ago, I couldn't imagine a life without him.

Now, I had no choice.

I collapsed onto the beach, flopping down in a heap without a care in the world that the water was now soaking my lower half with each wave that washed upon the shoreline. My ribs tightened around my already struggling lungs as I stared at my feet in the sand. I dug my toes in deep after each wave only to have the water wash away any attempt at hiding them.

All the promises we made in the hours where night kisses morning were broken now, the shattered pieces blowing away with every rush of the salty breeze.

"*I want you,*" he'd whispered against my neck that first time we touched, both of us shaking, panting, yearning.

"*I need you,*" he'd groaned into my mouth the night he told me about his dreams, the night he let me see what drove him and realized I wasn't laughing.

"*I love you,*" he'd confessed, unwillingly, his forehead against mine on this very beach, brows furrowed like the words pained him as much as they freed him.

Now, all those words were being washed away like the grains of sand around my toes, replaced by the truth that always existed beneath them.

We're nothing. We never were. We never could be.

Four months.

That's how long it took for me to fall in love with him.

Four minutes.

That's how long it took for him to wreck my whole world.

Chapter One

TWO YEARS LATER

POST-PRODUCTION CONFESSIONAL
CLOSE QUARTERS

SEASON 4

EMBER REED: CHIEF STEW

PRODUCER
Alright, Ember. Ready to get started?

EMBER
As ready as I'll be.

PRODUCER
You can relax. We promise – nothing to be nervous about.

Ember laughs softly.

EMBER
If you say so.

PRODUCER
We have the talking heads footage we captured on the boat, but now that you don't have guests to tend to, we hope to dig a little deeper. We're just going to go through and remind you of some of the things that happened this season, get your reaction and thoughts. These interviews will help tell the audience what you were feeling in that moment. You can start over as many times as you need to, and we just ask that you answer the question in a complete statement. For

example, "I was upset when the guests didn't tip us well, considering the hell they put us through." Make sense?

Ember gives a thumbs up.

PRODUCER
Great. To start, we'll just have you tell us who you are, your experience in yachting, and what you wanted when you agreed to this season – any goals you had. And just look at us when you answer, not the camera.

EMBER
I'm Ember Reed. I—

PRODUCER
Big smile! Remember, this is going to be the viewers' first impression of you.

Ember pauses, drinks water, resettles in with a beaming smile.

EMBER
I'm Ember Reed. I'm twenty-six years old and I'm from Fort Lauderdale, Florida. I've been a yacht stewardess for four years now and this is my first time as chief stew.

PRODUCER
Why don't you elaborate on that, tell us how excited you are.

Ember's smile wanes. She drinks water, exhales, smiles again.

EMBER
Being chief stew has been my dream for years. This is the opportunity I have been waiting for; so, when Captain Gary called me up and offered me the gig, I was over the moon. I'm so excited to finally show I have what it takes to run an interior team.

PRODUCER
And what's the main role of chief stew? Why are you so excited to have this opportunity?

EMBER

Working as a second and third stew for years now, I
know everything it takes to make the interior team
sparkle. It's not just serving the guests; though,
that is the number one priority. It's laundry and
cabins; it's table décor and pulling off perfectly
themed parties; it's booking local dancers for
entertainment. There's so much that goes into every
second a guest is on board. The goal is to make them
feel like it's a six-star experience without them
even noticing how hard we have to work to make that
happen. As for why I want this opportunity…

Ember shrugs.

EMBER
This is my chance to prove myself and open doors to
the career I've always wanted.

PRODUCER
Prove yourself to who… your father, perhaps?

Ember pauses, nods.

EMBER
Sure, that's always been a goal of mine. But it's
about proving to myself that I can do this, too. When
you're chief stew, you're the boss. I want to manage
a team. I want to create the best guest experiences
this show has ever seen. And, in the end, I want to
use this experience to get me where I want to be – a
purser on a private yacht.

PRODUCER
Wonderful, Ember. Okay… let's jump into the first
episode.

EMBER
Let's do it.

PRODUCER
What were you feeling as you walked up to Sinking Sun
for the first time?

EMBER
When I see Sinking Sun for the first time, all I
can think is how excited I am. There's something so

exhilarating about the start of a new season — all fresh with possibilities. The sun is shining, the breeze is cool and pleasant, and I have eight weeks of fun to look forward to. I mean… we're in freaking Italy. It's gorgeous here. I know it'll be hard work, sure — but yachting is a blast. It's why I chose it as my career. Well, that and the money, of course.

PRODUCER
How did it feel to be reconnected with Captain Gary?

EMBER
Walking onto the boat and finding Captain Gary in the bridge makes my heart soar. He's by far my favorite captain I've worked with. He's just so goofy and fun while also being stern enough to run a tight ship. I'm ecstatic to show him my chops as chief stew. This is my opportunity to solidify my new role, and I'm ready to take it.

PRODUCER
And how did you feel when Finn showed up?

Ember swallows, drinks water, smiles weakly.

EMBER
I don't suppose there's a next question option.

PRODUCER
Take your time.

EMBER
I never thought I'd see Finn Pearson again.

Long pause. Ember shifts in her chair, stares at shoes, lifts gaze back to producer.

EMBER
And I think we all know how I felt about it, don't you?

It was the worst-timed wedgie of my life.

Not only was it as hot as Satan's armpit, making sweat slide down my spine and into that lovely place where my underwear had decided to get real cozy with my backside, but I was also surrounded by cameras.

Therefore, there was no picking of this wedgie. I had no choice but to plaster on a smile and endure it.

One camera captured my profile at a distance, the man holding the behemoth of equipment following my every step. Another was down the dock at the foot of the gangway that led to the yacht I'd call home for the next eight weeks. Even though that lens was twenty yards away at the moment, I knew it was zoomed in, knew it was likely capturing every bead of sweat collecting at my hairline.

This was *Close Quarters*, after all — a reality TV show about the people just crazy enough to work the long, manic hours required to run charter yachts.

I'd heard of the show before they asked me to be on it, but I'd never watched a single episode — partly because I didn't really have time to watch television, and partly because I had a feeling it would piss me off at the way it misrepresented my career. But before I would agree to their offer, I knew I needed to watch at least one season of the show.

And that was all it took for me to know I was right.

The yachting seasons they showed on *Close Quarters* were shorter than what a crew would usually work, and each member was hand-picked by producers with the intention of stirring the pot once everyone was on board. It was common for the stars of the show to have worked together in the past, to have some previous drama from other seasons, or to be the complete opposite of one another in a way that would drive them mad. There were stewardesses with zero experience, green deck hands who did more damage than assisting when docking, and chefs with tempers and a short fuse.

These people typically had three things in common: they were young, hot, and willing to play right into the hands of whatever producer was pulling their puppet strings.

It was all drama, from the guests who came on board to the crew nights out — which, I knew now that I'd signed a contract, were a requirement. You *had* to go out if you agreed to be on this show, whether you wanted to or not. The only exception was if you were ill.

So, yeah — I knew that lens was zoomed in on me.

And I swore I felt the breeze whispering to me that I'd made a mistake.

I smiled wide despite that feeling, shaking it off and squinting even through the dark frames of my sunglasses as I took in the impossibly blue water of the Gulf of Naples. There was nothing like this feeling, the possibility and excitement of a new season in a beautiful part of the world most were never lucky enough to see in real life. Even with the unfamiliarity of the show aspect, I was still thrilled.

Nine charters of hard work lay ahead of me — but those weeks would also be the kind of chaotic fun that only comes with living the life of a yachtie.

We worked around the clock, catering to charter guests who paid six figures for just a few days on our boat. From the moment they stepped on board, we tended to their every need, giving them a luxury vacation experience while also keeping the boat pristine and functional.

The days were long, the nights never-ending, and yet we still found the energy to party whenever we had a day off.

I was born for it.

My father would hate to hear me say that. He was never afraid to let me know when he hated a choice I'd made, either. I knew all those years he pushed me to perfection, he imagined me becoming a doctor or engineer or lawyer or hedge fund manager.

The last thing he expected was for me to long to travel the world, to work in hospitality, to wait on other people the way we always had people waiting on our family when we vacationed.

He didn't understand this lifestyle I'd chosen. I knew he wasn't proud.

But this felt like my chance to show him why he should be.

I wondered if my mother had talked to him at all, if she'd tried to make him see the value in my career choice. I'd wager not, if I were a betting woman. My mom was kind and loving, the kind of nurturer any kid would be lucky to grow up with.

But she was also passive and agreeable to any and everything my father said.

At least, at the end of the day, I knew I could count on her to be waiting with a hug and some words of encouragement instead of a lecture.

I walked along a line of beautiful boats until I was looking up at the *Sinking Sun* — fifty-five meters of floating luxury.

And the first superyacht I'd be running as chief stew.

Excitement fluttered through me like a thousand freshly hatched butterflies, and I did my best to do as the producers had told me and ignore the cameras — and my wedgie — as I kicked off my sandals and carefully carried my suitcase across the passerelle.

It felt like coming home each time my bare feet hit the teak wood of a superyacht. And yet, as familiar as it was, this season was entirely different.

It was much shorter, for one — just a mere two months as opposed to the typical three-to-four months I'd worked on other yachts. I was also back in the Med after spending the last two years in the Bahamas, which was much more laid-back. Plus, the clients coming aboard were more high profile than I was used to, the kind of people I knew would put us through hell just for fun.

The biggest difference, obviously, was that every second of it was being filmed.

It was hard to forget that fact with the cameras surrounding me as I made my way past the main salon and down the stairs until I hit the crew quarters. The producers told me I'd be the first on board, the first to be introduced on the show after our captain, but it still felt strange. I was so used to arriving for the season with the chief stew already there and waiting for me, room assignment and plan of attack in hand.

This time, it would be *me* assigning the rooms and making the plans.

A smile bloomed on my lips at the thought as I took a quick peek around the crew quarters. As usual, they were cramped but functional — a space designed for necessity, not comfort. The small, galley-style kitchen was tucked into one corner, its stainless-steel counters gleaming under the harsh fluorescent lighting. A compact fridge hummed quietly beside a microwave that had likely reheated more instant noodles and late-night leftovers than actual meals.

A couple of well-worn tables filled the center of the room, surrounded by cushioned benches that had been patched up with duct tape. This was where the crew would shove our faces with whatever scraps the chef left for us, usually eaten in passing — quick bites grabbed between shifts, conversations cut short by radio calls crackling in our earpieces.

But these tables weren't just for rushed meals. They were the heart of our off-hours, the place where we gathered after long days, kicking back with stolen bottles of beer, trading war stories, and dissolving into fits of laughter that we tried to keep quiet enough not to wake the captain.

The crew mess was typically, like its namesake, messy — but it was ours.

I squeezed past a cameraman to assess the cabins next, noting that there were also cameras fixed in every corner of every room. They weren't kidding around when they said *everything* would be filmed.

The cabins were actually quite nice for a yacht this size, with built-in storage and just enough space to move without feeling completely claustrophobic. But the beds were still small, the mattresses thin enough to remind you this wasn't exactly luxury living, and the top bunk far too close to the ceiling. I knew from experience how easy it was to forget that fact and bang your head in the middle of the night or roll over too fast and nearly fling yourself off the side.

I dropped my luggage in the cabin I decided would be mine — claiming the bottom bunk, of course — before I bounded up the stairs and made my way to the bridge. It usually took me a few days to get the layout of a new boat, but the producers had provided all of us with a floor plan of *Sinking Sun*, and I'd be lying if I said I didn't study it like it was the key to the biggest test of my life.

From the hot tub on the sundeck to the crew mess in the bowels of the boat, I knew *Sinking Sun* like I'd already spent a full season aboard. The sundeck boasted loungers, a bar, and the all-important Jacuzzi for late-night drunk confessions and mid-day sunbathing. Below that, the bridge deck held the sky lounge and alfresco dining area — perfect for sunset cocktails. The main deck was all luxury, from the formal salon and dining room to the primary guest cabins, and of course, the galley. Beneath that, on the lower deck, were more guest cabins, storage, the laundry room, and crew quarters — where privacy was a luxury, and bunks were barely wide enough to turn over in. And all the way at the bottom, accessible only through a near-secret set of stairs, was the tender garage that doubled as a beach club, complete with a fold-down swim platform and lockers stocked with snorkels, floaties, and the dreaded gargantuan inflatable slide.

I had every inch mapped in my head before I stepped foot on board.

If this was my one and only shot to prove I was meant for this role, for this career? I was going to grab every opportunity to go above and beyond my duties.

"Trouble aboard," I called out with a rap of my knuckles on the open bridge door, smiling at the familiar bald head of our captain, Gary Parks. He whipped around, beaming at me with that toothy grin of his that was now framed by a neatly trimmed white beard. The man had tan, weathered skin from his earlobes to his toes, proof of his many years in the sun.

"Uh-oh, sound the alarm," he teased in his thick Australian accent, and then his arms were open for a hug that felt like the one a father would give his daughter.

Not that I'd know. My dad didn't do hugs — or feelings of any kind, for that matter. He was a man of few words, divvying out praise only when I did something to deserve it.

Which wasn't often.

"It's good to see you, Cap," I said when he released me.

"Great to see you, Ember." I always smiled at how my name sounded when he said it, the *R* disappearing altogether. *Em-bah.* "Ready for your first season as chief stew?"

"Come on, now. You know I've been ready for years."

He chuckled. "I do, indeed. This has been a long time coming. I'm keen to see you smash it." He glanced at his watch. "The rest of the crew should be trickling in soon. Why don't you go sort the crew mess and get started on provisions? We'll have a team chat once everyone's aboard."

I saluted him with a smirk. "On it, Cap."

"And Ember?"

"Mm?"

"Maybe don't order all the lobster in Italy this time around, yeah?"

Biting back a smile at the memory of our first charter together years ago when I'd accidentally ordered twenty cases of lobster instead of two, I gave him a thumbs up. Those closest to me knew a thumbs up was my version of flipping the bird, and the gesture earned me a hearty laugh that followed me all the way back down the stairs to the crew quarters.

After that, I fell into a steady rhythm, a familiar one that left me smiling and singing to myself as I ticked through my mental checklist. Sure, this was my first time *officially* working as chief stew, but I'd had enough experience that it felt like the job had been mine for years. From stepping up when other chiefs got sick to flying five hours to finish a season after one got let go, I had been thrown into the fire plenty of times.

And like a phoenix, I thrived in those flames. I rose from the ashes even better than before.

It was a product of my upbringing, the way this career suited me so well. Busy was my natural state of being. By the time I was five, my parents had thrown me into everything from swim lessons and soccer to piano lessons and Spanish as a second language. The praise my father gave me for achieving only encouraged me to continue to pack my schedule all the way through college. If I wasn't juggling at least a half-dozen clubs, extracurricular activities, sports and a job — I was bored.

I didn't know how to sit still for longer than what was absolutely necessary to get a decent amount of sleep to keep going.

And when it came to hard work, not only was I not afraid of it — I *craved* it. Nothing lit me up like kicking my own ass for days and hearing an *atta girl* at the end of it all.

It was how my father raised me to be. *Nothing in life comes easy*, he always told me. *You have to work hard for what you want.* With him, there was never a consolation prize. You were either the best or you had better keep trying. That was just one of the reasons I wanted to excel in this first season as chief stew. This was the highest position of the interior on a boat this size. That meant to be chief, you had to be the best. This was my chance to prove to him that what I did mattered, that it was a hard job with reward and recognition you had to earn.

What I lacked in affection for my father, I made up for with respect.

The man had always provided for me. He may not have been there when I had my heart broken or when I was crying in bed after a hard day, but he was a constant reminder that life kept going, that the effort I put into it was the one thing I could control.

And control I did.

In that moment of my life, standing in the crew quarters of

a new boat at the start of a new season, I felt a monumental shift.

On camera, all a viewer would see was me on the phone with the provisioner barking out a list of everything we needed for the first charter. They'd see my golden hair pulled up into a loose ponytail, one hand scribbling in my notebook while the other checked items off on the laptop. They'd see a young, smiling, ambitious girl eager to start in a new role.

But on the inside, a storm brewed.

Lightning sizzled in every nerve, thunder crackling down my spine with every checkmark I made. I catalogued those sensations as excitement, as opportunity, as a new beginning. In my heart of hearts, I believed it was one of those moments that tattooed itself onto your very soul when it happened, the kind you always knew you'd reflect on as *that time when everything changed*.

Now, looking back, I know better.

I know it had nothing to do with the season or the cameras or my new role at all.

It was just my body reacting before my brain could at the proximity of *him* — like it always had.

"Well now... would you look who it is."

The voice splintered my joy like a bolt of lightning to a frail, unsteady tree. I stopped mid-sentence where I was planning the schedules for my stews, pen hovering above the page in a hand that felt foreign, a hand that was already shaking.

I swallowed, looking up even when it took all my effort to do so, my heart kicking back to life from where it had halted in my chest.

And there he was.

Finn Fucking Pearson.

"Hello, Firefly."

Chapter Two

PRE-PRODUCTION CONFESSIONAL
CLOSE QUARTERS

SEASON 4

FINN PEARSON: HEAD CHEF

PRODUCER
Tell us a little about yourself.

FINN
I'm Finn Pearson. I'm twenty-eight years old from
Dublin, Ireland, and I'm a chef.

PRODUCER
Can you expand on that? Tell us a little about your
experience.

FINN
Ever since I was a kid, cooking has been my love
language. In fact, I don't think there's a better
way to show you love someone than by cooking for
them. When I graduated secondary school, I boarded
the first flight to the Netherlands to enroll in a
culinary arts program. From there, I found myself in
Switzerland, Italy, France… I was just traveling and
soaking up every bit of knowledge I could from some
of the best chefs in the world. One day, I got a job
offer for a yacht in the Mediterranean. It's damn
hard being a yacht chef. You're the only one in the
kitchen, for starters, which means you do it all —

the planning, the food prep, the cooking, and most of
the cleanup, too. But feck, it's fun - can I curse?

PRODUCER
It will be censored, but yes.

FINN
It's fecking fun, being on a boat in an exotic corner
of the world. The hours are long, but the money is
deadly. I was hooked from the first charter.

PRODUCER
You've taken a break from yachting for a couple of
years, is that correct? This will be your first
season in a while?

Finn drinks water, adjusts in seat.

FINN
That's correct.

PRODUCER
What were you doing in the time you took off?

Finn laughs.

FINN
Doing what every idiotic, dream-delusional chef does,
of course - trying to open me own restaurant.

PRODUCER
What made you come back to yachting?

Long pause. Finn cracks his neck, smiles.

FINN
Masochism, I suppose.

Blink.

I needed to blink.

I needed to blink, to smile, to fucking *breathe*.

I was all too aware of the cameras trained on us, trained on
me as Finn waited for me to respond. But the nickname I never

thought I'd hear again had sent an unwelcome warmth down my spine that had apparently seared my nerves and rendered me immobile.

This can't be happening.

He can't be real.

But he was. I knew it even as my brain tried to convince me otherwise. No defense mechanism was going to save me from the reality that Finn Pearson was in the crew quarters with me.

Two years had aged him, but only in ways that made him somehow even more attractive than he was the first time I met him in Greece. We'd worked the same charter there together for four months.

They'd been some of the happiest months of my life.

Until the memory of them became a repetitive heartbreak.

Finn and I had said goodbye at the end of the charter, and it wasn't a pretty goodbye.

His boyish eyes were older now, more mature, the edges of them crinkling a bit as he threw that signature smirk of his at me.

God, how that smile made me weak. Even still. Even after he left me broken on the floor.

My knees buckled as I grappled, reaching through the depths of my emotions for anger but coming up blank. It seemed I was going to settle firmly with shock and disbelief, instead.

I found safety in cataloguing all the ways he'd changed, so I let myself focus on that while my brain scrambled to catch up and make words again.

His chestnut brown hair was longer than the last time I'd seen him, the locks messy and curling a bit over the edges of his ears. It somehow looked styled and like he'd just rolled out of bed all at once. I finally managed to blink, but with that came a flash of a memory long ago — my fingers tangled in that hair, gripping, pulling...

Stubble lined his jaw and upper lip, framing his stupidly perfect heart-shaped face. There were shocks of white in that dark beard that should have been reserved for a man twice his age. That somehow made him hotter.

The bastard.

And amid all that dark hair, sitting right above that cocky tilt of his lips were the eyes that had once been my downfall.

They were the color of the sea; green and blue with flecks of gold.

And they were just as dangerous as the waves they emulated.

"Finn," I finally said, though it was more of a breath of disbelief than a name.

The sound of his name from my lips made the corner of his quirk higher.

"What—" I cleared my throat, turning my attention back to the provisions list on my laptop screen. *Was I really about to ask what he was doing here? It was pretty damn obvious, wasn't it?*

He was here for the season, for the show — just like I was.

Suddenly, I wanted to throttle the producers I had thought were so cute and pleasant, their smiles all wide and beaming every time I spoke to them.

Little weasels knew exactly what they were doing.

"It's been a while," I finally said instead, hoping my smile looked at least twenty percent less forced than it felt as I glanced at him and then back at my screen. "How have you been?"

Finn sort of chuckled, taking a step toward me before adjusting the duffle bag on his shoulder. He was dressed in white shorts and a sky-blue button-up tucked into one side, the sleeves of it shoved up to his elbows and a brown belt hugging his hips. He looked more like he was paying for a charter than like he was about to work one.

"So formal," he mused, and his hand inched forward, up — as if he were about to tuck the rogue strands of my hair that had fallen out of my ponytail behind my ear the way he used to. Instead, he shoved that hand into his pocket and nodded his chin toward my left ear. "Those are new."

I let my fingers ghost over the dainty jewelry that had caught his eye, the industrial and tragus piercings I'd had done just weeks after the last time I'd seen him. My neck heated when I remembered that he knew better than anyone that piercings and micro tattoos were my way of avoiding, of giving myself another softer form of pain to focus on when my heart was splitting in two.

"I like them," he said when I stayed silent.

The way my chest ached in that moment had me ready to double over, and I nearly did when my eyes met his again, when I saw his smile slip. There were a million words left unsaid flashing in those green irises, like ghosts trapped in glass and begging to escape.

He swallowed, his brows folding together and lips parting like he was ready to set them free. Before he could, what sounded like a herd of horses barreled down the stairs behind him.

"Ah, so this is where they hide all the beautiful people!"

Finn flinched as a large hand clamped down on his shoulder and squeezed, shaking him a bit from behind. That hand was attached to a very tan, very muscular arm — and a man with a smile so bright it was blinding.

He had long, dark blond hair with streaks that the sun had

turned a brassy gold, and where Finn was sharp and put together, this kid wore a t-shirt that had been ripped into a tank top, the arm holes of it gaping so much his entire rib cage was visible beneath it. That "shirt," if you could call it that, was paired with board shorts that looked so worn they were practically see through.

"I'm Elijah," he said, still grinning ear to ear as he took his hand off Finn's shoulder and held it out to shake his hand and then mine. "But you can call me Eli."

"Hi, Eli," I beamed right back, thankful for the distraction from the man standing next to him. "I'm Ember."

"Finn." Finn introduced himself.

"Right on. You the bosun?" Eli asked.

"Chef."

"Cheffy!" Eli grabbed his shoulders and shook them cheerily. "You'll be my favorite member of the crew, then." He patted his belly as if he had a big gut. In reality, it was a stone wall of ridiculous muscle. "Eli loves to eat."

I smirked at his reference to himself in the third person. I liked this kid already.

"I'm a deckhand, by the way. This is my first boat of this size, though. I fear I'm a bit green. And you?" he asked me next.

"Chief Stew."

My chest swelled with pride at that title and introduction, and I swore I felt Finn's eyes boring into the side of my head when I said it. He knew how much I'd wanted this, how long I'd worked for it...

How I'd chosen it over everything.

"Of course, you are." Eli saluted me with mock seriousness before picking up the bag he'd slung off when he'd barreled into the crew mess. "American?"

I nodded.

"Irish," he said, dragging his finger to Finn.

"Indeed."

"South African," Eli added, pointing to himself. "With captain up in the bridge, we've got half the world here."

He was so smiley and goofy it was hard not to smile right back, and I knew without a doubt he would be the biggest partier of the crew.

He'd probably also be the biggest flirt.

I didn't mind that, either.

"Right," he said, nodding his chin toward me. "Where should I set up, Queen Ember?"

Yep — I officially wanted to kiss that giant, muscular, smiley sonofabitch, because now I had something to focus on other than the anxiety bubbling in my stomach over the fact that the producers had surprised me with my ex on board.

"I've got you down here," I said, pointing to my right. "Back starboard cabin. You'll be with one of the other deck hands."

"Lekker," Eli said, and then he saluted me with a wink as he passed.

"You're down that way, too," I told Finn, muttering a curse word internally when I saw his name on my clipboard. How had I not put the pieces together? Probably because there were plenty of men in the world named Finn, and I certainly never expected to ever be reunited with *this* particular one.

Especially on a yacht — since he was supposed to be in Dublin running his own restaurant.

That gave me pause, stomach somersaulting as I wondered what happened to that dream of his.

It was that dream that had sent us crashing into the cold hard Earth two years ago.

Because he'd neglected to tell me about it until we were leaving, until I assumed we'd be leaving *together* and found out I was woefully wrong. I would be continuing my career in yachting while he went back to Dublin to open his own restaurant. Part of me wanted to go with him, but unless I wanted to get into sailing, there was no yacht season in the Irish Sea. Besides, Dublin was cold and wet. It wasn't for me.

No matter how much I thought Finn was.

I wondered how he'd ended up back in this world.

Did he want to be here, or was he here out of necessity?

I resisted the urge to look at him, knowing I couldn't get those answers just by staring into his eyes, and I definitely wasn't ready to ask the questions out loud. I kept my focus on the task at hand, picking up my phone to text a few additions to the provisioner and ignoring the way my body heated and raised to full alert as Finn squeezed past me and made his way back to his room.

Time passed quickly after that, the afternoon a blur of cleaning, prepping the boat, unloading provisions, and welcoming each new crew member as they came on board. My stews were the first to arrive, Leah and Bernard, both young and eager and, of course, attractive. I wondered if that was a stipulation for the show — to be hot. Leah was a pale, voluptuous, and perky blonde from Alabama with the kind of smile that dazzled like diamonds, and Bernard was a chiseled, cheeky Brit with warm brown skin and charisma in spades.

Palmer was the bosun, a biracial god-like creature from South Florida with short, black, curly hair and a physique so lean I was surprised to witness him lifting heavy provision boxes full of wine like they were nothing.

The second deckhand I met was Cameron, a Scottish dreamboat with dark ginger hair and freckles like constellations from his cheeks to his calves.

And finally, as I was inspecting where all the silverware and dishes were stored on the boat, our last crew member came aboard: a deck stew named Gisella.

"Hi!" I greeted as she made her way through the main salon, her wide brown eyes taking in the scenery.

She was gorgeous, the kind of beauty you saw on magazines and television screens. Her long, rich brown hair was pin straight and shining like silk, her skin a tawny brown, and she was petite — maybe five foot three with a lean, athletic build.

"*Hola*," she greeted in return, smile gleaming. "I'm Gisella," she said, and as we shook hands, I noted the lilt in her accent, a dead giveaway that she was Spanish.

"Ember," I said. "I'm the chief stew."

"I'm a deck stew!" she exclaimed. "I think I'm working mostly with the deck team for this season, but if you ever need help on the interior, I'm your girl."

"Be careful what you offer. I might be calling you down to laundry."

"Laundry is my meditation," she said with a wink. "Where are you from?"

"Fort Lauderdale. You?"

"Barcelona."

"Oh, I've always wanted to go to Barcelona," I exclaimed, squeezing her arm. "It seems so beautiful."

"Even more so than you can imagine. *Y la comida...*" Gisella made a chef's kiss gesture with her fingers pinched together. "*Uf, es para morirse.* When you come, I'll take you on a tasting tour."

"I love that we've only known each other two minutes and we're already planning dates."

"Ah, but don't get too excited. I don't put out until at least the third one," she said, wrinkling her nose with the jest.

I loved my new roommate already.

"Where should I...?"

She gestured to her luggage, and I clapped my hands together. "Oh! You'll be with me, actually, if you don't mind? I thought it would be best to let my stews room together so they can bitch about me in private."

"And what if I want to bitch about you?"

"Save it for crew night out," I said, and we shared a smile as I helped her get her luggage downstairs to the crew mess. Once I showed her to our room, I excused myself, giving her space to settle in.

And like Gisella had said, work *did* feel meditative, the flow of things making it so I almost forgot I was on the same ship with my ex.

Until Captain Gary's voice crackled over my radio.

"All crew, all crew, this is your captain speaking. Welcome aboard. Meet me in the main salon in ten minutes for our first team meeting."

Chapter Three

POST-PRODUCTION CONFESSIONAL
CLOSE QUARTERS

SEASON 4

BERNARD EVANS: SECOND STEWARD

PRODUCER
What was your first impression of your chief stew?

BERNARD
Oh, I liked Ember straight away. I mean, she's
fit, right? Fit and fun. Nothing better than those
qualities in your boss. She set the tone right away
that she wasn't going to be on our ass as long as we
did our jobs. I had a feeling she'd be fun to party
with, too. And I was spot on with that, wasn't I?

PRODUCER
Were you okay with how she structured things?

BERNARD
I loved that Ember didn't feel the need to
immediately assign the second and third stew
positions. She gave Leah and me the chance to show
her our specialties before those roles were given.
And since I knew I'd be an absolute knockout in
service, I wasn't worried. That second stew role was
mine.

PRODUCER
And what about the relationship between Ember and
Finn?

Bernard laughs heartily.

BERNARD
You're trying to get me in trouble.

PRODUCER
I just mean that it's an important relationship,
no? Chief stew and chef… they work pretty closely
together.

BERNARD
I'll say.

*Bernard smirks, arches eyebrow as he takes a drink of
water.*

PRODUCER
Care to elaborate on that?

BERNARD
There was something… electric between those two from
the moment we all stepped foot on the boat. They got
in each other's face, pushed each other's buttons.
There were few nights we didn't hear them screaming
at each other. But by the middle of the season, they
had a rhythm. They crushed it as a team.

PRODUCER
You said there was something electric between them.
What do you mean by that?
*Bernard chuckles, shakes head as he drinks water
before sitting back in his seat and folding his arms
over his chest.*

BERNARD
I mean, we all should have seen what was coming.
Where there is smoke, there's fire — and those two
were fanning the flames from day one.

The main salon exuded opulence, from the high ceilings adorned
with intricate moldings and a stunning chandelier to the dark
mahogany bar with sleek granite countertops. Floor-to-ceiling

windows framed the view of the marina beyond, natural light flooding the room and warming my already slick neck. Rich, polished wood accents complemented the soft, creamy beige of the sitting area where the crew was now gathered — all of us squished together on one of the couches as we faced Captain Gary and waited for him to kick off our season.

I, of course, sat as far away from Finn as possible.

He was at the edge of the couch opposite me, his arm draped lazily over the armrest and one ankle crossed over the opposite knee. We'd all changed into our polos since arriving, each of us working diligently in our respective areas to get the boat ready for our first charter. But it didn't matter that he no longer sported a posh button-up or that he'd broken a sweat getting the galley in order.

Even in a stupid red polo with a stained apron around his waist, he was hot.

I hated that fact as much as I hated that I noticed.

My brain still felt like it was short-circuiting at his proximity. I couldn't for the life of me figure out how the hell this had happened.

I was never supposed to see him again.

He was supposed to be in Ireland.

He was supposed to be running some stupid fancy restaurant.

He was supposed to be done with yachting.

He was supposed to be done with *me*.

I reminded myself — quickly, and with much emphasis — that he *was* done with me. Just because we'd somehow ended up on the same yacht in the Mediterranean didn't mean anything had changed.

In fact, it likely only meant that the producers of this show were out for blood when it came to packing their season with drama.

I didn't know *how* the hell they knew about us, but judging by the way they'd had cameras trained on my face when he showed up, they weren't oblivious. I wondered if they'd gone through our Instagrams, if they'd seen photos of us together two years ago — *that sunset picture on the beach with his sunburned shoulders and my drunken grin; a crew night out where we were both dressed in all white, his fingers curled around my hip as he kissed my cheek; a quick selfie captured before dinner service, me in my blacks and him in his chef's jacket, our tongues out and eyes crossed.*

I swallowed, the memories scattering like dry leaves caught in the wind — impossible to catch, impossible to ignore.

Had they dug up the past on purpose, piecing together the remnants of what we were to set the stage for what we could be? Or had they simply gotten lucky, striking gold in the form of unfinished business and unresolved tension?

Either way, I knew one thing for certain.

This wasn't just a coincidence.

It was a setup.

Well, I hoped they didn't waste all their ammo betting on the fact that I would play into this little game, because I wouldn't.

I didn't care that he was here.

I didn't plan on giving him any more attention than what was absolutely necessary to run the interior.

I was here for *me* — not for Finn Pearson.

In order, it was him, Gisella, Eli, and Leah on one couch, and then Bernard, Cameron, Palmer and me on the other. Our engineers and first mate — Rocco, Quest, and Liz, who would be excluded from being filmed for the show, the lucky bastards —

stood in the corners off to the side, their arms folded, shoulders leaning against the wood- paneled walls.

"Alright," Captain Gary said, sporting a toothy grin as he spread his arms wide. "Welcome to the *Sinking Sun*, crew. Are we ready to have a great season?"

We all clapped and did various little hoots and hollers of enthusiasm — mostly at the request of the producers. Bernard and I shared conspiratorial looks when the noise died down, both of us making fun of the situation. I already knew he'd be my drinking buddy come crew night out, and I couldn't wait.

My eyes flicked to Finn then, and my next breath shuddered in my chest when I realized his were already fixed on me. It was like a car crash, the way my body seized beneath those piercing blue-green eyes.

We watched each other for a long, rib-crushing moment — one that sent me flying back to another time, another version of myself.

"I love this look you get," he says, the corner of his mouth crooked, eyes sleepy as he runs his knuckles over my cheek.

"What look?"

"This dreamy-eyed one you wear when you talk about yachting. Travel. Seeing the world."

"It's the same one you get when you talk about food."

"Food makes sense. But getting your kicks from serving people? That one I'll never understand."

I smirk, climbing on top of him. We both laugh when I hit my head on the ceiling, his top bunk making the maneuver anything but graceful. We're both exhausted after a long day with a charter of particularly difficult guests, knowing we need sleep but not willing to sacrifice this time together to get it.

"I like serving you," I tease, biting my lip before I lower my mouth to his.

Finn groans with the kiss, his hands bruising my hips as he rocks into me. "And I like feeding you."

"Careful," I warn with a nip of his bottom lip. "You once told me food is how you show your love."

He pauses at that, sweeping my hair behind one ear, his eyes searching mine.

"I meant it."

I blinked, tearing my gaze from his and focusing on Captain Gary as my neck burned with a furious heat.

Captain started with a rundown of the yacht, detailing every feature of it from the length to the number of bedrooms. We all knew this was mostly for the show rather than for us, but we nodded and followed along.

After that, he launched into his speech — one I'd heard a half-dozen times before when I'd worked with him on other boats. I knew the way he ran his ship.

For Captain Gary, he wanted professionalism and top-notch service when we were working. If there were guests on this boat, we'd better be going above and beyond every second of every day to make their experience the best possible.

But when it came to our down time, he loosened that iron fist. He encouraged us to have fun, to enjoy our time in Italy as long as we were smart about it.

"When a charter ends, it's on you and your teams to get the boat sorted for the next one. After that, what you do with your time's your business. Go out, blow off steam, have a laugh — but don't let it mess with your work. First time one of you can't get out of bed because you're hungover, you'll be answering to me. I don't care if you party — just know your limits, and don't leave your crew mates hanging because you couldn't handle your booze."

We all nodded in understanding as he leveled a gaze at each of us, making sure we heard his threat loud and clear.

"Alcohol can also lead to a heap of drama, which I won't tolerate either. Past that, safety is my number one priority — the safety of our guests and of our crew, too."

Captain went on to explain what he meant by that, to review the importance of letting him know if there were any incidents on the boat, even if they seemed small. He reviewed our protocols for man overboard, fire, sinking ship, and other emergencies I hoped we'd never have to actually face, and then he was back to grinning.

"I want to give a couple of shout outs before we break here. First of all, let's give it up for Ember, our Chief Stew."

My cheeks flamed as the crew clapped. I wasn't expecting this little bout of being the center of attention, and right now, the last thing I wanted was eyes on me when I was still reeling from the fact that my ex was sitting on the couch opposite me.

Nope — not reeling.

I didn't care.

I didn't care.

"I've had the pleasure of working with Ember for years now, and there's no one who does a better table setting or a more superior dinner service. She runs an elevated interior from laundry to entertainment, and that's why I wanted her as my chief stew this season. I know she'll crush it. Let's make sure to support her in every way we can in this new role."

"Thanks, Cap," I said with a genuine smile.

He winked at me. "I'd also like to recognize Palmer here.

There's no one I'd trust more to help me dock this behemoth in such a tiny marina. He runs his deck team like a well-oiled machine, and I think you'll all find that everything on a yacht runs smoother when the deck team is in order. Let's just hope our green deckie here can hang," he added with a smirk at Eli.

"I won't let you down, Cap!" Eli saluted before leaning back and stretching both of his giant arms along the back of the couch.

Captain continued, giving little tidbits about each member of the crew that he was excited about. I blacked out a little when he was going on about Finn's culinary accomplishments; although, I didn't miss that he mentioned a restaurant in Dublin. I wondered when he opened it, how it had done, and was it still open now?

The fact that he was here was answer enough to that last question.

Which only made a dozen more pop into my brain.

"Now, I will say, there is one first for me on this charter that I am not particularly thrilled about," Captain said, his eyebrows raising as he shook his head. "But I've been assured there will be no issues."

A few of us frowned — me included — as Captain sighed and ran a hand over his bald head.

"This will be my first time working a season with two crew members who are a couple on board."

Did he just say... a *couple*?

For a moment, the entire crew was silent. Then, Bernard let out a whistle and threaded his hands behind his head, a smile on his face as he wagged his brows. "Oh, *this* ought to be good."

I was inclined to agree, the corner of my mouth climbing as I surveyed my new teammates. I couldn't help but try to guess who it was. Leah and Palmer, possibly? It obviously wasn't Bernard, and no way was it Eli — that boy was a walking flirt if I'd ever met one.

The camera operators stood completely still where they flanked us, but I swore I felt their lenses adjusting — zooming, fixating, capturing reactions.

"Like I said, this is one first I'm not exactly thrilled about, but as long as you two keep it professional on the clock — the rest's none of my business. Just keep the snogging to your down time in the crew mess or when you're off the boat, yeah?"

I surveyed the crew on each couch, waiting for the lovebirds to reveal themselves, but everyone looked just as confused as I did.

I glanced back at Captain Gary.

Wait... why was he leveling a gaze at Finn?

The question had barely formed in my brain before my body started to shut down as the obvious answer hit me like an anchor, sinking my stomach and the now racing heart in my chest along with it.

As if the boat had taken on water, everything warped to slow motion. I gradually dragged my gaze to our chef.

Just in time to watch him slide a hand over Gisella's knee.

My next breath lodged in my throat, eyes sticking to where his broad fingers were curling over her limb. I knew that hand intimately, knew the way the tan skin stretched over the bones, the scar on his middle left finger from when he nearly cut off the tip of it, the calloused heat of his palm when he wrapped that hand around my throat and tightened just enough to make me gasp and open for him and beg for more.

I didn't know what it looked like holding another woman.

I wished I'd never had to know that.

"Don't worry, Cap," Finn said, an affectionate smile aimed at Gisella as she batted her lashes and leaned into his side. "We'll be so professional, you'll forget we're dating."

"Yeah, I barely even like him, anyway," Gisella teased, wrinkling her nose in a way that somehow made her even more adorable than she already was.

I was going to be sick.

Acid burned my throat, my mouth watering in a most unpleasant way that reminded me of nights I'd drank well past my limit. I was all too aware of the camera duo positioned behind the couch opposite me, how their lens was directed squarely at where I sat.

Do not react.

Do not fucking react, Ember.

But my face felt frozen. I fired off all the signals to my brain to tell my stupid mouth to form a stupid smile, but nothing happened. I hoped my cheeks weren't as red as the heat I felt burning in them, hoped my jaw didn't look as unhinged as it felt, hoped the thick swallow I heard echoing in my ears wasn't obvious enough for viewers to see when this show aired.

"I'm sure it won't be a problem," Captain said in a way of finality, still grinning and shaking his head as he looked to the clipboard in his hand. "Right. We've got our first charter tomorrow, and this boat needs a lot of work before then. Let's get to it, shall we?"

"Let's do this!" Eli declared, hopping off the couch with so much energy I flinched. I hoped I covered that reaction quickly with the smile I finally managed as I peeled myself off the couch and stood.

The hair on the back of my neck prickled with the distinct

sensation of being watched, and when my gaze flicked to Finn, he was staring right at me again.

This time, his eyes were cautious, apologetic, the green-ish blue hue of them shadowed beneath his furrowed brows.

I'd had that man's attention in so many ways before. I'd been the object of his lust, the subject of his longing, the root of his affectionate jest.

But this wasn't any of that.

This was pity.

It soured my gut as much as it fanned the angry flame I hadn't realized was cresting to an inferno inside my chest. How dare he pity me. How dare he think he has any power over me anymore.

How dare he still have the capacity to love again when he completely obliterated mine.

Somehow, I managed to tear my gaze from his, but the reminder he'd given me of how love is flimsy and fleeting stuck to me like tree sap. I ignored the way my nerves were short-circuiting as I pinned my team with a smile, clapping my hands together and running over the list of items we still needed to accomplish before we called it a day. My voice sounded far away and foreign as I assigned Bernard to prepare the cabins while Leah was sent down to laundry. But this was how I'd survive. This was how I'd push past my discomfort and focus on the whole reason I was here.

I would continue inventory check and get started on the deep cleaning that needed to happen from bow to stern.

I would work — because that's what I was here to do.

I would work and I wouldn't think about Finn or Gisella or — *no.*

Another icy-cold realization slid down my spine.

Gisella was my fucking *roommate.*

I closed my eyes on a silent groan, knowing the producers were likely having a heyday with the fact that I'd unknowingly paired myself with my ex's new girlfriend.

This was the drama they craved, the drama they *created*.

Well, I wasn't going to feed into it.

I tilted my chin higher as the teams dispersed, even managing a smile and lighthearted joke as I passed Gisella on her way out to the sundeck.

"Ready for this, roomie?"

"*So* ready! I'm excited to get on deck. I need sun," she said, closing her eyes and extending her arms out like she was sunbathing. "What about you, *chief stew*?" She waggled her brows. "Ready to run this floating hotel like a boss bitch?"

"I guess we'll find out," I replied with a smile that felt as tight as my clenched asshole. *Why does she have to be so nice?* "If I start sleep-talking about charcuterie boards, just roll me over and tell me I'm pretty."

She giggled and promised me she'd do just that before she skipped out onto the deck.

Eli pretended like he was going to smack my butt when he slid past me next, but he held up his hands with a smirk at the last moment, casting me a wink and a comment about not calling HR.

I stood there for a brief moment when everyone was gone, savoring the newfound quiet of the salon.

And then I heard my name.

"Ember."

I closed my eyes for only a second, and then I popped them

back open, wide and focused, and clapped my hands together.

"Alright, let's get this boat in order," I said out loud to myself, to the cameras, to the viewers I knew would see this one day. I headed back to where I'd been working inventory before the crew meeting with the fakest smile I'd ever worn.

"Ember."

I ignored the way my heart raced as I wove through the interior of the boat, ignored the faint, familiar voice chasing behind me. I was determined to just focus on my job and the opportunity I'd worked so long for, to ignore the chaos the stupid showrunners were trying to create.

But when I made it to the pantry outside the galley, I was pulled to a stop, a warm hand catching me by the crook of my elbow and spinning me.

And I snapped.

"*What*, Finn?" My chest heaved, an exasperated sigh clawing out of me as I tore out of his grip. My forced smile fell along with my flimsy attempt at acting unaffected by the latest bomb drop. I lifted my hands and let them drop against my thighs. "What?"

That last word came out breathy and exhausted, almost pitiful, like a dying soldier begging to be put out of her misery. But there was no taking it back now.

I was safe from his touch, but not from his gaze — which cut through me like a scalpel as he stood less than a foot away. His jaw was set, the muscle of it flexing as his eyes flicked between mine.

He looked devastated, like I was a puppy he'd accidentally hit with his car.

"Stop looking at me like that," I whispered, swallowing, my gaze sliding to the floor between us.

"Ember, I didn't... I wouldn't have—"

The words died on his tongue, and even though I was narrowing my gaze at him and preparing to spit venom, I couldn't help but lean into whatever he was about to say. I wanted his excuses. I wanted to know what choices he would have made differently.

I wouldn't have lied to you if I'd known it would hurt you this badly.

I wouldn't have kissed you if I'd known you'd think we were more than just a casual hookup.

I wouldn't have let you go if I'd known I'd miss you this badly.

That last one was a stupid, aching kind of hope that I was a fool for even thinking. I knew the truth was likely more along the lines of *I wouldn't have agreed to this show had I known you'd be on it.*

Why *did* he agree to this show? I knew why I was here. I had my first shot at chief stew. This was my chance to prove myself not just to my father, but to other captains in the industry. A few charters of this size and I could get my dream job.

The money was fantastic, between what they paid us for each episode and the tips we'd get over the next eight weeks. But why would he need the money if he had his restaurant?

How the hell had he ended up back in yachting at all?

Was it because the restaurant had failed?

Was it because he missed me? (Again, that stupid hope.)

Oh, God... was it for *her*?

The likelihood of that made my stomach roil. I hadn't been enough for him, but clearly Gisella was. He was here with her instead of back in Ireland. He'd chosen yachting with her when he'd blatantly shut down that possibility with me.

Suddenly, a camera slid into the already cramped space we were in, the lens nearly knocking into the side of Finn's head with its entrance.

I cleared my throat, tucking my hair behind one ear as I retreated back several inches. "Yeah, I'll make sure to add some specialty cheeses to the provisions list. I think a charcuterie board when the guests arrive is a great idea."

Finn swallowed, his nostrils flaring with his next exhale as he watched me back away, knowing the camera was on us now.

Knowing there was nothing more to say even if it wasn't.

And with the last pretend smile I had in me, I turned, hustling through the galley and taking the stairs two at a time down to the crew quarters.

Chapter Four

POST-PRODUCTION CONFESSIONAL
CLOSE QUARTERS

SEASON 4

GARY PARKS: CAPTAIN

PRODUCER
Let's go back to that first day on board. When you
had the team meeting, how were you feeling about the
season ahead?

CAPTAIN GARY
Oh, I was absolutely buzzing. I mean, we had a great
crew. I had full faith we were going to run that boat
beautifully.

PRODUCER
You told the crew that you'd never worked with a crew
member couple on board before.

CAPTAIN GARY
That's right. It was a first for me.

PRODUCER
You weren't worried?

Captain Gary runs a hand over his jaw, shrugs.

CAPTAIN GARY
Honestly? No. But I guess I should have been, aye?

PRODUCER
Care to tell us what you mean by that?

Captain Gary chuckles, shakes his head.

CAPTAIN GARY
I don't know what you want me to say here. It wasn't
a problem until it was, and then it was quite the
problem, indeed.

PRODUCER
You knew there was a risk, though. Young people in a
relationship on a yacht with tight quarters, emotions
running high after stressful days working…

CAPTAIN GARY
Sure. I knew it was a risk. But I'm not the only one
who picked the crew, am I?

Captain Gary gives producer a pointed look.

CAPTAIN GARY
I was handed a stack of CVs for potential crew
members. I just culled from there. Other than my
recommendation for Ember, I was sort of along for the
ride. And had I known her history with Finn…

PRODUCER
Are you saying you wouldn't have hired Ember as chief
stew, had you known she and Finn had a past?

CAPTAIN GARY
I'm saying this whole couple on board thing wasn't
just as simple as a chef and a deck stew dating.
That I think we would have survived. But a chef and a
chief stew, who used to be in love, back together for
the first time in two years… and now she's rooming
with his new girlfriend?

*Captain Gary arches a brow, takes a sip of water,
shrugs.*

CAPTAIN GARY
Come now, mate. What the hell did we expect?

It was just past seven that evening when Captain Gary called a
preference sheet meeting.

We already knew the guests coming aboard in the morning, along with all their preferences. We *had* to know in order to provision the boat correctly. But this meeting was for the cameras. I knew from watching the show that this was how the viewers were introduced to the guests, how the showrunners foreshadowed any potential issues.

I was already exhausted as I made my way to the crew mess, the day having sped by in a flurry of vacuuming and polishing and organizing the boat. I mumbled curse words to myself on the way down the stairs, fumbling with the mic attached to me and trying to figure out how to place it where the clip and cord would be comfortably out of my way.

Knowing Finn would be at this meeting didn't help, and when I popped off the bottom stair and found he was the only one in the mess, I internally rolled my eyes as I slid into the booth on the opposite side of the table from him.

There were cameras everywhere.

An awkward pause stretched between us, me tucking a loose strand of hair behind my ear with a tight smile as Finn watched me with a thousand questions in his eyes. His expression still dripped with pity, and that made me narrow my gaze, my pathetic attempt at a civil smile dropping. I hoped my glare told him to *stop fucking looking at me like that* because I couldn't say it again with all these lenses pointed right at us.

I pulled out my phone, pretending to type something in my notes app when really I just wanted to avoid looking at him. It wasn't fair, how utterly attractive he was even after a day of sweating in the galley. In fact, I was pretty sure the sweat added to the allure.

He cracked his neck after a moment, which made me look up

at him again, and the way he was looking at me tied my stomach into tight knots.

"Ember, I—"

"Hey, hey!" Palmer announced himself as he skipped down the last few steps, and then he slid into the booth next to Finn, making Finn move more toward the center of the table. Palmer rapped his knuckles on the table in a quick little beat, his grin wide. "First preference sheet meeting. You guys excited?"

He was playing it up for the cameras — which was what I should have been doing, too. This was what we were paid to do. But I was too busy watching Finn and wondering what he was about to say before Palmer interrupted.

Before I could think too much on it, Captain Gary descended into the crew mess. I slipped my phone back into my pocket as he greeted all of us before plopping down next to me and giving me no choice but to scoot in on the bench.

Toward Finn.

I let out a frustrated exhale that I hoped I covered well with a smile as Captain Gary slid the packets to each of us. I crossed my legs as I picked up the stack of papers, and then promptly froze.

My ankle touched Finn's calf under the table.

It was innocent, that small touch, but electricity zapped through me as if we'd started dry humping right there for everyone to watch. My stomach hurdled to the ground at breakneck speed, a flash of memory from two years ago striking like another lightning bolt had a movie playing in my head.

His knees spreading my thighs. His hands in my hair. His breath hot on my neck as he bites it and curses my name.

"Fuck, Ember. You're so good. You're everything. I need this. I need you."

I ripped away from the touch like his skin had burned me, my cheeks heating furiously as I cleared my throat and focused on the guest photos staring back at me from the pages in my hand.

I thought I heard Finn chuckle.

I angled my chin, just enough to glance at him out of the corner of my eye.

The prick was smiling.

"Right," Captain Gary said, tapping the papers in his hands on the table to level them. "Let's get this party started, aye? Our first primary guest is Alistair Sinclair. A self-made tech mogul in his early 40s, Alistair made his fortune in cryptocurrency and AI start-ups. He loves the finer things in life and is expecting nothing less than six-star service."

"No pressure," I muttered under my breath.

"He's traveling with his wife, Theodora, who is a model and influencer. She would like candid photos taken of her as much as possible." Captain Gary paused, looking up at Palmer. "Think that's something you and the deck crew could handle when we're anchored or cruising?"

"Take photos of a hot babe in her swimsuit? Jeez, you're really asking a lot of me here, Cap."

Captain Gary grinned but chose not to comment. "Alistair also has his best friend, Benedict, and wife, Brielle, with him, as well as his older brother, Max."

"Since the guests are like gods in the crypto sector," I read off the page, arching a brow at that sentence as my fellow crewmates snickered. "They would like a 'Roman Empire Bacchanal' on night two, complete with gold togas, laurel crowns, and lots of high-end wine."

"Looks like Theodora will only eat organic, gluten-free, dairy-free, and *high vibrational* food," Finn read. "She also prefers no leafy greens, no red meat, is not a fan of poultry or soy, and despises raw fish." He scrubbed a hand over his short beard, tilting his head to the side as he re-read that last part. "Delightful. Love an easy first charter."

Captain Gary chuckled. "I have full faith you can pull it off, Cheffy."

Palmer took over then, reading off more of the guests' demands while on board. Although I'd already seen all of the requests, it wasn't hard to play up my anxiety for the cameras trained on us now. These weren't just regular charter guests. They weren't going to nap on the sundeck and go to bed after dinner. These guests were specifically chosen to bring us drama in one way or another, and with a primary who thought of himself as a god and a girlfriend who apparently only wanted to eat witchy berries — they were not taking it easy on us with this first charter.

Captain wrapped up the preference sheet meeting with me still in a daze, fingers absentmindedly playing with my piercings as I stared at all the requests and ran through a mental list to make sure I had everything I needed to pull off what they wanted. I'd asked the provisioner not just for the party supplies to get the theme right for the Roman Empire Bacchanal, but I'd also hired a local sommelier to come aboard with an expensive and exclusive selection of wine.

I knew Alistair's type before even setting eyes on him. He loved the power that came with being rich. He wanted to feel like he got to experience things in life that no one else did. It was my job to make him feel like this yacht charter was worth bragging about.

This was it. My first time at bat as chief stew.

I bit back a smile as that realization hit me. I'd worked so hard for this opportunity, years of literal sweat and tears under my belt to get me here. I didn't care if the charter guests asked for specific colored M&Ms or gold-painted pony rides on the beach — whatever they wanted, I was going to make it happen.

I was going to prove myself worthy of this title — and of my father's respect.

"What the hell am I going to cook for this girl?"

I blinked, realizing that Captain Gary and Palmer had already left the crew mess and it was just Finn and me left at the table. He was staring at the preference sheets just like I was, shaking his head as he looked through what Theodora couldn't eat.

"Macaroni and cheese?" I suggested.

"Cute, but she said no dairy, remember? Or gluten."

"Gluten-free macaroni," I said, snapping my fingers. "And vegan butter."

Finn rolled his lips together against a smile, and my stomach lurched at how familiar that grin was even after going two years of my life without seeing it. I'd blocked him on social media after realizing I couldn't survive a night drinking without making a fool of myself in his DMs.

I'd had to quit him cold turkey, and even now, I didn't feel clean sitting this close to my former addiction.

"Could you imagine? I just slather some gluten-free pasta with a heap of *organic* butter and call it a day?"

I smirked. "Garnished with a sprig of parsley for aesthetic."

"Sounds like a Michelin-Star meal."

I tapped the preference sheet. "What about a salad?"

"No leafy greens," he reminded me.

"Fine. A nice, juicy steak?"

"No red meat."

"Tofu scramble?"

Finn leveled me with a stare. "She doesn't eat soy."

I threw my hands up. "Air?"

That finally pulled a full-bodied laugh from him, his head tipping back as his shoulders shook. I tried not to let the sound of it affect me, but it was impossible — it had been my favorite sound once.

"Perfect. I'll serve her a nice plate of oxygen, seasoned with despair."

"If you're still as good as you were in Greece, it'll be the best plate of oxygen she's ever had," I said, and without thinking, my hand found his wrist and squeezed as an encouraging smile found my lips.

Of course, that smile slid off my face like butter on a hot skillet when that touch resonated, when Finn stopped laughing and stared at the point of contact. I swore I felt the heat of it crackle between us, like a live wire sparking, something dangerous and familiar in the way his gaze lifted — slow, hesitant, burning.

For one breath, neither of us moved.

For one breath, I considered what would happen if I let my touch wander up, if I leaned into him and pressed my lips to his just to see if it felt the same.

But on the next breath, I remembered his girlfriend was on this very boat with us.

I cleared my throat, yanking my hand away. My fingers clenched reflexively before I busied them in my ponytail. "Well, I think we both need a good night's rest to face these guests tomorrow. See you in the morning."

It wasn't just the stark realization that he was dating Gisella that had me scurrying off that bench. It was me remembering who I was now, who I had been after he'd left me broken and how long it'd taken me to recover. It was memories of late nights and whispered confessions, of hope curdling into heartbreak, of the years I spent trying to forget him — only to find him in front of me now, close enough to touch and yet so untouchable, unfamiliar and yet so familiar it hurt.

Finn didn't try to stop me as I left. He stayed silent and still until I ducked into my cabin, pressing the door shut behind me and leaning my head against it as a pained breath left my chest. My face burned, heart pounding like it wanted to rewind time to that moment before I touched him, before I let myself forget.

I knew the cameras had caught all of that, and it only had my stomach sinking more.

I had to get it together. I had to find a way to not let that man affect me.

And fast.

Chapter Five

POST-PRODUCTION CONFESSIONAL
CLOSE QUARTERS

SEASON 4

ELIJAH JOUBERT: DECKHAND

PRODUCER
Tell us about yourself, Eli, as if you were talking
to the viewer for the first time.

ELI
Well, my name is Elijah, but my mates call me Eli.
I'm from Cape Town, South Africa, and I've been in
yachting for a couple of years now. I'm pretty green
when it comes to a boat this size, but eager to work…
and play, of course.

PRODUCER
What made you want to work on a yacht?

ELI
You mean besides the money? I mean, come on –
traveling the world, working on luxury yachts,
jolling on my days off? That's the dream, isn't it?
Course, no one tells you about the actual job part.
Or the part where you're trapped on a floating tin
can with a bunch of beautiful, emotionally unstable
people for eight weeks straight.

PRODUCER
What was your first impression of the crew?

Eli snorts, shakes his head.

ELI
Mate. You ever seen a group of people so good-looking
and that bad at making good decisions? I clocked it
straight away - this was going to be a messy season.

PRODUCER
What made you think that?

Eli holds up fingers, counting them off.

ELI
One - half of us were clearly using this job to run
from something. Two - we were all so ready to let
off steam that we got gees'd every night out with the
crew. Three - there were exes on board, and that's
never a good thing.

PRODUCER
I assume you're referring to Ember and Finn?

ELI
Listen, I didn't know the full backstory at first.
But from day one? Ohhh, you could feel the tension.
The way they looked at each other? The way they
didn't look at each other? You didn't have to be a
genius to know there was history there. I scoped it
out early because Ember is mooi and I wanted to go
for her. Nothing like a fun little boatmance to get
you through a season, right? But I had to check with
the other okes, get a feel for where everyone's head
was at. And when I brought it up around Finn? When he
saw me flirting with her?

Eli whistles.

ELI
Should have seen his face. Oh wait - you did. I think
the way he blew steam out of his ears and nearly
chopped his finger was our first sign that we were
all in trouble.

PRODUCER
Did you think they'd be able to stay professional?
Once you found out they had history, that is.

Eli deadpans, sucks teeth.

ELI
Absolutely not.

*Eli pauses, laughs, kicks back in chair and crosses
ankle over knee.*

ELI
Nah, I mean, they tried. I'll give them that. But
let's be real - when you mix past heartbreak, close
quarters, long nights, and alcohol? Eish, something
was always gonna give.

PRODUCER
Are you still angry about what happened?

ELI
Angry? Nah, man - that's not really my vibe. Was I
disappointed? Sure. A bit gutted, even. But ja, it
is what it is. Life moves, and I happen to dig life
quite a bit.

PRODUCER
Do you blame Finn for ruining the season?

ELI
The only thing I blame Finn for is blocking my shot
with Ember after telling me he didn't have feelings
for her.

Eli winks at camera.

ELI
Ag, shame. I'll never forgive the dodgy bastard for
that.

The next day, I stood in a line with the rest of the crew as we
watched our first guests approaching after what was likely the
worst night of sleep of my life.

I usually started the season off energetic. The exhaustion
didn't come until a few charters in. But I'd tossed and turned last

night, especially when Gisella snuck into our cabin at well-past midnight. I wondered if she'd been with Finn, if they'd been in his bunk. And then I'd felt sick. And then I'd scolded myself for feeling anything at all.

Safe to say it wasn't a very restful night for me, but fatigue aside, I was still buzzing with excitement next to my fellow crew members as we prepared to welcome our tech mogul friends.

We were dressed in our whites — crisp, short-sleeved polos with the yacht's insignia embroidered over the chest, perfectly pressed skorts or tailored shorts, and deck shoes that somehow still looked fresh despite the abuse they took. Our hair was neatly styled, not a strand out of place, and not a single drop of sweat dared to stain our pristine uniforms despite the sweltering heat.

We were all smiling wide and talking shit to each other through our teeth.

"Here we go," I said to Leah and Bernard.

"These assholes better not destroy our toilets," Leah murmured back, her southern accent making the curse word cute somehow, and her smile brilliant, as she threw a wave at the guests now climbing aboard.

Finn chimed in from the other side of her. "Judging by the very little I'm allowed to cook them, I'd be surprised if they shit at all."

I bit back a laugh, holding the tray of champagne — Veuve, of course — steady as the guests dropped their shoes in the basket we'd provided and came aboard.

Unsurprisingly, they looked rich.

Theodora, the primary's girlfriend, led the way, dressed in an all-white crochet dress that clung to her body like a second skin, the bikini underneath barely visible through the intricate weave.

A designer tote dangled off her forearm, her manicured fingers adjusting her oversized sunglasses every few steps, as if to make sure the light hit her just right for the camera that was rolling behind her.

Our primary, Alistair, followed close behind, his salmon linen button-down unbuttoned halfway down his chest, revealing a golden tan and a chain that probably cost more than my yearly salary. He smirked like a man who had just bought an entire island and expected applause for it.

Benedict — the best friend — was already sweating through his designer polo, his Rolex catching the light as he clapped Alistair on the back. One look told me he was already blitzed out of his mind. And his wife Brielle moved like a woman who would rather be anywhere else, adjusting the strap of her cream-colored maxi dress with a pinched expression as she side-eyed her husband.

Max trailed behind the group, Alistair's older brother who stood out like a sore thumb with his plain white tee and well-worn linen pants. He looked like someone had dragged him here against his will, his hands shoved in his pockets and eyes surveying the luxury yacht like it was a floating prison, instead.

It was a chaotic symphony of voices then, each guest coming down the line of crew members to shake hands and introduce themselves. I was their last stop, handing them each a cold, sparkling glass of champagne with a smile that came effortlessly after all these years. It didn't matter that I knew they'd most likely be a pain in my ass — they controlled our tip at the end of this shit show, and it was my job to make sure it was a fat one.

"Welcome aboard the *Sinking Sun*," Captain Gary said, clapping his hands together.

The way Theodora and Brielle smirked at each other once he spoke told me they were already enamored with his Australian accent. I didn't blame them. Cap was hot.

"We're thrilled to have you with us for the next few days," he continued. "While the deck crew gets your bags settled and preps for departure, Ember will give you a quick tour of the yacht so you can get comfortable. Once we're underway, we'll be cruising along the Amalfi Coast, taking in the sights before dropping anchor near Capri this evening. If there's anything at all you need, don't hesitate to let us know."

He flashed them a charming smile, and I swore Theodora actually swooned. Brielle was side-eyeing her husband again, as if she were daring him to look even half as interested in any of the female crew members as she was in Captain Gary.

I handed the empty champagne tray to Bernard to take care of before sweeping my hand toward the main salon. "If you'll follow me, I'll show you around."

The guests followed, Alistair talking shit to his brother about loosening up while Brielle wrinkled her nose at the furniture like it wasn't up to her standard. We started at the bar, Leah standing behind it with a beaming smile ready to fill drink orders.

Benedict ordered a round of tequila shots — even though they still had their champagne — while I detailed all the features in the main salon. Leah got to work, and Theodora curled her lip at the spread of food Finn had prepared for light snacks. It was everything he knew she could eat — organic hummus with crudités (with no leafy greens), avocado and cucumber sushi rolls with coconut aminos (sans any raw fish, of course), sprouted seed crackers with cashew cheese, a fruit platter carefully arranged by color gradient, and a bowl of activated almonds that Finn had begrudgingly soaked himself — but she plucked at each dish with a long fingernail like she didn't trust it.

Then, as if she just remembered cameras exist, she gasped, smiled wide, and threw her arms around Alistair. "Bri, take a picture of us!"

Leah and I exchanged a look that said everything we couldn't speak out loud.

The tour continued through the formal dining area, where an elegant table was already set with fresh flowers and polished silverware; the sundeck, where plush loungers and a bubbling Jacuzzi waited under the afternoon sun; and the aft deck, where an alfresco dining setup promised the perfect spot for sunset cocktails. I pointed out the gym — though I doubted any of them would use it — walked them past the crew access areas with a well-rehearsed smile and a gentle reminder that those areas were restricted for guests, and finally led them to their cabins, where their luggage had already been placed.

In a performance worthy of an Oscar, I laughed with the rest of the guests when Benedict flopped onto the bed in his cabin without taking off his sweaty polo first, smearing a streak of sunscreen and God-knows-what across the pristine white duvet.

Brielle's lips curled in disgust. "Seriously, Benedict?"

"What? It's a bed. I'm using it." He stretched his arms behind his head, completely unfazed.

"We have to sleep in that bed!"

"And now, it'll smell like vacation when we do." He bolted upright with a grin and did a somersault backward off the bed. "Time for another shot!"

Brielle looked like she wanted to jump off the bow. I smiled through the tension, already making a mental note to have

Bernard swap the linens before she lost her mind.

I left the guests to settle in, unclipping my radio from my hip. "Interior, interior — go ahead and change into your reds," I said, jogging up the stairs two at a time to make my way into the galley.

"Copy," Leah said back.

I swung inside the galley just in time for a roar of laughter from Eli and Cameron. Finn was with them, too, but didn't seem to be in on the joke. He was focused on the white fish he was seasoning, not so much as a smirk on his lips.

"Oh boy, what did I miss?" I asked.

The laughter died instantly, Eli and Cameron exchanging wide-eyed looks before a laugh sputtered out of Cameron.

"Ach, better get on deck," he said, saluting me with a grin as he squeezed past me.

"Yeah, Palmer will have our arses if we bollocks up this first departure." But instead of sliding past me the way Cameron did, Eli put his arm around my shoulders, instead — beaming down at me with that toothy grin of his. "You look stunning today, by the way, Em."

I cocked a brow. "What do you want?"

"Just calling it like I see it." He bent and smacked my cheek with a loud kiss before I could register his intention. "Shot, *liefie!*"

Then, he bounded out of the galley with me slow-blinking and shaking my head.

"Okay..." I slid up on the other side of the counter where Finn was working. "What was that about?"

"Wouldn't know," Finn clipped, not so much as glancing up at me. "Some of us are working instead of feckin' around."

I frowned at the bitterness in his tone, but Bernard slung halfway into the galley with a little knock of his knuckles on the door panel. "They were going on about who's the fittest on the boat and who they'd fancy a round of naked Twister with by the end of the season," he said with a salacious grin. "You're a top prospect, ya cheeky little minx."

I chuffed a laugh. "Flattered, I'm sure."

Bernard did a little twirl before waving his fingers at us and saying he was off to change and then get the guests drunk. He and I would be on dinner service this first charter, with Leah handling cabins, laundry, and breakfast. I wasn't sure which of them I wanted to make my second and third stew yet.

I also had Gisella at my disposal; though, I tried to pretend I didn't. I already had to room with her, which was painful enough. My plan was to stay as far away from her as I possibly could during the day. Other than asking her to help with dishes and clearing plates at dinner service, I didn't want to need anything from her.

Finn aggressively chopping an onion startled me, and I eyed him cautiously, wondering what he was so tense about. I knew Theodora's preferences were annoying to work with, but I'd seen him deal with far worse on the boat we worked on in Greece. He was a pro. He could handle this.

So why was he strong-handing his knife like it owed him money and had the audacity to show its face in his galley?

"You okay there?"

"Ah, just grand."

"Yeah, you really seem it." I smiled, leaning my elbows on the counter. "Come on, what's going on?"

"Nothing."

"Convincing."

"Jaysus, will you ever bugger off?"

He snipped the words at me before sliding his hand across the cutting board, ushering the diced onions into a bowl in such a haphazard manner that a quarter of them flung to the ground.

"Feck's sake. I'm just trying to figure out what the hell to cook these people and don't appreciate the galley being used as the goddamn water cooler for gossip."

He slammed the metal bowl down, making me flinch, before angrily washing his hands with water so hot I could see it steaming from here.

I tongued my cheek, standing up straight. "Okay, Gordon Ramsey, dial it down a notch. You don't get to take whatever has your briefs in a knot out on me. I was just coming to see you about meal plans."

"And to be a pain in my arse, it seems."

"Well, now that I know speaking to you is an offense punishable by my hand being bitten off, trust me — won't happen again." I rolled my eyes, turning to write on the little white board we used for crew notes. I may have yanked the cap off the marker with more force than necessary. I was getting whiplash from this man not even forty-eight hours into the season. One second he's all cheeky and joking around, and the next, he's snapping at me like my mere existence offends him?

Well, I wouldn't be the one to turn the other cheek.

If he wanted a rematch from the last time we were in the ring together, I was more than happy to strap on my gloves and fight.

"They want lunch at three and dinner at nine. Work for you?"

"Yep," Finn clipped, still slinging dishes around like a cowboy with a lasso.

"Great. I'll stop by when you're finished with your impression of Mount Vesuvius and we can talk about what dishes you want used for each course."

Then I gave him a big thumbs up before leaving him to his fight with the vegetables.

Chapter Six

CHARTER CONFESSIONAL
CLOSE QUARTERS

SEASON 4, EPISODE 1
CHARTER 1

FINN PEARSON: HEAD CHEF

PRODUCER
Congratulations. Charter one in the books. How are
you feeling?

FINN
Considering the restrictions I had to work with?
Grand.

PRODUCER
Yeah, let's talk about the preference sheet meeting.
What was going through your mind when you saw all of
Theodora's dietary needs? Remember, this is talking
head footage, so it'll be playing alongside the
footage we captured of this charter.

FINN
This preference sheet is a feckin' disaster. High
vibrational food? Jaysus. I'm going to have to
really think outside of the box to give these guests
the level of food they're expecting with so many
restrictions.

PRODUCER
Great answer. How's the galley so far?

FINN
I've worked in better galleys, but this one isn't the worst. There's enough space for me to do what I need to do. It does get a little crowded in there during dinner service, though. I don't love all the chatter or feeling like I'm stuck in a can of sardines when I'm trying to focus.

PRODUCER
Yeah, let's talk about that first dinner service.

Finn laughs, folding his arms.

FINN
Let's not.

PRODUCER
I take it you weren't happy with how it went?

Finn sighs, scrubs hand over his face.

FINN
That first dinner service was an absolute bin fire.

PRODUCER
And whose fault was it?

Finn smirks, shaking head.

FINN
Depends on who you ask.

Out of all the things I discovered the first day of that first charter, perhaps the worst was that Gisella was absolutely lovely.

After an already grueling day with the guests requesting access to every water toy we had, Gisella bounded into the main salon asking if Bernard and I needed help setting up for dinner or if she could offer Leah some assistance with laundry. She was a bit sun-kissed from the afternoon, brightening every room she walked into with her pearly white smile. She did dishes from lunch so Finn could start dinner service with a clean galley, tidied up the crew mess after breaks had turned it to chaos, and took care of filling drinks so Bernard could focus on setting the dining table.

The guests adored her, the crew was motivated by her, and I couldn't help but feel the same — even though I wished desperately that I could.

I pretended I didn't see when she sat in Finn's lap during a brief break in the crew mess, me passing by them on my way to check on a dress Leah had steamed for Theodora. But I saw it. I saw his hands on her waist, hers in his hair. I heard her giggle after he murmured something low and deep in her ear.

I knew I'd need to get used to it. They were a couple, and if I was already having a hard time with their actions on the clock, I was really in for it when the crew went out after this first charter.

Maybe the *best* thing I discovered that first day was that Leah was going to be a great friend. She was the kind of stew who did what needed to be done before I even had the chance to ask, and the fact that she also did it all with a smile was a huge relief. More than that, though, she was kind and funny and sweet. We struck up conversation easily any time we worked together, and she did the same with every guest.

"Do you miss Alabama yet?" I'd asked her as I did a cabin check with her, ensuring she'd done everything to my standards. She was already great at it, and with a few pointers, I knew she'd have every room pristine.

"Not even a little bit."

"No?"

She'd shaken her head, and we paused long enough for me to show her how to fold the hand towels properly in the primary bath before she continued.

"I'm from a very small town where nothing happens. I couldn't wait to get out of there."

"I take it you don't have a boyfriend waiting for you back home then?"

She'd wrinkled her nose. "Ew, absolutely not."

I'd chuckled. "Yeah. Those are my sentiments about the guys I've tried to date in South Florida, too." I'd shivered at the memory of the few times I'd tried dating apps and lived to regret it. It didn't help matters that most of that regret came from ever thinking any other guy could live up to Finn.

I'd wanted to move on from him so badly, and in a lot of ways, I'd convinced myself I had.

Him showing up on this boat swiftly proved just how wrong I was about that.

"I'm sure you miss your family when you travel like this though, huh?" Leah had asked as we gave the mirrors another good wipe down.

It was like an iron chain squeezing around my rib cage as I'd tried to answer. "A little." I wasn't ready to dive deeper than that, so I'd turned the attention to her, instead. "How about you?"

Leah had given me a sad smile then, shaking her head. "No. No family back home for me. Mama walked out on us when I was a baby, and Daddy went home to God two winters ago."

"Oh, Leah. I... saying I'm sorry feels catastrophically wrong and weak, but I am. I'm sorry."

"Thank you," she'd said, and without thinking twice about it, I'd pulled her into a tight hug.

"Thanks for sharing that with me."

"You're easy to talk to."

"Let's hope you feel that way when you inevitably need to air your grievances against me as your chief stew."

"I doubt I'll have any to speak of," she'd said with a smile.

I'd hugged her tighter then.

Overall, it had been a nice first day, the beginning of friendships making me feel light on my toes and ready to conquer the season.

But once dinner service started, I didn't have time to think about Gisella or Finn or Leah or anyone else.

All my focus was on the guests.

The galley was alive with energy as crew members bustled in and out, Eli and Gisella washing dishes while Leah and I got plates or bowls ready for the first course in-between helping Bernard serve the guests who were already seated on the sundeck.

Somehow, Benedict had made it to dinner — which meant half the crew lost our bet that he'd be passed out by now. He was also still throwing back gin like it was water. It was kind of impressive, if not a bit terrifying.

The rest of the guests were still alive, as well. Alistair and Theodora had both drunk in moderation throughout the day, mostly champagne, and Brielle had drunk just as much as her husband but somehow managed to keep that air of annoyance over any kind of drunken demeanor. Max still looked like he'd been kidnapped and hadn't consumed anything other than water and lemonade. I'd noted him checking his watch at least four times during wine service. I didn't have the heart to tell him this was the main show and not something any of us intended to rush.

Dinner service on a superyacht was more than a dinner — it was a performance; a six-star experience where every detail, from the placement of the cutlery to the precise fold of the napkins, was a calculated stroke of artistry. The table wasn't just set, it was designed — chargers polished to a mirror shine, crystal glassware aligned with military precision, candles flickering in the exact right way to add ambiance without interfering with the aesthetic of the floral arrangements.

And if dinner service was an orchestra, then as chief stew, I was the conductor.

Every course, every pour of wine, every whisper between guests — it all flowed through me. I dictated the rhythm, the pace, the energy. I ensured the guests felt like royalty, that service was seamless, that my stews worked together like gears in a luxury timepiece — silent, seamless, exact.

The chef created the masterpiece, but it was my job to make sure it was delivered with the kind of precision and grace that made guests feel the money they had spent on this charter in every bite.

It was an honor to be in this position.

It was also so much pressure, I felt like a racehorse at the starting gate, every muscle tense, waiting for the bell.

I had done dinner service a hundred times, but never like this — never as chief stew, never as the one calling the shots. One mistake, one cold plate or forgotten garnish, and I risked Alistair and his guests walking away unsatisfied.

And on a yacht like this, unsatisfied wasn't an option.

I thought about my father, about how he might see me and the career I'd chosen differently once this show aired. When he saw how hard I worked, how sleep was fleeting and the days were long, how I put so much energy into every detail and made every guest feel special... would he understand then? Would he see that this was a profession built on all the things he valued?

Would he be proud of me?

"Hey."

I startled at Finn's voice, low and gruff from across the island. He was plating the first course, his eyes glancing at where Gisella, Eli, and Leah were goofing around before they slid back to me.

"You good over there?"

"Oh, so you're talking to me like a normal human being again?" The words had a bit of a bite to them as they rolled off my tongue, but I smiled when Finn slow blinked and flattened his lips at me.

Again. Freaking whiplash.

"I'm fine," I said on a sigh. "Just... nervous."

"Don't be."

"Easy for you to say. You've been head chef on a dozen charters. This is my first as chief stew."

Finn was quiet a moment, focused on his work. I allowed myself one stolen moment to watch him, to appreciate the artist he was. Every element on the plate was meticulously crafted, each dish a multi-sensory experience from start to finish.

I smiled a little when he frowned, a familiar line etched between his brows as he studied the presentation of the plate he was working on. I used to run my thumb over that line after the guests were asleep, when I'd sneak into his cabin and we'd steal a few moments together, no matter how tired we were.

"I've seen you step up to the plate and run dinner effortlessly when a chief has been down," Finn said, his eyes still on his dish. "And we both know you could have run that last boat we were on ten times better than Salina. You've been ready for this for years. Don't sell yourself short. Go out there and do what you do best."

"And what's that?"

"Dazzle them."

His eyes found mine at that, looking more blue than green at the moment. I swallowed under the intensity of that gaze, under the weight of those words.

He believed in me.

Even still.

"Alright," he said after a moment, stepping back and wiping his hands on the towel draped over his shoulder. "These are ready to go."

I took a slow breath, smoothing my hands down my uniform as I closed my eyes for just one moment. Finn was right. I could do this.

"Bernard, Bernard, Ember," I called into my radio. "We're ready for service."

"Copy, on my way," Bernard's voice crackled back.

Leah and I started grabbing plates, Bernard hustling down to join us before we were all carrying the first course out to the guests. I sighed when a cool breeze hit me once the sliding glass door opened and I stepped onto the sundeck. The guests all lit up at the sight of the plates in our hands, and I hit them with my biggest smile.

Showtime.

Everything went to shit.

It was like having a rug pulled out from under my feet, how quickly service had turned upside down. One moment, Alistair and his group were happy, the service smooth, the first course delivered on time and devoured by our hungry, drunken guests.

And then — somewhere between the entrée and the amuse-bouche — everything had fallen apart.

Finn had been slow plating, figuring his way around a new galley and realizing, often too late, that he was plating Theodora's dish with something she refused to eat. The time between courses started to drag.

Then, Finn had the audacity to yell at me and Bernard for not clearing fast enough. When he finally had dishes ready, they sat, losing heat, while Bernard and I scrambled to reset the table after an order was barked out from Finn over the radio.

After that, it was our fault for clearing *too fast*, the guests painfully aware of the stretched time between the main course and the palate cleanser with clean flatware waiting in front of them and not an ounce of food in sight.

It was a domino effect of dysfunction — guests waiting too long, plates going out lukewarm, wine pairings mistimed because the courses weren't moving fast enough.

Now, we were three-and-a-half hours into a meal that should have been wrapped up in just under two, and the guests were over it.

Alistair didn't hold his tongue over the last two courses we'd presented. He made it very clear that he was unhappy with the timing and the temperature of the food. Benedict had stopped drinking — *stopped drinking* — which was as clear a sign as any that things had gone off the rails. Even Brielle, who had been prim and proper all night, now sat slouched in her chair, swirling what was left of her wine as if debating whether it was worth staying awake for dessert. Theodora still took a dozen photos of every dish, bless her. The most difficult one and yet she seemed the easiest to please tonight. Max had already left, giving up on us after the roasted golden beet tartare with macadamia cream and citrus dressing.

It didn't matter that every course was beautiful, delicious, and made with every single one of Theodora's restrictions in mind.

The guests were tired.

I was frustrated.

And Finn? Finn was *pissed*.

All niceties between us disappeared after the third course, both of us taking to snipping at one another or not talking at all. It was almost impossible for me to recall his little speech of encouragement before dinner started now, and if anything, it felt patronizing.

"You've got to talk to me, Ember," Finn said as he smeared a perfect swoop of sauce onto the dessert plates, jaw tight. Only the stainless-steel island separated us, me on one side and him on the other. "You didn't even give me a heads up that you'd cleared after the main."

"Oh, I'm sorry," I snapped back, tension coiled in every muscle from my shoulders to my toes. "Was I supposed to let the guests sit there staring at dirty porcelain just so you could leisurely finish plating *coconut-kefir sorbet*?"

Finn's hand stilled mid-reach for a garnish, his eyes snapping to mine. "Leisurely?"

"Painstakingly slow? Torturously delayed? Or maybe you were planting, watering, growing and harvesting those edible flowers that were so important?"

He snarled, and the sound did more to my nether regions

than I would ever admit to anyone — most of all the peanut gallery standing around us enjoying the show.

"Did you want the food to actually look like something? Or should I have just slapped it on the plate and called it rustic?"

"I wanted it to be on the table before they started drafting their wills, Finn."

Behind me, I heard Eli let out the quietest *oof.* No one else spoke. No one moved. I'd sent Leah to bed after the second course, Gisella stepping in to help when needed, and she stood next to Eli now as he pretended to be focused on doing dishes and she waited for my cue.

Finn exhaled sharply through his nose. "Maybe if you'd been *communicating—*"

"I was too busy making sure the guests didn't start gnawing on the table linens while you were in here playing Picasso with the reductions to *communicate.*" I folded my arms over my chest, leaning into his space. It was only an inch, but I swore that inch ignited the air between us like a match to a gas leak. "And besides, *you* were the one who yelled at us for not clearing fast enough. So which is it, Finn? Too fast or not fast enough?"

Finn wiped his hands on his towel, nose flaring. "You have no clue what goes into plating at this level."

"And you have no clue what goes into *serving* at this level."

The tension in the galley was thick, charged, and the rest of the crew was watching it like a live-action soap opera. Bernard had given up trying to look busy or checking on the guests — who had told him three times now that no one wanted anything else to drink. He was looking at his nails, biting back a smile and glancing over at Gisella with a *this is juicy* expression in his eyes when he thought I wasn't looking.

And the cameras rolled on, catching every single second.

Finn clenched his jaw, grabbing the last of the garnishes and throwing them onto the plates with a little more flourish than necessary. "They're ready," he bit out.

"Great."

"Great."

Bernard and Gisella grabbed plates with me without needing to be told, both of them wide-eyed. I thought I saw Gisella give Finn a sympathetic tilt of her lips, but I stormed out of the galley before I could be sure. With a shake of my shoulders, I allowed myself one frustrated breath low in my throat before I plastered on that service smile.

And then I finished my job, somehow managing to save the night by regaling the guests with a story from the Bahamas while our chef threw his temper tantrum in the galley.

Chapter Seven

CHARTER CONFESSIONAL
CLOSE QUARTERS

SEASON 4, EPISODE 1
CHARTER 1

CAMERON DUNN: DECKHAND

PRODUCER
How are the sleeping arrangements? Like your
roommate?

CAMERON
Aye, Eli's sound. We're both here for a laugh, so the
energy's bang on. It's brutal when you get stuck with
a dry shite, but with Eli, I know we'll make the most
of the season. As for sleeping… well, it's easier
when there's not a full-blown scrap happening in the
crew mess, aye?

PRODUCER
A little too loud to ignore?

CAMERON
Are you kidding? I could hear every word of Ember
eviscerating Finn. Poor guy.

PRODUCER
Can you give us a reaction we can use? Maybe tell us
that they woke you up and then show us how you would
have reacted had you been in the mess.

CAMERON
I had morning shift, so Palm sent me down to sleep
pretty early. But then I woke up around midnight to
the sound of voices. I think they thought they were
being quiet but… aye, no. They were not.

*Cameron makes a face, lips drawn down in a yikes
expression.*

Producer laughs.

PRODUCER
Perfect. So, what do you think that was all about?
Just high tensions after an imperfect dinner service?

Cameron smirks.

CAMERON
Oh, aye…

Cameron winks at camera.

CAMERON
I'm sure that's all it was.

My father made me train for a marathon once.

I was not a runner, but Dad was, and he insisted running was
a lesson in persistence and determination for everyone. It wasn't
something that was negotiable, when he told me I was going to
run that marathon with him. It was an order. My father wasn't
a military man, but *his* father was — and that dominance was a
trait my grandpa passed down, apparently.

I hated every second of training, every mile I ran and every
ounce of pain my body went through in the process. But when
the day came, I was surprised by the overwhelming emotion
that surged through me when I hit the halfway point. I was
elated. Then, I was sure I'd never finish. I pushed through the
discomfort and the agony, and though I fell into a heap of bones

once I crossed that finish line, I felt the most intense pride I'd ever experienced in my life.

I'd done it. I'd finished something when it felt impossible — even when my body wanted to quit, when my mind convinced me I couldn't do it.

I remember my father standing over me with a hand to help me stand, and once I was upright, he'd squeezed my shoulder and said, *"Remember this feeling. Bottle it up and take a sip when you need a reminder that you can do hard things, Ember. You can achieve anything. And nothing worth having is easy to get."*

I reached for that feeling now as I checked in with Bernard one last time before turning in for the night. He assured me he could handle cleaning up and encouraged me to go get some sleep. He'd have a little later report time in the morning whereas I'd need to get up early to help Leah serve breakfast.

The perfectionist side of me wanted to stay up and make sure Bernard did everything right. We'd already royally fucked up dinner service — I needed everything else to run smoothly. But I had to trust him. That was part of being a leader, and I knew it was the hardest part for me.

Delegating meant things wouldn't get done the way *I* would do them, and that was never easy for me to accept.

Still, I was just tired enough to accept that I couldn't do it all. I dragged myself down the stairs to the crew quarters, rubbing my temples against the headache that had been throbbing for the last hour.

You can do hard things. This is nothing. The pain will pass. The fatigue is temporary.

I gave myself the best pep talk I could, but when I landed in the crew mess and found Finn waiting there for me, I sighed.

I knew he was waiting for me. There was no other reason for him to still be awake. The galley was clean, the dishes done, and he had to be up before I did to get breakfast going. But instead, he was leaned against one of the tables, arms folded, eyes on me.

"What?" I clipped. I wanted so badly to rip my mic off, but knew I couldn't until I was climbing into bed. It was part of the contract we'd signed.

Every word was up for public consumption.

Currently, there were no camera operators in the mess. But there were still cameras in every corner of the room. I did my best to ignore them, though I was cringing inside knowing every moment of the disaster of a dinner tonight would be broadcast.

My father wouldn't be disappointed in me — not yet. He always loved when I faced adversity, said it made me tougher.

It would be how I handled this failure that he would judge. It would be what I did next.

Finn exhaled, a long, slow breath through his nose. His arms stayed crossed, muscles tight under his chef's jacket. He seemed as exhausted as I felt, his hair disheveled and skin dark beneath his eyes. Even with his beard neatly trimmed, he looked wrecked from this hellish day.

"I wanted to apologize."

I blinked.

That was not what I'd been expecting.

"Oh?"

He nodded, pushing off the table and taking a step toward me. "I know dinner service was a mess. And I know you were under a lot of pressure. I didn't make it easier on you." His voice was softer, laced with surrender rather than the accusation it had held earlier.

The tension in my shoulders loosened, just a fraction. An apology was the last thing I thought I'd get from Finn, but hearing it now, I felt the sting of the night ease just a little.

But then, the prick kept talking.

"I should have accounted for how long it would take you to clear the plates, and I probably should have assumed you'd be a little slower than I'm used to."

The crack in the tension sealed back up, steel reinforcing my spine as I folded my arms. "Slower?"

Finn sighed, rubbing the back of his neck. "I just mean I've worked with more seasoned stews before. Ones who know when to clear, how to pace things. It's different when you're still learning—"

I scoffed. "Right. So I'm the problem."

His lips pressed together, frustration flickering in his gaze. "That's not what I said."

"It's exactly what you said." I took a step closer, heat crawling up my throat. "I'm still learning, so I should have expected to slow you down. Never mind the fact that you took so long plating the second course that the guests had finished their wine before they even took their first bite."

Finn's nostrils flared. "I was making sure the food was perfect, Ember. That's my job."

"And mine is to provide seamless service, but I can't do that when I don't know how long you're going to take! You said it was me who didn't communicate, but it was *you* who messed up and then didn't cue me in on how that would impact the rest of the service. I'm not a mind reader."

"I gave you estimates—"

"Which were all wrong."

His jaw ticced, his whole body coiled tight. "You rushed the clear on the fourth course and you know it."

"Because you threw a fit about me being too slow to clear on the third!"

We were toe to toe now, the heat between us sparking like an exposed wire. My chest heaved with frustration, with exhaustion, with the simmering rage that had been brewing since we first locked eyes at crew arrival. I was pissed at him for dinner service, but I wasn't too stupid to realize that it was more than just that.

I was pissed at him for being here, for being back in yachting, with *her*. I was pissed at how we left things, pissed he didn't try to come after me when that charter ended, pissed he had been living his life just fine and falling in love again while I still couldn't see through the rubble his love had left me under.

I hated him.

Because I still loved him.

And if two years without him hadn't cured me of that disease, I wasn't sure anything ever would.

Finn shook his head, his voice dropping lower. "You want me to say it was my fault? Fine. It was my fault."

My eyes narrowed. "You don't mean that."

"No, I don't," he admitted, a smirk curling at the corner of his lips. "But as much as I used to love watching you throw a fit just so I could spank it out of you, I'm knackered. So, for sleep's sake, you win."

My cheeks flamed as I shoved his shoulder with a scoff. He barely budged, but his eyes flashed, that smirk climbing higher.

His breath was heavy. So was mine.

And for a split second, the air between us shifted into something else entirely.

Something familiar.

Something tempting.

Something I couldn't — *wouldn't* — let happen again.

Not now that I knew better.

"I'm not trying to win. I happen to know that's impossible when it comes to you," I said, and when his eyes flicked to my lips as I said it, I had to use every ounce of willpower I had not to let my next breath shudder out of me.

"Is that so?"

"It is."

"You think you know me so well."

"I know all I need to. I know how much of a coward you are when you're wrong about something. And trust me, this time? I won't wait around for a real apology I know will never come."

I turned then, and the second I stepped out of that heated space between us, it was like a rubber band snapped, time catching up in a dizzying rush.

"And I hope you enjoyed those spankings, by the way," I threw over my shoulder when I reached the door to my cabin. "Because you'll never touch me again."

I longed to feel powerful vindication with those words as I slammed the door behind me.

But they devastated me, instead.

I was ready for bed — teeth brushed, face washed, hair wrapped around a silky, heatless curling rod — when Gisella dragged Finn into our room.

I heard her giggle and his low voice whispering something from where I was still in the bathroom. It almost sounded like he was protesting, but I suspected that was more my idiotic, unfounded hope than fact.

I groaned, letting my head fall back and closing my eyes.

What god did I piss off to have this as my punishment?

"It's fine," I heard Gisella say on another giggle, and then nausea bloomed in my throat at the sound of a kiss. "Ember is cool. She's not going to care."

I heard Finn's voice again, but couldn't make out what he was saying — just the low rumble of his baritone as I held onto the sink and tried not to hurl. I was so exhausted. All I wanted was to crawl into bed and pass out. But I knew with Finn in that room, there was no possible way I'd sleep.

With a sigh, I flicked off the bathroom light and opened the door just in time to find Gisella crawling up into her top bunk.

Finn was already there waiting for her.

"Hey, Em! We're just going to have a cuddle. We won't be loud, I promise." Gisella smiled that stupid, adorable, innocent smile and I still wanted to throat punch her.

"Yeah, no worries," I said. "I'm actually going to go have a glass of water on deck, get some fresh air."

Do not look at Finn. Do not look at Finn.

"Oh, perfect! It's just a little snuggle. We're both tired," Gisella said. "Turn out the lights, yeah?"

I gave her a thumbs up and grabbed the one long cardigan I'd brought with me, sliding it over one arm and then the next before wrapping it tight. I was only in a white spaghetti strap sleep top and my light pink sleep shorts, and I knew it'd be a bit chilly on deck this time of night.

"I won't stay long."

I stilled at the deep sound of his voice, at the apology I swore

I heard laced within it.

But I didn't dare look at him as I flicked off the lights and left them alone.

Bernard must have finished up and headed to bed already, because the boat was quiet as I made my way up. I did a quick run through the main salon — because *perfectionist* — and smiled at his work. Everything was spotless.

It made my next breath come a bit easier knowing he and Leah would be a good team to work with. At least, that's how it seemed so far. I knew that could change at any moment. I didn't know them well enough yet, but my first impression of both of them was that they were hard workers and competent in their respective roles.

I could work with that.

I stopped by the galley long enough to fill a glass with cold water, and then I climbed the rest of the way to the sundeck. It was chilly as I suspected, so I held my cardigan tight around me as I padded to aft.

The aft deck stretched behind the yacht like a private balcony over the sea, quiet and tucked away from the noise of the boat. The teak wood was cool beneath my bare feet, the salty breeze soft and noninvasive as it wrapped around me. I pulled my cardigan tighter, breathing in the crisp, briny scent of the water as it rolled in steady waves beneath us. Somewhere in the distance, a buoy clanged softly, and the yacht creaked with its own groans, like an old man settling into a long night's rest.

Overhead, the stars glittered in full view, untouched by city lights, a canvas so clear it made the whole world feel like it had shrunk to just this deck, this night, this breath. The wind toyed with the loose strands of my hair, the hum of the engines faint, just a distant vibration through the bones of the boat. The only other sound was the soft slap of the sea against the hull.

When I found Eli sitting in my destination smoking a cigarette and scrolling on his phone, I smiled.

"Hope you don't mind a bit of company," I said, announcing myself.

He looked up from his phone, long blond hair covering his face a bit as he grinned at me. "Not at all. Would love it, actually."

Eli set his phone aside on the teak, patting the other side of him for me to take a seat. We were protected from the wind in this little alcove of the boat, and I sighed when I finally sat down, my entire body aching and begging for me to carry my ass to bed.

Ten minutes, I told myself. If I could just make it ten minutes, hopefully Finn would be gone. Or if not, I could ask him to leave without Gisella thinking I was a bitch of a roommate.

"I'm on night watch," Eli said, taking a pull from his cigarette. "But why are *you* still awake?"

"Just need a bit to unwind, I guess."

Eli arched a brow at me like he didn't quite believe that lie, but to his credit, he didn't push. Instead, he offered me his cigarette.

"No, thank you," I said with a smile. "Although, I don't think I've ever wished I smoked more than I do right now."

"Ag, shame." He took another hit, his eyes assessing me. "Rough day, wasn't it?"

"Not the smoothest, that's for sure."

"For what it's worth, I think you did a great job. The guests were happy, loving the drinks, commenting on all the little things you and interior did to go above and beyond. Theodora was over the moon that you had a portable ring light for her to use to get the best lighting no matter where she was on the boat."

"Sadly, I don't think a ring light will make up for the train wreck dinner."

"Ag, you've got tomorrow night. It's the last meal that sticks in their heads, anyway."

I smiled. "Hope you're right."

"I usually am."

His next drag was long, and he watched me with that same intense, curious gaze. I knew this kid was a flirt, but in just five minutes alone with him, I could see he was also a predator. Anyone attracted to a man wouldn't last long with those eyes of his devouring them the way they were currently feasting on me.

My cheeks flushed under the gaze, and I bit my lip against a smile, looking down at where my hands were wrapped around the glass of water. I hadn't seriously dated anyone since Finn, but I'd kissed a few boys on past boats and tried my hand at a few app dates — just for fun, just to remember what it felt like to be wanted. I could see myself doing the same with Eli.

A big part of me knew I *should* do just that — because if I was kissing Eli, then maybe I wouldn't be so hung up on what it used to be like kissing Finn.

But the smarter half of me screamed not to even think about it. I'd learned my lesson about boatmances, and I was not encouraging any type of romantic entanglement while on board this time. I was a woman on a mission, and that mission did *not* include getting my heart broken again.

"So, how do you feel about the interior crew so far?"

"They're great," I said honestly. "Going to make my first go at chief stew easy, I think."

"Careful. Famous last words."

I knocked on the teak wood just in case. "How about you? Deck team cool?"

"Oh, yeah. Team's solid so far. Palmer's a good bosun, and I've worked with Cam before — good bloke, knows his stuff. Gisella might be stronger than him, though, judging by how she was hauling those provisions around yesterday. But hey, don't tell him I said that. Let's keep his ego intact."

He winked.

"You know anyone?" Eli asked next, pausing to finish the last of his cigarette. He put the butt out in the small ashtray he'd brought out with him. "From before the show, I mean."

Heat crept up my throat. "I do."

"Who?"

"One guess," I said, looking up at the moon breaking through the thin clouds above us. When I looked at Eli again, he smirked.

"Ah. Cheffy."

I rolled my lips together, eyebrows raising into my hairline as I pointed at him as if to say *bingo*.

"Any story there?"

I chuffed a laugh, draining the last of my water.

I was in love with him.

He said he loved me, too.

I thought we'd travel the world together.

He let me think it.

He said he was done with yachting, that he was opening a restaurant in Dublin.

Now, he's here, back on a superyacht.

With Gisella.

But I didn't say any of that.

I just stood, groaning a bit at the way my muscles protested the movement. "Not one worth telling. Goodnight, Eli."

"'Night, Em."

Chapter Eight

CHARTER CONFESSIONAL
CLOSE QUARTERS

SEASON 4, EPISODE 1
CHARTER 1

PALMER HUGHES: BOSUN

PRODUCER
Are you happy with your deck team after this first
charter? Feeling confident in a good season?

PALMER
I'm feeling… cautiously optimistic. We had a good
start, but I've got a green deckie, and his roommate
likes to horse around more than work. Still, they
got the job done, and I think with a little guidance,
they'll all make Captain proud.

PRODUCER
And what about Gisella? You two hitting it off?

Palmer shifts, sips water.

PALMER
Gisella is interesting. I haven't quite figured her
out yet. But like I said… I'm cautiously optimistic.
At least, until someone gives me a reason not to be.

"All crew, all crew — meet me in the main salon for our first tip meeting."

Captain Gary's voice crackled over the radio on my hip as I stripped the bedding in one of the guest cabins, and I smiled a bit when I heard various hoots and hollers ringing out from around the boat. It was everyone's favorite part of any charter.

We'd made it.

It was time to turn the boat, count our cash, and enjoy a night out.

I poured up tall glasses of champagne for everyone, delivering them to the main salon on a tray and letting Bernard hand them out. We all clinked our glasses together in a rowdy *cheers!* before kicking back on the couches, all our attention on Captain and the fat envelope in his hand.

He crossed an ankle over the opposite knee, slapping the envelope against his palm with a smirk. "Well, team, first charter's in the books."

A small round of cheers rippled through the crew, though we were all waiting for the real celebration — the number. We all got paid a salary, and we also got a bonus incentive for agreeing to be filmed for the show.

But the real money was in the tips.

Captain smiled at our antics, waiting until we calmed before he continued. "Look, docking went smoothly, cabins were spotless, drinks flowed, and as you saw when the guests disembarked, they left happy. That's what matters. Now, we all know dinner service the first night wasn't exactly textbook, but you lot turned it around. The bacchanal was a smash hit — seriously, they didn't stop talking about it. And Theodora told me this was the most 'high vibrational' trip she's ever had."

"Guess that means we're all spiritually richer," Eli said.

The crew laughed, but I barely heard it.

Because as soon as Captain mentioned dinner service, my gaze flicked to Finn.

He was already looking at me.

The sharp edges of the night we'd torn each other apart in the galley had dulled just slightly, softened by exhaustion and time. There was something unspoken in his eyes — something close to regret, but not quite. His lips pressed together, his jaw flexing, and then he gave me the smallest nod, like a peace offering.

And I smiled. Just a little.

Because the truth was, whatever disaster dinner had been, we'd found our rhythm again last night during the bacchanal.

I hadn't expected the bacchanal to go as well as it did — not after the disaster that was our first dinner service. But somehow, between the last-minute scramble to get the gold togas steamed and the wine list reprinted, everything had clicked.

Even me and Finn.

Of course, we'd nearly killed each other before we got there.

It started just before service, when I was checking the place settings one last time on the sundeck and Max — the broody, aloof older brother of our primary guest — wandered over with a glass of red in hand. He'd barely said ten words the entire charter, always lurking at the edge of the group like he regretted agreeing to come in the first place. I figured he'd hole up in his cabin again until dinner was over. But instead, he stopped next to me, looking uncharacteristically... amused.

"This table is like something out of a magazine," he'd said, nodding to the elaborate Roman-inspired décor. "I imagine that's your doing."

I'd smiled, brushing imaginary crumbs off one of the chargers. "Part of it, yes, but it's a team effort for sure. We aim to impress."

He'd looked at me for a long moment, the faintest hint of a smile tugging at his lips. "Well, consider me impressed."

And then, without warning, he'd lifted my hand and pressed a warm, slow kiss to the back of it.

The kiss itself meant nothing. He was tipsy. Grateful, maybe. And judging by the way his gaze dropped just slightly to my lips before he turned and walked off toward the deck bar, I'd say the wine had made him bold. My cheeks had flamed purely from the surprise of it, and maybe a little from the compliments. What girl didn't love to be doted on every now and then?

But the second I turned back toward the galley, ready to grab the amuse-bouches, I nearly collided with Finn.

Who had a tight jaw, pursed lips, and narrowed gaze aimed right at me.

It put me on the defensive before I even knew what I was being defensive about.

"What?" I'd snapped.

"Nothing," he'd clipped right back, brushing past me.

Except it wasn't nothing.

It was very much a something.

And that something came to a head ten minutes later when I popped into the galley to grab the first course, only to find Finn plating with slightly more aggression than usual.

"What's the ETA on the beet salad?" I'd asked lightly, already bracing for another round of whatever this stupid fight was we had going between us.

He hadn't answered right away — just wiped the edge of a plate and adjusted the microgreens with unnecessary force.

"Can I help with anything?" I'd tried again, softer this time.

"Are we serving all the guests?" he'd asked, still not looking at me. "Or just the ones who kiss your hand?"

Those words might as well have been the bell ringing.

I'd stared at him, stunned but ready to fight. "Excuse me?"

When Finn finally turned to face me, his expression was unreadable — not angry, not hurt, just... blank.

I couldn't figure it out.

"Forget it," he'd said, rubbing a hand over his face. "Forget I said anything. I'm just— It's been a long day."

"No, say it," I'd pushed. "You think I was being unprofessional."

Strangely, it was like *that* accusation shocked him — which had me second-guessing that I was correct in the assumption.

But if he wasn't judging my professionalism, then what the hell was his problem?

"I think," he'd said, exhaling hard, "that you're amazing at your job. And I think you know that. But I also think you're completely oblivious to how people look at you when you're in your element."

I'd blinked, throat tightening, caught off guard by the way his voice dipped on the word "amazing." But before I could respond, he'd closed his eyes, pinched the bridge of his nose, and sighed.

"Okay. Okay. Let's... it's fine. I'm sorry. Let's just work together on this, okay? We have one night to save this charter. Are you with me?"

I'd nodded slowly, my chest still tight, brain scrambling to catch up with wherever the hell he was. "Yes. I'm with you."

And somehow, with those words and a silent agreement to push pause on our feud — we'd found our groove.

From that moment on, we moved in sync, passing plates and glances like we hadn't spent the last twenty-four hours circling each other like animals backed into a corner and ready to strike. The guests were delighted. The food was phenomenal. The wine flowed. The bacchanal was everything they'd hoped for — indulgent, lavish, a little ridiculous in the best way.

Even Max raised a toast to the crew before disappearing back to his cabin.

The guests went to bed full and happy, high on gluten-free truffle gnocchi and thousand-euro bottles of Chianti.

And me and Finn?

We didn't say a word to each other once the last plate was cleared.

But I think we both knew — we'd done it.

We'd saved the damn charter.

No, we hadn't been exactly *friendly* to each other, but it seemed we both had learned from the night before — even if we would never agree on who was to blame for the chaos.

The way he plated and adjusted based on my timing, the way I read his body language without him having to say a word... it had been seamless, electric.

Just like before.

We were good together in a galley. Always had been.

When we weren't trying to choke each other, anyway.

And if we were going to make this season a success, we needed to find a way to keep that rhythm — without burning the whole damn boat down in the process.

I was still holding Finn's gaze at the tip meeting, still lost in the weight of it, when Gisella leaned over and kissed his cheek.

It wasn't possessive, wasn't anything more than an affectionate, absentminded gesture. But it hit like a match striking dry kindling, setting off a fire in my chest before I could stop it.

I tore my gaze away, back to Cap, to the money, to anything that wasn't Finn Pearson and his lingering looks and the infuriating way they still made my breath catch.

Gary smirked, lifting the envelope again. "Alright, speaking of being richer — let's talk numbers."

The entire crew leaned forward, collective breath held.

"Our first charter tip is... twenty-three-thousand euros."

The room erupted.

Bernard threw his head back with a whoop, Eli smacked the table like he was trying to wake up the spirits of yachts past, and Gisella and Leah let out almost identical squeals before crushing each other in a hug.

I smiled, and again, my gaze caught Finn's.

I didn't let that one linger.

"Bloody good start," Captain said over the chaos, lifting a hand for some semblance of order. "That comes out to about 2,180 US dollars each."

More cheers, claps, and whistles rang out as Captain Gary stood to distribute the tips. Off camera, I knew he'd already given our engineers theirs.

Bernard waggled his brows as he accepted his share. "Anyone else feel the sudden urge to make bad decisions tonight?"

Eli clinked his champagne against Bernard's. "Already ahead of you there, mate."

Captain Gary rolled his eyes, but his grin said he expected nothing less. "Alright, take your cash, enjoy your night, and let's make sure we're not dragging too hard tomorrow. We're turning the boat and getting ready for round two."

With that, he left us with a salute and a pointed look to not show up hungover in the morning. The energy in the room was palpable — our first tip in hand, a successful charter behind us, and a night of celebration ahead.

And as I clutched my own cut, I found myself exhaling for the first time since we left the dock.

I needed the break tonight.

I needed to figure out how to make the next charter stronger.

More than anything — I needed a drink.

Chapter Nine

CHARTER CONFESSIONAL
CLOSE QUARTERS

SEASON 4, EPISODE 2
CHARTER 1

GISELLA DÍAZ: DECKHAND/STEWARDESS

PRODUCER
Well, that first charter was exciting, wasn't it?

GISELLA
It was awesome! The guests were a riot. So fun.

PRODUCER
How did it go with the deck crew? Talk to us a bit
about how you feel about the team at the end of this
first charter.

GISELLA
El deck team *es un sueño*. I love working with Eli
and Cameron, and Palmer is such a great leader. He's
really calm under pressure, you know? It's kind of…
impressive. Makes me want to get to know him better,
learn from him. I like when the person in charge of
me is laidback like that.

PRODUCER
You helped out a little on service this charter, too.
How was that?

*Gisella hides face, peeking through fingers before
dropping hands to thighs with a sigh.*

GISELLA
To me, service is always the hardest part of
a charter. Working the exterior is hard work
physically, but we get to have fun with the guests.
On the interior, it's all about precision – and it
was clear to me very quickly that Ember runs her crew
differently than Palmer.

PRODUCER
Meaning?

GISELLA
Well… she's a bit of a perfectionist. And I guess
you sort of have to be to be chief stew. But she was
kind of cruel to Finn that first night, wasn't she? I
don't think it was that serious. It's just dinner.

PRODUCER
Yeah, that was pretty intense, huh?

GISELLA
So intense. Eli and I were torn between laughing and
staying as invisible as possible so we didn't get our
heads bit off.

PRODUCER
Why do you think Finn and Ember clashed so much that
first dinner?

GISELLA
Oh, I don't know. It happens sometimes with chefs and
chief stews. They work together really closely, and
they usually both have their own way of doing things.
It's normal to have some high tension. And look at
how great dinner was the next night. It all balances
out in the end, they just have to find their footing.

PRODUCER
So, you're not worried about it being a problem this
season?

GISELLA
No. I think this crew is going to be the best one
this show has seen.

PRODUCER
Love that energy! Yeah, maybe they just needed to
yell at each other and get some of that frustration out.
It's got to be hard working so closely with an ex.

Gisella frowns, tilts head.

GISELLA
I don't understand… ex?

PRODUCER
Yeah. Finn and Ember used to date.

GISELLA
They… *what?*

Once the boat was in decent shape and the post-charter interviews were done, we all retreated to the crew mess to get ready for the night out. It was all music and laughter, the doors to every cabin open as crew members flowed in and out, asking about outfits, getting opinions on colognes, and pouring pre-game shots.

When we piled into the two van cabs that would take us to dinner and then to the bars, I ended up sandwiched between Eli and Cameron.

Not a bad place to be, if I was being honest.

"Ember, this top…" Eli said, biting his knuckle as his eyes shamelessly raked over my cleavage. His other arm was draped around the seat behind me, and I didn't mind at all that we were touching from knee to hip.

"Easy, killer," Cam said from my other side. "You need to respect the authority on our boat."

"Palmer's my boss, not Em."

"I'm higher rank than you, though," I reminded him.

"Maybe I like a woman in power."

He smirked, casting me one of his signature winks that made me roll my eyes and shove at his chest. We were all already a bit tipsy, and even though I pretended to be annoyed by his advances, I welcomed them.

It was nice to feel wanted, and to take my mind off my ex who was riding behind us in the other cab with his girlfriend.

"Did anyone else catch the iciness from Gisella after interviews?" Leah asked from the backseat.

"I thought I heard her and Cheffy getting into it in his cabin," Cameron chimed in.

I frowned. "Like fighting? Why? They seemed fine at the tip meeting."

"Shit. You don't think Cheffy saw me whip G's ass with a towel when we were shammying, do you?" Eli pretended to be scared before sinking back with an even bigger smirk on his face. "Or maybe the horny bastard just wants a spanking himself."

I chuckled with the rest of the crew, but lost focus on the conversation as Leah shifted to talking about how hungry she was. I racked my brain, trying to think of anything that could have happened to make Finn and Gisella have a fight. Then, I chastised myself for caring.

It wasn't any of my business.

Still, I couldn't help but watch them as they climbed out of the van behind us when we pulled up to the restaurant. Finn offered a hand to help Gisella out, but she barely looked at him once her feet were on the pavement. She folded her arms over her chest, scowling.

And then, she turned that death glare to me.

I flinched a little at getting caught staring, but saved it with a smile.

Except Gisella didn't smile back.

I thought I saw her shake her head a little before she stormed toward the restaurant, sliding her arm through Bernard's and leading the way. Cameron and Palmer followed behind them, Eli ruffling Finn's hair like a kid, and then Leah and I took up the rear.

"I'm so excited to be off that boat for a while," Leah said, slipping her arm through mine. "The days blend when you're down in laundry."

"It's a shame you're so good at laundry."

"I *know*," she whined, giving me a wink. "Also a shame that I already adore my chief stew, so I'd do anything for her."

"I'll get you on service next charter, make sure you see some sun."

"It's really okay. I love laundry. I love the quiet routine of cabins. But, yeah, if we have a beach picnic or something... tag me in, okay?"

"Promise," I said. Then, I looked around at the restaurant, excitement blooming in my belly. "Ever had real Italian food before?"

"Never," she confessed with a dreamy sigh, gazing around the same as I was. "But I was born ready to devour pasta and cheese."

We dissolved into a fit of giggles, ducking inside the restaurant that was already teeming with life.

Trattoria del Mare sat on a quiet cobblestone street, tucked between towering buildings with weathered shutters and wrought-iron balconies overflowing with vines and flowers. Twinkling fairy lights draped from the awning, their soft glow mixing with the flickering flames of candlelit tables. The scent of garlic, fresh basil, and simmering tomatoes wafted through the open-air dining space, the sounds of glasses clinking and light laughter serving as the soundtrack.

The hostess greeted us with an easy smile and a *buonasera*, leading us past a wall of climbing bougainvillea to a large table in the back courtyard where ivy crawled up stone walls and a soft Italian love song played from hidden speakers. A bottle of chilled limoncello and a basket of warm, crusty bread were already waiting for us when we sat.

Eli pulled out my chair before dropping into the one beside me, draping his arm right back over my shoulders like it was second nature. "This place is lush," he murmured, plucking a piece of bread from the basket and tossing it onto my plate. "It's about to be a long night. You're gonna need fuel, babes."

I smirked at him, grabbing the bread and taking a giant bite right in his face. I moaned. "Still warm."

Eli paled at that, his eyes on my mouth. "Christ, Ember. I've never wanted to be a carb so bad."

"You want her to take a bite out of you?" Palmer challenged from across the table where he and Cam were already scanning the menu.

"If she makes noises like that? Hell yes."

"Oh, my God, stop," I said, shoving at his chest. I nodded to the menu. "Figure out what you're eating."

"Yes, Mommy." Eli then panted like a dog and let out a little bark.

Bernard twisted open the bottle of limoncello, shaking his head and pouring shots for the table. "To a fat tip and a night we won't remember," he declared, raising his glass.

Everyone clinked their shots together before throwing them back. The tart, citrusy burn warmed my chest, and I couldn't help but smile when I sat my glass down. I looked around, taking in the lights and the music, the faint scent of the sea, the pleasantly warm night air.

I was in *Italy*.

Sometimes it was easy to forget when I was caught up in the job. We worked long hours, long days, long nights — but in off times like this, I got to really soak it all in.

I kept smiling as I let my eyes wander over the crew, thinking about how we'd done pretty well working together. There were hiccups with that first dinner service, and my stews needed a little more training in the cocktail and cabin-cleaning departments, but it was promising that no one was fighting or not pulling their weight — at least, not yet.

It was almost easy to forget the cameras were with us. I was getting used to them, to the mic always clipped to my shorts and the wire under my shirt. Tonight, that mic was hanging on to the back of my skin-tight jeans for dear life, the cord visible where it snaked up my exposed back and then under the white crop top I had on. That top zig-zagged in the front, framing my cleavage in a way that I couldn't be mad at Eli for looking earlier.

Everyone was dressed up, ready to let loose and celebrate our first charter under our belt. And everyone was in good spirits.

Except for Gisella and Finn.

They were huddled together at the opposite end of the table from where I sat, Gisella speaking in hushed whispers, her expression sharp as she gestured with one hand. Finn's head was slightly bowed as he listened, his fingers tapping the rim of his empty shot glass. Whatever she was saying, he wasn't arguing back, but he didn't look happy, either.

I swallowed hard, forcing myself to look away before I got caught staring again.

It doesn't matter.

It's none of my business.

But when Gisella let out an exasperated sigh and pulled back from Finn completely, shaking her head before reaching for her shot that I hadn't realized she'd yet to take, my eyes floated to them once again.

She downed the shot in one go and smacked the glass on the table before turning to Bernard. "Tell me you ordered a bottle of wine."

"Two bottles," he corrected with a grin. "And an Aperol spritz, because we're in Italy, and I respect the culture."

Gisella hummed in approval, but as she picked up the menu to peruse it, Finn exhaled heavily, rubbing a hand down his face.

He flicked his gaze up, and for the briefest moment, our eyes met.

God, why did it always feel like a lightning bolt to the chest when he simply *looked* at me? It was like being struck with a thousand memories of the past along with the zapping reality of where we were now.

Finn swallowed, his gaze holding mine for just that moment before Gisella leaned over and whispered something else in his ear, her fingers trailing down his arm. She looked almost apologetic, or was it that she was expressing forgiveness to Finn?

What did he need to be forgiven for?

Whatever moment had been building shattered as I turned my attention back to my menu, gripping the edges a little too tight.

Eli leaned in close. "So, pasta or seafood, gorgeous?" he asked, voice low, lips just barely brushing my ear.

I forced a smirk and angled toward him slightly. "Why not both?"

His grin stretched wide as I reached for my wine glass.

I didn't dare look across the table again.

Three hours later, I was gloriously drunk and not thinking about work.

It always took a while for me to get to this point. Even at dinner, I found myself ruminating with Bernard and Leah about what we could do better on this next charter. I was launching into a whole theory about our dinner service issues when Palmer had reached for me across the table. He'd squeezed my wrist with a look that said *save this for another time*, and I realized then that poor Leah was yawning and Bernard was anxiously tapping his foot under the table while doing his best to keep that winning smile in place.

Palmer was right. It wasn't the time for corrections.

It was the time to blow off steam and reset.

So, I'd put my chief stew hat away for the night, and after copious amounts of wine at dinner followed by a round of shots as soon as we got to the club, and who knew what else I'd consumed since then... well...

I was drunk.

The bright lights of the camera crew surrounding us were like spotlights on the dance floor, and we weren't the only ones eating it up. Locals and tourists alike flocked to where we were, curious about the show and the people on it. Cameron and Eli reveled in the attention, dancing with groups of beautiful women and blowing their first tip on round after round of shots. But they were buzzing, alive with laughter and joy, and that was what it was all about.

Leah and I took turns doing ridiculous dance moves in a battle against one another, her hitting me with the running man before I shot back with the shopping cart. Gisella eventually joined us, but the poor girl couldn't dance awkwardly even if she wanted to. She was just inherently sexy, and eventually, the three of us were grinding in a sort of train, moving our hips to the heavy bass thumping through the club.

Somewhere between the limoncello shots and the second bottle of wine, Gisella got over whatever it was that had upset her. She was back to her bubbly self. Finn seemed to have relaxed with her shift in mood, too. He and Palmer were lounging in the VIP area the show had secured for us, which was a huge perk, because though I loved the high heels I was wearing, I couldn't last long in them before I needed to sit and take a break.

It was a little after midnight when I decided I needed to not only get off my feet, but to also get away from the heavy, fog-filled air of the night club. The lights were making my head throb, and I shouted into Bernard's ear over the music that I was going outside for a bit, but I'd be back. He smiled and nodded at me, though his attention immediately snapped back to the impressively tall and gorgeous Italian man whom he currently had one leg draped over, his hand toying with the buttons that ran down the man's chest.

A couple of camera operators followed me as I zig-zagged my way through the crowd and out to the back patio. The club butted up to the water, separated only by a narrow cobblestone street where people meandered between bars, gelato stands, and late-night eateries. Some strolled hand in hand, others laughed loudly, their voices carrying over the hum of Vespas zipping by. A group of musicians had set up near the curb, strumming guitars and singing in deep, throaty Italian, their melodies weaving through the night like smoke.

As soon as I stepped outside, relief washed over me. A cool breeze rolled in from the bay, carrying the briny scent of the sea, cutting through the thick, heady mix of sweat, perfume, and alcohol clinging to my skin. I inhaled deep, letting the salt air fill my lungs, allowing the distant sound of water lapping against the docks to slow the rapid beat of my heart.

"Not sure this will make for entertaining television," I said to the cameraman and the woman at his side who was managing the audio equipment. All the camera operators worked in pairs like that, and I knew after this first charter that the couple with me now were named Luke and Lexi.

They both just smiled, silent, their lens pointed right at me. Luke shrugged as if to say *just doing my job.* They looked spent, and I knew they likely couldn't wait until our crew called it quits for the night so they could go get some sleep at the hotel where the production crew was set up. Their counterparts would be the ones reporting early in the morning.

I found a tall, empty barstool and slid onto it, my feet tingling from the relief of not bearing my weight in heels for a moment. I leaned my arms on the railing that stretched the back of the patio next, taking reprieve in the quiet time. Not that it was quiet outside — between the club patrons on the patio with me and the people walking or driving by on the street, it was anything but.

Still, it was nice to not have music blasting in my ears or anyone screaming over it.

I allowed myself ten minutes of solo bliss before I decided I should probably get back inside. But before I moved an inch, someone slid up beside me, their forearms coming to rest on the railing next to mine.

"Sick of us already, are ya, Firefly?"

Finn's voice was low and gravelly, evidence of a long day and a rough charter evident in every syllable that rolled off his tongue. I turned to look at him, and he appeared as tired as he sounded. Unfortunately for me, the man was somehow even hotter when he was exhausted — something about that scruff on his jaw, the lines at the edges of his eyes, the curl of his sleepy smile.

"Just needed a little air," I said. "Quite loud in there."

"The Ember I know thrives in that kind of environment," he said. "There's nothing you love more than a night out, throwing shapes and getting into a bit of mischief."

There was a smile on my face that I didn't give permission to be there, and I bit against it as my gaze lowered to my arms on the railing. I blinked, and a flash of that night on the beach two years ago struck me like a car.

I instantly frowned.

"Yes, well. That was two years ago," I said pointedly, lifting my gaze to his. "You don't know me at all now."

"Maybe we should change that."

"Maybe we shouldn't."

Finn sighed, running a hand back through his hair as he let his gaze sweep over the dark water in front of us. "I'm sorry, Ember."

"If this is another shit apology that isn't actually an apology, you can save it."

"No, really," he said, turning back to me. "I'm sorry. I shouldn't have taken my frustration out on you during that dinner service. It was our first one together and we *both* made mistakes — me more than you, I'd wager."

I swallowed, the fact that he was offering a genuine apology shocking enough to have me silent.

"And then in the crew mess that night, and the whole thing with Max the next day..." Finn shook his head. "I'm not trying to make excuses because that was bang out of order. I just... I'm a bit thrown from all of this, aren't you?"

Fuck.

I'd been perfectly content to not call attention to the facts of this situation I knew neither of us could ignore, but when I looked into Finn's glazed eyes, I knew he was just drunk enough to cross that line and call all our ghosts into the light.

"There's nothing to be thrown from," I muttered.

"Don't do that."

I cracked at the tone of his voice, chest splintering as I closed my eyes and let my head drop.

"Don't act like we don't have a past, like things didn't end well, like we weren't sure we'd ever see each other again, and now we're working on the same boat."

"And that you have a girlfriend," I shot at him, neck snapping as I lifted my gaze. "Yes, Finn. I'm well aware of the situation. I'd just prefer not to torture myself, if that's alright with you."

Finn frowned, opening his mouth but then just letting it hang there.

I sighed. "Thank you for the apology. I'm sorry, too. Let's

just... let's try not to kill each other these next couple months, yeah?"

"That's exactly what I came out here to say," he said. I noticed he conveniently didn't comment on the girlfriend thing. "I thought maybe we could shelve all this... be friends?"

I tried not to laugh.

Truly, I tried.

But it bubbled out of me before I could stop it. Not a full on *haha, you're so funny* laugh, but one that sounded like I'd choked on that word he'd thrown at me.

"Sure, Finn," I clipped. "We can be friends."

I tried to ignore the way my chest was ripping apart as I slid off the barstool, ready to go back into the club and get my mind off this conversation. But before I could take a step, Finn's fingers caught the belt loop of my jeans.

He tugged me to a stop, pulling hard enough that I had no choice but to face him. My cheeks burned when I met his gaze again, when I saw his jaw set like that. It reminded me of the first night he touched me, the night I found out he wasn't just good with his hands in the kitchen.

"You look so pretty like this," he growls against my lips, hand splaying my throat before curling just enough to make me gasp and arch into the touch. "Wearing the way you want me like a red lipstick you want everyone to see."

"Finn..."

"That's it, Firefly. Call out my name. Beg for what you want."

I blinked, cursing the memory and the way it sent electricity straight between my thighs.

"I mean it," Finn said. He dropped his gaze to where I was staring at his fingers in my belt loop, and then cleared his throat, releasing the hold. "We need to work through this together. Especially with…"

He glanced at the camera I just remembered was with us, and I flushed deeper.

"Let's be a team," Finn added. "We make a good one, if you remember."

I'm trying to forget.

But I didn't say the words aloud. Instead, I sighed heavily, but nodded, leaning my arms on the railing again. As much as the idea of being *friends* with Finn Pearson made me sick, he was right. This was a huge chance to further my career, to secure myself gigs I couldn't even dream of at the moment.

It was a chance to prove myself to my father with the world watching.

I wouldn't waste that — especially not on feelings that should have been long dead by now.

"Fine," I relented. "Let's be a team. But only if you mean that. Don't take your little chef fits out on me. You can throw dishes and play Fruit Ninja all you want, but don't be a dick to me."

The corner of Finn's lips curved. "No dick behavior. Promise."

I smirked back, rolling my neck against the strain there. "I think I need another drink."

"I think I need my bed."

"Old man."

"Never felt that to be more true than this moment," he admitted, and right on cue, a huge yawn stretched his mouth.

I chuckled. "What happened to the Finn *I* used to know? You were always the last one back on the boat. You'd be out until you had to provision the next day sometimes."

"I guess we've both aged."

"Guess so." My smile fell a bit, eyes flicking over the new lines on his face, the way he looked older now. The floor dropped out from under me.

I hated that I'd missed out on those years.

"Is everything okay with you and Gisella, by the way?" I tried not to sound as desperate as I was to know the answer when the question left my lips. "She seemed a little... perturbed at dinner."

Finn sighed. "That's one word for it. She was fit to kill."

"Why?"

"The producers thought it would be fun to tell her during post-charter interviews that you and I used to date."

Shit.

I didn't know why, but guilt slid through me like a snake. "Oh."

"Yeah." Finn arched a brow at me, then smiled a little. "Don't look so scared. It's fine now. We talked. She was upset I didn't tell her first, but I didn't really have the time to yet, did I?"

I wished I had something to take a sip of because I didn't know how to answer that.

"We're good now," he assured me.

I pretended like that was a relief. "Oh. Great. I'm glad."

Silence stretched between us again, and I told myself to go back inside, but for some reason, I couldn't stop staring at him.

I blamed the alcohol for not being able to stunt my curiosity any longer.

"Finn."

"Mm?"

"What happened with your restaurant in Dublin?"

Every semblance of joy left his face in an instant, the light leaking out of him like a candle snuffed out by an unforgiving wind. He swallowed, the Adam's apple in his throat lurching as he tore his gaze from me.

"Some things just aren't meant to last."

I frowned, the urge to reach for him nearly strong enough to make me forget where we were, *who* we were... and who was watching.

"Em..." He croaked my name, jaw clicking. "You gotta stop looking at me like that."

"Like what?"

He didn't get the chance to answer. Gisella bounded out onto the patio like a bunny rabbit, smiling ear to ear as she threw her arms around Finn's neck and leaped onto his back.

"*Bebé*," she sang, kissing all over his neck.

Acid burned my throat as I cleared it, managing a smile at Gisella before I excused myself and rejoined the group inside.

My stomach never did settle that night.

Neither did my mind.

Chapter Ten

POST-PRODUCTION CONFESSIONAL
CLOSE QUARTERS

SEASON 4

GISELLA DÍAZ: DECKHAND/STEWARDESS

PRODUCER
Can you start by saying your name, where you're from,
and what you do?

GISELLA
I'm Gisella Díaz, I'm from Barcelona, and I've been
in yachting for two years now. I work as deck crew,
but I help on interior when needed.

PRODUCER
Do you prefer deck or interior?

GISELLA
Deck. No question. I'd rather scrub teak than cater
to a billionaire telling me his drink is exactly two
degrees too warm. I don't mind laundry, though. It's
therapeutic sometimes.

PRODUCER
Let's talk about that first charter. How did you feel
about the guests?

Gisella smirks, shrugs.

GISELLA
Oh, they weren't so bad. Benedict was only mildly

insufferable, and Brielle only looked like she wanted
to murder me for about ten seconds when her hair
got wet on the jet ski. I don't know. They were a
little difficult, I guess, but it's rare to have
charter guests who aren't. And honestly? That was the
happiest I was all season.

PRODUCER
Why's that?

GISELLA
Because back then, I thought the worst thing I'd deal
with was a tech mogul making me inflate the giant
slide, or an Instagram model making me risk going
overboard to get her the perfect shot.

Gisella shakes head, pauses for a moment.

GISELLA
I was on a yacht in the Mediterranean with my
boyfriend, making good money, catching a nice tan,
and having fun. I thought, *this is it – this is what
they mean when they say you're living the dream.*

PRODUCER
And that changed?

GISELLA
Yeah. Because back then, I thought my biggest problem
was going to be the guests.

PRODUCER
And what was?

GISELLA
The chief stew.

I was excited the next morning as we braced to welcome our next
charter guests.

For approximately twenty minutes.

Then, I found out Leah was sick.

I was on my way up to the deck, tightening my ponytail as I

swung through the crew mess to see what Finn had laid out for breakfast. When I saw fresh croissants, I moaned, snatching one to have with my coffee.

I was, surprisingly, not hungover — not that I was in tip-top shape, either, but I'd had worse mornings, for sure.

Unfortunately, that was not the case for Leah.

I heard the retching from the cabin she shared with Bernard even over the gentle hum of the washers and dryers going. Bernard slipped out of their cabin with a grimace, shaking his head at me. "It's an absolute crime scene in there."

"Hungover?" I guessed.

"Possibly, but she swears blind she isn't. Says she didn't drink enough for it to be the booze."

I tried to remember everyone's consumption from the night before, and had to admit I didn't recall her slamming down shots the way the guys had. She'd only had one glass of wine with dinner, too.

But if it wasn't the alcohol, then that likely meant...

"Fuck," I cursed under my breath.

"Food poisoning," Bernard finished the thought for me, crossing his arms and leaning against the wall. "She did have a whole bloody plate of oysters."

I winced as another violent retch echoed from the bathroom, then closed my eyes with a sigh, pinching the bridge of my nose.

This was not good.

"I'll check on her," I said. "Go grab a coffee, then can you start on cabins?"

"It would be my pleasure, m'lady."

He gave an exaggerated bow at the waist, one hand pressed

over his stomach like a royal guard. It pulled a reluctant smile from me.

"You alright?" he asked, his voice softening.

I tilted my head, one brow arched at his searching gaze. "Peachy. Why?"

"Just checking on my chief."

"Uh-huh. More like fishing for gossip. Spill. What have you heard?"

He flicked imaginary long hair over his shoulder, despite the fact his was cropped close to his beautiful head. "Only that you and ol' Cheffy in there used to knock boots."

Bernard stuck his tongue in his cheek as he inspected his nails, then flashed me a wicked grin.

"It's true, isn't it?"

I didn't know if I wanted to scream, cry, or yeet myself off the top deck — but in my delirium, all I managed was a groan muffled behind a grin. "It was a long time ago."

"Right. So long ago that rooming with his new girlfriend isn't awkward in the slightest."

"Cabins, Bernard."

He snickered. "Yes, yes, all work, no play." He gave my shoulder a quick squeeze on the way past. "It's going to be alright," he said, nodding toward where Leah was.

But he and I both knew the truth.

If there was a stew down, it was going to be hell on both of us.

"Leah," I said, announcing my presence with a gentle knock on her cabin door. I slid inside when she didn't answer, then inched the bathroom door open.

The poor southern belle was splayed out on the ground, her legs in a stag shape, arms draped over the toilet seat, head resting on her forearms. She groaned, turning just enough to glance up at me through her greasy hair.

"I swear, Em. I'm not hungover."

"I believe you," I said. I bent next to her, holding her hair out of the way as she dry-heaved into the toilet. When she caught her breath, I rubbed her back and sighed. "I think it's safe to say you need to be in bed today."

"No," she whined. "I'm fine. I... I just need..."

She vomited again, her shoulders deflating.

"You need rest and to hydrate. I'll call provisions and add some electrolyte drinks to our order. I'm going to bring you some crackers to nibble on, and when you're ready, Finn can make you some broth."

She gagged, then whined again. "I'm mortified. And putting you and Bernard in this position..."

"It's okay," I assured her. I was distantly aware of the camera duo just outside the bathroom door capturing this whole thing. "We'll figure it out."

Leah nodded and sighed, then smiled just a little. "Thank God for Gisella, huh? Not often you have a deck/stew on board who can help when something like this happens."

My insides coiled tight. I hadn't even gotten that far yet, but Leah was right — I was going to have to talk to Captain and see if we could use Gisella for this charter.

Which meant not only were we rooming together, but we'd be *working* together — closely — for at least the next two days.

"Yeah," I muttered, hoping my smile looked genuine. "Thank God for Gisella."

"Don't worry, *mi reina*. I got you." Gisella squeezed my arm where I was filling the champagne glasses to welcome our next charter guests, her smile bright and filled with assurance.

I wished I believed it.

Captain had agreed that it would be best if Gisella worked mostly with interior this charter while Leah recovered. He felt confident the guys on deck could handle everything without her and call on the radio for special circumstances, like docking or blowing up the giant slide that was always a pain in the ass.

I'd felt relief at first, but after provisions arrived and every moment since, that relief had slowly morphed into worry.

Gisella was sweet. She would definitely be able to serve with a smile. She was laid back.

But she was maybe a bit *too* laidback.

She'd moved at a snail's pace with laundry, and Bernard told me he had to go in behind her to tidy up the laundry room and get uniforms where they needed to be. She hadn't read the names on tags, so everyone had ended up with other people's clothes — including Captain, who also gave me a stern warning look when his epaulets went missing in the process.

Then, she'd taken nearly three hours to set the guest cabins, fluffing pillows and adjusting throws while simultaneously missing important things like tucking the corners of the sheets properly and making sure the mirrors were spotless. I'd had to polish up every single room when I checked her work, fixing everything she'd overlooked.

When we were provisioning, she spent more time learning how to make an espresso martini — something the guests had specifically stated they'd want in their preference sheets — than actually putting anything away. And yes, I needed her to know how to make that drink, but what I *didn't* need was for it to take half the afternoon. While the rest of us were knee-deep in organizing the fridges and dry storage, she was laughing at the mess she was making with the espresso machine like it wasn't adding to our list of shit to clean.

Not to mention the amount of times just since this morning that I'd caught her flirting with Finn instead of working.

I felt like we'd all been duped — me most of all. Because where Gisella had seemed like a rockstar with the first charter, she was more like a rock in my shoe for this one.

I forced a smile at her now as I continued pouring the welcome aboard champagne, hoping for my and Bernard's sake that it was just an off day. "At least these guests seem a little more relaxed than the last group," I said.

"They're certainly less picky eaters," Finn chimed in as he swept past us, tucking in his chef's shirt on his way to the main deck aft where the guests would come aboard. He smiled at me, making my stomach flutter like it was full of hummingbirds.

He'd almost made it through the sliding glass doors when Gisella grabbed his arm and whipped him back around, an expectant look on her face as she popped a brow into her hairline and leaned her weight on one hip.

"I know you weren't just going to prance by me like that without a kiss," she said.

Finn's eyes flicked to mine, and then he dipped down to brush a quick kiss over Gisella's lips, and all those hummingbirds in my belly died.

I swallowed, focusing on the task at hand and hoping my cheeks weren't burning red. "You can go ahead and get in line," I told Gisella. "I'll be right out."

"Sure you don't need any help?"

"I got it."

"Okay." But she stayed, tapping her nail against the marble bar, a slow, rhythmic click that grated on my nerves. "I just want you to know I'm not upset or anything."

I paused where I was pouring the last glass of champagne, arching a brow at her. "Huh?"

"About the whole Finn thing."

All the blood rushed from my face.

Shit.

"I mean, I wish one of you would have told me before the producers did," she amended, playing with her long dark hair. I made a mental note to ask her to put it up when this conversation was over. "Him being my boyfriend, you being my roommate..."

"Honestly, I didn't think it was worth telling you about," I said, filling the last glass and stashing the bottle of champagne away. "It was a very short-lived relationship, if you could even call it that."

"It doesn't take years to fall in love."

Her words were like a board sweeping under my feet. It felt like they'd thrown me to the ground, knocking the wind from me in an instant.

I knew the truth under them more than I'd ever admit to her.

"But I'm not mad or anything. We're good. I'm just glad it's all behind you guys and we can be professional. I don't know what I'd do if you were still obsessed with him or something." She laughed, flicking her hair over her shoulder. "*Drama!*"

She sang the word, stretching out the *ah* at the end like she was the carefree, fun one and I was the unhinged ex.

I somehow managed a smile, lifting the tray of glasses filled with sparkling gold. "No drama necessary. Finn and I are just friends."

That word still stung when I said it.

"That's what he said, too." Gisella's lips curled — a soft smile but with a biting edge to it. "I'm glad we're all friends. It would be a bit awkward otherwise, wouldn't it?"

She laughed again, but this time, there was something smug about it. Something that said, *I have him now. And you? You don't matter.*

You are not a threat.

My throat felt like I'd swallowed sandpaper.

Captain Gary called over the radio that guests were approaching, and I'd never been so thankful for a charter starting in my life. "Let's get out there. Pull your hair back for me, will you?"

"But it looks so much nicer down."

I smiled wider. "I understand, but it's more professional to have it pulled back and tidy."

"The guests won't care."

I ground my teeth. "Well, Captain Gary will."

"He's already seen me. He—"

"Gisella, put your hair up and get on deck." My voice was steel, my patience at its frayed edge. "We may be friends, but right now, I'm your boss. And you're wasting my time and energy arguing over something you should know after two years in the industry."

Gisella snapped her mouth shut, head popping back a bit like I'd surprised her.

Good.

She may have been stepping in to help, and she may have been the queen when it came to Finn now. But that was where her power ended.

I was in charge of this interior.

And I was not having another subpar charter on my watch,

no matter what the universe tried to throw at me.

If Poseidon were real, he was certainly sending us a gift with the current charter guests, because them being a cool group was the only reason interior wasn't completely falling apart.

Captain had Leah go to the hospital, mostly to make sure what she was suffering from really was food poisoning and not something the rest of the crew could catch from being in close contact with her. He also wanted her to get fluids to help her stay hydrated. She was back now, but still feeling rough, and I knew we were going to have to survive another day without her.

Bernard wore his exhaustion like an extra stripe as he helped me and Finn prepare for the beach picnic the guests had asked for. He'd been a rockstar on dinner service with me last night, despite the fact that Gisella had acted like she was an extra deckhand just floating around with nothing to do. I'd had to repeatedly call for her on the radio to help carry plates when they were ready to go. As soon as we served them, she was gone again. But she always had an excuse when I called her on it.

I was checking cabins.

False. Because Bernard had already done them.

I was working on laundry.

False. Because it was still a mess in there when we wrapped dinner service, and *I* had been the one to sort through it all.

Palmer needed me on deck.

False. We were anchored, the water toys were already put away, the sun had set, and there was nothing more to do until Eli cleaned while on night watch.

The only reason we were surviving right now was because the

guests were clearly not used to the yacht life, or they were just ridiculously gracious. Because I knew that dinner service had been clunky and slow, drinks while they relaxed on the sundeck before had been delayed, their cabin refreshes during dinner were mediocre at best, and we were now running thirty minutes behind, and counting, for their beach picnic.

"Oi, you're smashing it," Bernard said, pausing where he was packing coolers long enough to grab me by the shoulders and give me a little shake. I'd been pinching the bridge of my nose and forcing some calming breaths, but I didn't feel any more at peace than two minutes ago.

I tried to force a smile. "Thanks. You okay?"

"Fit as a fiddle," he lied.

"I want you to go down for a break once you get the cabins in order," I told him, checking my watch. "I'll have Gisella make the welcome drinks for when we get back."

He arched a brow. "You certain?"

"You need rest."

"So do you."

"Chief stews don't rest." I winked at him through my sleepy smile. "Alright, let's get these coolers in the tender."

I called for Eli and Cameron's help over the radio, and once they'd lugged the coolers away, it was just me and Finn in the galley.

"Okay," I breathed, running over the list in my phone. "We've got the drinks, glasses, ice, tables, décor... napkins, plates, flatware... towels, sunscreen..." I paused where I was checking off items long enough to call to Palmer on the radio and make sure he had umbrellas and the tent for shade. Once he confirmed, I continued. "And you have everything you need?" I asked, finally looking up at Finn. "All the appetizers already prepared, everything you need for the grill?"

Finn was wiping down where he'd prepped the citrus and herb couscous salad that would be served as a side.

He was also watching me in the most curious way.

His mouth was tilted at the edge, his eyes shining like the water outside the small galley windows behind him.

"What?" I asked.

"You were built for this, you know that?"

The words were soft, lilted by his accent and subtle appreciation.

I chuffed a laugh. "Yeah. I'm slaying it."

"You are."

"If we're judging by these first two charters, I think everyone in the world would argue the opposite."

"No one in the world knows you like I do."

He said it casually, but the moment the words were in the space between us, the air grew heavier. Finn paused where he was cleaning, his smile waning, and I furrowed my brows as I looked at him and waited.

For what? For him to apologize, to explain those words away?

For him to double down and say them again?

Neither happened, because Gisella swept into the galley, and I cleared my throat, turning my attention back to the list on my phone.

"I'm so sad I don't get to go with you to the beach," Gisella pouted, throwing her arms around his shoulders. "It's not fair."

I rolled my eyes, and that was just enough of a glance in their direction for me to see Finn swallow.

"Trust me, it'll be more fun on the boat with the guests gone.

Beach picnics are hard work."

"Sure, such a misfortune." Gisella sighed. "I guess it will be nice to get a bit of a break. I feel like I've barely come up for air this charter, balancing both deck and interior."

I couldn't help it. I snorted a sarcastic laugh that felt as awkward as it sounded. Both their gazes slid to me, and I tried to cover it by pretending to cough, making my eyes water.

"Something in my throat," I muttered through another fit. "I'm going to head over with this tender and start getting everything set up. Gisella, I'll radio when we're ready for the guests. I told Bernard to go down for his break as soon as we're gone. Can you take care of cabins and make sure we have a welcome drink for the guests when we return?"

"So much for that break," Gisella said to Finn, as if it was quiet enough that I wouldn't hear when she pinned me with a fake smile. "Yes, ma'am."

Ma'am.

As if I were ten years her senior.

I wanted to smack that smirk right off her gorgeous face, but in a feat of restraint I was surprised I had, I mirrored her smile and just said, "Thank you."

Before heading to the beach, I popped down to Leah's cabin, knocking softly and sitting on the edge of her bed in the dark room.

"How are you feeling?"

"Getting better," she said, wincing as she maneuvered her way to sitting up. She took a sip of the electrolyte drink next to her. "Although I'm absolutely devastated to be missing this beach picnic."

"I did promise you I'd let you get off the boat as soon as we had one, but…"

"Yeah. Throwing up on the guests probably wouldn't make for a good tip."

I smirked, squeezing her knee.

"Y'all okay?" she asked.

God, no, I wanted to reply, but I forced a smile, instead. "We're just fine. You rest up and we'll all be back to normal soon."

"I feel awful, Em."

"I know. But it's okay. I promise."

I patted her leg, ready to tell her to get some rest and I'd check in on her later, but she stopped me.

"Em?"

"Yeah?"

"What's the story with you and Finn?"

My gut churned. "What do you mean?"

"Well, you guys used to date, and now you're here together again, but he's with Gisella… and I don't know, I just feel like there's some animosity there. Was it a bad breakup? Were you together long?"

I blew out a breath. I shouldn't have been surprised that the whole crew knew about me and Finn now, the way gossip travels on floating tin cans like this. I was fairly certain the producers had a hand in the wildfire spread of our past, too.

"It was only four months," I said, though my body betrayed how casual I made those words sound.

"A lot can happen in four months. Especially on a boat."

I nodded.

"Why did you end it?"

"I didn't want to," I confessed softly. "I thought we were

leaving the boat together. We talked about it all the time — where we'd work next, how we'd spend some time off traveling together before we took our next job. I had a friend in the Bahamas who hooked us up with her captain. We had all these plans…"

I shook my head, the pain so fresh even two years later that I half-expected to look down and see blood gushing from a wound.

"But the last night of the season, he told me he was going home to Dublin to open a restaurant," I said, swallowing. "So… I guess I'd never really been a part of his plans. He let me think it, let me live in my delusional fantasy until the very last moment."

"Oh, my God… why would he do that?"

"To have a little fun on a boat and not have to face the consequences, I guess." I shrugged. "It was just a boatmance to him. I was stupid for thinking it was more."

Even as the words slid from my lips, I didn't believe them. I'd spent two years trying to get myself to face reality — that I'd meant nothing to Finn. But he'd played my heart so expertly that I still wanted to believe he cared about me, even when I had all the proof that he didn't.

"He never let on that it was just a fling to him?"

At that, I let out a soft, painful laugh. "He was a mastermind," I whispered, meeting her gaze. "I swore he loved me. Everyone else on that boat swore it, too."

That admission had everything inside me going sharp and sour, the memory of how broken I'd been when I'd walked off that boat slamming into me like a cold block of ice. I'd thrown myself into my next charter, desperate to fill my time and stay busy so I wouldn't think about how much I missed him. I got a new piercing. I got a new tattoo. I drank and partied with my new crew. I tried to build a new life without him.

None of it made me feel any better.

Eventually, I moved on — but not in the "I'm over him! I'm healed!" sort of way. I moved on because time gave me no choice. I moved on because I put one foot in front of the other, and eventually, weeks turned to months, and then to years.

And now here we were, two years between us, and all it took was one look at him for me to spiral.

I asked my mom once what it was that kept her and dad together all this time. They'd been college sweethearts, and it just seemed like a miracle to me that they could survive that youth, and then graduating, jobs, marriage, buying a house, having a kid.

She'd looked at me with a small smile as she washed dishes and said, "Some people come into our lives and then fade out, and we miss them, but not in a desperate way. We think of them fondly, but we can go on living without them. But others come into our lives and something inside us clicks into place, like a missing gear that has the power to make our whole system work properly. We can't let those people go — even when it gets hard, even when common sense says we should. They're a part of us. We will go to battle for them without a second thought. We'll lay down our own lives for them, no questions asked." She'd shrugged then, her eyes that mine mirrored swinging my way with a twinkle. "Some loves are inevitable — meant to be. And when you stumble upon that kind of love, it becomes an impenetrable force. Nothing can break it — not trial or time or distance. It just... survives."

I remember smiling at her like I got it, but really, I was just thinking about her and Dad. I was trying to understand how she put up with a man who could be so cold sometimes. It helped me make sense of them. It helped me see their love in the soft moments I witnessed them share and I realized that Mom didn't need a man who doted on her or showed up with big, grand gestures — she just needed Dad.

But I couldn't really relate.

Not until I lost Finn.

I understood her fully now.

Except where her love for Dad survived and kept her thriving, my love for Finn survived and killed me, little by little, day by day — even still.

And it wasn't even real to him.

"Maybe he did love you," Leah said. "Maybe there's more to the story."

I offered her a small smile, patting her leg before I stood. "Well, if there was, he had his chance to tell me and didn't. He just... left. Left yachting, left the Med, left me." I shrugged. "And now he's back, with Gisella, so maybe it's just that I wasn't what he wanted in the long run."

Leah frowned, reaching out to squeeze my wrist. "I'm sorry. It must be kind of weird, being back in close quarters with him." She winced. "Oh, God. That was so cheesy. I bet the producers will love that line."

I chuckled, but her comment made my gaze flick up to the blue light of the camera rolling in the corner of the cabin. "It's fine. We're all adults. And what Finn and I had is in the past."

My stomach roiled with the lie.

"Well, I'm here if you ever need to talk about any of it. Or if you want to, like, print out a picture of him and throw darts at it."

Palmer called over the radio that we were set to head to the beach and set up, and I smiled at Leah, nodding my thanks.

"Get some rest," I told her. "I don't need to talk about my ex, but I *do* need my stew to feel better."

"On it," she said with a salute, and then she crawled back under the covers.

Five minutes later, I was in the tender with the guys headed toward the beach, the salty wind in my hair and one of the cameras pointed right at me. Between the growl of the engine, the slap of waves against the hull, and the occasional holler from Palmer as he steered us toward shore, it was too loud to hear anything.

And my thoughts were the loudest of all.

Finn's voice echoed, over and over, the words looping like a broken record: *No one in the world knows you like I do.*

Each repetition peeled back another layer, revealing memory after memory I'd tried to bury. His hands in my hair. His laugh in my ear. His whispered promises in the dark. And then, silence — the space he left behind when he walked away.

My chest tightened, breath shallow as I clenched the edge of the cooler between my knees and forced myself to focus. There was work to be done, a picnic to set, a show to run. But no matter how much I tried to drown him out, his voice cut through — softer than the wind, sharper than the salt in the air.

No one in the world knows you like I do.

I squeezed my eyes shut against the sting behind them, the truth of it sinking in like an anchor.

He was right.

And I hated it.

Chapter Eleven

CHARTER CONFESSIONAL
CLOSE QUARTERS

SEASON 4, EPISODE 3
CHARTER 2

CAMERON DUNN: DECKHAND

PRODUCER
Charter two under your belt! How are you feeling?

CAMERON
Like a bloody pack mule after a week in the Highlands.

PRODUCER
Tell us about beach picnics. Are they common on yachts?

CAMERON
Aye, beach picnics are a right pain in the arse. First, you've got to find a beach in the first place, which is a nightmare, because these guests all want something 'exclusive' – white sand, crystal-clear water, nae a soul in sight. Then, you've got to haul every bit of furniture and food over like we're setting up a five-star restaurant in the middle of the feckin' jungle. After that, serve them, cater to their every whim, break it all down again, and then drag it all back to the boat just in time to do more work.

Cameron shakes head.

CAMERON
It's never fun for the crew. But if you pull it off
right, it can mean a hefty tip.

PRODUCER
How do you think this one went?

CAMERON
It was about perfect, wudn't it? The food was spot
on, the beach was a stunner, and service was smooth
as a fresh pint of Tennent's Lager. Not much more you
could ask for.

PRODUCER
Did the guests seem happy? And what did you think
about them?

CAMERON
This was one of those charters you thank God for. The
guests were sound — proper nice, easygoing, and up
for a laugh. I had a blast with them on that beach,
and you could see they were loving every second of
it. Of course… they weren't the only ones, were they?

Cameron smirks.

PRODUCER
What do you mean by that?

CAMERON
Oh, come on… I'm not the only one with eyes.

The beach picnic was going off without a hitch, which was both a
relief and a small miracle.

The guests — a wealthy family from the Midwest celebrating
the father's sixtieth birthday — were easygoing, the kind of
laidback rich that made for a drama-free charter. They didn't
have any outrageous demands, there were no passive-aggressive
complaints, and they seemed genuinely excited over the setup

Cameron and I had put together. White linen tablecloths flapped in the salty breeze, the crystal glassware catching the golden sunlight, and Finn's spread of fresh seafood and gourmet sandwiches had been met with enthusiastic approval.

And for the first time since this charter kicked off, I had a break from Gisella.

Maybe that was why things were going so smoothly.

I pushed the thought away as I worked on clearing the table, surveying the guests where they now lounged near the shoreline. John, the primary, was waist-deep in the water with his wife and son, all three of them laughing at something Cameron was saying from where he stood on the shore. The rest of the family was sprawled out on the lounge chairs the guys had set up, sipping the light spritzer I'd whipped up and soaking in the late afternoon sun.

"Not bad for your first official beach picnic as chief stew." Finn's voice came from behind me, low and warm like the sunshine hitting my neck.

I turned to find him standing close, arms folded over his chest, a small smirk playing on his lips. He had rolled his sleeves up to his elbows, exposing forearms dusted with flour and a small streak of something — maybe olive oil? — on his wrist. His apron was long discarded, leaving him in just his white polo and tailored navy shorts. The sight of him like that made sparks flutter low in my belly. He was relaxed, his job done for now, the guests fed and happy.

Food wasn't just his job, it was his passion, his love language.

Up until now, I swore I felt something dark and weighted holding onto him. Maybe it was the death of his restaurant. He just seemed... lost. Half-whole, almost. But now, standing in the shade of the pop-up tent covering the leftover food, he looked like the old Finn.

The one I fell for years ago on a boat miles from here.

"Not bad at all," I agreed, exhaling. "Though I can't help but wonder if that's because Gisella had nothing to do with it."

I cringed internally as soon as I said the words. The last thing I wanted was Finn to think I was some jealous ex, but my comment had nothing to do with them and everything to do with the fact that Gisella was supposed to be making this charter easier on me, and so far had done nothing but the opposite.

"Harsh," he said, but it was with a laugh that made the stress of explaining myself float away. Gisella was his girlfriend, but maybe he could see past that and acknowledge that she wasn't exactly an A+ student on this yacht.

"Honest," I corrected.

Finn hummed in response, his smirk deepening.

I crossed my arms, mimicking his stance. "Still, with the way things have been going, I half-expected some kind of disaster. A tipped-over champagne bucket, a seagull stealing a sandwich, a rogue wave sweeping the whole table out to sea."

"All things out of your control, even if they did happen."

"As chief stew, it's my job to be in control of *everything*."

"You're doing a great job, Ember." Finn's voice was quieter now, sincere. "Really. You should be proud."

I blinked, caught off guard by the praise. For some reason, it meant more coming from Finn, just like I knew it would if it came from my father.

Because they knew me. They knew how hard I'd worked over the last several years, how much this chance meant to me, how far I was willing to go to make my dreams happen.

No one in the world knows you like I do.

I swallowed, muttering a thanks before I finished clearing the table. I ran out to check on the guests, refilling drink orders and double-checking on what time they wanted to head back to the boat. When they were content again, I joined Finn under the shade once more.

"They won't stop talking about the food," I told him, my smile widening when his cheeks flushed a little. "John is making jokes about offering you a job as head chef for the family."

"Is he joking, or is he serious?"

"If it's the latter, you're going to break his heart. I know you well enough to know you wouldn't be satisfied cooking for just one family."

He shrugged. "I don't know. Maybe the Midwest is where I'm meant to be. I feel like I could thrive in... where was it they're from again?"

I blinked. "Illinois."

"I've heard Chicago is great."

"*Southern* Illinois."

"I'm not sure what the difference is."

I laughed a little as I dug my fingers into the muscle running from my neck to my shoulder, trying to work out the tension. "You'd figure it out real fast."

"Here, let me."

I didn't have time to react before Finn reached out and pressed his hands to my shoulders, thumbs kneading into the muscle. There was no time for me to be shocked at him offering, no chance for my body to buzz to life once he touched me. One second, it was my hand massaging my neck, and the next, it was his.

I melted.

I was so tense, so sore, so fucking *exhausted* that just that minor touch from another human had me sighing. My eyes fluttered shut for half a second, body going as limp as it could while still keeping me upright. The stress of the last few days turned to liquid under his touch, rolling off me like a slow-trickling waterfall with each careful roll of his thumbs.

"Mmm," I exhaled, my body leaning into him without my cue. "God, I forgot how good you are at this. Remember the first time you massaged my feet after that charter where the guests demanded an all-night dance party?"

I let my head drop back against the wall, groaning as Finn digs his thumbs into the arch of my left foot. "Fuck, Finn. That feels so good."

He swallows, nostrils flaring, his eyes lifting to mine.

"I'd like to hear you say those words when we're both wearing less clothing."

"Dirty," I tease with a smile.

"Like your feet."

Then he tickles me as I squeal and laugh, trying and failing to wriggle out of his grasp. Soon, I stop trying. Soon, I pull him into me, instead — hands fisted in his shirt and tugging him in until he's on top of me, until our laughs turn to kisses, until I feel him harden between my thighs.

I blinked out of the memory, peeking over my shoulder. I expected to find Finn smirking at the memory, too, but his gaze was focused on the back of my neck.

"This one is new," he mused, thumb gliding over where I knew delicate black ink stretched over my skin.

It was a tiny northern lapwing bird.

The bird of Ireland.

My chest strained with the effort to breathe properly because I had no idea what to say. Finn was well aware that I used piercings and micro tattoos as a way to sort through or, sometimes, *avoid* pesky emotions. It was another thing about me I was sure my father didn't love.

But I didn't want to admit out loud what I knew Finn had just figured out.

That one was for him.

One of the guests let out a peal of high-pitched laughter as a wave soaked her up to her chest, and Finn and I both snapped our gazes to the sound.

That's when we saw the camera duo that was sent to the beach with us.

Their lenses were pointed right at where we stood.

My stomach lurched, and Finn hastily removed his hands, quickly busying himself with cleaning the grill while I awkwardly cleared my throat and pulled my ponytail behind my shoulder again, as if it could hide the tattoo I'd nearly forgotten was there. Needing to move, I pretended like there was still packing up to do, opening and closing coolers like an idiot.

When neither of us had anything left to fake it with, Finn sighed, running a hand through his hair. "I know it's not my job to do it, but... I want to apologize for Gisella. Safe to assume she hasn't been the saving grace you expected when Leah went down."

I was surprised by his acknowledgement of the situation, my eyebrows creeping up into my hairline as I folded my arms over my chest, eyes on the guests in the water. I was also relieved that we were moving on from the tattoo, that my body was cooling a bit now that his hands were no longer on my shoulders.

"It's fine," I said. "Hopefully Leah will be good as new in the morning. I will admit... I was hoping for the version of Gisella that we had the first charter. Not sure what happened in between."

He glanced at me, his expression unreadable. "She... doesn't really take anything too seriously."

"I've noticed."

We shared a smile, the tension from before floating away on the soft breeze. I relaxed a little, enough so that I finally asked what I'd been wondering since that first crew meeting.

"How long have you been with her?"

Finn's throat bobbed. "It's pretty new. Just a few months."

Even though I'd asked, the answer didn't bring me any sort of relief. I stared out at the horizon, letting the sound of the waves fill the space between us, wondering how serious a few months could really be.

Then I remembered we'd only been together four months, and my stomach pitched more.

"So... why is she here? If she doesn't take this seriously, I'm assuming that means she doesn't really care to advance. What's her end goal?"

Finn shrugged. "She loves to travel. The money's good. She thought being on a show would be fun."

"So she doesn't really have any ambition?"

Finn's expression flickered, his shoulders tensing slightly. "I didn't say that."

"No, sorry," I backtracked, suddenly feeling like I'd stepped on a nerve. "I just... you have so much desire, so many dreams. I guess I'm a little surprised you'd be with someone who..."

Finn was watching me closely as the words died on my

tongue, his jaw tightening.

"But I guess that's kind of nice," I added quickly, forcing a lightness into my voice. "Because I'm sure she supports your dreams. And if she's not tied down, that means she can follow you wherever you want to go."

The last words were quieter, the bitter truth of them like an ice pick to my chest.

She would follow him.

Like I didn't.

A muscle in Finn's jaw ticced. He was silent for a long moment before he blew out a slow breath. "Actually... Gisella helped me see that the restaurant was a mistake."

My head snapped toward him, brows furrowing. "What?"

Finn didn't meet my gaze.

I scoffed, shaking my head. "Please tell me that's a joke..."

He still wouldn't look at me, his body tight from the muscle straining his neck all the way down to where his feet were planted in the sand.

"Look, I don't know what happened, but that restaurant wasn't a mistake, Finn. It was your dream. I mean, it meant so much to you that you walked away from yachting."

It meant so much that you walked away from me.

He finally looked at me then, his expression dark, something simmering beneath the surface. "You're right. You don't know what happened."

The accusation in his voice turned me to stone.

"Because you weren't there."

My breath stalled in my throat.

The air between us was dry and hot, crackling with

everything we had left unsaid for two years. And that betrayal I'd almost forgotten about seeped in like sludge, slowing my heart.

He was right. I didn't go with him.

Because I didn't know he would be going in a different direction until the night before we were set to leave.

And he was forgetting to mention a big piece of this puzzle: he didn't come with *me*, either.

Now, he was back in yachting with another woman.

Which told me loud and clear that I had never been enough for him.

I let out a hollow laugh, my mouth falling open. "Right. Because I'm a woman, so it's me who should drop everything to cater to whatever *you* want, right? Fuck my own aspirations?"

Finn blinked, like he'd been in a spell and my words had snapped him out of it. Regret shaded his gaze. "That's not what I meant."

"Save it," I spat. "We've already had this fight, remember? No need to do it again."

I turned before he could say another word, my pulse roaring in my ears as I grabbed the pitcher of spritzer and headed toward the guests, plastering a smile on my face.

Business as usual.

Even if everything inside me was still burning.

Chapter Twelve

POST-PRODUCTION CONFESSIONAL
CLOSE QUARTERS

SEASON 4

PALMER HUGHES: BOSUN

Palmer watches footage, shakes head, runs hand over jaw.

PRODUCER
That second crew night out was a memorable one, huh?

PALMER
I mean… it didn't feel like it then. We'd survived a charter being one stew down, the guests were happy, the tip was bigger than the last one… Everyone was drunk, yeah, but that's what you do on a crew night out. You get wasted and forget about work for a while. It seemed fine at the time.

PRODUCER
And now?

PALMER
I'm surprised none of us saw the flashing neon sign warning us of what was to come.

PRODUCER
Do you think that night was significant, then?

Palmer laughs.

PALMER
I think it was the first crack in the dam, but none
of us noticed the pressure building until the flood
hit.

"How does it feel to not have your head in a toilet?" I teased Leah, looping my arm through hers in the back of the cab. Drop-off day had gone swimmingly, the guests leaving with big smiles on their faces and big money in our hands. Now, it was time for the crew to let loose and celebrate, and I was ready.

I'd managed to mostly avoid Finn the rest of the charter, acknowledging him only as necessary to get our jobs done. Dinner service was fine, breakfast was exactly as the guests ordered, and now I didn't have to deal with him professionally until our preference sheet meeting tomorrow.

I needed the break from him most of all.

Of course, he was in the same freaking car with me at the moment, so the break wasn't exactly all-encompassing.

"Ugh, I am still so mortified." Leah groaned, burying her head in my chest as I smirked and pet her hair. "Second charter and I go down, leaving you and Bernard to fend for yourselves."

"Thankfully, they had me!" Gisella piped in from the seat in front of us. She was practically sitting in Finn's lap, her lipstick stained on his cheek. Finn didn't look too happy about it. But then again, he didn't look too happy *period,* so it likely had nothing to do with Gisella. In fact, if I had to guess, that mood of his was more to do with our spat on the beach than anything else. "But personally, I'm glad you're feeling better. I'm ready to get back on deck. Not that I don't enjoy interior, but I want to be in the sunshine, not locked up doing laundry."

She tilted her head back as if she were sunbathing now, a wide smile on her face. When she opened her eyes again, she grinned down at Finn and nuzzled his nose.

I wrinkled mine, and Leah fought back a laugh as she sat up and tucked her hair behind one ear. "Yes, Gisella. We're all very lucky you were able to fill in for me," she said. "Can't imagine what we would've done otherwise."

Leah and I shared a look, me gripping onto her knee as I did my best not to roll my eyes. Leah could barely contain her smirk.

"No oysters tonight, yeah?" I said as we pulled up to the restaurant.

Leah grimaced. "Never again."

Finn hadn't said a word in the cab, brooding to himself and letting Gisella talk his ear off.

When we all started piling out of the cab, he stood at the door, helping Gisella out, then Leah, and finally extending a hand for mine.

I stared at it a beat too long, heat rushing up my spine at the sight of that scarred hand and all the memories it evoked for me. Those tan fingers had once traced every inch of me, learning me like a map he wanted to know by heart. Just the thought of sliding my palm against his again made my skin prickle, my breath hitching in my throat.

My fingers twitched toward his, heart thumping a little harder as I closed the distance — until another memory made me pause.

His words at the beach echoed in my mind, sharp as broken glass.

You weren't there.

Like it was *me* who'd driven us into the ground instead of him.

Like it was *me* who was the bad guy for not turning my back on all my goals to follow him as he pursued his.

The reminder stung like dry ice to my skin, chasing away any warmth.

I acted as if I were going to let him help me, but at the last second, I pulled my hand back, flipped him off with a sweet smile instead, and hopped out on my own, brushing past him to catch up with Leah and Bernard.

"I need a drink immediately," I declared, and I felt the determination to numb myself drowning out all the memories vying for my attention.

Bernard slung his arm around my shoulder with a grin. "Time for our first round of shots?"

Leah gagged and we all laughed.

Everyone except Finn.

I'd almost grown used to the cameras now, their presence feeling more normal than I ever thought it could. All through dinner, I forgot about them, talking and laughing with the rest of the crew as we devoured each plate of food placed in front of us. It almost felt like a normal yacht season, like I was on one of the many boats I'd worked, and it was a regular crew night out.

Until the conversation turned a direction I didn't see coming, and those lenses felt like sunbeams through a magnifying glass trying to take me out like an unsuspecting ant.

I was content, sipping a delightfully dirty martini as I listened to Cameron tell us all about growing up in Edinburgh.

He was a self-declared mama's boy with two younger brothers he helped care for. It was sweet, listening to how he wanted to work his way up to captain and make it where his mom never had to work another day in her life. That was something I loved about yachting — we worked together toward a common goal as a crew, but we were all from different backgrounds, different *countries*, with different reasons for being here and different dreams for the future.

"I told my mum that, one day, I'd buy her a house," he finished, holding his glass up with a proud gleam in his eyes. "And that's exactly what I'll do."

Bernard and Gisella lifted their glasses to his, the rest of us following suit. I noticed Palmer wearing an appreciative smile, like he wanted to help Cameron as his bosun to achieve that dream. When I glanced next to me, Leah had practically turned into a heart eye emoji. I cocked a brow at her, but she flushed and waved me off.

"What about you, Em?" Eli asked, pinning me with a tipsy, crooked grin from where he sat across the table from me. "What's your family like?"

I froze, drink hovering at my lips where I'd been about to take a sip. I finally managed to take one, slowly, smiling though my heart was already starting to race. "Oh, I don't have a story to tell, really."

"Come on," Palmer chided. "Everyone has a story."

It wasn't warm enough to sweat, but I felt myself start to as all the eyes of the table fixated on me.

"Mine is pretty boring," I said, hoping the laugh I gave with it would convince them to leave me be.

"Try us," Leah said. Her smile was genuine, curious, and it shouldn't have been that big of a deal for me to answer the question. They wanted to know about my family, just as most of them had already shared about their own.

But I was suddenly very aware of the cameras, of the fact that my father would watch this on television, and that I needed to be very careful with my words.

I shrugged. "I don't know, my family is pretty normal, I guess."

"Normal." Bernard snorted. "Is there really such a thing?"

"My mom is a wonderful mom... quiet, but smart. She's been a great partner to my father all her life and always made sure I was nurtured. My dad..." I paused, my fingers tracing the stem of my martini glass. "He's a businessman. Real estate, mostly — but not the flashy kind you see on TV. He's more of a numbers guy. Commercial acquisitions, development deals, asset management. The whole nine."

Bernard let out a low whistle. "Bloody hell, so you're definitely not here for the money then, are ya?"

A few of them laughed, and I forced a smile, even though my stomach tightened like a fist wringing out a towel.

"Seriously," Palmer added, nudging my elbow. "Are you like a trust fund baby?"

I shook my head. "Not even close. My father has always believed you should earn what you have. No handouts. No freebies. If you want something, you work your ass off for it."

"Sounds like a proper hard-ass, your dad," Cameron said.

I shook my head immediately, taking a long sip of my martini to buy myself some time to say the right words. I wondered if I'd say anything different if the cameras weren't around, but knew in my heart I wouldn't.

I was protective over my father, even if I struggled from his lack of affection.

"No, no, he just expects me to be great, you know? Like any parent, I guess. He wants me to make smart decisions, earn respect, make something of myself."

The table grew eerily quiet.

"That's a lot of pressure, Ember," Gisella said softly. I winced under the soft empathy in her gaze, both surprised and annoyed by the presence of it. I didn't want her pity, and yet something in me cracked at her words, like I was thankful someone said what I couldn't.

"Well, all I know is he's gotta be a proud papa bear," Leah said, lifting her glass in the air like a cheers toward me. "Chief stew on a superyacht? On a hit reality show? Come on — you're killing it."

I used all the energy I had to smile at her, my throat tightening so fast I had to swallow hard to force it open again. I tried to speak — to agree, to say something witty and deflective — but nothing came out.

Because I knew my father wasn't proud of me.

I wasn't sure he ever would be, with the path I'd chosen.

No matter how hard I worked, no matter how many promotions I earned or how many charters I crushed or how much praise I got from captains and guests alike — I wasn't sure I'd ever change his mind about my career and the value of it.

And suddenly, agreeing to be on this show in the hopes it would prove my worth to him felt naïvely silly.

The silence dragged a beat too long, my insides churning under the weight of it along with the alcohol buzzing through me. But then, from across the table, Finn cleared his throat.

"Well," he said, sliding into the conversation with that easy, charming smile of his. "I come from a long line of terrible cooks. Me ma could burn water if you gave her half a chance, and me da once made boxed mac and cheese with powdered sugar instead of flour for the roux."

The table laughed, and just like that, all attention shifted to him.

"But my granny... God rest her soul. She could cook like no one I've ever met. Sunday dinners at her house were a religious experience, and then she moved in with us and brought that magic to our home every night."

I snapped my gaze to him then, frowning, my heart thundering for a different reason now. It'd taken him almost a month to tell me about his grandmother when we'd worked together on our last boat, longer than that to admit what she'd meant to him. And even then, he was hesitant to talk too much about her. It was too hard. It hurt too much. The wound was too fresh from her passing.

But he was doing it now, after only two charters, with a bunch of strangers.

Did he just feel more comfortable with them?

Or was he doing it to save me?

I knew it was the second, even if the smarter part of me didn't want to latch onto that like it provided some kind of hope for something I knew would never exist again. But the truth was, Finn knew my issues with my father intimately. He knew the quiet resentment I held for my mother for never offering me anything else. She was always so content to just let my father run the show, and he'd done so with an iron fist.

Finn knew that. He knew me.

And he saw me struggling. He saw what no one else did, that my hands were trembling and I desperately needed the attention off me.

So, he was doing what he could to make that happen.

The realization made me dizzy, my heart dancing in my rib cage even as my brain attempted to squash it with the heels of its boot.

"Gran taught me everything I know. Every dish I make, every recipe I write, it's all a tribute to her," he said. His voice was low, eyes a bit distant as he stared at the dark beer his hand was wrapped around.

Gisella covered his wrist, her brows tugging inward. "I didn't know that."

Finn tried to smile, but the lift of his lips fell quickly. "Not many people do."

His eyes found mine, and the conversation spun off from there, but it was muted to my ears. It was like time had stepped its feet into quicksand and slugged to a stop around us.

I was still fuming from his words at the beach, but now,

that anger was clouded by gratitude. I hoped he could see it even though I couldn't say it. I hoped my silent *thank you* was loud enough for him to hear.

His expression softened just enough to let me know he understood, and my eyes stung.

Leah frowned from her seat beside me. "You okay, Em?"

I waved her off with a laugh, blinking the wetness from my eyes before any tears could form. "Yeah, girl. I'm just ready to dance."

"Yes!" Bernard shouted, pushing up from his seat and throwing his napkin down like a gauntlet. "Let's go. I'm ready to shake my arse."

A chorus of cheers followed as Bernard did just that, hiking one leg up on his chair and giving us a little twerk. I let myself get swept up in the celebration, grateful for the distraction.

But as we left the restaurant and spilled into the night, I felt something precarious stirring inside me, like a distant roll of thunder warning of an impending storm.

I was just one little huff and puff of breath away from losing the balance I was barely holding onto.

And Finn might as well have been the big bad wolf.

Chapter Thirteen

CHARTER CONFESSIONAL
CLOSE QUARTERS

SEASON 4, EPISODE 3
CHARTER 3

EMBER REED: CHIEF STEW

PRODUCER
So… how are we feeling this morning?

Ember glares at producer, winces a bit, drinks coffee.

Producer chuckles.

PRODUCER
A little hungover, I presume?

EMBER
I'm fine. Just need to eat and I'll be good as new.

PRODUCER
Well, we'll let you get to it. We just wanted to get some talking head footage about the crew night out. Did you have fun?

Ember sips coffee, forces smile.

EMBER
It was such a great night out. We all got to spend some quality time together as a crew and I think that was needed. We get a little time together during

charter, but it's the off nights where we get to know each other more. I think we all became more like a family last night.

PRODUCER
Do you see any friendships forming… or anything more?

Ember smiles.

EMBER
I mean… we all saw Leah and Cameron making out on the dance floor. I'd say they're pretty friendly.

PRODUCER
Can you give us a little reaction to show with that footage? What were you thinking in the moment?

Ember's jaw drops. She smiles, eyebrows raising. She pumps her hands in the air, does a little dance.

EMBER
Okay, Leah, yes. Go girl. Get you that fine Scottish man.

Producer laughs.

PRODUCER
And what about you and Finn?

Ember stops laughing, clears her throat.

EMBER
What about us?

I was dangerously close to falling over that delicate line that separated *drunk* and *disaster*, but I didn't care.

I slammed back another shot, anyway.

Bernard picked me up by the waist and twirled me around as I winced, still trying to make sure the shot *stayed* down, and Eli was clapping, shaking his head at me like I was a marvel.

No sooner had Bernard planted my feet back on the ground than Leah was dragging me out onto the dance floor.

We'd found ourselves at a different club this time, one that was more of a bar with some cheap lights and a jukebox we'd completely taken over with our own song choices. It was an older clientele in the bar for the most part, but they were a hoot, all of them clapping and laughing as they watched us dance. In the last hour or so, a few other younger groups had rolled in — one that was a bachelor party from the States and one that we guessed was made up of study-abroad students taking a weekend holiday. They joined in with us, our groups merging as they asked what the cameras were for and how they could get a little time on the show.

I was thankful for Leah's love of dancing, because when I was on the floor, I could get away from Gisella hanging all over Finn. She was just as drunk as the rest of us, and she'd been practically trying to get Finn to fuck her at the bar since we left the restaurant.

I sighed internally at myself as Leah found us a good spot on the dance floor, throwing her hands up for us to dance. I joined in, smiling and laughing, though inside, my stomach churned.

Gisella was a sweet girl. A bit lazy and full of herself, maybe, but kind, nonetheless. And funny. In another world, I'd be ecstatic to have her as my roommate. We'd have inside jokes and talk shit to each other at night. We'd share clothes and makeup.

She didn't deserve me being a bitch to her, even if I wasn't voicing my bitchiness out loud.

She hadn't done anything to me to deserve my distaste.

Other than be wonderful enough for my ex to fall in love with, anyway.

A stronger woman would have been fine. A better version of myself would have wiped her hands of the whole situation as soon as she found out Gisella and Finn were dating that very first day. I wished with everything I was that I could watch them together and not feel anything, that I could be happy for Finn, that I could befriend Gisella and assure her that everything between me and Finn was so far in the past that I never thought of him anymore.

But I had never been a good liar.

The truth was seeing them together made me sick, and while I was fairly decent at pretending I was fine when I was sober and working, I lost all ability to do that once I had a few drinks in me.

The dance floor was sparse, which meant Leah and I had plenty of room to do our silly dance moves. She did the cabbage patch before I hit her with the lawn mower, and then the battle continued, back and forth again and again until we were both wheezing from laughing so hard. Eventually, the song changed, the beat heavy and melodic. Leah started swaying her hips and I followed suit, both of us falling into a rhythm.

I turned, lining my back up with Leah's front, her hands on my hips and mine winding into my hair. When I glanced over at the bar area where the rest of our crew was, I caught sight of Gisella straddling Finn, her mouth trailing kisses and bites along the column of his neck.

I tasted bile, bitter and burning.

And then I glanced up, and found Finn watching me.

His hands were on Gisella's hips, his jaw angled down toward her, but his eyes were locked on me.

Heat flooded my face, and I tore my gaze away, throwing my arms up and letting myself get lost in the music. The song shifted, and then I felt Leah's absence. I stopped dancing, assuming she was ready to go get another drink, but when I turned, I found her dancing with Cameron.

For all of two seconds — and then, they were kissing.

Bernard screamed from where he was across the dance floor talking to Palmer, who let out a wolf whistle when he saw what Bernard did. I laughed and clapped as Leah flipped us off before grabbing Cameron's shirt and pulling him closer, kissing him more earnestly.

I was on my own then.

I looked around, wondering if Eli was close and I could wrangle him into dancing with me. But he was nowhere to be seen, and I assumed he was outside smoking or off flirting with someone. Doing my best not to feel awkward, I threw my arms up again, dancing by myself.

I closed my eyes, letting the music fill me as I matched the sway of my hips to the thump of the bass. Lights flashed behind my lids, the last shot I took catching up to me and making everything feel slow and heavy.

Before the song ended, I felt a pair of hands on me — tentative, a soft touch before the grip fastened. I smiled, assuming it was Eli, but when I looked over my shoulder, it was a man I didn't recognize.

But *damn*, was he handsome.

He was tall, lean, and tan with jet black hair and a thick beard. I wondered if he was Italian. I wondered how old he was. I wondered if he was a tourist or someone who frequented this bar often. But I only wondered those things for a split second before I decided I didn't care, and I leaned into his touch, letting him guide me as the song changed.

I thought I heard some guys holler encouragements, and I smiled, wondering if this was one of the men with the bachelor party. I ground against him, dropping my ass low as he strained to follow before I planted my hands on the floor and straightened my legs, shimmying against him as I rolled back up.

More whistles rang out, and I laughed when I heard Bernard yell, "Be gentle, Em!"

I let my eyes flutter open, enjoying the pleasant buzz flowing through me along with the music. Bernard shook his head at me, mouthing *naughty girl* with a wag of his finger that made me laugh again.

I flushed when I glanced at Palmer next, who crossed his arms and arched a brow with his lips curling. Eli came up behind him, clutching Palmer's shoulder at the sight of me. His hand thumped against his chest like I'd sent an arrow through it, and he stumbled back, making a whole show of it.

I shook my head, still keeping rhythm with the guy behind me as I chuckled.

But then my eyes crashed into Finn's.

And that laugh died in my chest.

His gaze was stone cold, his jaw set, hands curling into fists at his sides. I had no idea where Gisella had run off to, but when I realized Cameron was with the guys at the bar, I wondered if she and Leah had gone to the bathroom.

Of course, I couldn't think straight about anything with Finn's eyes on me like that.

Like he was pissed.

Like he wanted to murder the man touching me.

Like he wanted *his* hands on me, instead.

Oh, my God, Ember.

Get a fucking grip.

I blew out a breath, breaking eye contact with him as I laughed at myself, my chest still tight even as I willed my hips to stay loose. I closed my eyes, letting my head fall back against the guy behind me and trying to get lost in the music again.

But I didn't get the chance.

Because less than ten seconds later, a hand slid into the crook of my elbow, and before I knew what was happening, I was being hauled off the dance floor and out the door of the bar.

"Hey!" I blinked, feet stumbling to keep up as I looked behind me at the confused guy who had just had his hands on me and then whipped my head back around to the person gripping me now.

My throat tightened at the sight of unruly brown hair and broad shoulders.

I let my gaze trail down his arms, the muscles in them strained before I found a familiar hand still holding me tight at the elbow.

Part of me melted at that touch.

But the louder part of me bucked like a wild mustang.

"Finn, what the hell?" I tried to rip out of his grasp, but he held tight until we poured out of the noise and into the quiet night.

My ears rang as he kept tugging me until we were down the cobblestone street and away from the patrons smoking near the bar entrance.

"What are you doing?!"

Only when we were around the corner did he release me. "Rescuing you from that gobshite," he said. "You're welcome."

My mouth popped open. "Are you fucking *kidding*—"

"You're locked."

Locked — in other words, drunk as fuck.

"No shit, Sherlock. It's crew night out, or did you forget?"

"So crew night out means you throw yourself at whatever

random prick decides to grind on you?"

My mouth snapped shut at that, jaw clenching as I stepped into his space. I pressed on my toes so I could at least try to match his height, and I pointed my finger right in his face. "Don't. Don't you fucking dare."

Finn's nostrils flared, but he didn't back down.

"You don't get to be jealous," I seethed. "You lost that right when you left me behind."

"When *I* left—" It was his jaw hitting the ground now, and he barked out a laugh, shaking his head before he turned and gave me his back.

"I don't need saving," I spat, already making my way back toward the bar. "Especially from you."

I took one step before his hand found my wrist, tugging until I pivoted.

"Finn, what the fu—"

"I never meant to hurt you."

"So why did you?!"

The words might as well have been a foghorn in a cave for how they echoed in the space between us. Finn's jaw muscle ticced, his hand releasing me, but I didn't try to run this time.

"Why didn't you tell me about the restaurant until the night before we were supposed to leave?" I asked, chest heaving. The question felt like a rusty nail driven into my heart. "Why did you let me assume you were serious about us when you weren't?"

You're wearing a mic.

They're watching you.

I didn't care.

"I was," Finn croaked, his Adam's apple bobbing hard. "I *was* serious about us. That's why I couldn't tell you."

I frowned, shaking my head. "What? That makes zero sense."

"I was torn between opening a restaurant to honor the woman who practically raised me, who gave me my life's passion, who instilled the love of food and cooking so deep in my soul it's forever a part of me…" He paused, rolling his lips together, his eyes flicking between mine so fast it was dizzying. "And you. The woman I loved. The woman I knew I'd lose in the process."

All the blood drained from my face, a numbing sensation sliding over me like a cold waterfall.

"It wasn't black and white, Em. It wasn't easy. It fucking killed me."

I didn't know if it was his words or the alcohol or a combination of the two, but I suddenly felt very unsteady, the world spinning around us in a violent swirl of colors. I reached my hand behind me until I found the brick, then I let myself lean back, hoping it would steady me.

"The restaurant was for her?"

Finn swallowed, but didn't confirm. He didn't have to.

"You never told me that."

"When could I? As soon as I told you about wanting to open the damn thing, you shut me out."

I opened my mouth to argue, but slammed it shut again.

"Do you know how bad that hurt?" he asked, stepping closer. "I'd never told anyone about it. You think I didn't know it was stupid, that it was a long shot? *Young chef wants to open their own restaurant*, how fucking original." He threw his hands up and let them slap against his thighs. "It wasn't just a pipe dream for me. It was a way to honor Gran and her legacy, to do what she always wanted to do but never could because she was too busy taking care of her kids, her grandkids, our whole fucking family. Telling you, telling *anyone* meant exposing the rawest parts of me."

He wet his lips, breath coming in ragged pulls.

"I was already afraid of failing. I was already afraid I wouldn't live up to her memory, that I wouldn't do her justice. And then the first person I felt safe to tell proved to me why I was so scared in the first place. You dismissed it. You dismissed *me*."

I blinked, over and over, my heart thundering in my ears and lungs struggling to give me oxygen. I pressed a hand against my aching rib cage as my mind raced to catch up.

"I didn't know," I whispered. "I... I'm sorry, Finn."

"No, don't," he said instantly, pinching the bridge of his nose. "I know it was on me. I should have told you sooner. I just... I didn't want to until I was certain it would happen. I was waiting to hear from my potential business partner, and I didn't... I *couldn't* tell you until I knew for sure."

I chewed the inside of my cheek, nodding. My brain was still swimming from all the alcohol. My mouth was dry. I needed water. I needed sleep.

"Look at me," he whispered.

When I did, tears pricked my eyes.

"You think I didn't try to find a way?" he asked, stepping more into my space. He was just inches away, his eyes searching mine. "You think I didn't scour my brain for any possible chance I could have both — you, and the restaurant? But like you were so quick to point out that night on the beach, there's no yachting season in Dublin, Firefly."

I closed my eyes at the nickname, at how it still made my stomach flip.

"I knew it wasn't the place for you to chase *your* dream." He swallowed, waiting until I opened my eyes again before he continued. "And still, I asked you. I asked you to leave your passion so I could chase mine. It wasn't fair, and I can see now why it hurt you. I didn't get it then, even though I should have, because you shared everything with me. I was just angry and thought you were choosing yachting over me." He shook his head. "Feckin' eejit, I was — thinkin' what I was buildin' mattered more than what you'd spent years fightin' for. It was selfish and I'm sorry. But what I regret most is that I never asked the obvious next question." His eyes flicked between mine. "I asked you to walk away from yachting. What I never asked was if you'd make Dublin your home in the offseason."

My heart cracked.

"I never asked," Finn repeated, nostrils flaring. "And *Jaysus*, do I regret it. I was just... young. Scared. Pissed off. Wanting it all. I convinced myself that if I waited to tell you until everything was set in stone, until I had this grand plan... I thought..." He shook his head, dropping his gaze to the ground.

"Finn..."

"I didn't want to ruin what we had. It was... fecking magical, wasn't it?"

I covered my shaking lips with one hand, squeezing my eyes shut and freeing the tears that had been pooling.

Finn thumbed one away, and I choked on a sob as I leaned into that touch, into what we used to be.

"Maybe naïvely, I thought by the end of it all... I don't know. I thought maybe we were so in love, you'd come with me."

For the first time since that night, I wondered why I hadn't.

I'd been so angry, so hurt. He'd hidden his true intentions from me all season. He'd let me think we were leaving together when that was never his plan.

I understood now why he did it, but it didn't make it hurt any less.

And why hadn't *I* thought about the option of being in Dublin in the offseason? Why hadn't I looked for any way to make it work?

I was just as guilty as he was for turning my back on us.

I was the same — young, angry, wanting to prove a point.

God, it seemed so terribly stupid now.

"But listening to the way you talked about your dad tonight," Finn said, snapping my attention back to him. He shook his head. "About how you've risked disappointing him because you love yachting so much, because it makes you so fucking happy... I knew you two had a strained relationship, but I didn't realize, Em... I didn't realize how much this all means to you."

"You didn't realize how much you meant to me, either," I shot back, pushing off the wall to stand straight again. My chest brushed against his sternum when I did. "You still don't."

Finn swallowed, staring down at me over the bridge of his nose. He opened his mouth, and then we both jumped, a high-pitched scream ringing out in the night as footsteps barreled toward us.

"There they are!"

It was Palmer's voice, he and most of the crew spilling out from the bar. The footsteps and scream belonged to Gisella, who threw herself into Finn's arms with a wide smile and me still standing just inches from him.

Finn caught her easily, swinging her up into his grasp as she locked her ankles behind his lower back and started kissing him all over.

His eyes were still on me until I peeled my gaze away, blinking over and over as I struggled to clear my mind through the haze of the alcohol.

"Babes, you okay?" Eli asked, slinging his arm around my neck and grinning down at me with tipsy eyes. "I'll go bliksem that oke if he was getting too handsy."

He hooked a thumb over his shoulder toward the bar where I'd been dancing with a stranger, but I shook my head, forcing a smile.

"He was harmless. I just... needed air. I was about to get sick."

"Ag, that must be why Cheffy hauled you outside, hey? He saw the signs from when you two worked together before."

Finn caught my gaze again, and I swallowed. "Exactly. And he got me out here just in time. That last shot was my death warrant."

"Well, on the bright side, I've never known someone to barf and have as nice of breath as you do right now," Eli said, tapping my nose. "I'd still kiss you."

"Gross, bru," Palmer said, wrinkling his nose. I didn't miss how he kept that grimace in place as he watched Gisella maul Finn.

Everyone laughed as the cabs pulled up to the curb. We piled in, ready to head back to the boat and call it a night.

My mind whirled the entire way, the alcohol working to actively erase my memory of what was said between us before I could even properly digest it.

I was still uneasy when we got back to the boat, and while everyone else was getting changed to go to the hot tub, I just needed to be alone.

I grabbed my phone charger, toothbrush, and something to sleep in before retreating to a guest cabin.

But it didn't matter what I was wearing.

I wouldn't sleep a wink that night.

Chapter Fourteen

POST-PRODUCTION CONFESSIONAL
CLOSE QUARTERS

SEASON 4

FINN PEARSON: HEAD CHEF

PRODUCER
So, the editing crew would like to have some talking
head footage from you for episode four just kind of
explaining your love of cooking, how you came into
it, why you love it so much. Sound good?

Finn gives thumbs up.

PRODUCER
Great. So, you already told us a little bit about how
cooking has been your love language since you were a
child. How did it all begin?

FINN
I fell in love with cooking when I was about five,
I think. After me grandad passed, me granny moved in
with us. We didn't have a lot when it came to food,
but somehow, she always whipped up the most magical
meals. Nothing against me ma or da, but cooking was
never their strong point. We got by, we ate grand,
but with Granny? We ate like bloody royalty. I
started offering to help - mostly because I wanted
to spend more time with her - and from the start,
she treated me like I was capable. She didn't hand

me some daft little job just to keep me busy. She
showed me how to hold a knife proper, how to dice
onions without crying all over them, how to thicken
up a sauce when it was too watery, or stretch a meal
when there wasn't enough to go round. At first, it
was just fun. But soon, it became an obsession. I
loved making delicious meals from scratch. I loved
hearing the praise when I got something right. I
don't feel confident many places… but I'm at home in
the kitchen.

PRODUCER
Beautiful, Finn. We find it really fascinating that
you use the specific term of food being your love
language. In a previous interview, you said, "I don't
think there's a better way to show you love someone
than by cooking for them." Can you explain that a
bit?

FINN
It's intimate, isn't it? Cooking, baking, all of it…
It takes creativity, thought, energy, and time. When
you cook for someone, you're not just feeding them
– you're saying, I see you. You're thinking about
what they love, what'll make them smile, what reminds
them of home. It's not just picking out a card at a
grocery store or ordering some flowers that someone
else arranges and delivers. It's personal. When I
cook for the guests, it's my job, sure, but it's also
me making this the vacation of a lifetime.

PRODUCER
And when you cook for your family, or your friends?

FINN
Ah, it's even more special then. Feels like a proper
love letter, doesn't it? It's like putting the kettle
on when someone's had a shite day, or warming their
coat for them before they head out into the rain.
It's a small thing, but it says, *I care. I'm thinking
of you.* It's comfort, it's celebration, it's even a
way to say sorry when words won't come. In my family,
we're not the best at talking feelings out – but you

know you're forgiven when a plate of your favorite
biscuits lands in front of you.

PRODUCER
Would you say you quite literally use food to declare
your love, then?

FINN
One hundred percent.

Finn pauses, frowning.

FINN
What episode did you say this was for again?

The groans of a crew sharing mutual hangover woes carried
through the crew mess like the wails of ship-wrecked ghosts.

I could barely stomach the coffee I very much needed as
I wrapped up the interview with the production team. They
wanted to get some reactions to the crew night out. I imagined
they also wanted to capture how miserable we all were today on
camera.

Brilliant jerks.

I escaped the interview mostly unscathed; although, they
did question me about why I slept in the guest cabin. They also
reminded me that every word between me and Finn last night had
been caught on camera — but I dutifully ignored that point. My
conversation with Finn had already played on repeat in my head
all night long. I didn't need the production crew to remind me of
it, too.

I ducked into my cabin just long enough to swap my pajamas
for my uniform — crisp polo, tailored shorts, hair slicked back
into a bun. The boat was already in good shape after the work
we'd done before heading out last night, but there was still plenty
to tackle before the next guests arrived. We'd need every minute
of the morning to make sure every surface gleamed and every

pillow was perfectly fluffed.

And I'd need every bit of distraction work would offer to not think about Finn.

I didn't think it was possible, but I felt even more confused and unsettled after all he'd confessed. Suddenly, he'd given power to the voice inside me that had always wanted to believe he gave a shit. All this time, I'd thought he was a player, that he'd just said and done what was needed to get me in his bunk for a season.

Even when it felt wrong to think it.

Even when, deep down, I felt I was wrong about that.

Maybe I just thought it was safer to feel angry and scorned than to admit that I'd been so deeply hurt.

Now, after last night, I had no fucking idea *what* to feel.

Fortunately, my cabin was empty when I popped in to get changed. Gisella was likely on deck already and Finn in the galley, but I wondered if he'd slept here with her last night since I had been in the guest cabin.

I caught myself looking at the rumpled sheets of the top bunk for a beat too long before I grabbed my radio, strapping it to my belt and heading for the crew mess. I needed sustenance to make it through the day.

"Mornin'," Cameron greeted me gruffly from where he was already devouring a plate of scrambled eggs.

"Good morning. How are you feeling?"

"Not my best," he admitted, pointing his fork at the plate of eggs in front of him. "This is helping, though. And Cheffy made baked beans for me. Absolute angel, he is."

"I could go for a greasy cheeseburger right about now," I said, then grabbed a plate and started shoveling eggs and breakfast potatoes onto it. "But eggs will do, I guess. I—"

My next thought flew out of my head like a bird from an open cage, eyes catching on a plate of food I didn't expect to see.

"Aye, I don't know what Cheffy was thinking with those," Cameron said around a mouthful of eggs. "Who the hell wants something sweet when they're hungover?"

I swallowed, heart thumping hard against my chest. "Me, actually."

I just barely whispered the words, my gaze still fixated on the plate.

Cameron shrugged. "Well, I'd wager you're the only one in this crew, so eat up. They're all yours."

I covered my mouth with one hand as a smile slowly spread on my lips. I felt dizzy with the simple kind of giddy joy that can only come from a reborn memory.

"You're kidding. Pancakes?"

I bite my lip and nod as Finn shakes his head at me. "What? They're delicious! Especially banana ones. Those are my favorite."

"Alright, Jack Johnson."

I lift his palm to my mouth and playfully bite where his thumb meets his wrist. "You asked! Don't be a bully about my breakfast choices."

"Well, as far as day after drinking food preferences go, that may be the worst answer I've heard. Eggs, bacon, a Bloody Mary… hell, even cold pizza would be more acceptable."

"Make fun of me all you want. I don't need you to make my breakfast, anyway." I pop up out of his bed, nearly tripping on the sheets we were tangled in before I find a pair of shorts and tug them on. "I can make my own damn pancakes."

"You better not."

"Watch me."

But before I take a step, he wraps me up from behind, his warm arms taking me back toward the bed as I giggle and pretend to try to get away. He hauls me up into the top bunk in a feat of strength and balance unmatched by anyone I know.

"I *will* make you pancakes," he growls in my ear, spanking my ass for good measure. "With bananas and whatever other weird shit you want in them."

"*Right now?*"

"*Right now,*" he confirms, and then he turns me in his arms, sweeping my hair from my face as his eyes settle on mine. "*And tomorrow. And every day for the rest of your life, if that's what you want.*"

I blinked out of the memory and swayed a bit, reaching my hand out for the edge of the table to steady myself.

"Whoa, there. You alright?"

I nodded, righting myself as I came back to the present, back to the stack of perfectly cooked banana pancakes in front of me. They were even dusted with powdered sugar, and there was a ramekin of raspberry compote to top with instead of syrup.

I instantly recognized it for what it was: not just a plate of pancakes, but an apology.

It was Finn's way of starting over.

My pulse stuttered with the memory of the night before, all the words he said dancing in a dizzying blur in my mind. For two years, I thought he'd lied to me. I thought he'd played some sick game to get what he wanted from me before leaving me behind.

Now that I knew the truth, I realized it was nobody's fault.

We were both young. Emotions were high. Time was short. I was stubborn and he was prideful.

But it was what it was — a messy, unfinished story neither of us knew how to end. And those pancakes? They were an invitation to write a new chapter.

Leah and Bernard poured into the mess, both groaning at the sight of the feast Finn had prepared for us. I greeted each of them before plopping two pancakes on my plate and smearing them with the compote. I grabbed a fork next, told my crew to meet me in the main salon after breakfast, and then padded barefoot up to the galley.

I climbed the stairs with the plate balanced carefully in both hands, my stomach a knot of nerves and nostalgia twisting tighter with every step. It was just breakfast, I told myself. But it felt like something more.

Cooking had always been how Finn expressed himself when no words would work, and I was trying my damndest not to read too much into whatever the hell he was trying to tell me with these pancakes.

I paused just outside the galley to gather myself, smiling a little at the symphony of sounds coming from within. I could hear the rhythmic chop of a knife against the cutting board, the soft scrape of metal on wood, the faint hiss of something simmering on the stove.

And then, I saw him.

Finn moved through the galley like a gold-medal-winning figure skater — fluid, effortless, completely at home. His hair was damp, unruly from a quick shower and half-hidden beneath the hat he wore backward. He'd already worked his sleeves up to his elbows, exposing forearms I knew too well. I hated that my pulse jumped at the sight of him, that after all this time, all this hurt, my body still reacted like a violin only he could play.

For a moment, I just watched. It was impossible not to — the way he chopped herbs with quick, sure strokes, the way his brow creased in concentration, the way his lips moved silently as he mentally ran through the day's prep. It was so painfully familiar, like a song I'd forgotten existed but knew all the words to once I heard it play again.

Then, as if sensing me, Finn glanced up — a quick flick of his eyes toward the doorway before he returned to his work.

But a beat later, he froze.

He looked back at me, this time really seeing me, and the shift in his expression sent a bolt of heat through my chest.

I swallowed hard, lifting the plate in a small, uncertain offering, my smile shy and unsure. "I'm surprised you remembered this."

Finn's gaze flicked to the pancakes, then back to me.

"Not much I forgot, Firefly."

My breath caught, heart stuttering in my chest at the quiet honesty in those words. There was no teasing, no armor, just a truth so simple it knocked me off balance.

I shifted my weight to one foot, my grip on the plate tightening. This was dangerous territory — memories like this one were booby-trapped. One wrong step, and the explosion would take us both out.

But instead of poking at it, instead of demanding more or asking him why the hell he'd made these for me after everything that happened, I just nodded.

Apology accepted.

"See you at the preference sheet meeting later?" I asked, my voice lighter than I felt.

This time, Finn's smile fully broke free, and my stomach flipped at the sight of it. "Let's just hope these guests don't want anything high vibrational."

I snorted, shaking my head as I turned to leave. "Careful, Cheffy. Keep talking like that and you might make me like you again."

"Wouldn't want that now, would we?" he tossed back, but his voice was softer than his words.

I escaped before I could get caught up in whatever was hanging between us. That smile, that easy banter... it was confirmation that I'd been right in my assumption about the breakfast being a peace offering. And I'd accepted it.

I had no idea what would happen next.

But I'd never tasted pancakes so sweet.

I ambled into the crew mess later that morning to find Captain Gary housing a handful of Galatine candies.

I cocked a brow. "Breakfast of champions?"

He blinked at me mid-chew, the corners of his mouth stretched with guilt and sugar. "They're milk-based. Practically health food."

"Uh-huh. And I suppose the bottle of limoncello in the fridge is just fermented citrus juice?"

"I'm boosting my calcium intake," he argued, popping another tablet in his mouth like he was doing his bones a favor. "You should be thanking me. I'm trying to avoid breaking a hip on this charter."

"You're more likely to choke on one of these than fall on deck," I said, plucking the candy bag from his hand and holding it just out of reach.

He narrowed his eyes at me, but I could tell he was fighting a smile. "Give those back, Chief Bossy Pants, and no one gets hurt."

"I outrank you when it comes to snack management."

"God help me," he muttered, folding his arms as he leaned back in his seat. "You were less insufferable when you were a second stew."

"I had less power then. Now I wield it like a saber."

That earned a laugh, and he shook his head, his expression softening as he watched me take the seat across from him. I set the candy bag on the table but didn't slide it back.

Then, just as I was about to make another snarky remark,

Captain leaned forward, his eyes sincere.

"All jokes aside, I see what you're doing on this boat, Em." He arched a brow, making sure I was listening before he continued. "You've got a strong team, happy guests, a clean ship, and even with cameras in your face and a contractual agreement to go out every night between charters, you've handled yourself like a pro. I'm proud of you."

The breath caught in my throat, my chest blooming with something warm and tight. It was the words I'd always wanted to hear from my father but knew I likely never would.

Hearing them now — here, from Captain Gary, who had taught me more about being a leader than anyone else — meant more than I could voice without breaking down.

A slow, stunned kind of smile spread over my face. "Thanks, Cap."

He winked. "Don't let it go to your head."

"As long as you try not to let *these* go to your gut," I challenged, sliding the bag of candy toward him with a grin.

Captain made a face, mocking my words and earning a laugh from me as Finn and Palmer jogged down the stairs to join us. Captain scooted toward the middle of the table — fist clutched around his candies — and Finn and Palmer slid in beside him with a curious smile aimed at the two of us.

"Alright, charter three," Captain Gary said, his grin wide as he tapped the preference sheets on the table. "And no one is sick this time."

"Hallelujah," I muttered.

"Let's get into it. Our primary guest is Nicole Irving. She's a mom of three who has made her fortune in the pornography industry."

Captain's bushy eyebrows shot into his hairline at that, all of us sitting up a bit straighter. We had the guest preferences before this point — what they wanted to eat and drink, the themed parties they preferred, et cetera — but the producers left out the guest details until we had this meeting on camera.

Now I knew why.

"Oh, this is going to be a circus," Palmer said, rubbing his hands together with a grin.

"Nicole is traveling with her husband, her sister and brother-in-law, and two girlfriends from the industry as they celebrate Nicole's latest film winning a Nudey Award."

Finn whistled low. "I gotta ask — what category?"

I laughed, which made Finn grin wider, which made my neck heat.

"Best Group Scene," Captain Gary read off the page, adjusting his glasses. "And before anyone asks — I will not be googling it."

"Coward," Palmer teased.

I scribbled down quick notes, smiling to myself as I realized now why the provisions list had been so... interesting.

"You look thrilled over there, Ember," Captain mused, arching a brow.

"Listen, I grew up in a very reserved household," I said. "I think my father still assumes I don't know pornography even exists. But we worked with some guests in the industry on our last season together, remember?"

Captain chuffed. "How could I ever forget?"

"They were amazing," I said. "So fun, so kind. This is going to be great. Besides, how often do you get to throw sex-themed parties as your *job*?"

"You and I have very different ideas of fun," Captain said, but he was smirking. "Speaking of parties, for the first night, they want a 'Studio 69' theme. Think disco balls and platform heels, but with way more... skin."

"Oh, my God. I can already see the outfits," I said excitedly. "Palmer, do you think you and the other guys would be up for helping us serve?"

"Why do I feel like I will *not* be wearing my black uniform for this?"

"I was thinking more like tiny silver banana hammocks," I said, waggling my brows.

He laughed, running a hand back through his hair. "Eli is going to eat this up."

I caught Finn staring at me, a soft curl on his lips before he flipped the page. "What about food? Are we talking lobster tails and caviar, or are they more of a pizza rolls and Jell-O shots crowd?"

"A bit of both," Captain said. "Nicole's husband, Mark, is a big foodie and specifically requested a tasting menu for the first night — paired with wine and cocktails. But then they want 'guilty pleasure' snacks served at midnight."

Finn grinned. "I can work with that."

We continued on through the rest of the preference sheet, which included a request for a Nudey Award "after party" theme for night two, complete with a red carpet and champagne wall. They also wanted a photoshoot on the beach in Positano... on a giant circular bed. I had a feeling that photoshoot wouldn't exactly be family friendly, so I would need to do some calculations to figure out how to pull it off without breaking every maritime rule in the book.

But I wasn't overwhelmed or worried — I was excited.

These were the kind of charters I lived for. Every night had a theme, every guest had a dream of what their yacht experience would be like, and I was the one with the key to make it all happen.

From the moment they stepped on board, it was my job to make fantasy reality, to take a bare table and transform it into a Studio 69 wonderland, to plan menus and excursions that felt like magic, to read their minds and anticipate needs they hadn't even thought of yet.

It was a kind of creative chaos that fueled me — part high-stakes event planning, part luxury hospitality, part performance art. And I was damn good at it.

My father would never understand. To him, real success had a corner office, a six-figure salary, and a respectable title that made people nod with approval when you said it at cocktail parties. To my mom, success was a family and a clean home.

But this? This floating paradise of gold confetti and six-star service? This was my canvas. My stage. My proof that I was exceptional at something, even if it wasn't the career my parents once imagined for me.

It killed me that I still longed for their approval, even knowing it would likely never come.

Would my father see this show and finally understand it? Would he see the way my brain worked, how I could take a list of absurd requests and turn them into a seamless, spectacular few days at sea? I wanted him to understand how hard I worked, how much thought and care went into every place setting and party playlist and flower arrangement.

And I wanted him to see how much joy it brought me — not just doing the work, but nailing it. There was an art to this, and I wanted my father to appreciate the craft: seeing a guest's face light up when they walked into a themed dinner that was better than they'd dreamed, hearing them laugh until they couldn't breathe during a ridiculous game I orchestrated, watching them actually relax because they knew they were in capable hands.

I created memories.

I left my mark on guests from all over the world.

That was success to me.

That was the kind of work that mattered.

"Couple more notes," Captain said, glancing down. "Nicole doesn't drink tequila after an unfortunate incident at the AVN Awards. Mark doesn't eat anything purple. And they want a 'Naughty Nautical Brunch' on their last day — complete with penis-shaped pancakes and mimosa towers."

Finn rolled the preference sheet package and tucked it into the front pocket of his shirt. "You know it's a party when I pull out the penis molds."

"This is going to be the most insane charter of the season," Palmer said, but the way he rubbed his hands together showed he was just as excited about it as I was.

Captain stacked the pages, shaking his head with a weary grin. "Here's hoping they tip like porn stars, too."

"Don't worry," I said, flipping my notebook closed. "If they want the wildest, most unforgettable charter of their lives... they came to the right boat."

Chapter Fifteen

CHARTER CONFESSIONAL
CLOSE QUARTERS

SEASON 4, EPISODE 4
CHARTER 3

LEAH BROOKS: THIRD STEWARDESS

PRODUCER
Welcome back! How are you feeling?

LEAH
I'm feeling so much better, but also still mortified.
How embarrassing to get sick on the second charter,
and *after* a night out. I just hope Captain doesn't
think I was hungover. Not a good look!

PRODUCER
Well, I think everyone is glad to have you back. Are
you excited about this charter?

LEAH
Oh my God, yes! These guests are so freaking fun. I
mean, I have seen more ass and titties in the past
twenty-four hours than in my entire life, I think,
but they're super nice.

PRODUCER
It was quite… interesting, unpacking for them,
wouldn't you say?
Leah covers her face and laughs.

LEAH

Yeah… definitely wasn't prepared for all the… toys
I'd find in those giant suitcases. No wonder the boys
nearly threw their backs out lugging them on board.

PRODUCER

Can you give us some commentary on that to run with
the footage? A live reaction of what was going on in
your head?

Leah drops jaw, blinks, laughs.

LEAH

Wow… okay, then. I think it's safe to say these
guests came to party. I have never in my life seen a
dildo this big.

Leah does a little dance, humping the air.

LEAH

But hey, no judgment here. Express yourselves, babes.

PRODUCER

Perfect. The guests do seem nice. They were thrilled
with dinner, but that didn't stop them from wanting
midnight snacks.

LEAH

Oh… yes, I heard about this. Poor Ember was up so
late!

PRODUCER

Finn, too.

LEAH

Rockstars, both of them. It's not easy to smile and
serve after such a long day like that. You know, I
can totally understand how they were together in the
past. They make a great team.

PRODUCER

Has it been weird at all, having exes on board? Any
sticky situations?

LEAH

They've been professional, as far as I can tell.
Bicker at each other like an old married couple, but
other than that, I think it's been fine.

Leah tilts head, arching brow at producer.

LEAH
But your cameras have seen more than I have, haven't
they?

The first day of the charter passed in a blur of champagne corks, shrieking laughter, and the unmistakable slap of bare skin against our freshly cleaned sun pads.

Our guests wasted no time making themselves at home. By the time they'd finished the tour, Nicole was topless, her girlfriends were taking turns trying to flash the drone camera operators, and Mark was already flirting with Leah and boasting how he and Nicole had an open marriage. That was especially charming, considering he was wearing nothing but a gold thong and sunglasses that spelled out *Daddy* in rhinestones.

I, of course, checked in with Leah to make sure no one was making her uncomfortable. It was one thing to do whatever it took to please the guests and get a tip, but another entirely if anyone crossed a line and made my crew feel unsafe.

But bless her heart, Leah was just happy as a clam to be back with us, and she said she felt about as threatened by Mark as she did a goldfish.

I shuffled through my to-do list with an impenetrable smile. Guests like this were a nightmare for logistics, but they were a hoot once on board, and they usually tipped well. Besides, their over-the-top antics were the exact kind of chaos that made for a memorable charter.

I knew the producers had to be happier than toddlers with fresh containers of Play-Doh.

Leah had tumbled into the crew quarters when we were all

changing into our polos, breathless, eyes wide. "Uh... Em? I need you to come look at something."

She'd dragged me to the primary's cabin, where Nicole's luggage lay open like a crime scene. Among the designer dresses and strings that made up her swimsuits, if you could call them that, was... a weapon.

In the form of a dildo so large and so aggressively pink, it looked like it belonged in a museum — or a horror film.

Leah and I just stared at it, slack-jawed, until Bernard poked his head in to see what had us mesmerized. One glimpse and he was howling, and then Leah put on gloves and winced as she carefully laid the thing out on the nightstand along with a bottle of lube like they were a tray of chocolates. That had me and Bernard laughing even harder, until we were both gasping for breath and clutching our sides.

And that was the vibe all day.

The crew was buzzing from the energy the guests brought on board, everyone wearing smiles — in fact, the guests wearing nothing *but* smiles as they sunbathed on the top deck. Dinner was flawless, the Studio 69 theme landed perfectly with mirror balls hanging over the table and disco-themed cocktails glowing in neon colors. Finn's tasting menu blew everyone away, from the decadent lobster and caviar bites to the playful chocolate fondue fountain at the end.

"Finn! Marry me!" Nicole had shouted across the table, licking melted chocolate off her fingers.

"Sorry, angel," Finn had called on his way back to the galley. "Already taken."

Gisella had beamed at that, the guests *oohing* and *awwing* while I busied myself re-filling drinks and dutifully ignored the way my ribs constricted.

The party raged long after dinner, the deck turning into a glittering karaoke lounge under the stars. They sang 70's hits so badly the dolphins probably swam for quieter waters, and they drank enough champagne to have them dancing in nothing but sequined underwear — though I doubted they needed any booze to reach that level of bravado.

It was after midnight when they began to quiet, and I was aching for my bed and a good night's rest. I was tidying up their glasses and wiping down surfaces, just biding my time until the last of them headed off to bed.

But suddenly, Nicole gasped from where she lounged on the luxe cream sofa in the main salon. "Ember! We need snacks!"

Mark was still up with her, along with one of her girlfriends, Megan, and her brother-in-law, Luke. They all gasped in sync, clapping at the revelation, and I internally groaned while plastering on my best smile.

"Of course. Finn already prepped some for you. Let me go grab them."

I ducked into the galley, stifling a yawn as I pulled out the trays Finn had put together earlier in the day — a gorgeous midnight spread of crudités, charcuterie, fruit, chips, and dips.

But when I returned, Nicole pouted, Megan picking up one of the pieces of fruit with a wrinkled nose and a very serious frown.

"No, no," Nicole said, shaking her head. "We need *snacks*, Ember. Grilled cheese. Nachos. Cheese fries. Mozzarella sticks."

"Basically anything dripping with hot cheese," Mark chimed in on a laugh, throwing his arm around his wife. "My baby *loves* steamy, wet, hot—"

"Got it!" I said with an uncomfortable laugh, already on my way to the galley. "Your wish is my command. Do you need any refills before I get to work?"

Luke lifted a half-full bottle of champagne. "Don't you worry about us, darling."

I hoped my smile didn't reek of exhaustion as I nodded and excused myself, and as soon as I made it to the galley, I let out a long sigh.

Fuck my life.

I didn't want to wake Finn. He'd kicked his ass all day between the welcome aboard snacks, the fresh lunch, and the multi-course dinner. He'd had to cook for the crew in between, too.

We all needed sleep, but he needed it most.

Besides, how hard could cheese fries be?

It was fine.

I could do this.

I hummed a little to myself as I started pulling out ingredients, checking them off in my mind as I thought of everything I needed to bring this cheese parade to life. The worst part was that we didn't have frozen fries I could just pop in the oven. No, Finn made everything from scratch, which meant I was going to have to figure out how to do the same.

Thank God for Google.

I was halfway through cooking bacon — expertly, if I do say so myself — when a voice slid down my spine like a slow, wicked hand.

"What the hell are you doing?"

Finn stood in the doorway, barefoot and sleep-rumpled, hair a mess, t-shirt clinging to his chest in a way that made me want to slide my hands under it and feel the warmth of the skin it clung to.

I tore my gaze away and back to the task at hand, ignoring the very strong zip of electricity that slid between my thighs at the thought.

"Didn't want to wake you," I said, flipping the bacon. "I see I failed in that mission."

"Bacon has a very distinct scent, and since I'm the chef on this boat, I was more than a little worried when I smelled it in the middle of the night."

"Well, no need to worry. I'm just whipping up some—"

"Stop." He crossed the galley in two long strides, taking the spatula from my hand like I was a child caught playing with knives. His hand wrapped around mine in the process, a fleeting touch, but it seared my skin like lava.

It was insanely hot, the way he commanded control with the snatching of that spatula.

And it did not help the unwanted tingles situation I had going on.

"Go to bed," he growled.

Hot.

Why is it so hot?

"I've got it," I argued, even as he maneuvered me out of the way.

He swatted my ass — a sharp, playful smack that made me yelp. "I said go to *bed*."

My mouth dropped open. "Finn!"

"Let me do my job, love." He grinned over his shoulder as he took over the bacon and then began expertly cutting the potatoes I'd peeled, knowing the guests wanted fries without me even saying it.

I was still standing there with my jaw on the floor when he peeked at me again, arching a brow.

"You just going to stand there when you could be sleeping?"

I blinked out of my daze, but his handprint on my ass might as well have been a tattoo for how impossible it was to ignore. I rolled my lips together, popping a hip against the nearest counter and folding my arms.

"As chivalrous as your demand is, as long as *they're* awake," I said, nodding toward the main salon. "So am I."

"Then I guess you're keeping me company."

I smirked, watching him as he effortlessly took over the mess I'd created and began turning it into a masterpiece.

It was frustrating, how good he looked — even half-asleep, bossing me around. Maybe *more* so with the whole bossing me around part. The easy way he moved around the galley reminded me of all the late nights we used to spend just like this, cleaning up after service, stealing kisses between washing dishes and checking on guests.

I swallowed hard against those memories, shoving them down as I picked up a piece of bacon and took a bite, the *crunch* of it so satisfying I moaned.

"Oh, yeah," I said, shaking the bacon at him before I took another bite. "Nicole is going to cream her pants when you throw this on a bed of cheese and sandwich it between two slices of sourdough."

"Is that what that little moan was? You creaming yours?"

I narrowed my gaze, taking one last bite of the bacon before throwing the last of it at him. "Shut up."

He laughed as it bounced off his nose and hit the floor.

"I heard about the, uh, *discovery* Leah made while unpacking today," Finn said, arching a brow at me. He held up the ball of mozzarella I'd pulled out with a frown.

"They want it fried. Cheese fries, grilled cheese, mozz sticks…"

"They don't want to shit tomorrow. Got it."

I chuckled. "Maybe it helps with the whole toy situation. I can't imagine anything that big coming *near* my ass, but different strokes for different folks, I guess."

"What exactly *is* the appropriate size for things coming near your ass?" Finn asked with a smirk. "Just so I can pocket that information away."

"That's for me to know and you to lie awake at night dreaming of."

"I'll never sleep again."

He smiled with the comment, seasoning the potatoes as my stomach did a little flip.

Was he flirting with me?

That felt like flirting.

I told myself not to read too much into it. After the fight last night and the pancakes this morning, I had no idea where the hell we stood. Throw in that little ass slap, and I was more than just a little confused. But whatever we were now felt better than what we had been the first day we walked onto this boat — so I'd take it, no questions asked.

I ran out to check on the guests, laughing when they cheered at my announcement that Finn was awake and creating a cheesy paradise for them. When I slid back into the galley, I found Finn staring at what he'd assembled so far with a frown like he was making sure he hadn't forgotten anything.

He was twisting a ring on his right pinky finger.

My breath stalled out at the sight.

His grandma's ring.

He'd told me about it one morning as we had coffee on the dock in Greece, our feet swinging beneath us as we watched the sun rise higher over the diamond blue water.

"I don't know any other guys who wear a pinky ring," I say, *nodding to the simple gold band gleaming from where he holds his coffee mug.*

"Ah," he says, smiling down at it. He wears his exhaustion on his face and somehow it makes me even more attracted to him. I wish we could spend the day snuggled in a hotel bed. "Me granny's."

"Really?" I reach out for his hand, and he lets me inspect the ring closer. "That's so sweet."

"She left it to me when she passed, along with her best cookware. She didn't have much in the end, since she'd moved in with us, but... she knew I'd appreciate the little she did have."

"It's really nice that you honor her memory by wearing it."

He cracks his neck, growing quiet before he takes a sip of his coffee. "One day, I hope I can do more."

I hadn't understood what he meant by that then, and our radios had gone off in the next instant, our captain calling a crew meeting.

Now, I knew he meant the restaurant he'd yet to tell me about at that time.

His words battled through the fog of the alcohol from the night before, though I struggled to remember it all clearly.

I didn't want to ruin what we had.

I thought if I had a grand plan... you'd come with me.

If I were a more confident woman, maybe I would have. Maybe Gisella would have if she were in my spot then. But Finn had triggered me, even if it wasn't his intention. He'd made me feel the way my father did, like my career wasn't important, like my dreams weren't valid.

And worst of all, him leaving me in the end confirmed my deepest fear.

That I wasn't enough.

I wasn't enough to stay for, to change course for, to be honest with, to fully let in.

Staring at this man in the galley now, I wondered if it had been his fears ruling him that night, too. I wondered if love, or lack thereof, wasn't to blame.

Love never stood a chance against bad timing and two scared kids trying to figure out who they were.

Finn startled a bit when he realized I was back. "They good?"

I smiled. "They're fine. Drunk and hungry, but fine." I edged closer, placing my hands on the opposite side of the stainless-steel island where he worked. "I love that you still wear that."

He followed my gaze to his ring, flexing his hand before he curled it into a fist.

"Never take it off."

"Finn." I waited until he looked at me again. "What happened to the restaurant?"

His hands stilled where he was working, his eyes searching mine for a long moment. "Put my trust in the wrong eejit, didn't I?"

"What does that mean?"

He sighed, cracking his neck before he was back to work. He seemed to do everything with a little more gusto, frustration rolling off him in plumes. "It means I thought I had a proper partner. Turned out I'd hitched my wagon to a bloody crook."

He poured the dipping sauce he'd been making for the grilled cheeses into a ramekin — some sort of maple glaze — then tossed the silver mixing bowl into the sink without care. The clang of it made me flinch.

Finn rested his hands on the edge of the sink for a moment, smoothing out his breaths. "Everything was perfect, Em," he said softly, shaking his head. "It feels impossibly hard when you open a new restaurant. There are a thousand ways you could fail... a shit location where no one can find you, a menu that tries too hard to impress everyone and ends up impressing no one, staff that's either incompetent or just couldn't give a shite, margins so razor-thin you're bleeding out before you even open the doors... but everything worked out for us." He hummed a little laugh like he still couldn't believe it. "The location was great, the community was welcoming, the reviews were glowing, the staff keen to make it a success. We struggled in the first couple of months, but before we knew it, every table was filled for dinner every single night of the week. We had a waitlist." His nostrils flared. "It was too good to be true. I knew it, but I thought maybe..."

His voice faded, and he pushed away from the sink, getting back to work on finalizing all the dishes. It smelled amazing in the galley, all the cheese and garlic and onions and bacon. Even with pain etched into his face, he worked like it wasn't work at all.

"So, this business partner..."

"Ronan," Finn said, and his jaw tightened with the name. "He was a family friend, lad I knew since we were in nappies. He came into a big sum of money when his grandparents passed. We ran into each other at a bar a couple months before I left for that charter I met you on, and as we were catching up, I told him my plans for the restaurant." Finn shook his head. "He knew what Granny meant to me, what this was all about. He told me he'd look into things and see if he could help.

"I couldn't believe it. I mean, it was like a sign from the universe. Then, about a month before our season was up, he called and said he was ready to go into it with me as a partner — fifty-fifty. He said he believed in the restaurant. He made *me* believe in it." His eyes found mine. "And then he bled us dry. By the time I clocked it, there wasn't a prayer of saving the place. I tried, but it was hopeless. We went under so fast I didn't have time to abandon ship even if I wanted to."

"You never would have anyway."

He swallowed.

"I'm so sorry, Finn." My chest cracked with the words. I couldn't imagine working so hard for something like that, for a dream so hard to accomplish, and then to have it all disappear in an instant...

"Thank you," he whispered. "It just... *Jaysus*, Ember, it really fucked me up." His voice broke a bit with that, and the vulnerability of it made my throat tighten. "I've never felt such shame in all my life."

"There's nothing for you to feel ashamed of," I said with a frown. "You did everything you could. You would have made your grandmother so proud. You—"

"Should've seen the signs plain as day," he finished for me, eyes hitting mine. "Now I don't trust me own bleeding shadow, don't trust me judgement at all anymore — on anything. On any*one*."

"Not even Gisella?"

Oh, God.

My eyes widened at the words I couldn't *believe* I'd let slip out, but Finn didn't seem fazed by them at all. He just finished plating the midnight snacks, one of his shoulders inching up a bit.

That was all the answer I got before it was time to take the food out to the guests. Finn helped me, both of us plastering on wide smiles and Finn even doing a little bow to the applause from the group when we delivered the trays. It was a performance worthy of an Oscar from him, considering the topic of conversation before.

The guests dove in, moaning their appreciation as I got them each situated with bottles of water before Finn and I retreated back to the galley.

The tension was still right where we'd left it.

Wordlessly, we both began cleaning up, Finn focusing on wiping all the surfaces down while I got started on the dishes. He eventually joined me, taking over drying after I washed and rinsed.

"How did things start with you two, anyway?" I asked. "You've been dating for a few months... but how did you meet?"

There was no way to make the question sound casual, no way to stop my throat from closing in around the words as they escaped.

Finn took the pan I'd just rinsed and began to dry it, his eyes skirting up to me before he focused on what he was doing. "You really want to know that?"

No.

Yes.

I don't fucking know, Finn.

I didn't trust myself to try to answer. After a moment, he took away the choice.

"She was there when everything happened," he said. "Gi was in Dublin for the offseason the first time I met her, working at a hotel not too far from where the restaurant was. She came in one night for dinner with some of the other employees and we struck up a conversation when I checked on their table. After that, she became a regular, most times coming in to eat by herself. She'd come late, usually our last seating of the night, so sometimes I'd sit with her when I was finished cooking and we just... became friends."

Acid burned my throat.

Why the *fuck* did I ask?

"I admit I was still... hung up," he said, his eyes darting to mine only briefly before they were back on the dishes he was drying. "And I guess part of me thought I needed to start moving on somehow. I thought maybe she was the way."

Our hands brushed when I handed him a large knife, his fingers wrapping around mine on the handle before I pulled away with my neck burning.

"She left for another charter season, and when she came back, it was just in time to watch everything go to shite." Finn finished drying the last of the dishes and wiped his hands on a towel before throwing it over his shoulder. "She was there for me."

He left it at that, letting me fill in the gaps. I wished I'd never asked and then again, I felt better for having the knowledge.

"I'm glad you have her," I said, and even though the words felt like nails being driven into my tongue, I meant them.

He deserved to be happy.

He deserved to have someone reliable by his side.

"You said she helped you see the restaurant was a mistake," I reminded him. "What does that mean?"

Finn sighed. "Just means she saw better than I did what a waste of time it all was. She told me I didn't need the stress of a business like that when I could make a killing as a private chef, whether it be on yachts or for a wealthy family somewhere." He shrugged. "I knew she was right. I just... it's hard to hear, I guess."

"It wasn't a waste of time," I said softly. "And if you ever wanted to try again, that wouldn't be a waste, either. It's never a waste to pursue your dreams."

Again, one of his shoulders hitched up, but he didn't comment. Instead, he changed the subject.

"What about you?" he asked, letting out a long breath as he folded his arms and leaned a hip against the sink. "You ever..."

"No," I said before he could even finish the thought. I tried to smile, but my lips only curled a moment before they fell again. Finn's eyes were hard on mine, but I didn't waver, and something about that quiet galley in the middle of the night made me brave. "I've kissed a few boys, cuddled after a crew night out, maybe, but... never anything serious." I shrugged. "I think my heart still belongs to a chef on a boat in Greece."

I whispered the words, but they struck Finn hard. I watched as his breathing intensified, his eyes flicking between mine.

"Firefly..."

"I'm sorry, Finn," I interrupted, and I hated how my eyes flooded with tears, but I didn't bat them away.

I was so good at running from emotions, so used to that being my modus operandi. But I wanted to feel all of it tonight. I wanted to surrender.

"I'm sorry I didn't listen to you. I'm sorry I assumed the worst. I'm sorry I didn't even consider going with you, in any capacity. You regret getting into business with Ronan? Well, I regret the night I walked away from us."

His brows pinched together as he stepped into my space. He

reached out his hand, thumb catching a tear my blink had set free. I closed my eyes and leaned into the touch as my heart throbbed in my chest.

I wanted to stay there. I wanted to bask in what it felt like to have his hands on me again. I wanted to breathe him in, sink into him like a warm bed after a long shift.

My body betrayed me, leaning just a fraction closer before my brain caught up and yanked me back.

I rolled my lips and pulled away quickly, laughing at myself as I wiped my hands over my wet cheeks. "But hey," I said, voice thin and brittle, "at least we can be friends now, right? I guess the universe works in mysterious ways, bringing us back together like this."

Finn's expression was unreadable. He didn't smile, didn't nod, didn't move.

He just watched me, gaze heavy enough to make my pulse stutter.

And suddenly, I felt the urge to bolt rushing through every cell in my body like water from an unleashed dam.

"Ember!"

Nicole's voice sliced through the quiet, making us both flinch like we'd been caught doing something we shouldn't. My smile was weak, but I held it as best I could as I slid past Finn, patting his shoulder.

"Duty calls," I said, my voice hollow.

He caught my wrist before I could take another step.

I didn't turn. I *couldn't* look at him again — not now, not with my heart splintering in my chest and my composure hanging on by a thread. I was barely holding it together, and I was afraid even one more glance in his direction would have me falling apart at his feet.

The weight of his hand around my wrist was like an anchor, holding me to this spot, to this man, to everything unresolved between us. My body hummed with a dangerous energy the longer he held me, both of us breathing like our lungs were on fire. I waited for him to speak, but he never did.

Just when I thought I couldn't take it anymore, he let me go.

I stumbled forward, dragging that hand he'd just had in his grasp through my hair in an attempt to steady myself as I headed for the main salon. My breath was shallow, my chest caving in around my lungs.

I swiped a large tray from the counter as I passed it, ready to gather up whatever dishes the guests were finished with, and that's when I saw it.

A soft, glowing blue light in the corner of the galley.

My heart lurched.

I'd completely forgotten about the cameras.

Chapter Sixteen

CHARTER CONFESSIONAL
CLOSE QUARTERS

SEASON 4, EPISODE 4
CHARTER 3

GARY PARKS: CAPTAIN

PRODUCER
With three charters done, we're a third of the way
through the season. How are you feeling so far?

CAPTAIN GARY
Oh, mate, can't complain. We've had a few hiccups —
deck crew needed a bit to find their sea legs with
docking — but I reckon we're on the up. Interior's
running like a dream, six-star service every charter,
and no more bickering between the chef and chief.
From where I'm standing, we're sitting pretty heading
into the back half of the season.

PRODUCER
So, you'd say the crew is working out well?

CAPTAIN GARY
Yeah, solid crew. Food's been top-notch, guests are
loving the deck crew's entertainment, and Ember's
absolutely smashing it as chief stew. She was made
for this gig. Service is spot-on, boat's sparkling,
guests can't stop raving about the little ways she
made their charters special. I knew she had it in
her.

Gary laughs, shakes head.

By the time charter four wrapped, we had found our rhythm.

It wasn't perfect — not by a long shot — but the chaos felt more controlled. Palmer and the deck crew had Cap beaming with their docking, not a single line touching the water and every meter of distance being called correctly. Leah seemed hell-bent on proving herself after being down a charter, the laundry executed perfectly and cabins polished to perfection, and Bernard had fully settled into his role as my second stew. I could trust him implicitly with dinner service, knowing he would not just help me pull off every theme with the table scape, but that we'd work together seamlessly to provide luxury service to every guest.

I did hear Palmer complaining to Cameron about Gisella one morning as they uncovered the chairs on the sundeck, something about her moving with zero sense of urgency. I had yet to ask for her to do more for interior than run a few plates at dinner service or help Leah touch up cabins in the evenings. She was a deck/stew, which meant she was just as much at my disposal as Palmer's, but I was happy to run the boat without her help as much as possible.

And Finn and I had found whatever this new normal was between us.

We spoke when we needed to, coordinated service with tight efficiency, and put on a united front for the cameras. But beyond that, I stayed away.

I had to.

Because if I'd learned anything from that late night in the galley, it was that my body wasn't my ally when it came to Finn Pearson. And if I wasn't careful, I'd end up making the kind of mistake that couldn't be undone.

But just because we were all working hard and finding our groove didn't mean there wasn't *plenty* of entertainment for the production crew to capture.

The fourth charter had the usual guest dramatics. One of the primary's friends insisted on wearing heels everywhere — on the deck, on the tender, even on the jet ski. The entire crew watched in horrified fascination as she attempted to climb onto the swim platform in four-inch Louboutins for a picture, only to slip and send one flying into the water. Eli had to dive after it before it sank, and I had to dry the pair out with a hairdryer while she wailed about their impending ruination.

On our crew night out after that charter, sparks flew between Leah and Cameron again, the two of them giggling to each other at one end of the table at dinner before grinding on one another the rest of the night at the bar. I'd turned in early that evening, catching a cab back with Palmer who seemed just as intent on getting sleep as I was.

During the fifth charter, poor Eli lived out his most embarrassing moment of the season. He'd been tasked with repositioning one of the jet skis, a simple enough job. Or, at least, it should have been. But within minutes of him pushing off from the yacht, he'd realized he didn't have the key.

Or his radio.

Production had a field day capturing the footage of Eli slowly floating away as he waved his hands in the air and whistled, trying to get someone's attention. Of course, not a single producer or cameraperson said a thing. It wasn't until Gisella spotted him, and she'd had a full-on laugh before radioing for Palmer.

It was reality TV gold.

Laundry was another disaster. At some point during turn day between charters, Gisella had tossed her brand-new red bikini into a load of whites Leah had going, turning every last towel, sheet, and guest robe a lovely shade of pink. Leah had nearly burst into tears, Bernard had dissolved into a fit of laughter so long I was afraid he'd need an oxygen mask to breathe again, and Captain Gary had taken one look at the stack of blushing linens before shaking his head and muttering, "Just tell them it's the latest trend in luxury."

Thankfully, provisions had been able to save the day, delivering fresh linens to fill the gaps for what we didn't have on board. It would cost us, though, and no yacht owner liked to be surprised with things like that from a charter season. Still, it was better than some of the things that *could* rack up a bill — like a bad docking or a tender running aground.

At the end of both charters, the guests left happy — and left decent tips, too. We were exhausted but satisfied as a crew, and with charter five under our belts, we were officially over halfway through this shortened season.

Captain Gary had pulled me aside after the guests disembarked, checking in on me and the interior while taking a moment to tell me again how proud he was of me. Like Leah with the laundry debacle, I'd nearly lost it, but the tears I held back were of joy. It felt incredible to be recognized for my hard work, to have everything running so smoothly on my watch.

I was doing exactly what I came to do.

Where Captain was proud of me for the interior, I was proud of me for something I couldn't brag about to anyone.

I'd barely thought about Finn outside of work hours.

I was keeping my distance and keeping my focus on the charter guests and the interior.

And when I caught him looking at me, when I swore his eyes held something deeper... I reminded myself what I already knew.

Finn Pearson wasn't mine anymore.

When Captain dismissed me from the bridge after our little chat, I'd let out a slow breath full of relief, like I'd been a raft filled to the point of nearly popping and finally got to release the pressure.

Five charters done, four more to go.

We had a night off ahead of us, another fat tip in our pockets, and no guests for the next eighteen hours. I had just enough time to unwind before the next wave of stress hit.

But first, I had a call to make.

After an afternoon of deep cleaning and turning the boat for our next guests, I slipped away to my cabin, pulling the door shut behind me. Gisella was still on deck, finishing up her duties before she'd start getting ready for our night out and it would be a tornado of hair spray and flying clothes in here. She and I had found our own little truce of sorts, even joking with one another and talking a bit at night before we'd pass out.

She wasn't so bad, and maybe I hated that most of all.

I did wish she was cleaner, though. I was just as bad as she was at destroying this little cabin when we were getting ready to go out, but I'd tidy my space back up in the end. She, on the other hand, seemed to be testing my patience with how much makeup she'd smear on the bathroom counter, mirror, and towels before

I'd break down and clean it all up.

The crew quarters were unusually still — no clinking dishes from the galley, no banter from the mess. Just silence. The kind that left too much room for thinking.

I sat on the edge of my bunk, phone in hand, thumb hovering over the screen. I didn't even have to search for his name — Dad was pinned at the top of my contacts. It had been since I got a phone. He was reliable, steady, the person I would call first when something went wrong or when I had something to celebrate.

My leg bounced as I stared at the phone, chewing the inside of my cheek. I could already hear his voice in my head — clipped, calm, faintly amused, like he was always a step ahead and I was just trying to keep up.

Calling my father shouldn't have felt like such an ordeal, but it did. Because it was never simply checking in. It was always a test. I felt as if I needed to have my report card ready, posture straight, all emotions tucked neatly away.

I took a deep breath.

And then I hit call and flopped back onto the bunk, staring at the ceiling. It rang twice, and then that voice pierced through my anxiety.

"There's my girl."

I swallowed, spine snapping straight like a soldier called to attention. That greeting — warm and proud — always hit like a paradox. It wrapped around me like a soft blanket and sank like a stone in my stomach all at once.

"Hey, Dad."

"It's been more than a month since I've heard from you."

"You know, the phone works both ways."

"Well, I never know with your... job if you'll be able to answer.

I just assume you'll call me when you can."

I rolled my eyes. Just one of many of my father's assumptions.

"And here you are!" he continued. I could almost see his bright grin, the way it took up his whole face like a politician's smile. "How are you? *Where* are you? Oh, your mother is here, too."

"Hello, darling," Mom's soft voice called from the background. "So good to hear from you. I've been hoping I'd see you post an update on Facebook but haven't seen anything."

I chuckled. "No offense, Mom, but I only post on Facebook because you and Aunt Zoe beg me to. You need to download Instagram. Also, I can't post anything until the show airs, remember?"

There was a beat of silence, like they'd both completely forgotten about the show.

Or maybe they'd hoped it wasn't real.

"Oh, that's right," Dad said with that tone I was so used to hearing over the years. It was the same one he used when he and Mom hosted a party and he got caught in a conversation he wasn't particularly interested in, or one he didn't agree with. "So, you went through with that, did you?"

"I told you I was." I tried not to grit those words through my annoyance that they were pretending like this was surprising news. "And it's going great, which is why I wanted to call. We just wrapped up the fifth charter, got four more to go. Captain Gary has told me a few times now how proud he is of me." I sat a bit straighter at that, my smile genuine. "He says he knew I'd be a great chief stew and that I'm proving him right."

There was another long pause. I wondered if my parents were exchanging that look they thought was so hard to read when I knew exactly what it said even if no words left their mouths.

"Well, it doesn't surprise me that you're good at making cocktails and doing laundry, Ember," my father clipped. "You've been great at everything you've put your mind to all your life. I just wish you put your mind to something a little more respectable."

Ice pricked my veins just as there was a knock on my cabin door. It flew open before I could say a word, and Eli swung in with one hand on the doorframe and a wide grin on his face. "Em, what are you—" He clapped a hand over his mouth when he saw me on the phone, mouthing a *sorry*. But instead of backing out of the room, he took one look at my face and frowned, easing inside and plopping down on the bed next to me.

"It is respectable, Dad. It's hard work. You know how many years I've hustled to earn this title."

"And *you* know there is a position waiting for you here with me that would pay four times the amount you're making there — if not more."

"It's not about the money."

Dad's laugh made my jaw ache. It was a placating kind of laugh, and I knew he was likely shaking his head, too. "And that's how I know you're still young, my sweet daughter. You may think I'm being harsh, but I push you because I love you. I want the best for you. You've never had to live a life where money is tight. You've never experienced the things I did as a child — and I'm glad for that. I'm happy your mother and I could provide a better lifestyle for you than either of us had. But you don't think about money because you've never *had* to."

I swallowed, my chest flushing with something between rage and shame. He was right, of course. But I hated that he was using my privilege to discount my passion.

"And as your father, sometimes I have to play the bad guy in order to set you up for success."

Mom had either left the room or was staying silent, as usual. How I wished she was the kind of mom who would step in at times like this. How would it feel to hear her hush my father for once, to tell him to mind his business while she asked me more about whatever it was that made me happy?

What would it be like, to have the support of even *one* parent?

"I'm happy, Dad," I said, and Eli put a hand on my knee, squeezing. My eyes stung with that little sign of support. "I'm making a name for myself. I *am* successful, and some day, I'll be running a superyacht all on my own as the sole purser."

"And you'll never be home for a holiday again."

I sighed, pinching the bridge of my nose. I was all too aware of the camera that had sidled up outside my open door to watch this all unfold, as well as the eyes that flicked my way as they passed. I looked up just in time to see Finn pausing behind the cameraman, his brows pinched together in concern.

Gisella pulled him away, and I blinked.

"You're working for other people right now when you could have other people working for *you*."

"I do have a team working for me," I corrected him. "I'm chief stew, Dad. I run the entire interior. I have three stripes, each one hard earned. You always told me to work for what I want in this life, and now I'm doing that and you're telling me it's not enough."

"Now don't go putting words in my mouth." His voice turned stern, all the sweet cadence gone in an instant. "You are a young lady with free will to make the choices you deem appropriate for your life. But I am your father. And it is perfectly acceptable for me to want better for my child than cleaning toilets."

I closed my eyes, my throat tight with the effort to hold in my emotion.

"Okay, Dad. Well, I just wanted to call to check in," I said, and my voice sounded as cold as I felt on the inside. "I love you. Give Mom a hug for me."

"We love you, too. And I'm..."

He sighed. I almost thought he was going to apologize, but I knew he was too proud for that.

Besides, he'd meant every word he said.

"I'm sure the show is exciting. Maybe when I watch it, I'll understand more. But... this isn't a real career, Ember. It's a phase. A detour. You're smarter than this. And I just want you to know you always have other options. You can always change your path."

My ribcage constricted at the thought of them watching the show.

Just like when I'd accepted the offer, I knew this was my chance to let them into my world. It was my only opportunity for them to see what I did and truly understand it, to value it, to value *me*.

Which meant I needed to tighten up.

Because if I did get their attention, if they really did watch the show? I wanted my parents to see their daughter working hard and making moves.

Not making a fool of herself over some boy.

"Bye, Dad," I whispered, and then ended the call.

I'd almost forgotten Eli was there until he blew out a breath.

"Okay, then?"

I nodded, but my eyes were welling when he pulled me into his massive chest for a hug.

"Ag, shame, *liefie*," he said, kissing my temple before he pulled back. "Listen, your old man doesn't know what he's missing. You're killing it here. And tonight, it's about you, me, and enough drinks to forget he even called, neh?"

He gave me a playful nudge, eyes twinkling warmly, before standing up and offering his hand.

"Now put on one of those lekker little numbers you packed and let's go dance."

I nodded again, wiping my face when he released me. Eli was right.

It was my night off, and I was determined not to let my father's words ruin it.

Chapter Seventeen

PRE-PRODUCTION CONFESSIONAL
CLOSE QUARTERS

SEASON 4

BERNARD EVANS: SECOND STEWARD

BERNARD
Look, I love a flirt, but a boatmance? Never had one, never will. Mark my words.

PRODUCER
You wouldn't pursue it, if there was someone on board you were attracted to?

BERNARD
From the crew? Not a chance.

PRODUCER
Why is that?

BERNARD
It's messy, innit? Shitting where you eat. We're crammed in together 24/7, stress levels through the roof. Even if you fancy someone, it's got disaster written all over it — one likes the other more, someone catches feelings when the other's just after a shag, you split and then have to act professional? Yeah, right. Like that ever happens.

PRODUCER
Do you think a boatmance can ever make it past the charter season?

Bernard laughs loudly, shakes head.

BERNARD
I've never seen a boatmance last a full season, let alone beyond it. We're all from different places, working jobs that keep us moving. Plus, let's be real — everyone's young, fit, and up for it. Trusting your partner to stay faithful on another yacht? Mate, you're asking for heartbreak. What do they think is gonna happen? It's not like any of us are buying a house with a white picket fence anytime soon.

PRODUCER
So I guess it's best to just have a little fun and leave it at that, then?

BERNARD
If you want a bit of fun, find a local. But if you actually want a season without drama? Don't shag the crew. Best bet is to keep it professional.

PRODUCER
And if you don't?

Bernard shrugs.

BERNARD
Then you've only got yourself to blame when it all goes tits up.

"Fucking hell, Leah, that arse deserves a standing ovation!" Bernard said loudly over the music, splashing water at Leah. She was twerking her ass in the hot tub, hands braced on the edge to keep her steady as she danced. I hollered, too, marveling at how talented she was at making her booty shake while the rest of her torso was perfectly stable. She was blessed with juicy curves, and as a more athletic build myself, I was mesmerized watching her move.

Cameron looked ready to propose where he watched her from

his corner of the Jacuzzi. I jokingly reached over and pretended to wipe drool off his chin. That was when Gisella came running across the teak and all but jumped into the hot tub, joining right in with Leah without missing a beat. We all cheered, and Palmer leaned back against the edge with his arms spread wide. "This is what they mean when they talk about the good life."

It had been a perfect night out — no drama, no one so inebriated they were being an asshole or throwing up or passing out, and most importantly, no thoughts of my dad making me turn into a sad drunk. Dinner had been filled with great conversation and laughter, and instead of going out to a club, we'd all decided to head back to the boat and enjoy the hot tub we were usually serving the guests in.

Now, it was like a Vegas afterparty. Eli acted as DJ on his portable speaker, playing mostly EDM. Bernard had whipped up some strong cocktails for each of us — after we took a round of tequila shots, of course — and Finn was throwing together some snacks. There was dancing and laughter and not a single frown in sight.

"God, I'm starving," Leah said, a bit breathless after her twerk session as she sank down in the hot water. "Where's Finn?"

"Finn! Finnn," Gisella sang, and then Bernard joined in, followed by Cameron, Eli, Palmer, and finally me until we were all calling for him so loudly, I was afraid we'd wake Captain Gary. Finn eventually appeared in the main salon, visible to us through the glass doors, and we erupted into cheers. He smirked and shook his head as the doors slid open. He was balancing two trays of food, everything from grilled paninis and potato chips to pickles and bar nuts.

"Oh, my God, I love you," Leah proclaimed, snagging a

panini with cheese melting over the edges of the crust off one of the trays before Finn even had the chance to set it down. The rest of the crew followed suit as he chuckled.

He acted coy, like it was no big deal that he'd gone to work while the rest of us changed into our swimsuits and continued to fuck off. But I saw it in his eyes, that pride that cooking gave him, that joy he experienced at the sight of someone enjoying what he'd created.

Finn was such a strange type of familiar to me now. I knew so much about him and yet hadn't a clue what he'd done for the last two years. He'd lived life without me, just as I had without him. There was a separation that could never be undone.

But there was a bond that couldn't be broken just the same.

I still remembered the first time we met, the first day I knew what it was like to be in a world where Finn Pearson existed.

My duffle bag digs into my shoulder as I make my way through the boat, eyes wide and taking it all in. I pass through the galley on my way to the bridge to greet the captain, and that's when I see him.

He's bent over an open drawer, organizing knives by size, sleeves shoved up to his elbows, brown hair curling around the edges of a backward facing hat. I don't even say a word and yet somehow, he senses me.

He looks up.

Our eyes lock.

The earth shifts beneath my feet when I take in those ocean blues, when a smile curls on his lips.

"Hey there," he says, straightening to his full height. "You must be a stew."

I smile back, nerves fluttering. "That obvious?"

"Only 'cause you're still looking around like this boat is full of

gifts for you to open on Christmas morning instead of months of hard work and exhaustion."

"Guilty. I'm afraid I love this job."

"Have to, don't you?"

We share another smile.

"I'm Finn," he says.

"Ember."

He cocks his head. "Like a burning ember of flame?"

"Wow. Never heard that one before." I roll my eyes.

"Fiery. Just like your namesake. And you've got the looks to match, too."

He winks with that, and I snort, stepping past him with a smirk. "Flattery won't get you out of doing your own dishes when you make a big mess, Chef. And you can cool it on the name play."

"Mm. If you hate Ember so much, I'll call you something else." He leans against the counter, eyes tracing me like he already knows everything about me.

I find I kind of want him to.

"How about Firefly?"

I turn, curious, one hand still gripping the strap of my bag. "Firefly?"

"It suits you better," he says, that magnetic smile softening. "You light up the room. Can't help but follow the glow."

My face flushes when he hits me with a sexy, mischievous grin. That tilt of his lips does something to my belly that feels like an invitation and a warning all at once.

And then he's back to work and I'm on my way to the bridge.

I have no idea I've just met the man who will destroy me by the time the season ends.

"Wait, why aren't you in your swim trunks?" Gisella asked

with a pout, snapping me back to the present.

"Ah, I've done my bit. You lot are fed, my work here's done," Finn said, nodding to the food. "But I'm knackered. I'm off to bed."

"You what, mate?!" Bernard asked, aghast.

"Noooo," Gisella whined.

There was a chorus of shared sentiment from the rest of the crew, protests muffled by mouths full of Finn's delicious food. I stayed silent, though disappointment sank like an anchor in my gut. I'd barely talked to him all night, and I was sad he wasn't joining us.

Which is stupid, I reminded myself with an internal groan. I didn't know why I wanted him to stay. Did I really want to torture myself with watching Gisella hang all over him in the hot tub? Because that was the truth of it — he would be here with *her*, not me.

I hated that I still had to actively fight so hard against the natural instincts I had with him. I wanted to spend time with him, talk to him, laugh with him — as if nothing had ever happened, as if we were still the same people we were two years ago. It was like my brain was planted firmly in the reality of today, but my heart still lived in the past. And my body wasn't any help. That traitorous bitch was either absolutely clueless or willfully ignorant.

"Come now, bru, don't be a chop," Eli said, picking up the cocktail Bernard had made for Finn that had since sat untouched on the teak rim of the hot tub. He tried handing it to our chef. "You're off the clock and there's a hot tub full of half-naked people begging you to join them. What could be better than that?"

"Sleep, mate. The real luxury in life," Finn quipped back

with a grin, clapping Eli's wet shoulder and giving it a squeeze.

"Boo," Cameron jeered playfully. Palmer was the only one keeping quiet about it all, a fellow head of department showing respect, I guessed. It made my own silence feel more reasonable.

"Stay," Gisella pleaded, catching Finn's wrist with her bottom lip protruding. "It'll be fun."

"I have no doubt it will be, darlin'. You enjoy. I'll see you in the morning." He bent down to peck her on the lips, and I dragged my gaze away with acid burning my throat like he was still mine and I was watching him cheat in live time.

"You can't be *that* tired," Gisella tried, still holding onto him when he went to walk away. "And besides, you can sleep in a little in the morning!"

"I'll need to prep for the next charter."

"We'll help!" she said. "*Venga, porfa, mi amorrr.*"

When batting her lashes didn't work, she pouted more. Then, she gasped, gaping at him like she'd just realized something very obvious that the rest of us had missed.

"Wait a second... this isn't because of your silly *tattoo*, is it?"

"Tattoo?!" Bernard and Leah echoed, jaws popping open.

"Cheffy, let's see it, then!" Cameron added, devouring the last bite of his panini before he spun his finger in the air.

"Finn doesn't have any tattoos."

Regret sliced through me as soon as those words left my mouth, because everyone grew silent, and all eyes swiveled to me.

Fuck.

Gisella narrowed her gaze. "Well, seeing as how I'm the only one on this boat who has seen Finn naked recently, I think I'd know better than you, wouldn't I?"

I wanted to shrivel up and cease to exist.

"He *does* have a tattoo," she finished, then a strained smile found her lips as she turned back to him. "And it's cute. Come on, babe. Don't be a *muermo*. Join us. No one is going to make fun of your drunken mistake under an ink gun."

"I might," Palmer teased with a wink.

Gisella splashed him.

Finn's jaw was set, and I could tell any playfulness he'd been trying to hold onto had vacated the premises.

"Nothing to do with that. I already told ye, I'm tired," he clipped. "You lot have fun."

He tried to walk away, but Gisella caught his shirt, giggling as she pulled at it hard enough to expose his midriff. He wasn't stacked the way Eli or Cameron was, but he was lean, his abs defined and dusted with a light trail of hair.

I tried not to look, but it was impossible. I still remembered the way it felt to wrap myself around that body. I remembered how warm he was, how he'd tremble when I ran my fingertips from his chest all the way down to the band of his briefs. If I closed my eyes, I knew I could recall exactly what it felt like to lay my head on his chest.

My heart ached.

I should have prayed for mercy from those memories, but instead, I found myself wishing they'd never fade.

"Gi, that's enough," Finn said, but she was still giggling, and everyone else was so drunk they laughed and egged her on. She tugged and lifted until we all caught sight of the tattoo she'd spoken of, and my heart stopped.

It was small, just a spattering of black ink on his left rib cage just below his chest.

Below his heart.

"What is it?!" Eli asked, standing to get a better look before Finn ripped away and tugged his shirt back down.

"A firefly," I whispered.

Finn's eyes snapped to mine.

It must have only been a split second, but time snagged like a fishing line on a tree for me, yanking my entire existence to a halt. My pulse thundered in my ears, and though I knew I should look away and play it off for the crew and the cameras watching, I couldn't.

I just stared at him, and he stared right back.

"All these tattoos," he murmurs, tracing the small lines of ink on my arm with his fingers first before he begins to kiss each one.

I bite my lip and squirm under his touch, hooking a leg over his hip and pulling him closer.

"Tell me what they mean."

"Which one?"

"All of 'em."

"That might take a while."

"We have forever."

I laugh, stealing a kiss when he reaches the tattoo at my collarbone before he's rolling on top of me and admiring the ones on my abdomen.

He points to the little lion on my hip bone.

"Leo," I answer. "My sign."

Finn smirks, trailing that finger until it touches the little cowboy hat inked on my inner thigh.

"For a book series I love."

His finger glides slowly over my cotton panties, making me whimper. He smirks as if he's innocent before his touch stalls at the little star beneath my bikini line.

"A reminder that we're star dust."

He continues his perusing, asking about every tattoo until I'm driven so mad from his touch that I'm pulling him on top of me and begging for relief.

After, with my head on his chest, I ask him, "Do you have any tattoos?"

"Not one."

"Think you ever will?"

"Nah, probably not. Can't think of a thing I'd ink onto my skin forever. It'd have to be something important to me — something I never want to lose."

I tried to swallow but couldn't as the memory replayed on a loop.

He had a tattoo.

A firefly.

Emotion strangled me like a fist wrapped tight around my throat.

Was it for me?

"Nah, that's tame, bru," Eli said, shrugging it off. "Check this out!"

He stood and ripped his pants down before any of us had a chance to look away, showing us his pale ass and a shitty, faded tattoo of a rubber duck that looked more demented than cute.

"Christ Almighty, Eli! No one wants to see yer arse, ya weapon!" Cameron yelled, shielding his eyes. Everyone else was laughing.

I was still staring at Finn.

Finally, he cleared his throat, breaking our gaze and offering a flat-lipped smile to the group. "Goodnight."

"Awww, we were just having a laugh, Cheffy," Palmer called

after him. "We love you!"

Finn threw his hand up in a wave, but didn't turn around. He disappeared inside the glass doors, and I watched until he was no longer in view.

"He'll be fine," Gisella promised. "Now, who's up for a game of Truth or Dare?"

I blinked like I was coming out of a trance, and when my eyes met Bernard's, he was watching me with a quirked brow.

He'd been in the galley when Finn used my nickname during this last charter.

And he was watching me now like he knew every secret I was trying to hide.

Gisella's game of Truth or Dare started off tame.

Eli had to take a tequila shot off Bernard's abs (which Bernard ate up like the cheeky bastard he was). Leah admitted she'd faked an orgasm with a guy on a past boat (to which Cameron loudly declared that it would never happen with him, earning laughter and a playful shove from her). Palmer was dared to run a lap naked around the deck (which had Daria, the poor camera operator still with us, flushing a furious shade of red when he ran past her with his dick swinging).

On the outside, I thought I was holding it together quite nicely. I laughed along with everyone else, hooted and hollered when appropriate, and sipped on my cocktail.

But inside, my mind was still trapped in that split-second of time when Finn's eyes locked on mine, when I saw that tiny mark inked just beneath his heart.

I needed to go to bed.

That thought was loud and clear, shoving its way through the rest of the noise until I had no choice but to address it. The last thing I needed was to drink any more, or to let my brain wander any further into dangerous territory.

Besides, it was late, we were all wasted, and this game of Truth or Dare had the potential to get ugly if we didn't call it soon.

I started to push up from the water, ready to call it a night, when Bernard's voice cut through the chatter. "Cameron, truth or dare?"

"Em! Don't go!" Leah tugged on my wrist until I flopped back into the water.

Well, shit.

Cameron grinned, shaking wet hair out of his face as he stretched an arm along the rim of the hot tub. "Dare, obviously."

Bernard's eyes gleamed. "Kiss Gisella."

The second the words left his lips, my stomach plummeted.

I wasn't the only one who stiffened. Palmer's smile evaporated, his brows furrowing as he shot a glare at Bernard.

Leah froze next to me, her drunken smile melting off her face like ice cream in the hot sun. She showed her cards for only a moment before a forced smile found her lips when Cameron looked to her, as if asking for permission. She took a sip from her martini glass like she was entirely unaffected.

I knew better than to believe her, but apparently Cameron didn't, because he turned to Gisella and arched a brow as if to ask *want to do this?*

Palmer tried to save it. "I don't think Gisella will be a willing partner in that dare, bro. She's got a boyfriend, remember?"

Gisella pursed her lips with an innocent lift of one shoulder. "Well, Finn went to bed, didn't he?"

The entire hot tub shifted.

Fuck.

This was not good.

Cameron hesitated for all of a second, his gaze bouncing to Leah again. But when she just stared at the bubbles she was pushing together with her hands, he shrugged.

And then he crossed the hot tub, Gisella met him in the middle with a sultry smirk, and they kissed.

The cheers started before he even reached her. Bernard splashed water and Eli whooped loud enough to wake half the marina. Palmer shook his head like he already knew it was a mistake, taking a drink of his cocktail, but he watched the train wreck right along with the rest of us.

All I could focus on was Leah — the way she suddenly wasn't smiling, the way she'd abandoned her drink on the rim of the tub and curled her arms around herself.

The second they kissed, I swore I watched my third stew break into a thousand pieces.

It wasn't just a peck, either. Gisella hooked her arms around Cameron's shoulders, pulling him flush against her. Cameron's hands found her waist, his fingers splaying over the wet fabric of her swimsuit as she deepened the kiss, tilting her head and parting her lips, which just made Bernard scream louder.

That was all Leah could take.

She climbed out of the tub with no one noticing. The water streamed off her body in rivulets as she stepped onto the deck, wordlessly reaching for a towel and wrapping it tight around herself like armor. The cheers didn't stop. No one asked why her lip trembled or saw the way her shoulders tensed as she turned on her heel and walked inside.

I closed my eyes on a long breath, the pain on her face making my own chest squeeze. Quietly, I climbed out of the hot tub, ignoring Bernard's questioning glance and the way Cameron and Gisella were still tangled up in each other. I was already stepping toward the doors when Gisella's voice stopped me in my tracks.

"Oh, relax, Chief. You're off the clock and your stew will be fine. It's just a little fun — nothing to be so uptight about."

I turned, narrowing my gaze. She wasn't kissing Cameron anymore, but she still clung to him. "You really think Finn would be okay with what you just did?"

I expected her to waver. I expected guilt, or regret, or even a flicker of uncertainty.

But instead, she just smiled.

"I know he would," she said, her voice honey-sweet and menacing all at once. "Because he's *my* boyfriend."

Her brow ticced up in a challenge, like she only wished I'd try to fight her. But I had neither the energy nor the desire.

Maybe she did know Finn better than I did now. Maybe he *was* fine with it.

Even if he wasn't, it was none of my business.

And I reminded myself of that fact the entire way down to the crew quarters to check on Leah.

Chapter Eighteen

CHARTER CONFESSIONAL
CLOSE QUARTERS

SEASON 4, EPISODE 7
CHARTER 6

GISELLA DÍAZ: DECKHAND/STEWARDESS

PRODUCER
So… the hot tub got a little crazy last night, huh?

GISELLA
It was so fun!

PRODUCER
Have you talked to Finn yet this morning?

GISELLA
I just rolled out of bed. He's been up for a while,
I'd guess. Probably hard at work in the galley
already! I'll go see him as soon as we wrap up here.

PRODUCER
Are you going to tell him about what happened last
night?

GISELLA
What do you mean?

PRODUCER
You and Cameron.

Gisella flicks hair over shoulder, laughs.

GISELLA
Oh, my God. It's not that big of a deal! I mean,
sure, I'll tell Finn, but he's not going to care.
It's just a kiss. I kiss everyone.

PRODUCER
So, you'd be okay if Finn kissed someone else?

"Alright, crew. Charter six! Here we go," Captain Gary said, passing the preference sheet packets around to each of us. He was oblivious in his cheer, probably still riding the high of a successful charter five.

Meanwhile, Palmer and I watched Finn warily as he wordlessly took his packet and flipped through the pages. He wore a mask of indifference, his blue-green eyes lined with exhaustion, but otherwise seemingly unaffected.

But in my gut, I knew better.

I'd been vacuuming the main salon when I heard the commotion from the galley earlier. I went to inspect, but was stopped dead in my tracks by Bernard, who was huddled in the staff prep galley just outside the main one. It was where we'd wash cocktail glasses and make juice or coffee, a little nook that was out of the chef's way.

Bernard had been pretending to prep lime slices when I'd found him, and he'd held a finger up to his lips to quiet me before I could say a word. He'd arched a brow, tipping his head toward the galley just as a deep voice cut through the clattering of dishes.

"Why the hell would you assume I was okay with it?"
Finn.
"It was just a kiss," Gisella had whisper-yelled. "It's not like I

slept with him or something. Relax. You went to bed, remember?"

"So you kiss someone else? Jaysus, Gi." The sound of pots and pans being thrown around had met my ears next. "Do you hear yourself?"

"I didn't realize I wasn't allowed to have fun in your absence."

"And I didn't realize your idea of fun was cheating on me."

Gisella had scoffed. "Don't be dramatic."

Bernard had grimaced, his eyes finding mine before he was looking to the galley again. I'd felt guilty for listening and told myself to go back to what I'd been doing.

But my feet were rooted in place.

"Don't be dra—" Finn hadn't finished the echo before he was laughing, a deep, maniacal laugh that faded as the sound of a knife aggressively hitting a cutting board filled the air. "Right. Okay. I was knackered and wanted rest, so my girlfriend first makes me the butt of her joke, shows the entire crew something she knows is private to me, and then snogs another crew member once I'm gone — and I'm *dramatic* because I'm upset about it?"

"Are you seriously mad that I showed the crew your silly tattoo, Finn?" Gisella had laughed. "No one gives a fuck that you drunkenly got a bug tattooed on your ribcage."

"I'm mad that my girlfriend kissed someone else!"

The next clattering of dishes was so loud I'd jumped, and then I'd shaken my head, ducking out of the pantry and heading back to the main salon to finish my job. It wasn't my business what was happening between them.

But somehow, in the time that had passed since then, Finn and Gisella must have worked things out. I'd found them hugging in our cabin just before this meeting, and I'd slid to a halt and backed out quietly, hoping they hadn't noticed me.

Now, Finn was quiet, but not in the way of someone who was just tired. He seemed... resigned.

That scared me more than if he were still angry.

I couldn't help but peek at him out of my peripheral as Captain Gary went over all the details of our charter guests. Every muscle from his jaw to his shoulders was wrought with tension, his fingers gripping the papers a little too hard. I silently begged him to look at me, but he never did.

I wondered what was going through his head. Clearly, Gisella had been wrong about him being fine with her kissing Cameron. But then again, they were also okay now... so had he just needed to get a little fight out of his system and now he was past it? I couldn't imagine being in his shoes. I knew how badly I would be hurt if it were me — the same way Leah was hurt by Cameron's actions, and they weren't even officially dating.

But maybe Finn wasn't threatened. Maybe he had just been a little embarrassed, but now that they'd talked about it, he was fine. Maybe she'd promised it wouldn't happen again. Maybe he didn't care if it did, as long as he was notified beforehand.

My head spun and I squeezed my eyes shut against the noise, giving myself an internal shake.

It wasn't my business.

And I had a job to focus on.

Our new charter guests consisted of a group of eight women jointly celebrating their fiftieth birthdays together. The primary, Deborah, had booked the charter as a surprise to her best girlfriends. She was a brain surgeon, and her friends ranged from a dentist and veterinarian to a kindergarten teacher and sandcastle artist.

One of them was also a chef at a Michelin-Star restaurant in Chicago.

And as soon as Captain said it, my eyes flicked to Finn again.

"Oof," Palmer said, clapping him on the shoulder. "Bet you love to hear that."

Finn offered a flat-lipped grin that fell quickly, his eyes focused on the list of food restrictions and desires from each guest. It was never a good time for a chef when another chef came aboard. Inevitably, they would be the harshest critic of the season when it came to the food, and the pressure to perform and impress was extremely high.

Which was not ideal, considering what Finn had already had to face this morning.

"On night one, the guests would like a seven-course tasting menu and a celebratory birthday cake," Captain continued. He smiled at Finn. "Ah, nothing for you, Cheffy. You got this."

Finn nodded at Captain like he wasn't worried, but I saw his hands under the table.

He was twisting his grandmother's ring, his knee bouncing uncontrollably.

"Deborah would like to have an 80's themed pajama party after dinner," I noted, trying to take the focus off Finn so he could catch his breath. "Oh, that will be fun! I can get provisions to bring some black lights and make a little glow corner. We'll set up bean bags and sleeping bags, but make it luxe. Bernard can whip up some retro cocktails with fun names, we'll do a candy bar... Oh! We can set up *Sixteen Candles* on the projector! And I'll have leg warmers and big scrunchies ready for them. Maybe I could convince Eli to dress like John Cusack and do a bit with a boombox."

"I don't think much convincing will be necessary," Palmer said with a grin.

"That's brilliant, Em." Captain beamed. "You're gonna smash it. We all are," he added, rolling up the preference packet and playfully smacking Finn's arm with it. "Right. Let's get to it, shall we?"

Palmer and Captain hopped up first, chatting about where to anchor as they made their way up to the bridge. But I stayed back, waiting until they were gone to turn and face Finn.

My chest caved in when I finally let myself really look at him.

"Hey," I said, reaching over to squeeze his forearm. "Captain's right, okay? You've got this. Don't stress."

He swallowed, nodding, but couldn't even manage a smile.

He couldn't look at me, either.

Instead, he slid out of the booth, pulling away from my grasp and trudging up to the galley with his shoulders slumped like a prisoner sent to walk the plank.

"Don't say a word when we get back to the galley," I whispered to Bernard, both of us balancing plates and flatware in our hands.

"You mean, don't tell Finn that our little Michelin-Star chef friend called his rustic potato soup sewage water?"

I grimaced. "Exactly that."

It was our first dinner with our new charter guests, and while most of them were pleased, a couple were not — and those voices seemed to be the loudest. First, Marley — the dentist — wrinkled her nose and picked at the salad presented as the first course, like all the lettuce was still covered in dirt. She barely took two bites, which Finn noticed when we brought her full plate back to the galley.

And Regina, the chef, had sent hers back nearly untouched, as well.

Bernard carried her full bowl of soup back now, and I knew if Finn saw it, the night would spiral.

"Get rid of that before he sees it," I said to Bernard, nodding to the bowl. "We can save this, but not if—"

My thought was cut short by a frustrated growl from the galley, followed by a clattering of dishes. Bernard and I shared a look before he went one way into the pantry and I ducked around him, dropping off my stack of plates to be washed before I found Finn.

He was a man unglued.

His hands splayed wide on the stainless-steel island, the muscles in his arms strained, his head hanging between his shoulders. The remaining courses stretched out in various stages of prep all around him. He breathed heavily, eyes manic as he scanned each ingredient with a tight jaw. Gisella was next to him, and she tried to touch his shoulder, to whisper something I assumed was encouraging, but he shrugged her off.

His stormy blue-green eyes caught mine only briefly before he stormed over to the stove.

"You can save your breath," he called over his shoulder, fire lapping at the edges of the pan in his hand as he sautéed something that smelled incredible. "Gi already told me the soup was trash."

"I didn't say that!" Gisella let out an exasperated sigh. "And I don't know why you're getting all huffy at *me* right now. I'm just trying to help."

He spun in place to face her. "By telling me I should *maybe do a little better* with a chef on board?"

My jaw dropped, and I pinned Gisella with a glare of disbelief.

"You did not say that..."

"Oh, don't act like you're not thinking it, too," Gisella shot back with a glare of her own. "I'm his girlfriend. I don't have to tiptoe around his feelings. The dinner isn't going well, and he deserves to know."

"The dinner is going wonderfully for everyone except two guests," I corrected. "Who, in all likelihood, wouldn't be pleased no matter what we did. And besides, *I* am the chief stew. I am the one whose job it is to communicate with our chef about dinner service."

Gisella opened her mouth to argue, but I wasn't in the mood, and I didn't have the time.

And yes — maybe I was still just a little pissed off at her for kissing Cameron, for hurting both Leah and Finn, and for being a little brat about it.

So, I didn't give her the chance to speak.

"If you would like to be helpful, might I suggest offering a hand to Leah in cabins or assisting Cameron with the stack of dishes we just brought in? Your input is not needed in the galley at the moment."

I thought I heard a noise from behind me, something that sounded like Bernard was coughing to cover up a laugh, and Gisella snapped her mouth shut with her jaw grinding as she narrowed her eyes at me.

Fortunately, she was smart enough not to argue.

She shrugged past me, nudging my shoulder hard on the way past, but I didn't react. Instead, I turned to Finn.

"Everything is fine," I told him. "Regina didn't care for the soup, but everyone else devoured theirs — including Marley."

"Oh, joy," Finn said, flicking off the burner as he removed a glorious cream sauce with mushrooms and garlic from the stove. "I've managed to please the dentist."

I flattened my lips as he blew on a spoonful of the sauce to taste it. "Finn, it's fine. Now, what is the next—"

"Goddamnit!" he cursed, and before I could stop him, he slung the sauce into the trash before throwing the pan into the sink.

"Finn!"

"It's fucking shite," he said, and the lamb he was planning to smother in that sauce went to the garbage next. "All of it. Trash. A swill bin. No, worse than a swill bin. Pigs would be offended if I served this horrific mess to them."

I gaped at him as he stormed around the kitchen trashing everything needed to build the next course, and though I wanted to scream at him to stop, I knew it was no use.

This was it.

This was his breaking point.

I wasn't the only one staring at him as he lost it, and I knew that didn't help. He felt every pair of eyes on him as he lost himself, and eventually, his back hit the stainless steel of the freezer and he slid down it into a heap on the floor, dragging his hands through his hair. They caught on his hat and he ripped it off, tossing it to his feet before he sat there, resigned, breathing like a freight train as all his spirit seeped out of him like a slow gas leak.

My heart broke at the sight.

For a moment, I stared at him along with everyone else. Then, I cleared my throat, turning to face the crew.

"I need everyone out."

"But—" Gisella started to argue.

I held up a finger. "Out. Please. Give me five minutes." I

didn't wait for her to respond before I turned to Bernard. "I need you to stall. Refill wine glasses. Make a fun in-between-courses shot. Dance on the table if you have to."

Bernard saluted me before he was jogging out of the galley, and Palmer helped shoo everyone else out behind him. Our bosun's eyes snagged on mine, one brow arching as if to ask if I needed help. I hoped my eyes told him I had this even though I didn't feel entirely sure.

Once they were all gone, I turned back to Finn.

I didn't have time to second guess anything. We had eight guests out there waiting for their next course and two of them were already in a mood. If we were going to save this service, we had to do it fast.

I crossed the galley in quick strides, plopping down in front of Finn on the hard tile floor. I didn't care that it had food scraps from him prepping. I didn't care about anything other than getting my chef back in order.

Getting my *friend* back to himself.

The word struck my chest like a hot iron as usual, but I ignored it.

"Hey," I said softly, tapping his knee. "Look at me."

He shook his head, bracing his elbows on them instead. "It's over, Ember. I blew it."

"No, you didn't."

"Yes, I did." His voice cracked, low and rough like it hurt just to admit it. And in that moment, I wondered how much of this was the dinner and how much was what happened with Gisella.

He was hurt by her kissing Cameron.

But judging by the way Gisella had played things off, he didn't feel like he had a right to be.

Was this him shoving it all down in an attempt to stay professional and do his job, to not be *dramatic*, as she'd called him?

"I'm not cut out for this," he said, his eyes losing focus on the floor between his feet. "I thought I could make something of myself again, but clearly, I was wrong. I failed in Dublin, and now I'm failing here, too. Maybe I'm just... done."

My chest ached. "You don't believe that."

He let out a humorless laugh. "Don't I?"

Resolve settled in over me as I watched him break in front of me. This wasn't him. This wasn't my Finn.

I had minutes to pull him out of this, and I wasn't afraid to pull out the big guns to do it.

"No. You don't believe that. *I* don't believe that," I said firmly. "And you know who else wouldn't believe that for a second? Your gran."

His head snapped up at that, his eyes finding mine with the kind of wounded resistance that told me I needed to tread carefully.

But there wasn't time for that.

"What would she say if she saw you now?" I asked, my voice gentle but unwavering. "Would she tell you to give up? To throw away perfectly good food and sulk on the floor while some influencer chef with a superiority complex calls your soup sewage water?"

He said nothing.

"Would you be able to look her in the eye and say you quit?"

His throat bobbed as he swallowed. Still no answer.

"Exactly," I whispered. "You wouldn't, Finn. Because she believed in you. And she was right to. Because she knew everything you're capable of."

Finn exhaled hard through his nose, dragging a hand over his face.

"You are not a failure," I continued. "You're a genius in the kitchen. You're the reason our guests have literally wept over a grilled peach. You're the guy who nearly made me convert to a religion over a spiritual experience with a scallop, Finn. A scallop."

That earned me a twitch of a smile, the ghost of it haunting the corner of his mouth.

"You can do this. You've done it before, and you'll do it again. One bad course doesn't define you. One rude guest doesn't negate the magic you create every single day on this boat."

I leaned in, catching his eyes again, holding them with everything I had.

"This dinner isn't over. And neither are you."

His jaw ticced, eyes searching mine. "I... I don't know what to do. I don't think I can save this."

"Yes, you can." I leaned forward even more, wrapping my hands around the back of his neck. My fingers slid into his hair and I held him with my eyes never wavering. "Imagine it's me at that table. What would you do?"

At that, his hands hooked around my wrists where I held him, and he brought our foreheads together. Instead of his breaths steadying, I watched his chest struggle even more for air.

Suddenly, I was struggling, too.

"It's you at the table," he repeated.

"Yes."

"And it's just us on the boat?"

"It's just us," I confirmed. "No one else. What would you do?"

Finn wet his lips, his tongue darting out for just a split second. It was enough to make a bolt of electricity zip through me, and my thighs squeezed together instinctively.

He lifted his head, just a little, just enough to look me in the eyes again.

"I don't think I should say."

The words were just a whisper, a pained one laced with so much insinuation that I wasn't sure if I was reading too much into it, or convincing myself it was innocent when I knew it wasn't.

He licked his bottom lip again.

And this time, his gaze fell to my mouth when he did it.

"Finn..." I warned.

He moved, just a centimeter closer, but then froze at the sound of a harsh voice ringing through the quiet galley.

"Right, they're happily distracted with an Eli special at the moment," Bernard said, swinging into the kitchen. He slid to a halt at the sight of us, his eyebrow ticing up, but he didn't falter. "But there's only so much a shirtless South African and a round of neon blue vodka shots with dry ice fanatics can do."

Gisella came in on his heels, and when she saw me and Finn on the floor, an unreadable expression darkened her gaze.

I cleared my throat, breaking all contact with Finn and pushing to stand. I didn't rush it. I didn't act guilty even if somewhere inside me I felt it. I just ignored the stares drilling holes into my back and extended a hand down for Finn.

"You can do this," I promised him again. "Now get off the damn floor, Chef. We've got a dinner to finish."

For a long moment, he stared at my hand. When his eyes met

mine, I wondered if he felt the same heat buzzing through him that I did from our close proximity.

This was exactly why I'd stayed away from him.

And it was exactly why I couldn't stay away for long.

Finally, Finn took my hand, though he barely needed my help as he jumped up from the floor. His eyes flicked between mine for a quick second before he clapped his hands, swiping his hat off the floor.

"Right." Finn's voice was stronger now, more certain, like he was snapping back to the chef I knew he was.

He tugged his hat back on, adjusted his apron, and turned to the crew like a general before battle.

"We're scrapping the original main," he said, rolling his shoulders back. "I want halibut fillets out and thawed now — gently. Palmer, can you handle that?"

Palmer was already moving toward the freezer.

"Em, I want you to prep the sous vide. We'll do a miso-butter glaze with a charred corn and shishito hash. I want it plated on that black ceramic, minimal garnish."

I couldn't fight the smile that spread on my face. "Yes, sir."

He was alight again, his eyes sparkling a little as he smirked at me and winked.

"Gisella, we're adding an intermezzo," he said next, turning to face her. "Grab the cucumbers and fresh mint from the walk-in. Juice the cucumbers and I'll blitz them with mint and a touch of lime. We need to get it in the freezer fast — we're doing a cucumber mint granita in the coupe glasses. Ice cold. Clean."

"And dessert?" I asked, already working on the sous vide. I pulled out the vacuum sealer as Finn handed me spices.

"Lemon olive oil cake," he answered without hesitation.

"We'll cut rounds and toast them. Mascarpone whip, honey drizzle, thyme. Light, floral. It'll feel like the Amalfi Coast whispering goodnight."

The corner of my mouth climbed again, and I shook my head.

I knew he could do it.

Finn clapped once, loudly. "I need all of you if we're going to make this happen. Let's move!"

The galley came alive again — knives tapping, burners igniting, steam rising. Each word from Finn was a spark, each movement a gear locking into place. The kitchen was a machine, and he was its heartbeat.

In the chaos, he paused and found me.

His hand reached for mine, rough palm sliding down my arm and over my wrist until he could wrap my hand in his own. He squeezed, his eyes sincere.

"Thank you," he said. "For reminding me who I am."

My heart clenched as I squeezed his hand in return.

It was only a second, a quick exchange before Finn broke contact and hustled to jump in on prep. But I stood there a long moment with that touch searing my skin, with his words surrounding me like a cozy, warm blanket on a frigid day.

I exhaled, smoothing my hands over my uniform and taking a moment to get myself together. I knew my cheeks were burning but prayed they weren't red enough for the cameras to notice.

When I snapped back into action, I glanced toward the walk-in and found Gisella watching me from where she was juicing the cucumbers.

Her gaze narrowed.

And suddenly, the cameras were the least of my worries.

Chapter Nineteen

CHARTER CONFESSIONAL
CLOSE QUARTERS

SEASON 4, EPISODE 8
CHARTER 6

CAMERON DUNN: DECKHAND

PRODUCER
Six charters behind you, just three more to go. How
are you feeling?

CAMERON
Been better, if I'm honest.

PRODUCER
Oh? Was this charter a particularly rough one?

CAMERON
The charter was sound. Those ladies were a laugh —
easy to please, at least on deck. Can't speak for
interior. But they were mad for the water toys, loved
the snorkel trip. Especially loved when Eli or I
peeled our shirts off.

PRODUCER
So what's the issue?

Cameron sighs, runs hand through hair.

CAMERON
Aye, fucked it, didn't I? Snogging Gisella.

PRODUCER
Ah. Having regrets?

CAMERON
I was steaming. Wasn't thinking. And now Leah won't
even glance my way, let alone speak to me.

PRODUCER
Think it's over, then? Your boatmance?

CAMERON
I hope not. I need to pull off something epic to win
her back. Good thing we've got a crew day off coming.
Owner's footing the bill for a full-on catered beach
bash. Feels like my shot.

PRODUCER
A crew day off should be fun. I'm sure everyone is
excited.

CAMERON
Oh, the vibes are flying already. This is what we
live for, innit? We work our arses off for weeks,
and then we get one day to go full send – drink like
guests, dance like we're on holiday, pretend we're
not walking HR violations.

Cameron grins.

CAMERON
Problem is, beach days? They always bring trouble.
Too much sun, too much rum, not enough clothing…
things get messy.

Cameron leans back in chair, shrugs, scratches jaw.

CAMERON
I'll be focused on Leah. But everyone else… well,
let's just say it should be interesting. Beach days
have a way of making bad ideas feel like good ones.
You mix sunshine with free booze, and suddenly,
everyone forgets the cameras are rolling.

"Oh, yes. Yes," Bernard said, dragging out that last affirmation as he sank back into his lounge chair. He stretched his legs long, taking a sip of his frozen cocktail before he sat it on the table between our chairs and folded his arms behind his head. "This is exactly what Daddy needed."

Leah giggled from where she was stretched out on her stomach on the chair next to me. "I love the way you say that. Your accent is the best. Say it again."

"What, daddy?"

Leah fell into another fit of giggles, proof that the frozen daiquiris were treating her well. "I love it so much. I have to marry a British man just so I can hear that all the time."

"Not a Scot, then?" Bernard asked with a quirk of his brow.

Leah deflated a bit. "Jury's still out on that one."

From the other side of Bernard, Gisella sat up in her lounge chair, her beautiful brown skin shining with oil. "I really am sorry about that, Leah."

Leah waved her off. "It's okay. You've already apologized, and all is forgiven."

I bit my tongue at that. I already knew Leah was a better woman than I was, and her easy forgiveness of Gisella proved that. But I also wasn't sure it was a warranted forgiveness, and I felt protective over Leah like she was my little sister.

She might have been over it all, but I still had my guard up.

"I'm just not sure I want to pursue things with someone who isn't taking it seriously, you know?" Leah shrugged. "I don't want a boatmance. I want a relationship. And it's fine if that's not what Cameron wants, but I need to set boundaries."

I smirked, though my heart ached for my stewardess as I reached over to squeeze her ankle. I knew all too well how it felt to be the person who wanted more in a relationship.

"I'm proud of you," I told her.

"Thanks," she said, but then she giggled as she drained the last of her frozen drink and held up the empty glass to signal our waiter for another. "But don't judge me for what I do after this next daiquiri."

We all chuckled at that, placing an order for another round of drinks when the waiter stopped by. We couldn't have been set up with a lusher beach experience. We had our own private stretch of the sand, multiple cabanas with shade, plush lounge chairs to soak in the sun, and all the booze we could drink delivered by someone serving *us* for once. It was the perfect crew beach day off, courtesy of the owner of the *Sinking Sun*, and we were greedily eating it up.

I'd watched a full season of *Close Quarters*, and while it did show a lot of truth when it came to working on a yacht, there was plenty the show didn't cover. One thing I felt like it couldn't fully encompass was just how long and how hard we all worked, day in and day out. We were lucky to get six hours of sleep, and we didn't just work an eight-hour shift like a normal person might — no, we were on the clock from the time we opened our eyes until our head hit the pillow again. Our breaks were few and far between, quick and filled with one purpose usually: feed ourselves or sneak in a quick nap. And though the people watching the show saw us running from one end of the boat to the other, they didn't fully understand how that wore on us. We were barefoot most of the time, running plates up and down stairs, lifting heavy equipment or provisions, loading and unloading suitcases packed to the brim.

All that to say — we needed a break, and we were making the most of the one given to us on that beach.

"Well, I'd wish you luck with Cam, but frankly, my dear, I don't condone boatmances of any kind," Bernard said when the waiter was gone. His sunglasses slipped down his nose and he pushed them back up on a shrug. "They're always messy. No way to avoid that. And I don't think any boatmance can last."

"Well, so far, I have no evidence to prove you wrong," Leah said with a longing sigh.

"Hey, it can happen," Gisella chimed in from the other side of Bernard. "I've seen relationships born on boats that lead to marriages. And look at me and Finn."

"Yeah, but you two didn't *meet* on a boat," Bernard pointed out.

"So? We're working together on one."

"And it's going so well, isn't it?" Bernard pursed his lips with a little dance of jest.

"It is," Gisella said defensively. "Yes, I know I kissed Cameron, but it really wasn't that big of a deal. We're both over it."

Hearing her talk about Finn always made my stomach sour. I wanted to be happy for them, but the truth was I just couldn't be, especially after what she'd pulled.

And if she thought Finn was fine with it, she didn't know him at all.

"It was just a kiss, a stupid dare, everyone was drunk." Gisella huffed and leaned back in her chair. "Besides... it's not fair of him to hold it over me when he's been such a prude all season."

"Prude?" Leah asked.

Gisella chewed her lip, looking around like she was afraid someone might overhear us. But it was just the four of us stretched out on the lounge chairs. Eli, Cameron, Palmer, and Finn were playing a game of beach volleyball down near the water.

"We haven't slept together *once* since we came aboard," she whispered.

The bottom fell out of my chest.

He... hasn't slept with her?

I froze, careful not to let my expression shift. But inside, something detonated.

It lit up inside me like a flare, so bright and blinding that it took everything in me not to squint against the glow. I didn't want to feel it — I *shouldn't* feel it. But God, I did.

I was giddy.

Because I remembered how he used to be with me. How he could barely keep his hands to himself. How just a glance could unravel both of us.

The idea that he hadn't touched her that way, not even once in all these weeks...

It rattled me.

I should have been ashamed at that internal reaction.

But some bitter part of me — sharp and shameless — was thrilled.

Bernard slid his sunglasses down so we could all see his wide eyes. "You're kidding. Gi... it's been like six weeks!"

"You think I don't know that?!" Gisella peeked over at where the guys were playing before turning back to us. "*Me está volviendo loca*, okay? I mean, I can get him in my bunk for a cuddle but that's it. He won't make a move, and he won't respond when I do. He just keeps saying it's unprofessional and rude. I even tried to get him to take me to one of the guest cabins, but he refused."

"Ouch," Leah said. "That's brutal. Even Cameron and I have shacked up."

"Wait, *what*?!" Bernard and I said at the same time, and then we were laughing and smacking her ass and demanding details.

When the chaos quieted, Gisella cracked her neck and sank back in her chair with a sigh. "I mean, look, we've never rushed anything. Took him forever to want to do anything physical with me. He was kind of broken when we got together..." She frowned. "But I don't know. I feel like I'm missing something, like I've got the whole puzzle put together but there are two pieces I can't find to finish it."

Her gaze swung my way then as she reached up to grab more tanning oil, the movement slow, deliberate. She uncapped the bottle and poured some into her palm without looking away from me.

"What do you think, Ember?"

I stiffened, ice sliding through me at the unexpected spotlight — at the sudden shift in the air. Her tone was light, borderline casual. But something in it didn't sit right. It was just a little too breezy. A little too... staged.

And then there was the eyebrow — the slightest lift, just enough to feel like a dare.

Everyone's eyes were on me now. And I had no idea what to say. Because while the reason could have been anything, I couldn't help but wonder if Finn was abstaining because of me.

Was it because he didn't want to hurt me, didn't want me to overhear it or walk in on anything?

Was it guilt? Courtesy? Some deeply buried instinct not to hurt me?

Or was it something else... something that pulsed between us every time our eyes locked. Something unfinished. Something neither of us could name out loud, but both still felt in our bones.

That it wasn't over between us.

I lurched up in my chair as the thought passed over me. I

couldn't believe I'd let myself think it at all.

Don't be stupid, Ember. He's just trying to be professional.

It's not about you.

You are the past.

"Oh, I mean, I don't know," I said, trying to smile. "I'm sure it's just what he's been saying, that he doesn't want to be rude. Besides, all these cameras around," I said, waving to the camera people who were almost too easy to forget about now that we were this far into the season. "He probably feels weird about that. But you know him better than I do."

I didn't mean for those words to sound so spicy when I said them, but Bernard bit back a smile as he took a drink, and Gisella pursed her lips.

"Yes. You're right. I do. And I'm sure it's fine. There will be plenty of time for him to rail my brains out once the show is done."

Acid burned my throat as I reached for my cocktail, trying again to smile.

"What about you, Em?" Leah asked. "You going to have any fun before this season is over?"

"I'm the chief stew," I reminded her. "My job is to stay professional."

"Eli will be crushed to hear that," Bernard said. "Poor thing is like a lost puppy when it comes to you, just following you around like a mutt begging for scraps."

"Oh, my God, stop, he is not," I said on a laugh.

"You're blind if you don't see it," Leah said. "He's been into you since the first charter. And I don't see why you can't have some fun, if you want to. I bet he'd be a great lay."

I flushed so hard Bernard ran his hand over the condensation from his cocktail and rubbed it on my cheeks.

"Oh! If not him, maybe Palmer?" Leah suggested next. "He's hotter than a Montgomery summer."

"Palmer isn't interested in any boatmances," Gisella snapped, still irritated by the whole conversation, it seemed. "He's a bosun."

"Exactly. Gisella is right. We're both here to do our jobs and get paid — that's it."

But Bernard was eyeing Gisella curiously. "And just how do *you* know what Palmer wants?"

She waved him off. "Doesn't take a genius to read the neon signs."

"Uh-huh." Bernard narrowed his gaze, but then snapped his smile back to me. "What about Cap? He's newly single. Very daddy-like. Could spoil you rotten, too. You don't mind an age gap, do you?"

"And on that note," I said, standing up and stretching my back. "I'm going to take a stroll by the water."

"Should we send Eli to join?" Gisella teased.

I gave them all two big thumbs up, and their chorus of laughter followed me all the way down to the water.

The warmth of the sand gave way to cool relief as I stepped closer to the shoreline, my feet sinking into the soft grains with each step. The breeze off the Mediterranean carried hints of sea salt and lemon, and I let it lift my hair off my shoulders, breathing in deep as I walked.

The laughter from our lounge chairs slowly faded behind me, muffled by distance and the rhythmic sound of the waves lapping against the shore. Out here, away from the teasing and the cameras, it was quiet. Still.

I wrapped my arms around my waist, not from any chill — because the Amalfi sun was generous — but from the ache that was blooming in my chest.

Six charters behind us and just a few left now. It was almost over.

And what a season it had been.

There were so many moments I thought I might break under the pressure — under the expectations, the long hours, the chaos. But somehow, I hadn't. I'd kept things afloat, managed every detail, every guest tantrum, every crew conflict. I'd stepped up as a leader and earned the respect of the captain and crew. I was damn proud of that.

And still...

My father's voice haunted me.

"This isn't a real career, Ember. It's a phase. A detour. You're smarter than this."

I blinked hard against the sting that came with the memory. It didn't matter how many times I reminded myself that he didn't understand; that he'd never even tried to. It still hurt. Worse than that, it made me doubt.

Was he right?

Was I chasing something fleeting? Something unworthy? Was I wasting time instead of building the kind of life that would make him finally look at me with approval instead of disappointment?

My eyes lifted from my toes in the sand to the horizon. Everything in me wanted to believe I wasn't wrong. I wanted to trust that surge in my heart for this job, this life, for the people I'd grown to love and the passion I felt for what I did.

It meant something.

But even as I stood rooted in that truth, doubt whispered like the tide around my ankles, washing over me, pulling me back, tempting me to give in.

I sank into the sand where the surf kissed the shore, arms draped over my knees, toes half buried. I watched the waves, letting their rhythm soothe the war in my chest. I wanted to just have fun. It was a beach day, for fuck's sake. And when I was with the crew, the alcohol buzzing through me made me silly and happy and carefree.

The moment I was alone, it made me sad.

I didn't hear him approach, too lost in my own thoughts, but I felt the moment his shadow passed over me.

Finn settled into the sand without a word, close but not touching. I didn't look at him, not right away. I just kept watching the sea, heart thudding at the nearness of him.

I felt his eyes on me.

Always, I felt him.

And just like the sea, he unsettled me — familiar and wild, beautiful and dangerous, capable of saving me or pulling me under.

"Hello, Firefly."

I turned to face him, and then all the anxiety was swept from me with the next wave that hit my toes.

Because he was grinning at me, his hair a mess from the wind, his shoulders sun-kissed, and something about that made all the heaviness vacate my chest in an instant.

"You're drunk," I mused, tapping his red nose.

"I am," he confessed.

"And you need sunscreen."

"You going to rub it all over me?"

I rolled my eyes, nudging him with my shoulder before I looked back out at the water.

"I'm glad you're letting loose," I said. "You deserve to after that charter."

"Wouldn't have made it without you."

"Yes, you would have."

He didn't respond, so I turned to look at him again, and the playfulness had left him completely.

"I was ready to give up," he said. "But you pulled my head out of my arse. You're a good friend." He swallowed right as the word pierced my lungs. "But more than that, Ember, you're a fucking fantastic chief stew."

The corner of my mouth lifted. "Thanks."

"I mean it," he continued, his words slurring a bit. "I know your dad makes you feel like it's just cocktails and cleaning, but it's more than that. You're a leader, Em. You saved that dinner service. You made a luxury vacation for those women that they'll never forget. It takes a special person to touch lives like that."

It was like my ribs were crushing my lungs, his words both healing me and adding pressure at the same time. How did he know? How could he walk up here and just *know* exactly what I was in my head about?

Suddenly, my stomach somersaulted as a memory of the last time we sat on a beach like this hit me like a crate of bricks.

I'm sitting where the water meets the sand on Kontokali Beach, the night closing in around me like a black hole. I feel his presence without looking to confirm it.

I don't need to turn my head to know he's walking the dark beach toward me, that his haunted eyes are set on my hunched-over form in the sand. My body alerts me, buzzing to life the way it always does when he's near.

I am the orchestra and he, the maestro.

I press a hand over my racing heart, the one he conducted without care, closing my eyes and trying to find a steady breath through the ringing in my ears.

Any attempt is thwarted the moment he says my name.

"Em..."

"Don't," I beg, not recognizing my voice as it croaks out of me. My throat is dry and raw, tongue like sandpaper in my mouth, but I force myself to open my eyes and look up at him. I hope he sees the desperation, hope he sees how I'm crumbling, hope maybe he will grant me this one mercy. "Please, Finn. Don't."

Even in the dark, I notice his jaw tighten.

I told him not to follow me.

I pleaded for him to let it go, to let me go...

But he just can't.

The selfish bastard.

Rage simmers in my chest, pushing away the harder, deeper emotions I've been surrendering to on this beach. And I welcome anger. I embrace her like an old friend.

It's easier to be mad.

This is how it's always been with us — everything is just... big. Big lust, big jealousy, big possession, big love. All of it is too much for of us to hold onto together, let alone by ourselves. And yet we let it crush us, over and over, the weight a welcome pain.

"I wish I never met you," I murmur, knowing it's a lie.

"You don't mean that."

"I do."

I stand, not bothering to brush the sand from my legs or wring the water from my shorts.

"Damn you for following me." I mean to spit the words at him like venom, but instead they leak out of me like a sad last breath. I'm so tired, the burning flame he lit inside me the past four months

slowly flickering out and leaving me numb in its wake.

I take a step in the direction of the marina, but he stops me, his hand catching my hip.

"What am I supposed to do, Firefly? Just watch you walk away?"

The irony of that question combined with the pain his nickname for me now elicits has a harsh laugh barreling out of my chest, because the alternative would have been for him to come with me.

Which is exactly what I'd asked him to do.

Not to come with me here, to this beach, on this night — but to the Bahamas, to the next boat, the next adventure. We were supposed to leave this island together. We were supposed to walk hand in hand into our next gig as a couple. All summer, I thought that was the plan.

I thought that because he'd let me.

"You were supposed to mean what you said," I tell him, more dejected now, my voice soft and weak. "You were supposed to come with me, Finn."

There it is again, that tight jaw, that grinding of bone. It's too dark to see the color of his eyes — are they sea green tonight or more of that ocean blue? — but I feel them piercing through me just as much as if it were high noon.

I wait for a response, and when it doesn't come, another sad laugh leaks out of me like helium from a pricked balloon. I laugh at him and at myself, too.

Fools, we are.

Love-drunk fools.

Wiping my nose with the back of my wrist, I shrug, the bottle of wine I'd toted to the beach with me making a sloshing sound in my hand. "Go on, then. You came here to say something? Say it. Say what you haven't already."

"Ember, I don't—"

"Say it," I snap, using my free hand to shove against his chest. My body lights up with longing the second I touch him, even for that brief second, every cell within me yearning to give in, to collapse into his arms and let him hold me — even if just for one more night. "Go on. I'm all ears. Tell me what—"

"Come with me."

For a split second, the words have me speechless.

Hopeful.

But then anger slides right back in.

"Come with you," I deadpan. "To Ireland. Where there is no yachting season. Where I walk away from my career, my aspirations, for you."

"And what, it's somehow fair for you to ask the same of me?"

I try to sharpen my gaze at him then, to pierce him the way his words were cutting me. But I feel it, how I soften, how my shoulders deflate and my eyes sting with the all-consuming sadness that's ripping me apart.

"I never asked anything of you," I whisper. "Except for you not to lie."

His nostrils flare. "Em, I didn't—"

"Don't tell me you didn't lie. Don't try to make me feel crazy. I was there."

"I never said I wanted to stay in yachting."

"You never said you didn't!" My chest heaves. "All those times I laid my head on your chest and talked about what came next, all the nights I dreamed aloud of where we'd go, the places we'd see together — you never stopped me. You never told me the truth."

He closes his eyes as I step into his space, my chest pressing just below his, face angled up as I dare him to look at me and tell me I'm wrong.

But he can't.

"I… I begged you, Finn. I begged you not to hurt me." I hate how my eyes gloss with tears when those words croak out of me. "And you looked me right in my eye and told me you wouldn't — all the while knowing you would."

"Stop."

"You wanted to use me up for the summer."

"Stop."

"Was it some masochistic game to you? To make me fall in love with you, knowing I meant nothing?"

"Stop, Ember! Jaysus," he yells, pulling back from me and stalking two feet in the opposite direction. He rakes his hands through his dark hair, and for a moment I'm jealous of those hands, jealous that I'll never feel those silky strands between my own fingers again.

When he turns back to me, he rolls his lips together, Adam's apple bobbing in his throat as he stares at me like I'm the one holding the gun.

We both know it's always been him.

"You… You're breaking me right now. You're fucking killing me, Em."

There it is again, that ache in my chest, that incessant need to throw my arms around him and pretend like none of this is happening, like we're still the people we were just twenty-four hours ago instead of the ones we are right now.

But I can't.

I owe it to myself to be strong, to see that his actions are speaking far louder than his words.

"Good," I say, voice cracking. I refuse to blink, but a hot tear *slides down my cheek despite my attempt to hold it at bay. "I hope you hurt. I hope you never forget this pain." I swallow, stepping close enough that I know he can see I'm not shaking when I say it. "I hope you never escape the rotting death of what we could have been if you'd actually loved me the way you said you did."*

I'd left him on the dark beach with those words.

And when I boarded my flight the next day, I thought I'd never see him again.

The memory had my throat tight and dry. I didn't trust myself to keep talking about my father now, not with my emotions all stirred up like bay water in a hurricane. Between the booze and the sunshine and my heightened state of emotions, I felt two seconds away from bawling my eyes out.

But that memory held onto me.

Curiosity did, too.

And I gave into it, asking what I'd wanted to since that night in the hot tub.

There had been other, more pressing things to worry about since then — Gisella kissing Cameron, Leah being hurt, Finn having an absolute meltdown.

But now, we were alone on the shore — aside from the cameras I was sure were watching us still, even if from a distance — and I couldn't wait any longer.

"So," I said, poking him in the ribs just below his heart. "What's this?"

Finn's grin climbed. "You know what it is."

My blood buzzed beneath my skin, a smile curling on my lips at his playfulness. I hated that he was like this right now, that he was all airy and light, no shame as he let his eyes devour me in my bikini. It was confusing as hell, and entirely too easy to pretend we were the people we were two years ago, that we were just flirting and teasing and biding our time until we got the other alone.

"I was right, then? It's a firefly?"

He nodded, wiggling his toes in the wet sand as he stared at me.

"Is it for me?"

My stomach bottomed out when I finally asked.

"What? No." He looked out at the water with his mouth downturned like the thought was absolutely ridiculous. "It's because of the glow worms that used to fill the yard of the cabin I'd go to with me parents in the summer. It's nostalgic. A little reminder of childhood."

My cheeks flamed with embarrassment. "Oh."

But before I could apologize for the idiotic assumption, Finn sucked his teeth and laughed, turning to face me again. He slid his sunglasses off so I could see his glazed blue-green eyes, the colors even brighter against the sea.

"Come now, love, don't be daft," he said, shaking his head. "Of course it's for you."

The words crashed over me like a tidal wave. He said them so simply, so confidently, as if they wouldn't mean a thing.

But they meant *every*thing.

His grin softened the longer I stared at him, shocked from his confession. Finally, I found the nerve to speak again. But I could only manage one word.

"Why?"

Finn slid his sunglasses back on, shrugging. "Took a page out of your book, didn't I?"

"It helped you heal from us?"

"Something like that," he said, and his voice was hoarse now, the playfulness abandoned.

I thought we were going to let it go, but he moved an inch closer, every nerve in my body firing to life as he turned to face me again. He reached out, his fingers walking up my spine until his hand found the back of my neck. He tickled the skin there, making chills burst out from the point of contact all the way down to my toes.

"And what about this, Firefly?" he asked, voice low and gruff as his finger traced the ink I knew was there. "This for me?"

He palmed the back of my neck then, fingers wrapping around until I had no choice but to look at him. His throat bobbed, and I was thankful I couldn't see his eyes through his dark sunglasses, thankful I had at least one small barrier between us.

I didn't get the chance to answer him.

There was a loud chorus of cheers from where our crew was on the beach, and then Eli was sprinting toward us, sand flying in his wake. He had a shit-eating grin on his face, and he swung his arms down to scoop me up without warning.

"Dibs on Ember!"

Somehow, a laugh managed to break free of the tight knots my body had been coiled into just moments before. "What are you doing?!"

"It's what are *we* doing, babes," Eli corrected me with a drunken grin, already jogging us back toward the beach setup. "And we're playing beer pong."

"Oh, they're all going down."

"I know that's fucking right," he said, smacking my ass with a holler that sounded like a war chant as he dropped my feet into the warm sand.

I glanced over my shoulder at Finn, heart still racing, skin still tingling where his fingers had touched the back of my neck.

He was already walking toward the crew, the corners of his mouth pulled up in that crooked, lazy grin he wore so well. From this distance, he looked relaxed. Breezy. It was like nothing had happened at all, which only added to my confusion and unrest.

Gisella popped up beside him and wrapped her arm around his waist, pulling him into her side. He let her. And jealousy sank its claws into me deep enough to break skin.

With me still watching them, Finn reached up and slid his sunglasses down the bridge of his nose — just enough to glance at me over the top of them.

The look he gave me wasn't casual. It wasn't friendly.

It was molten.

But I didn't heed the warning of the imminent volcano eruption until it was too late.

Chapter Twenty

POST-PRODUCTION CONFESSIONAL
CLOSE QUARTERS

SEASON 4

LEAH BROOKS: THIRD STEWARDESS

PRODUCER
Do you feel like the crew beach day was a turning point for you and Cameron?

LEAH
Oh, yeah. I was content to stay away from him the rest of the season and just do my job. I was hurt, you know? But Cameron made an effort, and I appreciated that. I felt like he regretted what he'd done.

PRODUCER
Do you think Gisella regretted it, too?

LEAH
Well, she apologized to me, which was nice, but… I don't know. I don't think she felt bad for what she did. I think she'd do it again, if we could turn back time. She wanted attention and she got it.

PRODUCER
Finn's attention?

Leah shrugs.

LEAH
I mean… I think anyone's attention would do.

The sun had dipped below the horizon while we were still elbow-deep in a fiercely competitive beer pong tournament — half the crew versus a pack of rowdy tourists who'd somehow roped themselves into our beach day. Shirts were swapped for team colors, dares were shouted over music, and Eli played the entire last round wearing a snorkel mask, claiming it was a strategic advantage. It definitely wasn't, and when we lost, we made *him* run the naked lap around our cabana. He somehow managed to do so without the local authorities noticing. Or maybe the Italians and tourists on this beach didn't care about someone running around with their dick slinging so long as everyone was having fun.

Now, hours later, the beach glowed under warm string lights woven between driftwood posts and leaning cypress trees, casting golden halos over a sea of people swaying to music. A local Italian cover band played from a stone terrace just off the beach, their sound a dreamy fusion of acoustic guitar, soft percussion, and the occasional saxophone. They were taking American pop hits and spinning them into smoother, slower remixes. It felt like being at a forbidden speakeasy jazz bar, except under the stars with the smell of salt wafting in from the sea.

The air was charged.

I stood in the middle of it all, barefoot in the sand and buzzed just enough to feel like the world was on tilt in the best way. Leah was curled up against Cameron on my right, her cheeks flushed and lips kiss-swollen. The hot tub incident was officially ancient history now, if the way they couldn't stop touching each other was any indication. They laughed at something I missed —probably another joke about Cameron's failed, behind-the-back beer pong shot that nailed Palmer square in the forehead — and I smiled, warm and loose-limbed and grateful for the night off.

Finn stood to my left.

Where I swayed and sipped the cocktail in my hand, he was solid and still. He still seemed just as buzzed, if not more so, than he had been when we sat by the water earlier, a lazy smile on his lips, but I saw what I was sure most didn't.

He was somewhere else.

I saw it in the way his eyes glossed over as he watched the band, in how he'd blink back to the present moment every now and then and attempt a wider smile at whoever was trying to talk to him.

He kept a small but noticeable space between where he stood and where I was, but the tension still coiled in the inches that separated us. Gisella danced on the other side of him, rotating between hanging on him and joking with Eli and Palmer. She tugged on his arm until he bent enough for her to say something in his ear over the music, and she let out a laugh that had her tilting her head back and eyes watering from exertion. Finn only gave a lazy half-smile in response, but his eyes didn't leave the band. He didn't lean into her or let his touches linger on her skin. He didn't pull her into him and move with the beat. And when Gisella didn't get the reaction she wanted from him, she turned back to Palmer and Eli.

I shouldn't have cared, shouldn't have been so tuned into them that I missed an entire song, but I was drunk and the kind of tired that made it harder to ignore the tug in my chest every time I glanced his way.

What happened on the shoreline earlier still stuck to me like a leech, no matter how I tried to pluck it away. I watched the band, trying to keep my focus on singing and dancing with Leah when she took a break from making out with Cameron. I sipped my drink. I sang along to words I knew. I did everything I could to let the memory of Finn's hand on my neck dissolve into the sea air.

But I felt like a forest in a drought — just one stray spark from burning too hot and too fast to be contained.

With a long exhale, I surrendered to the music. I was dizzy from drinking all day, but not in an unpleasant way. My buzz vibrated through my sore muscles, and I let it carry me, humming through my bones as I moved in time with the smooth, slow melody.

I'd needed this.

We'd *all* needed this.

Six charters behind us and just three more to go, and the long days were catching up with everyone. We were still working together nicely, but there were small moments when the little nit-picky things slipped — like Eli making a joke about Cameron taking yet another coffee break, or Leah muttering that she never got to see the light of day from being stuck in laundry, or Palmer popping back at me when I asked for his help on service and he pointed out that he hadn't had a break all day.

We were all strung tight and exhausted, and without this day off, we likely would have snapped.

There was still the chance even after a break, if I was being honest.

But I chose not to focus on the what ifs.

I swayed with the rhythm of the music, hips rocking, hair sticking to the back of my neck, my smile widening with each passing second. My eyes slipped shut, the world narrowing to the pulse of the song and the fizz of liquor in my veins. And I let go

— of the tension, of the stress, of *him*.

Just for a moment.

When the band ended the song and introduced another, I finally peeled my eyes open, and the scene around me had shifted.

Gisella and Palmer were gone. I assumed they'd gone off to get new drinks or take a break from the crowd. Eli was at the bar with Bernard and a gaggle of locals, slamming back shots and howling with laughter. Cameron and Leah were still nearby, though they'd moved closer to the front of the stage, and they might as well have been alone with the way they were tangled up in each other.

One camera duo was with Eli and Bernard at the bar, the other had tired of the endless footage of Leah and Cameron drunkenly making out and was nowhere to be seen. I wondered if they'd taken off with Gisella and Palmer.

I scanned the space, registering it with the kind of lazy awareness only alcohol and exhaustion could bring.

And then I felt it — the faintest touch on my left hip.

It was the graze of a knuckle, rough and warm, curling just under the tie of my bikini like a question mark.

Feather-light, so much so that it was almost nothing at all.

But it seared my skin like a branding iron.

I didn't have to look to know who it was.

My heart lurched into my throat, strangling me as it stalled out. I froze. I couldn't will my hips to sway to the music anymore, not with that touch anchoring me to a past I realized I'd never escape.

Finn's warmth invaded my space even though he was still a safe distance away. I chanced a glance, secretly, tilting my head to the left like I was looking at the bar when really I was cataloging him in my peripheral. And there he stood, his eyes on the band, head bobbing a bit to the beat like there was nothing out of place.

But his knuckle dragged along the skin beneath my bikini, from the front of my hip to the back, and then he slid his finger beneath the tie.

That was the spark.

I went up in a blazing inferno, heart stuttering back to life before it kicked hard and fast like a snare drum in my chest. I swallowed, keeping my eyes on the band, but I felt it when Finn moved in closer, when he slid to stand behind me.

His finger toyed with my bikini again.

Oh, God.

I should stop this.

I should walk away.

But I was rooted in place, drunk off hours of alcohol and the heat of his forbidden touch.

There was no question — he knew what he was doing. It didn't matter that he kept his eyes on the band and pretended to be innocent. His halo was askew, flickering and threatening to burn out altogether with every millimeter of space he annihilated between us.

We were hidden by the crowd, tourists and locals dancing all around us with their hands in the air. I once again found myself scanning for the location of the cameras, and when I found them focused elsewhere, my insides liquified.

Because I knew Finn noticed their absence, too.

He slid up fully behind me, confident and careless all at once as his other hand found my hip, too. He had me framed in his grasp now, and his fingers bit into my flesh as his hot breath washed over the back of my neck.

My eyes fluttered shut, tongue sweeping out to wet my bottom lip as I desperately tried to hold onto my morals. But they were washing away quickly, the buzz dampening my inhibition, the darkness of the crowd daring me to test my limits, the heat of Finn's touch too intoxicating to resist.

I gasped when Finn pulled me closer, one hand still holding fast to my hip as the other wrapped around me and splayed across my abdomen. The tip of his nose ran along the back of my neck, a groan vibrating out of him when I let myself fall into his touch.

My body melted into his, back to chest, and that devilish hand of his slid up higher until his thumb slipped beneath the string between the two triangles of fabric covering my breasts.

I whimpered, both desperate for myself to come to my senses and stop this and desperate for him to keep going, to push the boundaries more, to throw all caution to the wind and take me as his willing prisoner.

Memories of our past assaulted me one after another as the lights acted as a film reel over my closed eyes. A flash and we were there in my bunk in Greece, laughing and shushing one another as we peeled off every article of clothing. Another flash and we were walking hand in hand through the streets of Kontokali, pointing at the mansions and guessing who lived there, what their lives were like, before the conversation turned to what *our* lives would be like.

Together.

Flash of light. His wide beamed smile. *Saxophone riff.* Me straddling his lap. *Whip of cool sea breeze.* Him inside me for the first time, shaking.

His warm breath on my neck brought me back to the present,

to a moment so wrong it somehow made it all the way to the other side and felt nothing but right. He was so close I heard him swallow even over the music, like my mind was tuned into only him and had blocked out every other noise and possible distraction. I wanted to ask him what he was doing but I was too afraid to speak, too scared I'd shatter the fragile, illicit moment.

Finn was barely touching me and yet his cock was hard against my backside, like being near me at all was his undoing. That's how it was for me, too.

One touch, one look, one breath from him had me ready to risk it all.

His lips parted, brushing my neck as he nosed the shell of my ear and sent electric tingles cascading down my body like a waterfall.

I angled my chin toward him.

His eyes caught mine — too close and out of focus.

Our breaths hitched, mouths just an inch apart.

And I covered his hand with mine, sliding it under the fabric of my suit and over until he was palming my breast, until I could find relief for the insatiable ache within, until I was sure he could feel how hard my heart was beating from his touch.

His eyes slammed shut, a deep, guttural groan ripping from him as he squeezed and I arched and we crashed through the gates of Hell, unrepentant.

"Em..." he groaned.

I could have come right there, right then, just from that sound, from that touch. One more flick of his palm over my nipple and I was going to surrender.

But in an instant, all his warmth was gone, the absence of

him sweeping over me like a frigid whip of wind.

Somehow, I knew without looking to confirm that it was because someone was coming. And so I played it off, acting like I was dancing and my heart wasn't about to kick its way out of my chest. I swayed and lifted my hands into the air, smiling despite how I could barely manage my next breath.

Suddenly, Eli was at my side, throwing his arm around me with a goofy, blitzed grin. He smelled like cigarette smoke and rum, and I instantly missed the scent from before. Finn's scent. Vetiver and black pepper and fresh ocean air.

"Had a quick chat with some of the brus at the bar and we all agreed — you and me? Way overdue for a date."

I blinked my eyes open, hoping no one could see the heated flush of my skin under the lights strung above. "Oh yeah?"

"Yeah," he said, and then he bopped my nose with his finger, swaying us side to side a little too quickly for the current beat.

I laughed and tried to blend into the new moment, leaving the heavy one behind me, but it felt like a fish trying to fit in with a pack of wild horses.

When I chanced a glance over my shoulder, I found Gisella with her arms around Finn's neck. He had a lazy smile on his face as he listened to whatever she was saying. She laughed and threw her head back.

And then she kissed him.

And I wanted to die.

The sight of them together was a rope around my neck and a boot kicked against my back, pummeling me forward no matter how I tried to resist.

I knew Finn well enough to recognize the hollowness behind

his smile, the stiffness in the way he held her, the resistance in his share of the kiss. But it didn't matter. Because it still happened.

She kissed him, and he didn't stop her.

He'd had his hands on me, his breath in my ear, both of us on the edge of something I couldn't even attempt to reach for now, it was so far gone.

And now he was letting Gisella press her mouth to his like none of it had happened.

I turned away too fast, the world blurring at the edges as I laughed at something Eli said without hearing a word of it. I forced my body to move, to dance, to pretend like I wasn't clinging to the phantom sensation of Finn's hand on my skin, like I didn't still feel his lips at my ear, like I wasn't aching so fiercely it felt like every nerve ending had been exposed.

I was so stupid.

How many times was I going to let him do this? How many times would I fall for half-measures and quiet looks, for words that said one thing and actions that screamed another?

I blinked against the sting in my eyes, swallowing hard, willing the heat rising in my throat to settle.

Soon, the group started gathering to leave. Eli wandered off to find Bernard. Gisella clung to Finn as they rejoined the others. And I slipped away before anyone could notice the battle raging inside me.

I climbed into the back of the first cab that pulled up, pressing myself into the far corner. Cameron and Leah took the front, still giggling and kissing, and Gisella clambered in after them, tugging Finn along with her. He paused at the door, eyes flicking to me, but I turned my face to the window before he could latch that gaze on too tightly.

My heart was an open wound, and every glance in his direction poured salt in it.

I didn't want his fucking loaded looks.

I didn't want his confusing words.

I didn't want *anything* from him.

I curled in on myself, arms around my middle, eyes locked on the passing lights outside. I could see our reflections faintly in the glass — the others bathed in shadow and streetlight, the space between Finn and me feeling like a canyon, even though we were barely a few feet apart.

My thoughts raced, each one louder than the last.

What are we fucking doing?

This wasn't some harmless flirtation. This wasn't a few lingering stares or accidental touches. This was full-on submission of our self-control — a reckless, spiraling mess that neither of us had the guts to stop.

That neither of us *wanted* to stop.

But why did he let it start in the first place?

I thought about all of it — the way he looked at me when no one else was watching, the way he talked to me in quiet moments like our past still haunted him, too, the damn tattoo inked into his skin, the press of his hand on my neck earlier as he asked about mine, the way he gave into sin on the beach tonight like we were the only ones in the world, like there were no consequences to face.

For a short, stupid moment, I thought that was him claiming me again. I thought it was him saying Gisella didn't matter, that what they had wasn't anything compared to what we did...

That it was still us for him, just like it was for me.

But he'd snuffed out that hope with a press of his lips against Gisella's.

My chest cracked wide open as the world blurred past, confusion bleeding into shame. I closed my eyes against the pang of it, how it made me want to pack my bag and leave in the dead of night without facing anyone. How could I room with Gisella and pretend like nothing had happened?

What kind of monster was I becoming?

Yes, she had kissed Cameron, but she'd immediately told Finn about it. And though I was fairly certain he was far from okay with what happened, he'd clearly forgiven her and moved on.

So... maybe they were finding themselves in some kind of open relationship.

I scoffed internally at myself even as I thought it because I knew for a fact Finn didn't have the okay from Gisella to do what he did tonight.

And I hadn't even thought of her — not for a single second.

I really was a monster.

It was tempting, to give into that track of thinking, but before it could sink its claws into me and pull me under, fury slid in and took the wheel.

This wasn't all on me.

Finn was the one who'd touched me tonight. It was *him* who was crossing the line and tempting me to test it with him. Was it because he missed me? Did he have regrets?

Oh, God... was he using me to get back at Gisella for what she'd done to him?

My gut soured at the thought, and that's when resolve sank in deep.

I was done.

He didn't get to play both sides.

And I refused to be the girl who let him.

No more.

This ended here, now, tonight, in this cab, without a word of declaration.

Starting tomorrow, Finn Pearson would be nothing more than a coworker. No more lingering looks. No more small, stolen touches. No more talking about a past that needed to stay buried.

If cutting him out meant bleeding for a while, I'd take the pain. Eventually, the bleeding would stop. Eventually, I'd scab and heal and only have the remnants of a soft pink scar, one I could easily ignore.

This was it for me. The final straw.

He could keep the memories.

I was done living in them.

Chapter Twenty-One

CHARTER CONFESSIONAL
CLOSE QUARTERS

SEASON 4, EPISODE 9
CHARTER 7

PALMER HUGHES: BOSUN

PRODUCER
How are you feeling about the charter guests coming aboard for charter seven?

PALMER
It's not the guests I'm concerned about — it's the weather.

PRODUCER
Uh-oh. What's going on?

PALMER
These guests pay a small fortune to come on this yacht for a few days, and they expect it to be everything they ever dreamed of: crystal blue water, soft white sandy beaches, endless cocktails served on a sunny upper deck, all the water toys they can think of, six-star service… but all that goes right out the window when a storm moves in. A little rain is one thing, but thirty-five knot winds, a gale warning, lightning, and buckets of rain?

Palmer shakes head.

PALMER

That's when it becomes a nightmare – especially for the interior. Because suddenly, you've got to make a yacht charter worth $100,000 without even leaving the dock. The food has to be impeccable, and the whole crew has to pull together and figure out some way to entertain the guests.

PRODUCER

Does it eat into the tip, you think?

PALMER

Oh, absolutely. There's only so much you can do when rich people have had their expectations shredded. Our tip will suffer – and so will we.

PRODUCER

Sounds like it's going to be a tough one.

PALMER

For sure. And there's nothing like a high-tension charter to test a team of crew members already on edge.

PRODUCER

On edge? It seems like everyone is doing great after yesterday. The beach day off was a hit, right?

Palmer scrubs a hand over his jaw, shaking his head.

PALMER

You're really going to pretend like you didn't see, huh?

PRODUCER

What do you mean? Did something happen last night?

Palmer laughs, stands.

PALMER

Good call. Save it for the reunion.

Palmer exits.

If the weather outside was gloomy, then the mood on *Sinking Sun*

was an outright hurricane.

Rain pelted the harbor like bullets from a gun, wind whipping so hard the deck crew had no choice but to bring everything inside or hide it away in the locker. Inside, the air was thick with nerves, exhaustion, and whatever invisible toxin made an entire crew collectively want to throw themselves overboard.

We'd been docked for thirty-six hours.

Thirty-six hours of non-stop complaining from our current charter guests — a group of middle-aged tech investors who looked like they'd just rolled out of a cigar lounge and brought their sugar baby starter packs with them. Their girlfriends were runway hot, chronically bored, and wore their distaste for the men who paid for this little adventure like diamond necklaces, bright and brazen and impossible to ignore.

The primary's girlfriend, Jewel, had gotten so blitzed at our make-shift wine tasting last night that she'd openly admitted that she and the other girls were hoping to pick up guys at the beach. Not that her boyfriend, Robbie, or any of his friends noticed — they were too busy yelling over each other about how the weather was "ruining the vibe" and asking Captain, *"Is it really even that bad? This boat would be fine out there. It just seems a little windy."*

We'd somehow survived the first night and got them drunk enough that they slept in. Finn made brunch a whole ordeal, and Bernard and I made sure service was nice and slow-paced. But the dishes were clear now, and the weather still sucked.

It was only 1 PM.

"Okay," I said to the interior team, hoping the calmness in my tone would wash over them and bring them both down a notch.

They looked two seconds from quitting on me, and it was up to me to find a way to keep them motivated and hanging on. "Let's recap. We've already done a spa day, a wine tasting, a trivia night, and the most traumatic game of charades I've ever endured. What else can we pull out of our magic hats here?"

"Group therapy?" Bernard offered. "Because I'm quite sure Robbie is on with his best mate's girl. And the oldest cat, Derrick? Yeah. He most certainly has zero interest in the blonde bombshell he's been toting around. In fact, I'd bet my tip that it's our primary he fancies."

I arched a brow. "While I don't doubt you, I hardly want to test those theories while we're stuck on board with them. Even a superyacht feels small with that kind of drama." I turned to Leah.

"I say we let them loose in the galley and call it a team-building exercise," she suggested, stacking folded napkins with the aggression of someone one straw away from a breakdown. "Let Finn handle them for a while."

"Because I'm sure he'd love that," I muttered.

"Where is the deck crew?" Bernard crossed his arms. "If Cameron is napping again, I swear on my life..."

"Focus, team." I clapped my hands together, forcing a smile at one of the girlfriends as she passed us. Her name was Tempany and she asked if we'd make her a Miami Vice. Once I assured her we'd get it done right away, I turned back to Leah and Bernard. "Look, I know this isn't fun. But we're an all-star crew. We can handle this. Come on — think. We just have to make it through today and then this nightmare is over. What can we do to ensure that our tip isn't completely invisible tomorrow?"

Bernard sighed, but tilted his head in thought. And then

Leah snapped her fingers. "Casino night?"

I pointed at her. "Now we're talking."

"I used to put these on with my brothers all the time in Alabama. I mean, we were usually playing with real money, but we can still make it fun for the guests. We'll get chips and fake money and have prizes they can use their winnings to bid on. Oh! Maybe we also have a punishment for the biggest loser of the night, like…"

"They have to choose someone to cover in whipped cream and lick it off?" Bernard suggested.

A laugh barreled out of me. "Oh, *that* will be motivation for the girls to win for sure. Okay, this is perfect. I'll call the provisioner. Leah, you said you're tired of laundry, so let's put you to work. You'll help me serve dinner and set up the casino night after. Bernard, I can see you need a break from this lot, so hit laundry and cabins and then work on what the different prizes could be. See if Captain Gary is willing to help. Maybe he'll let them use their fake money to buy their way into the Captain's lounge or something."

"Brilliant," Bernard said, and then with a sigh, he hurried off to the cabins as Leah and I continued brainstorming — while making a sweet, sticky, frozen cocktail.

The blender was not helping my headache.

I was holding on by a thread — and it was fraying fast.

Finn walking around the boat like he hadn't had his hand under my swim top two nights ago wasn't helping things, either.

He'd been nothing but sunshine and easy smiles all day yesterday, like he'd received news that he'd won the lottery rather than that we would have to fight our way through a rainy charter. He was making jokes with the guys, humming in the galley as he sliced and diced, and throwing me looks I refused to catch.

And the more I ignored him, the more he turned up the heat.

It was maddening and alluring all at once. I willed myself to keep the image of him and Gisella front and center in my mind so I wouldn't be fooled by his longing blue-green eyes or the way he seemed to be finding ways to touch me when there was no reason to — a hand at the small of my back as he passed me in the crew quarters, a firm grip steadying me when I slipped a little on the wet teak deck greeting the guests, a brush of his fingers as he plucked one of my freshly cut limes for the dish he was prepping.

I felt like he was even trying to speak to me through cooking when he prepared a glorious spread of Cuban food like ropa vieja and stewed plantains for the crew lunch, complete with the most amazing Key lime pie I'd ever had. It reminded me of South Florida, of home, and when I'd said so to Leah as we ate, I didn't miss how Finn had smiled.

So far today, I'd done a decent job staying away from him. Other than relaying food requests from the guests for brunch, I hadn't had contact. But as soon as I sent Leah off to serve Tempany her Miami Vice and get the other guests' drink orders, my luck ran out.

I was about to hit dial on the provisioner's number when I nearly ran into Finn in the pantry.

"Whoa, easy there," he said, his smile charming and infuriating as his hands found my arms before I could fall. "Someone's in a rush."

My cheeks flushed, body betraying me in every way as it yearned for me to smile back and lean into his attention. "Yes, well, if you haven't noticed, some of us are busting our asses to save this charter from being a complete disaster."

I tried to move past him, but he side-stepped to block me. "And I'm not one of the ones pulling me weight, is it?"

I gritted my teeth. Of course he was. If anything, the food would be the *only* thing to save us. But I didn't want to admit that to him.

The longer I stood there without answering, the more his smile slid into a frown. His eyebrows knitted together, hand reaching out to touch the side of my face.

"Hey, you need a break? I can call the provisioner and take that off your plate, make you some tea?"

I knew I was far past exhausted then because tears pricked my eyes, my throat closing in on the words I wanted to scream at him.

I shrugged away from his touch. "I don't need anything from you."

Shoving past him, I finished dialing the provisioner as I jogged down the stairs, but I only got one ring in before Finn reached over my shoulder and hit the "end call" button.

"Hey!" I spun to face him, the two of us caught in the cramped stairwell with not nearly enough space between us. I was one step below him, but I jutted my chin high in defiance. "Can you back off and let me do my job?"

"If you talk to me first."

I laughed. "I can't think of a single thing I'd like to talk to you about."

"No?" he challenged.

"Nope."

"Hmm, not *one* thing, huh?"

He stepped down with that question, forcing me to do the same. My defiance melted a bit, heart picking up its pace inside my chest.

"Don't," I warned.

"Don't what?"

This time, the words were low and teasing, the corner of his mouth tilting up at the corner. Goosebumps erupted over my skin.

I wanted to kiss him.

I wanted to throttle him.

I wished he'd tell me I was his again.

I wish I'd never been his to begin with.

I didn't trust myself to bicker back without my voice betraying me, so I withdrew, shaking my head and descending another stair.

"Jaysus, Firefly — what's the bleedin' story?"

Ignore.

Ignore, ignore, ignore.

"Did I miss the memo where I became public enemy number one?"

That made me stop, my feet like Velcro stuck to the bottom stair. I whipped around, glaring at him and hoping he felt the daggers I wanted to throw with that gaze.

"You may have missed my memo, but I got yours loud and clear. If you're so desperate for something to do, why don't you go make out with Gisella somewhere?"

That wiped the smirk clean off his face.

"I mean, isn't that your move?" I seethed, taking a step toward him now, the flames of anger finally overtaking the nostalgic ache. I was fairly certain the stationary cameras couldn't reach us here, and there were no floating cameras nearby, but I turned down the volume on my mic and whispered my next words, anyway — just in case. "Touch me like I still belong to you, make me think for one second that maybe I'm not losing my goddamn mind — and then turn around and press your mouth to hers like none of it ever happened?"

Finn's jaw flexed. "Ember—"

"No." I held up a hand, eyes snapping shut before I slowly opened them again. "You don't get to say my name like that. Like it still means something, like *I* still mean something when you've already proven I don't."

He tried once more to speak but I wouldn't let him.

"I'm done, Finn. I'm done being confused, done wondering what's real and what's just some twisted game you're playing with your own guilt. I don't care if you're still figuring it out or if you're trying to punish her or punish me or punish *yourself.*"

I shook my head, lips trembling but voice sharp.

"You picked your side, Chef. Now stay there. Because I won't be a weapon you use against another woman, and I damn sure won't be your little memory doll you pull out to play with when you're bored."

I turned, the sound of my footsteps down the last of the stairs muffled by the downpour outside as I flicked the volume on my mic back on — but all I could hear was my thundering heart.

I didn't look back at him.

I couldn't.

I didn't trust my rearview mirror anymore.

So I ripped that motherfucker down.

Chapter Twenty-Two

CHARTER CONFESSIONAL
CLOSE QUARTERS

SEASON 4, EPISODE 10
CHARTER 7

ELIJAH JOUBERT: DECKHAND

PRODUCER
Wow, you look snazzy. Ready to celebrate making it
through that charter?

ELI
Ag, ja, always ready for a bit of a joll. But first —
got bigger plans. I'm taking Em on a date.

PRODUCER
Is that so?

ELI
Damn right it is. Been laying the foundation, bru. A
girl like Ember? You can't just rock up with a wink
and a cheesy line. She's sharp. Classy. Built like a
fortress of boundaries. You've got to earn your way
in. So I've played the long game — flirting, check-
ins on deck when she can't sleep, compliments without
being a creep. You know, gentleman vibes. I've shown
her I'm not just here to party and play games — I'm
into her.

PRODUCER
And she said yes to the date?

ELI
Said yes with a little smile, too. Not that I was
nervous or anything - I mean, come on. I'm charming
as hell.

PRODUCER
So you think this is your shot?

ELI
No doubt in my mind, boet. And believe me when I say
I don't miss. Not goals, not vibes, and definitely
not a chance with Ember Reed.

"So, are you considering it?" I asked Leah the next night as I curled my hair. We'd somehow made it through the nightmare charter. The casino night turned out to be a big hit with the guests, and by the time they were leaving, all the complaints we'd had to hear over the days spent with them melted into praises.

And they left a pretty fat envelope for a group that never left the dock.

Now, while most of the crew was napping and prepping for another night out, I was getting ready for a date.

With Eli.

My stomach tumbled to the ground. I wished it was filled with butterflies and I was giddy at the thought of spending a night with him, but truthfully, I was dreading it. It didn't make sense why I was dreading it — Eli was hot, hilarious, fit, and driven. He hadn't moved in too aggressively, but he also had made his feelings for me clear. In every way, he was playing the game to win.

The problem was I had been playing a different game altogether with Finn.

And I'd definitely lost that one.

Though, I wasn't sure there was a winner. Maybe Gisella, if we were drawing straws.

Either way, I wasn't excited for my date, but I pretended like I was and kept myself distracted by listening to Leah detail her next steps with Cameron.

Which, currently, was to go back to Scotland with him when the season ended.

"I don't know," she said, blowing out a breath. "I mean, I want to. If I'm not thinking of any possible consequences, then my answer is a resounding yes. But... what do I expect to happen here? I mean, we go spend some time in Scotland and then... what?"

I offered a sympathetic smile as I started curling the next section of my hair. "I wish I could tell you it's the happy ever after you've read about all your life, but... in our world?" I shrugged. "It's hard to say."

"Exactly. I mean, maybe we end up on the same charter together again. Or maybe we go do our own thing but meet up in the in-between." She paused, kicking her feet where they hung off my bunk. "But then it's like... a dead end. It's not like he's going to marry me and move to Alabama."

My chest tightened at her words. They were so similar to the ones I'd thought when everything went down between Finn and me. Except where Leah was smart to see the end in sight already, I'd pretended we could make it. I convinced myself we could work together, travel the world together, and one day, make a life of our own together. I never pictured us settling down, but rather building our own dream — owning a little sailboat, maybe, and circumnavigating while we worked odd jobs here and there to make ends meet.

I'd been a fool.

And yet I still wanted to have hope for Leah and Cam.

"Maybe you reframe it," I suggested. "Instead of thinking

so far down the line, what if you focused on the now? Just on whatever comes next? Right now, that's going to Scotland for a while after the show ends. Then we have the reunion. Then... you figure it out." I finished my last curl and grabbed my hair spray, ready to force these girls to stay in place even battling the Mediterranean humidity. "Could you be okay with that?"

Leah nodded, contemplative. "Yeah. Yeah, I really think I can. I mean, I don't need to be planning our wedding already. We've known each other like two months." She laughed. "I just fell hard for the sucker, didn't I?"

I chuckled as I sprayed my hair, then turned to face her with a knowing smile. "Trust me — I get it. Easy to do when you live in such—"

I caught myself before the words *close quarters* could leave my mouth, and Leah and I both groaned before she laughed and threw a rogue bralette at me.

"Is that what happened with you and Finn?"

Her question knocked the laugh from me, my next breath sharp and hot. I swallowed, touching up my makeup in the mirror before I slipped into the room to get dressed. Gisella had scurried off somewhere after the deck team was released for the night. I half-wondered if she was in Finn's bunk and wholeheartedly decided I did not want to know. But it was just Leah and me in my cabin now, and I wanted to be honest with her.

But I couldn't — not with the cameras watching.

"Something like that," I murmured, offering her a sad smile before I disappeared under the bright blue dress I was pulling over my head. When I emerged again, Leah was watching me curiously.

"Do you still have feelings for him?"

I should have immediately answered no and laughed her off

at the audacity, but the question made me freeze.

"You do, don't you," she said softly. "Oh, honey..."

"It's fine," I said quickly, trying to regain my composure as I strapped my wedges on. "Some flames take a while to burn out, right? I just never expected to see him again."

"And then he shows up here. With Gisella."

My smile was tight. "Yep."

"I'm really sorry."

"It's fine."

"For whatever it's worth, I don't think you're one-sided in those feelings. I've seen the way Finn looks at you. Maybe you should talk to him... see what he's thinking."

My throat was dry as I tried to swallow. I managed to shake my head, keeping my focus on my shoes.

"He's thinking about Gisella," I said pointedly, lifting my eyes to hers. "As he should be."

"Maybe," she combatted with a shrug. "But like you said, big flames die hard — and who's to say Gisella isn't just some sort of rebound?"

"It's been two years since we split," I said, throat rough. "I think the rebound period has passed."

"So, Eli isn't a distraction for you?"

Shit.

"I'm just saying... there are relationships, and then there are love stories. I don't know what it was like with you two, but... just being around you in the galley? I know there was chemistry back then because it's still there now. And it's not like Gisella is some angel. She made out with my boyfriend the second hers wasn't around."

I smirked at her. "So he's your boyfriend now, huh?"

"Stop trying to change the subject." She flushed, fighting back a smile before her eyes turned serious on me again. "I mean it, Ember. They're not married. I'm not sure Gisella is even that serious about them at all. And maybe he feels the same. What if it's not supposed to be over for you two yet? What if there's more to your story than what's already been written?"

There was a knock at the cabin door, and Eli's deep greeting on the other side.

I stood, checking my reflection one more time in the mirror before I pulled Leah up and into a hug. Her words battled to break through the walls I'd built up around my heart in the two days since Finn had his hands on me, but my forces stood strong. I wanted so badly to play into her *what ifs*, but when it came to Finn, I'd had enough pain to last a lifetime.

"Our story might've been cut short," I said softly. "But the ending would've been the same no matter how long it dragged out."

I released her, smoothing the hem of my dress with a steady breath.

"So I'm done rereading it," I added with a small smile. "Time to write something new."

And with that, I opened the door and let Eli take my hand.

I wished I was drunk.

It would have been so easy to make my wish come true. If I would have ordered a wine with my dinner when Eli ordered his beer, or if I would have taken him up on the shot he suggested we take before we joined the others, or if I would have slammed back a double the moment we got to the bar.

But I didn't do any of that.

No matter how much I craved the numbness I knew alcohol

would bring me, I resisted it. I was wary of the stuff since that night at the beach. Had I been sober, surely I wouldn't have done what I'd done with Finn. That was what I'd convinced myself. And besides, I had wanted to be clearheaded for my date with Eli — I wanted to be in tune with every emotion so I knew for sure how I felt.

Well, my plan worked.

And I felt absolutely nothing.

Okay, that wasn't exactly true — it was nice going on the date with Eli. He was gorgeous and funny, and the conversation flowed easily between us. But there wasn't a spark in sight, not even a little tingle when he kissed me after dinner. He'd smiled against my mouth and swept my hair back and kissed me with the mouth of an expert, and I'd smiled and giggled and willed myself to feel something.

I only wanted to run.

Now, we were back with the group at the club. It was the same one from our first night out, the liveliest we'd found all season, and everyone was letting loose.

Gisella was happily draped over Finn at the bar, her eyes glossy and smile wide as she talked to Bernard, who sat next to Finn. Finn seemed lost in space, his eyes half-focused on one of the televisions broadcasting sports highlights. If I didn't know better, I'd say it looked like he was drinking water, but it must have been vodka. I would have asked him, if it were any other night.

As it was, I did my best not to look at him or wonder anything about him.

Palmer was next to me at the other end of the bar. I'd been trying to kick up a conversation with him, but he was short with every answer. He seemed pissed off, but I couldn't figure out why. The way he glared at Gisella made me wonder if maybe she'd fallen short on her duties on deck. God knew I understood that feeling all too well after our second charter.

Leah, Cameron, and Eli were on the dance floor, the first two tangled up in one another while Eli danced by himself like it didn't bother him one bit. He kept finding my gaze and nodding for me to join him, but I'd just shake my head or laugh him off. The last thing I felt like doing was dancing.

And yet... I decided maybe I should.

So what, I didn't feel a connection right away? Eli was nice. He was putting in the effort. Maybe it would be a slow burn with us. Not every romance felt as explosive and all-consuming as the one I had with Finn did. In fact, I'd bet that most stable relationships felt the opposite: warm instead of hot, comfortable instead of unpredictable, safe instead of adventurous.

Maybe I just needed to give Eli a chance.

Once again, I found myself wishing to be drunk, but I somehow found courage despite being sober and made my way to the dance floor.

Eli threw his hands up in victory. "There she is!" He let out a loud wolf whistle that had Leah laughing and Cameron jumping in with a few hollers of his own.

My cheeks were on fire by the time I made it to them, and I realized just how much of a crutch alcohol was for me in that moment. Because where I was never shy dancing when I had liquor running through my veins, I found everything awkward about my current attempt. My limbs felt stiff. The beat pulsed around me, but I couldn't quite find the rhythm.

Fortunately, I didn't have to do it alone.

I barely put my hands in the air and moved my hips before Eli was there, pulling me into him. His grin took up his entire face, mischievous and unbothered, and then his hands were on my waist, warm and confident and touching me like the simple kiss we'd shared after dinner was the checkered flag for him to start the race. His leg slid between mine, thigh pressing just enough to jolt my senses, and he rocked us to the rhythm like we'd been dancing together for years.

He didn't give me a chance to think. He just moved — wild and smooth, grinning, spinning me in a circle before yanking me back against him. My laughter came easy then, surprising me with how genuine it felt, how *easy* it felt. His arm wrapped around my middle, holding me flush to his chest as we moved together in time with the bass that thudded like a second heartbeat.

And still, I felt nothing past a friendly affection.

Eli was giving it his all — smiling, touching, moving with me like we were the only two people in the club. And I was trying. *God*, I was trying. I looped my arms around his neck, let him tug me closer, let my body lean into his.

But it was like I was watching someone else dancing, I was so disconnected.

What was wrong with me?

Eli was everything I should want. Gorgeous. Kind. Confident. Fun. He wanted me and he was showing me that. He didn't have a fucking girlfriend — which was a big plus considering where my brain wanted to go.

I was still stuck in a memory I couldn't crawl out of.

And alcohol or not, I found myself wondering if Finn was watching.

I told myself not to look.

I put all my willpower into smiling with Eli, into mirroring his movements with my own and staying in the present moment with him. I tried rationalizing with that very foolish, very loud voice inside my head.

But a few minutes was all I got before I folded like a house of cards.

My gaze drifted to the bar, to the far right where I knew he'd been, and sure enough... there Finn was.

Sitting with that same drink in his hand.

Watching.

His eyes weren't half-lidded or distracted now. They were on me — locked in, challenging, burning. Like he knew exactly what I was doing. Like he was daring me to keep going.

Gisella was gone. Bernard, too. It was just Finn left at the bar. And without any threat of someone seeing, I found it impossible to tear my gaze away.

And for the first time all night, I ignited.

It was absolutely unhinged behavior, grinding against Eli with my eyes on Finn. I hadn't felt an ounce of electricity from Eli alone, but now, I was molten. Sweat pricked the back of my neck, my skin flushing, heart racing out of my chest.

I should have dragged my gaze from his.

Instead, I gave him something to watch.

I turned back to Eli with new fire in my veins. My hands slid up his chest, slow and deliberate, curling around his neck. He grinned, surprised at the sudden shift, and before he could say a word— I kissed him.

It was an awkward clang of teeth at first, but then his mouth opened to mine instantly, like he'd been waiting for it, like he'd been dreaming of it. His hands roamed as our tongues tangled, the kiss deep and messy and hot. But I knew I didn't feel that heat from the man kissing me.

It was the one watching us from across the bar who held the torch.

A sudden jerk of Eli's shoulders had us breaking apart.

Cameron practically climbed on his back like a monkey, ruffling his hair as Eli laughed and spun him around. Leah grabbed me by the arm, and I leaned into her in a fit of giggles before Eli dropped Cameron to the ground and snatched me by the waist, pulling me into him again.

"Damn," he said, his tipsy eyes dragging the length of me. "Where've you been hiding *that*?"

I just smiled, pulling back, fingertips trailing down his chest as my heart continued to race.

"I need to hit the ladies' room," I said. "I'll be back."

He held onto my hand even as I walked away, and I laughed when he finally released me and then dropped to his knees and pretended like he was praying to God. Cameron played into his dramatics, and even Bernard joined in, the two of them fanning Eli as he faked passing out and they carried him off to the bar.

Leah looped her arm through mine to join me in the bathroom, but before we made it, I pulled to a stop.

"I actually think I just need some air," I said over the music, squeezing her wrist. "I'll catch you back out there?"

She nodded, a happy, drunk smile on her face, and then she made a beeline for the restrooms and I took the first exit outside.

The door was only shut for thirty seconds before it banged open behind me.

I didn't have to look to know who it was.

Chapter Twenty-Three

POST-PRODUCTION CONFESSIONAL
CLOSE QUARTERS

SEASON 4

EMBER REED: CHIEF STEW

PRODUCER
We'd like to go back to the night of your date with
Eli.

EMBER
I'm sure you would.

PRODUCER
As you can probably imagine, that episode was when
everything really shifted for the crew. You weren't
very forthcoming with talking head footage on the
boat, so we were hoping we could get some of your
thoughts now.

EMBER
Any idea of why I wouldn't have been keen to do
interviews after that night?

PRODUCER
Because you felt guilty?

Ember laughs, shakes head.

EMBER
Of course I did, but even guilty people have their
shot at a fair trial. That wasn't the case for me.
You all decided to make me the villain.

Ember shrugs.

EMBER
So, that's who I became.

Now, I was buzzing.

Not a drop of alcohol in my system, and yet every nerve was alive as I casually walked around the corner of the building and into the small alley, gathering my hair in my hands and fanning my neck like I was innocent.

As if I didn't know who was storming after me.

As if electricity wasn't prickling my skin in anticipation of what he'd do once he reached his target.

It was sick. *I* was sick.

And yet I wouldn't have taken the remedy even if there was one.

The fabric tie fastening around the waist of my dress pulled taut, yanking me to a stop just as I disappeared in the shadows of the dimly lit alleyway. I didn't gasp as I turned. I didn't even try to act surprised.

I was humming, ready for the fight.

And when I saw Finn's tight jaw, everything inside me lit up like a firework show.

"You're actually fecking kidding, right?"

"Sorry?" I pulled free of his grip on my dress, crossing my arms.

"What the hell was that back there?"

"A kiss. Where's your *girlfriend?* I'm sure she'd be glad to show you what it's like."

Finn's nostrils flared. "He's a kid, Ember. And you're leading him on."

I laughed. "Eli is far from a kid, Finn, and I'm not leading anyone on."

"You know damn well that's a lie."

My chest was on fire, my skin hot to the touch. I was so angry at his audacity and yet I expected it. I bet on it.

I craved it.

"It's not a lie," I combatted. "And I'm not sure where you get off thinking you know so much about me."

Finn took a large step into my space, the move so quick I backed up without my brain firing off the signals to my body at all. It was instinct, prey being cornered by a predator. My back hit the wall of the building, fingertips pressing into the brick, heart leaping into my throat as Finn brought his face within inches of mine.

"I told you once and I'll tell you again — no one in the world knows you like I do. And I know you're leading him on. Want to know how?" Another inch of space destroyed — along with my composure. "Because I tick the same twisted way you do, Firefly. I beat to the same fucked-up drum. And that kiss back there?" He pointed toward the end of the alley. "That was all a show. For me."

I bit my lips together, shoving against his chest even as my voice sputtered out weakly. "You wish—"

"I don't have to wish, love. You wanted me to watch? You wanted me to fume? To chase after you? Well, you got what you asked for. I'm here. Now," he said, pressing in another centimeter, just enough for my breath to catch in my throat. "Look me in the eyes and tell me what you really want to say because I know it isn't that you're over me and moving on with that cuttlefish."

My labored breath betrayed my arrogance. "Real mature."

"I think we're done pretending we're that, aren't we?"

I skirted the wall, slipping past him as I rolled my eyes. "Eli's nice. And interested. And, perhaps the best bonus of all, he doesn't have a girlfriend." I gave a tight-lipped smile with that. "Speaking of which, maybe you should focus on Gisella and stay out of my business."

I turned with those words, ready to sway back inside and leave him there fuming. I had no idea what game I was playing at. I couldn't untangle my emotions, all of them blurring together until I wasn't sure if there were ten different strings or if it was just one very long string in a very complicated knot.

Was I angry or was I excited? Did I hate him or love him still? Was my heart racing from the adrenaline of revenge or from the anticipation of his next move?

I didn't get the chance to figure it out.

Because I took two steps and then a hand caught me by the elbow, spun me hard, slid into my hair, curled around my neck — right where that lapwing tattoo was — and pulled me in.

Finn kissed me.

And every nerve in my body detonated at once.

My lungs collapsed, something between a gasp and a moan rumbling out of me as my hands found his shirt and gripped the fabric tight. I was already kissing him back before my brain even registered that it was happening — before the consequences could catch up, before I remembered the cameras, the crew, Gisella.

But *God*, he felt the same.

His hands were still strong and sure where they gripped me, one fastened around the back of my neck and the other sliding in to frame my face, his thumb hard on my jaw. His lips were still warm and firm, his tongue tasting like a thousand memories as it swept inside my mouth and eviscerated any other thought.

It was just a kiss, and yet it was a sensation overload.

Everything was right again — even though what we were doing was so, so wrong.

I melted into it, into *him*, my fingers curling into his shirt and pulling him closer. Two years evaporated like boiling water turning to steam, all the bad blood whisked away on the next whip of cool sea breeze against our skin.

This was why Eli could never measure up — why no one would.

No one felt like Finn Pearson.

No one could unlock me when he still held the key.

He kissed me like a man possessed — like he hated me for making him want it, like he'd punish me with pleasure just for tempting him. My back hit the wall again and I didn't fight. I let him pin me, let him take, let myself fall, mouth greedy and open, hands grasping for more, more, more—

And then reality broke through the haze.

I broke away, panting, shoving at his chest until we were an arm's length apart.

Finn let me put the space there, his eyes wild, chest heaving as he strained to pull his hands off me. His fingers curled into fists at his sides like he had to use all his willpower not to touch me again. My heart ached for him the second we were separated.

A hundred words rushed through my mind, each desperate to be the ones I'd pluck and use to put together a sensible sentence: *we have to stop, we can't do this, you have a girlfriend, there are cameras watching.*

But my body overrode the system, and I launched myself back into his arms.

The next kiss was harder.

Desperate.

Worse.

Better.

I whimpered at the feel of his body surrounding mine, brows

folding together as I fought to understand what I wanted. I pulled him into me one second and then shoved at him the next, but this time he wrapped his arms around me — holding me steady and firm as if he could keep me safe when we were the very thing that was dangerous.

"I'm glad the restaurant failed," he murmured against my lips before he was kissing me even harder. "You hear me? I'd take the pain of losing it a thousand times over if the outcome was the same. Because I lost that dream, but then I found my way back to you, and I realized that dream doesn't mean shit if you're not a part of it."

"Finn," I breathed against his lips, but another kiss stole my protest.

"I tried to fight it, this pull between us, but I'm helpless against it and I think you are, too. I can't *stay out of your business*, Firefly. Because my business is you. Everything you say, everything you do — I'm tapped into it. I'm hanging onto every word. I'm silently begging for your eyes to find mine in a crowded room, for you to come close enough for me to make up some fecking excuse to touch you."

I was going to combust. The combination of his words and his mouth as it slid from my lips to my throat and along the line of my jaw and back again was going to take me all the way out.

"We can't," I spoke the truth, and yet I held onto him with more fervor, my hands betraying my words. "It's wr—"

"Wrong? No. Fuck that. Don't you say that because I know you don't believe it. You know it's not true. This? You and me?" His hands cradled my face, forcing me to look at him, and I swore I died and was born again in the depth of his sea-green eyes. "This is the only thing that's right."

I shook my head even as my hands weaved into his hair and held him close.

"It's why we can't fight it," he said, his forehead falling to mine. "Why we never could. We were doomed from the day we walked onto that boat and saw each other again when we thought it was over. What's *wrong* is us being apart. What's wrong is me pretending anyone could ever matter more than you. What's wrong is you pretending you weren't just thinking of me the entire time you let him kiss you. There's no tattoo or piercing you can get to erase me, Em, and I'll never drink myself over you."

Another bruising, passionate kiss had my knees giving out, the weight of me falling into him as I surrendered even before I could find the words to say so.

"The cameras," I tried.

"Don't care." His mouth was on me again, and I was losing my already fragile grasp on what was right. "I'm so fecking tired of fighting my feelings for you because of what other people might think. I'll take the blame. I'll be the bad guy." He kissed me harder, shaking his head as his hands tore at my hair, my skin, like he was afraid I'd disappear in the next breath. "Just let me have you again and I swear I'll do anything it takes to keep you."

A broken sound ripped from my throat, but it was cut short by another kiss, by Finn sweeping me up as if he could shelter me from all the consequences of our choices. I was dizzy from his words and the all-consuming rush of *yes* coursing through me like the best high of my life, but I was also desperately trying to hold on to my morality.

"Gisella," I finally managed, and the sound of her name was like a shotgun blast. Finn froze, and I swallowed, hand at his chest and putting space between us while I had the chance. My eyes floated up to meet his. "We can't..." I shook my head. "This is wrong. We can't do this to her. You have to make it right. You have to end it with her if we—"

"I already have."

Finn's throat constricted with the words just as my heart constricted with their implication.

I frowned, head tilting to the side, but before I could question what the hell that meant, there was a burst of noise from around the corner.

The music from the club spilled out into the night air along with the distinct sound of our crew members, and panic seized me by the throat.

"Go," Finn said, nodding toward the streetlamp as he dipped farther back into the shadows. "I'll catch up."

The cameras had already seen everything, but the crew was none the wiser. I didn't have time to thank Finn for giving us the chance to keep it that way — at least for now. I hustled toward the light, running into the crew just as they rounded the corner, all of them cheerful and boisterous and completely oblivious to what had just transpired.

My heart was a snare drum in my ears as Leah wrapped an arm around me and started on about some dance off I'd missed as we ambled toward the waiting cabs. Finn must have gone around the back, because two minutes later, he was jogging out of the club and flying into the cab behind mine.

I touched my swollen lips with shaky fingers as the van started to move, the driver steering us back toward the boat. I was shaking all over. My stomach was in knots. I was dizzy and burning and aching for relief. Everyone in the cab was loud, Cameron singing while Bernard and Leah laughed and egged him on, but it was all muted for me — as if my kiss with Finn had sunk the ship and I was watching them from my new underwater grave.

But there was one thought loud enough to clear the haze.

I already have.

What the hell did that mean?

Chapter Twenty-Four

**CHARTER CONFESSIONAL
CLOSE QUARTERS**

SEASON 4, EPISODE 11
IN-BETWEEN CHARTERS 7 AND 8

GARY PARKS: CAPTAIN

Captain Gary groans, runs hand over face, shakes head, drinks coffee.

PRODUCER
We know you have a lot on your plate this morning, so we'll try to keep this brief.

Captain Gary nods.

PRODUCER
So… in your own words, can you tell us what's happened?

CAPTAIN GARY
Let's just say I woke up thinking today would be about fuel levels and guest preferences. Didn't expect I'd be managing a full-blown scandal before breakfast. And if I don't handle this right, it's not just reputations on the line — it's my boat.

I was still in a daze when we made it back to the *Sinking Sun*. It felt like I was watching someone else take off their shoes and pad along the teak deck into the main salon, down the stairs, and into the crew quarters. Everyone was shouting about going to the hot tub or making snacks. I was focusing on breathing.

When I walked into my cabin, the lights were off and white noise was blaring from Gisella's speaker. It sounded like a rushing river. One glance at her bunk confirmed she was already there, a large lump of a body under her comforter and pillows stacked all around her.

I frowned, trying to fight through the haze in my brain to remember if she'd left at the same time the rest of us had. The other cab did get here before ours did, but it wasn't long enough for her to already be passed out. Was it?

I considered asking if she was okay, but thought better of it. I was fairly certain that if she *was* upset, it wouldn't be from her knowing what happened between me and Finn. But guilt still slithered down my spine like a cottonmouth snake, and I was too cowardly to face the possibility.

Using the light from my phone screen, I debated my next move. I needed to change, but would I change into my swimsuit and join the crew in the hot tub?

Was Finn joining them?

Or should I just change into my pajamas and get some sleep?

Would I be *able* to sleep after what just happened?

I stood immobile for a full three minutes just staring at the chaos of clothes and shoes in my shared room with Gisella before my phone vibrated in my hand.

I turned it toward me, squinting against the screen now that my eyes had adjusted to the dark, and then my stomach hit the deck.

**TEXT FROM DO NOT CALL HIM EVER NO MATTER HOW
DRUNK YOU ARE STOP DON'T DO IT:**

Come to the primary cabin.

I'd been too weak to delete our messages when I finally cut myself off from Finn, and though I'd blocked him on social media, I couldn't bring myself to ever block his number.

Just in case.

Now, I was staring at the first text from him in two years.

Just above it was a string of ones from before, inside jokes and kiss emojis and dirty promises we kept. I stared a little too long at the one that read *I sleep better when you're in my bed, Firefly* before I clicked the screen off with my heart hammering in my chest.

I debated for all of two seconds before I was changing into my pajamas, brushing my teeth, checking my appearance in the dimly lit mirror of my cabin bathroom, and sneaking out as quietly as I could.

There were voices from the main salon followed by a loud burst of laughter and the distinct sound of glasses clinking. I tiptoed through the crew mess and up the stairs, peeking my head into the galley before I crossed through it and over to the stairs that led to the guest cabins.

My heart was racing the entire time, like I was some secret agent on a mission, and if one person caught sight of me, I was done with. But no one spotted me. I cringed a bit when I heard Eli ask Leah if I was coming into the hot tub, and when she answered that she wasn't sure, he started singing out my name. Bernard eventually hushed him and warned not to wake Captain, and then their voices slurred together until they were snuffed out by the sliding glass doors closing behind them as they disappeared outside.

The silence their absence left the boat in made every step I took feel like I was a bowling ball crashing through glass.

The camera duo following me certainly didn't help, and I wanted to tell them to fuck off, but knew I couldn't. So I let them trail me all the way to the primary cabin, and then I knocked so softly I wasn't sure I made any noise at all. I looked back over my shoulder with my ears thrumming, but I was alone, and the camera crew had paused at the end of the hallway, their lenses focused on me but giving space.

Finn opened the door, and then he snagged me by the wrist and pulled me inside. He shut the door before the camera crew could get more than a glimpse of us.

"Give me your mic."

Finn was already yanking his from where it was wrapped around his midriff, and the sight of him dragging his shirt up to do so had me temporarily frozen before I snapped into action and followed suit.

"We're not supposed to take them off."

"I don't fucking care."

As soon as I had the mic cord free from where it had been snaked under my thin silk pajama top, Finn plucked the device from my hands. He tossed it onto the floor in the corner of the cabin along with his, the clattering of them loud enough to make me jump.

"They'll still be able to hear us," I pointed out. "Maybe not as clearly, but—"

"Come here."

Finn hooked his finger under the waistband of my silk shorts and tugged until I was in his arms, until he could wrap me up and lower his mouth to mine. He let out a long, sated exhale the moment our lips touched, as if he'd been holding his breath since we broke apart outside the bar and could finally find relief now that I was here.

That thought had me melting into him, and I almost forgot about all the questions my brain had been screaming since I hopped into the cab. It felt so fucking good to just kiss him and be kissed that I almost didn't care about anything else.

Almost.

"Finn." I broke away just far enough to part our lips, my forehead against his, fingers still curling in the fabric of his shirt. "I want nothing more than to lose myself in you right now, but you... you've got to talk to me. You've got to tell me what the hell is going on because I'm... I'm going out of my mind trying to figure it out."

I was panting between the words, my entire body trembling even as Finn's hands fought to hold me steady. When I lifted my gaze to his, he looked wrecked by my admission, and he pressed a swift, sweet kiss to my lips before he dragged me over to the bed.

He sat, pulling me to sit next to him, but he didn't allow even a centimeter of space between us. His thigh was against mine, his hands wrapping mine up and holding them tightly in my lap. He angled himself toward me, his eyes flicking between my own.

"I haven't touched Gisella since the moment I saw you."

Those were far from the first words I expected him to say.

"I'm serious. All the times she dragged me into your cabin to cuddle? I felt fucking sick, Em. She always wanted to do more but I refused. She'd try to come to mine in the middle of the night and I'd essentially play dead. I told her I didn't want to be unprofessional or make anyone uncomfortable, but the truth is I couldn't lie to her or to myself. I couldn't hurt her like that. I couldn't pretend." He swallowed, his thumbs smoothing over my fingers where his hands were laced with mine. "If I took her to bed, I knew it would be you I'd be thinking of."

His words lit the fuse I'd had to stomp out when we broke apart outside the club, and I felt the countdown start. The longer he stared at me, the more he said? The closer that spark got to the dynamite piled inside of me.

I thought about the crew beach day, about how Gisella had confessed to us that she'd been frustrated with Finn for not touching her. It was one thing to hear it from her, but to hear his side of it now...

It was terribly wrong, how good it made me feel.

Still, I shook my head, a full-body shake rocking over me. "I... I don't understand."

"That makes two of us, Firefly," Finn said on a short laugh. "I don't even know where to start. I hate myself for what happened between us two years ago. I've tortured myself these past two months just wondering what would have happened if I would have asked you to be with me in the offseason, if I would have told you sooner about the restaurant, if I wouldn't have thought I was so fucking smart with my grand plan to get you to fall in love with me and abandon everything else you care about."

"I was young and stupid, too," I told him, my eyes welling with tears. "I was just so proud. I couldn't stop the anger long enough to be reasonable. I wanted to hate you because it was easier than admitting I was hurt."

"I hate myself enough for the both of us for hurting you."

I shook my head, but Finn kept on.

"And I'm sorry for not doing something sooner, for not pulling my head out of my ass the second I saw you and realized nothing about the way I felt for you had died. I was just... fucking confused. Scared. I didn't want to hurt Gisella, even though I knew it was inevitable. I didn't know where you stood, if you would even hear me out if I tried..."

His eyes dropped to our joined hands, his thumbs brushing lightly over mine as he searched for the right words.

"And all those times I was a dick to you in the beginning — snapping, picking fights, lashing out over stupid shit like dinner service — that wasn't about the job. I was reeling. Seeing you again wrecked me. I didn't know how to function with you that close when you weren't mine. It was like fate had slammed us back together but locked the fucking doors. I felt trapped by my own choices... and by how badly I still wanted you.

"I thought you hated me, and you had every right to, but then we'd have these little moments, and I thought... maybe not. Maybe she feels the same way I do. But then I'd do something stupid, and I was so fecking defensive." Finn rolled his lips together, then shook his head with a breathy laugh. "You turn me into a bleeding eejit, you know that?"

I choked on something between a sob and a laugh, and the corner of Finn's lips curled up, his eyes dancing between mine.

"But during that dinner service with the chef on board, when I broke down, when I lost control..." He swallowed. "You saved me. And I realized right then that I couldn't pretend anymore. I realized it didn't matter who I hurt or what anyone watching this bloody show would think of me. I realized I couldn't let the possibility of you shutting me down keep me from putting myself out there and telling you how I really feel — not again." He shrugged. "So, at the beach…"

Fire licked along my spine at the memory — his words by the water, his hand on the back of my neck, his tentative touch when he thought no one was looking, when we were covered by the shadow of night.

But acid scorched my throat when I remembered what happened next.

"You were drunk," I said icily. "And you kissed Gi not even two seconds after you wrecked me with your touch."

"She kissed me," he corrected. "And I broke away as soon as it happened. I also explained why she did it in the note I gave you."

I blinked. "Note?"

"The note? That I slipped under your door the next morning?" Finn frowned the longer I went staring at him like he had a screw loose. "Shit… tell me you got the note, Firefly."

I shook my head.

"Fuck." He tore one hand from me long enough to run it through his hair. "Gisella…" He tongued his cheek, laughing to himself and shaking his head before he turned back to me. Finn took my hands in earnest then, his eyes locked on mine. "I had already broken things off with her, Em."

My next breath lodged in my throat. "You… *what*?"

"That night after the dinner disaster. I took her up on the sundeck and told her I couldn't do it anymore. She tried to talk me out of it, thought it was because she'd kissed Cameron, but I assured her I would have felt the same regardless. We talked for hours. We cried. I care for her, Em, I do. She was there for me at a really vulnerable time in my life. I didn't want to hurt her. But I couldn't let her think I still felt the same when I knew I didn't, when my every waking thought was consumed by you."

I was speechless. My wheels spun faster and faster as I tried to track through everything. "But at the beach... she was talking like you—"

"Were still together? Yeah. She wasn't ready to let anyone know. She begged me to wait a few days, to let her do it on her terms. She wanted to have a big breakup where she was the one who called things off. I told her she could do whatever she wanted." He shrugged. "Like I said last night — I'll be the bad guy. I don't fecking care. As long as I have you."

My jaw was unhinged but I couldn't think of a single word to say.

"I thought she'd do it last night, make a big scene or whatever, but she didn't. So yeah, she was still hanging on me, still stealing a kiss here and there. But she knew where I stood. She was just using me for whatever game she's playing at." He shook his head. "I still can't figure it out, but I respected her enough to at least try to let her have it the way she wanted it. But then I saw you tonight with Eli, and I..."

Finn's nostrils flared, his Adam's apple bobbing as his eyes darted between mine.

"I fucking lost it, Em."

"I wanted you to," I confessed.

"You think I don't know that?" He laughed a little then, reaching up to thumb my chin. "It was a dare. A challenge. And I knew as soon as you walked outside that I was over all the pretending. I didn't care what Gisella wanted anymore. I was done with the games. I was going to kiss my girl and I was going to get her back — cameras and public opinion be damned."

Sparrow wings tickled my stomach as the corner of my mouth

lifted. "Your girl, huh?"

At that, Finn slid his hand over my jaw, hooking me behind the neck and pulling me into him. "Damn right."

He kissed me, and those flutters I'd felt in my stomach from his words dipped lower, igniting a part of me I'd thought was dead. I'd tried so hard to use other people as a distraction since we broke up, but it never worked.

And now that my body was firing up from the simplest kiss, I remembered why.

Sharing intimacy with anyone after having Finn was like trying to substitute a shot of whiskey with a non-alcoholic beer. It didn't burn. It didn't tingle. It didn't satisfy.

"I'm not even drunk," I whispered against his lips before I was seeking another kiss. "I can't blame any of this on alcohol."

"I haven't had a single sip tonight."

I laughed, and then I was on the move, crawling into his lap with my mouth traveling along his stubbled jaw. "We're terrible."

"Truly awful," he said breathlessly, his hands fastening to my hips and helping me climb him.

"They're going to hate us."

"Absolutely loathe our existence."

Each sentence came between a heated kiss, a passionate roll of my body against his, a claiming grip of his fingertips in my skin.

"No one will understand."

"*We* understand," Finn said, and this time he stopped everything long enough to lock his eyes on mine. "That's all that matters to me. I know what I want. I know I'll risk everything to have it." He swallowed. "But I'll walk out of this room and leave you alone forever if you don't feel the same. If this is too much…"

"Shut up," I breathed against his mouth, and then the words and confessions faded away as I raked my hands through his hair and held on tight.

I sat fully on him, rocking my hips, the sensitive heat between my legs finding the sweetest friction against his hard shaft. We groaned together, my body trembling as Finn's hands slid from my hips to my ass and gripped hard. He used the new handle on me to help me roll, to pull me flush against him as he bucked his hips up to meet mine.

It was too much and not enough. I needed more of him, and also felt I'd die from even one more touch. Every sensation was overloaded — my head light, skin buzzing, blood pumping.

This was it.

The dynamite explosion.

For years, I'd convinced myself I'd never have him again. My body had mourned the death of his touch and now it was being revived. Shock and disbelief mixed with such an intense longing and sense of *right* that I had no choice but to submit to the confusing ecstasy of it all.

I fell into the dark, passionate, bottomless pit.

And Finn caught me.

His touch was everywhere — hands dragging from hips to hair and back again, lips trailing fiery kisses along the column of my throat, down the lacy neckline of my silk top, over each swell of my breast and back up to my mouth.

We couldn't catch our breaths, both of us panting and moaning and gripping and clawing. We were torn between savoring each taste of skin or shredding every piece of clothing still separating us.

A man possessed. A woman consumed. The kind of passion that ends wars or starts them.

Maybe it was toxic. Maybe we were the villains.

But *fuck,* to me?

This felt like the victorious sunset ride as the credits rolled.

Chapter Twenty-Five

**CHARTER CONFESSIONAL
CLOSE QUARTERS**

SEASON 4, EPISODE 11
IN-BETWEEN CHARTERS 7 AND 8

FINN PEARSON: HEAD CHEF

PRODUCER
Are you alright?

FINN
Oh, I'm absolutely grand.

PRODUCER
Really? You're not… I don't know, feeling any certain
type of way right now?

FINN
Can't imagine what you mean.

PRODUCER
You don't feel guilty or bad or worried or…?

*Finn smirks, wipes hand over jaw and leans forward,
elbows balancing on knees.*

FINN
There's a reason guilt is subjective, isn't there,
mate? All depends who the judge and jury are. And I'm
curious… have you asked anyone else on this boat if
they feel guilty?

PRODUCER
Should I?
Finn shrugs, sits back.

FINN
Guess that depends. Have you already made up your
mind about the narrative for the show?

PRODUCER
We don't spin a narrative. We just capture what
happens.

Finn laughs, stands to leave.

FINN
Right. We'll go with that.

⊕

I was on fire.

Finn slid his fingers under the silk hem of my top and bunched
the fabric, dragging it up slowly in a silent request for me to lift
my arms. As soon as I did, he peeled the shirt over my head, my
hair gathering in the neck hole before it fell over my shoulders in
waves as the silk was flung somewhere behind me.

A groan and his hands were on me, each palm testing the
weight of my breasts as I arched into the touch. My hands wove
into his hair and Finn took me in his mouth, his tongue swirling
around one nipple before he kissed his way over to the other one.

"I'm so fecking torn right now," he groaned, thumbing my
nipples as he bit his lip and watched me squirm under the touch.
"I don't know if I want to spend the whole night worshiping these
perfect tits and kissing every inch of your skin I've missed for the
last two years..." His hands moved to my hips again, fisting the
silk there. "Or if I want to shred these shorts and bury myself
inside you right fecking now."

A wave of chills broke over me at the raw edge of his voice, and I rocked against him until my clit sparked to life enough to make me tremble.

"I could come just like this I think," I whispered, rolling again as he flicked his tongue over one nipple and toyed with the other. "I've missed this so much. I feel like... like..."

I panted and moaned in lieu of continuing that sentence, wondering if Finn felt the same need coursing through him like a wildfire.

"I know, I know," he assured me, slowing his perusal with his tongue. "I feel it, too."

"It's only with you."

"Only ever you."

He kissed me long and hard with that declaration.

"Before we go any further, I want you to know that I have always used protection," Finn said, and he didn't really need to say it because I already knew. We'd always used protection when we were together in the past. "But tonight... Em, I want you bare. I want to feel you — *really* feel you. No barriers, no holding back. I'm so feckin' tired of everything that's come between us."

"I want it, too," I whispered against his lips before I kissed him to seal the need. "I need it. To feel you inside me."

"You've nothin' to worry about with me, Em."

"I know. You're safe with me, too. And I'm—"

"On the pill?" He growled, nipping at my bottom lip. "I know. Watched you take it every morning, wondering who you were shagging instead. Drove me bloody mad."

I laughed into his possessive kiss at that. "Oh, my God, you brute. I mostly take it so that my period cramps don't kill me." I pressed a hand into his chest. "And for the record, I've only slept with one person since we split. Not that I owe you an explanation.

You don't own me."

"But you own me," he said, and he slowed our kiss just long enough to hammer that point home with a very purposeful sweep of his tongue over mine. "Now, no more talking about other people. It's me and you now."

"Me and you."

Finn smirked against my lips, the tip of his nose nudging mine. "You said you could come like this," he mused. "Go on, then. Show me."

A bolt of electricity struck me hard and fast when he rocked his hips up to meet mine, timing it perfectly with a swirl of his tongue.

"Finn," I breathed, and already the edges of my vision were sparking.

"Jaysus, yes. Just like that," he praised, and then his hands found my hips and added just the right pressure. "Say my name while you're grinding on me like a desperate wee thing."

A moan ripped from me, every nerve screaming to life at his degradation. He knew I liked it, that I wanted it, that I craved the surrender of him taking control and letting me give myself to him fully. And I knew he'd whisper these dirty words against my skin now and cover them with praise as soon as we were finished.

He was right — he knew the way I ticked. He understood me like no one else.

This was why we were inevitable.

We were current and tide — pulled by the same moon, bound to the same rhythm. No one else would fit. No one else would do.

I picked up my pace, grinding against him as he paid homage to my breasts. I threw my head back as the first orgasm crested — and I knew it would only be the first of many. This was our favorite game to play, after all. How many times could we get the other off? How much energy could we spare before we were both truly spent?

"I hated seeing you with her," I rasped, pulling his hair until he lifted his chin and looked up at where I rocked and writhed against him. His eyes meeting mine lit another wick within me. "I want to punish you for torturing me that way."

I ground against him harder, enough to make him suck in a hiss of breath and grit his teeth a little. But he didn't pull away. Instead, one hand snaked around to cradle the back of my head and pull me into him for a bruising kiss while the other helped me ride him harder.

"Punish me, then," he breathed against my lips. "Make it hurt."

I surrendered to the need coursing through me, my hips wild and pace quick. I didn't care if I was putting too much pressure on him, and he welcomed the pain, holding me to him, kissing me through the crest of the first wave. I came with a hitched breath and my hands clawing at his back, and Finn smirked against my mouth, helping me ride out the last of it.

He took the weight of me when I melted, my heart racing against his chest as he pressed a kiss to my hair.

"That's one," he mused, and then he spanked my ass and helped me off his lap.

My shorts were dragged down to my knees in the next second, Finn helping me step out of them as I balanced with my hands on his shoulders. I was shaking like a leaf, still panting from my first release, but Finn's hungry gaze only intensified once I was fully bare for him.

"Christ, Firefly," he groaned, biting his lip and shaking his head as his eyes drank me in. "You're a masterpiece."

He was up and kissing me silent before I had the chance to reply, his mouth fixed on mine as his hands deftly grabbed at each layer of clothing still separating us. My trembling fingers fumbled with the lower half of his buttoned shirt while he took care of the top, and when we met in the middle, he shrugged out of it, hands sliding into my hair the moment his arms were free.

He kissed me long and promising, heat rolling off him like a steam engine, and then his hands were gone again. He made quick work of his belt and slacks, ripping them down and kicking out of them. Then, I was hoisted up, one hand at the back of my neck and the other holding my weight as I wrapped my legs around him.

Finn fell back into the bed, taking me with him, and as soon as my knees hit the mattress, his hands were free to roam. He cupped my backside and squeezed, giving me another little spank before one hand slid around my thigh and between us.

The moment his fingers brushed my clit, I whimpered.

"*Christ*, I've missed this perfect cunt," he growled into my mouth, smirking as he spread my lower lips with one thick fingertip. I was soaked from my first release, and he slid his digit along my seam with a satisfied moan before plunging one finger inside me and curling it just the way I liked.

I buried my head in his shoulder, barely keeping myself upright for him to work his magic as my arms shook on either side of his head. Finn reached up to grab behind my neck and pull me down for a kiss, a second finger joining the first just as his tongue swept in and danced with mine.

"Sit that pretty cunt on me face. Let me taste you, love. I want to drown in your next orgasm before I fuck you to your third."

I wanted to talk back. I reached for the sassy bite I knew I had inside me but came up empty as a shell. My first orgasm had hollowed the fight out of me. I was in full surrender now, ready to do any and everything he asked me to.

My heart thundered in my ears as I climbed up his body, Finn helping me maneuver as he slid down and off the pillows enough for me to straddle his face. He spanked me with a satisfied groan when I was seated, his hands taking my ass in full handfuls before he made me spread wider and drop lower. My hands shot forward for the padded wall that served as a headboard, and I held on for dear life to whatever I could grab as Finn took his first taste.

It was a slow drag; a flat, hot tongue covering me from where his fingers had stretched me to where I was still overly sensitive from my first climax.

I dissolved under his touch.

My head lolled back as I let a moan roll through me, hips rocking to find another lash of his tongue. He rewarded me with what I craved, licking me from seam to tip again and again before he cupped his lips around my clit and sucked.

"Oh, fuck," I whispered, my voice strained against the second orgasm already building. I was so wound up from months of little touches and looks that I felt like an exposed nerve. Every lick had the power to undo me, and Finn seemed hell bent on tearing me apart.

My moans got louder with each flick of his tongue, each slow suck that drew me closer and closer to the edge. I was drenched — in sweat, in want, in the sheer fucking heat of his mouth on me after all the little games we'd played.

Finn held me firm, coaxing me lower like he wouldn't be satisfied until I was sitting on him fully and trying to suffocate him. His tongue flattened and curled, his lips sucked and teased, and when he slipped two fingers inside me again, my hands flew into my hair, body winding as I gave into my need and fucked his mouth.

"That's a dirty girl," he praised, curling his fingers in time with the rhythmic sucks of my clit. "Ride my face like I know you can't wait to ride my cock."

I shattered.

The orgasm tore through me with violent grace, a full-body quake that had me crying out into the night. Distantly, I realized I should try to be quiet, but there was no sense to be had in that moment. I was fully committed to sin.

I pressed my forearm to the padded headboard, forehead collapsing against it as the world turned white and hot and wild behind my eyes.

"Finn," I panted. "Fuck—FUCK."

He didn't stop. His tongue and fingers danced in time until the aftershocks were nothing but twitches in my thighs and soft pleas from my lips. Only then did he ease me off his face, pressing one last lingering kiss to my inner thigh.

When I looked down, his mouth was glistening — and his lips were turned up in a smile.

"Fecking hell, Firefly," he rasped, voice gruff and filthy and beautiful. "I think I could have come just from *that*."

I slumped forward on a laugh, breathless and shaking, trying and failing to catch up. But Finn was already moving, already sitting up with those strong hands cradling my waist as he helped me ease down onto the mattress.

"Come here, love," he murmured, crawling up over me until our bodies aligned again — until he was staring down at me like he'd just found religion.

With that look, the moment shifted, the frenzied passion of it melting into something deeper. I could feel Finn's heartbeat against mine, could hear my blood buzzing in my ears, could feel every tingle of nerve endings from my neck to my toes.

"You alright?" he asked, brushing the back of his hand down my cheek, his touch featherlight now. Reverent. Worshipful.

I nodded, still dazed. "I think I'm in shock."

"From the orgasm?" he teased with a smirk.

"Maybe." I wove my hands into his hair. "Or maybe just from you. From this. From…" I shook my head. "I never thought I'd have you again."

He nodded, solemn. "I know."

"Is this a dream?"

A firm shake of his head. "No, love. It's real." He kissed me, slow and long. "Real fecked up, maybe, but still real."

I laughed at that, winding my arms around his neck and holding him to me for another lazy kiss. We stayed like that for a beat, our ragged breathing the only sound between us, the tension morphing into something softer, something sweeter — but no less intense. My entire body was buzzing, sated enough to sleep.

But I needed more of him.

"Finn."

"Mm?"

I slid my fingers beneath the band of his briefs. "Off."

He smirked against my neck, kissing me there before he leaned back on his knees. Without breaking my gaze, he reached for his waistband and slid the fabric down slowly, the muscles of his abdomen flexing as he freed himself.

My mouth parted before I could stop it, breath catching at the sight of him — hard and thick and heavy, the tip flushed and glistening.

A foreign noise rumbled in my throat, but I couldn't find it in me to be even slightly embarrassed. I could have stayed just like that, staring at him for hours like he was a painting in a museum. He was more beautiful than I remembered, the shadows of the room playing with all the lines and mounds and valleys of his body. I reached forward instinctively, fingertips trailing goosebumps over his flesh as I dragged them down his abdomen.

"My turn to taste," I tried, but before I could even wrap my hands around his shaft, he snatched me by the wrists and pushed me back into the mattress.

"Not a chance, Firefly," he said, punctuating that statement with a hard kiss. "I need to be inside you."

"You don't play fair," I whispered, nipping at his chin.

"Says the one who purposefully drove me to my limit tonight."

"Zero regrets."

That earned me a deep chuckle and another swift kiss. Then, he pressed back up to his knees and hooked his grip under my thigh, hiking up my left leg.

My heart was a free-running stallion as Finn wrapped his large hand around my ankle and brought it to his lips. He kissed the sensitive flesh just below the bone, along the curve of my calf, and up the inside of my knee. Every touch of his mouth felt like a promise, like an apology, like a poem written on my skin.

When he reached my inner thigh, he sucked in a breath like being inside me was jumping off a cliff into ice cold water, like he was bracing for the excitement and the pain, too.

"You're wreckin' me," he murmured against my skin, voice rough as his teeth scraped just enough to make me gasp. "Always have."

And then he bit down, marking me.

I let him.

With a moan, my fingers twisted in the rumpled comforter beneath us as he eased my leg up and settled it over his shoulder. His hands slid beneath my hips, tugging until I was right where he needed me, and with one last look — one filled with equal parts heat and heartbreak — he sank into the space between us.

The moment his cock brushed against me, I trembled, black invading the edges of my vision.

And the second he began to push in, I knew.

This wasn't just sex.

It was resurrection.

We both came back to life the moment he flexed and filled me that first inch. I saw the way he fought the urge to plunge all the way in, to satisfy himself no matter the cost. He groaned and battled with restraint to pull out and edge back in, over and over, the wetness from my first two climaxes coating him a little more each thrust.

A flex and a kiss.

A moan and a sigh.

Then, he was fully submerged, so deep inside me I wondered where I ended and he began.

And we were home.

If I thought I was shaking before, it was nothing compared to now. I trembled relentlessly, fingernails digging into his shoulders and back as Finn held fast to my hiked-up leg and withdrew only to bury himself again.

The groan that vibrated through him filled every need I had, that sound better than any word he could have uttered. He was overwhelmed with the feel of me, with the feel of *us*. His pace quickened from deep, rolling thrusts to punishing flexes. He couldn't get enough. He wanted to be like the tattoos spanning my skin — painful and lovely and permanent.

And I wanted to mark him just the same. I wanted to pierce through his soul and fasten myself like a tungsten ring. He could never cut me out. He could never rid himself of my love.

I knew he'd never want to.

It was dizzying and obscene, the way we crashed together without any hesitation, without any regard for the impact of the earthquake we caused. The waves of our decisions could wash away an entire city and we'd make the choice to do it again.

The truth wasn't always beautiful and pure.

Still, he felt so right. This moment, this surrender — it was heaven disguised as sin. I knew even as I lost myself to Finn that night that everyone would judge us and find us guilty. No one would understand.

But we were meant to be.

Words were lost to the sea the longer Finn found himself between my thighs. When he came, his body locking up tight before it shuddered beneath my fingertips, I found my third release, too. I clung to him, and he buried his face in my neck, his cock in my cunt, his heart in my soul.

We barely finished that round before the next one began.

I rode him slowly and passionately. We limped to the shower under the guise of getting clean only to give in to even more filth once the steam was rising around us. Finn helped me crawl into the sheets only to crawl in behind me, pull me flush against him, and rock himself inside me once more.

Night had bled into morning by the time exhaustion became too heavy for either of us to fight.

"I should go back to my cabin," I tried, but Finn hooked his arm around me and pulled me closer.

"Stay."

"Finn..."

"I'll set an alarm," he promised. "We can sneak back to our cabins in a few hours. We can figure out what we do next tomorrow. But tonight, just..." He sighed, his lips feathering a kiss to my spine. "Stay."

My heart surged out of my chest at the desperation in his voice. I nodded, letting him roll away from me only long enough to set the alarm on his phone like he promised before I was clinging to him again. I burrowed into his embrace — his leg between mine, my thigh hitched over his hip, our arms wrapping one another up like someone was trying to tear us apart and we refused to let them.

I fell asleep with my head on my ex-boyfriend's chest.

And woke to complete fucking chaos.

Chapter Twenty-Six

POST-PRODUCTION CONFESSIONAL
CLOSE QUARTERS

SEASON 4

BERNARD EVANS: SECOND STEWARD

PRODUCER
Let's go back to the drama that unfolded between charters seven and eight.

Bernard rubs hands together, smiles.

BERNARD
Well, if you insist.

PRODUCER
Were you shocked by what the crew found out the morning that charter eight started?

BERNARD
Yes and no. Was I surprised to find our chief stew and head chef tangled up together in the sack? Not really. But I was surprised by how it all kicked off after. Thought they might try to play it cool — instead, it was fireworks.

PRODUCER
And what about how the rest of the crew responded?

Bernard laughs.

BERNARD
Ah. Shit show, that was, wasn't it? But you've got
to understand - emotions were running high. We were
all on fumes by that point, and seems like half the
boat had been biting their tongues for weeks. That
morning? That was the snap.

PRODUCER
Were you hurt by anything that was said?

Bernard shrugs, leans back in chair, grin unfading.

BERNARD
Nah, mate. Then again, I wasn't the one who found my
boyfriend in bed with my superior, was I?

The alarm didn't go off.

I knew it the second I creaked one eye open and saw sunlight playing through the slats in the blinds.

Panic hit me before the grogginess could, my breath catching as I bolted upright — or tried to. Finn's arm was draped across my waist, heavy with sleep, his bare chest rising and falling against my back.

Fuck.

"Finn," I whispered, trying to shake him awake. "Finn, we overslept. We—"

SLAM.

The door burst open.

And my heart jumped into my throat when I locked eyes with Gisella.

I barely had time to yank the sheet to my chest before she was in the room, eyes wild, face flushed, jaw clenched like she was already coming for a fight before she even knew there needed to be one.

"You have got to be fucking kidding me." Her voice was sharp and high, gaze slicing from me to where Finn was hastily snapping into action beside me. I expected him to curse and jump out of bed and run to her, begging for her to give him a chance to explain.

Instead, he put his body in front of mine like a shield, his hand squeezing my knee under the covers in a silent reassurance that we'd be okay.

I wasn't so sure.

Gisella cataloged the movement with her tongue in her cheek. She shook her head and barked out a laugh. "How chivalrous, Finn. You're a lying, cheating sack of shit — but hey, at least you're a gentleman to your whore."

The cameras and production crew had already squeezed their way into the cabin, too, and I buried my face in Finn's back as I imagined what they were capturing.

Oh, God.

What have we done?

Everything felt so right in the moment. When Finn held me and kissed me and touched me, when he told me how he felt, how he'd felt for weeks — *years*. Last night, we were just two people in love against all odds, floating in our own little bubble.

Well, that bubble had officially been popped.

And the reality of our carelessness was crashing over me like a tidal wave.

Gisella looked between us — the tangled sheets, our clothes scattered around the room, Finn's calm but protective demeanor.

"This explains a lot," she said, her voice rough. "Guess I know now why you got so pissed at me kissing Cam. Hard to stomach the thought of me cheating on you when you were already doing it to me?"

"That's not—" I balked, shaking my head with wide, pleading eyes. "We didn't, Gisella. I swear. Last night was the first—"

"Don't insult me with a lie." Her eyes narrowed, full of fire. "At least have the decency to own your shit, *zorra cobarde de mierda.*"

Before I could say another word, Eli appeared in the doorway, concern etched into his face as he stepped inside. But one glance at the scene — the discarded clothes, Finn shirtless in front of me, the way I clutched the comforter to my chest — and his expression flattened into something I hadn't seen from him before.

Disappointment.

His gaze swept from Finn, to the floor, to me.

"Wow," he said, voice flat. "Real nice."

He turned on his heel, shaking his head, and let out a sharp, humorless laugh that felt like a punch to the gut.

My stomach sank further, the weight of his judgment heavier than the luxury comforter I gripped like a lifeline. Voices stirred outside the door — hushed, then louder, pressing for answers — and Eli must have shoved right past them without a word because the muttering turned to footsteps.

And then the crew flooded in, drawn to the drama like moths to a flame.

One by one, they crowded the cabin doorway, peering over shoulders, ducking under arms, gasping as they took it in.

My heart beat loud and unsteady in my ears as each one of their gazes landed on me.

Finn squeezed my knee again.

Bernard was the first to speak. "Well," he drawled, the corner of his mouth ticking up like a man watching his favorite soap opera. "This is awkward."

"Shit," Palmer muttered under his breath, rubbing a hand over his face.

But it was Leah's wide, wounded eyes that sucker punched me.

"Em," she whispered. "I thought we told each other everything."

I opened my mouth to explain — to say I didn't know I was going to do it either, that it was a mistake, that it wasn't supposed to happen — but I couldn't possibly hand her another lie.

And it would be a lie to say I felt anything about last night was a mistake.

Cameron stepped forward with a scoff before I could figure out what to say. "Safe to say that little moment with Eli last night was just for show then, yeah?" he said, arms crossed, his tone full of venom. "Guess you were just soft launching this disaster."

"Cam, stop," Leah hissed, smacking his arm.

He shrugged her off. "What? They're lying cheaters and she led my mate on. Why are we pretending this is some tragic love story when it's just bullshit?"

Bernard chuckled, suddenly turning toward the cameras with his hands up. He whipped out an Australian accent and crouched low like he was on a safari. "And here we have a rare sighting of chief stew and head chef in their natural habitat. If you look closely, you can see—"

"God, Bernard, will you *shut up*," Leah snapped, rounding on him. "You probably encouraged all of this, didn't you?"

Bernard blinked, caught off guard. "What's that supposed to mean?"

"It means you're a little pot stirrer and you know it. Wouldn't surprise me a bit if you egged this on just for the drama of it. You're the one who dared Gisella and Cameron to kiss — knowing she was with Finn, and knowing Cameron was with me!"

Bernard scoffed, crossing his arms. "Babe, don't be mad at me. Hate to break it to you, but your man's got free will. He could've said no. He *would've* said no... if you actually mattered to him."

That did it.

Cameron lunged like a viper set to strike.

Palmer grabbed him just in time, locking his arms around his chest and dragging him back as Cameron barked, "Say that again, you Sassenach bastard, and I'll wring your fecking neck."

Bernard just laughed, shaking his head as Palmer struggled to keep Cameron from losing it. "Upset I called out the truth, are we, my sweet Scot? Aww." He made a pouty face. "You'd really be suffering if Leah found out you and Gisella continued to have a little fun after she and Ember went inside, wouldn't you?"

Ice pricked my skin like a thousand little needle points, the shock of Bernard's words hitting their intended targets perfectly. Gisella turned bright red, her fingers curling into fists as Cameron lunged for Bernard again. He was firing off a string of curse words in such a thick Scottish accent that I couldn't understand him, but I was too busy watching Leah to pay much attention anyway.

And she was breaking like a fragile vase knocked off the highest shelf.

"Leah," I tried as her eyes flooded with unshed tears, but her jaw hardened, her chin lifting.

"Don't pretend like you're my friend," she spat to me, and then she stormed out of the room with the guys still clamoring for a fight behind her.

As soon as she was gone, another face appeared at the door.

This one was all business.

"ENOUGH!"

Captain Gary's voice cracked through the room like a whip.

Every head turned to where he was in the doorway. I knew with one glance that he'd yet to even have his coffee. His eyes were wide, jaw locked as he slammed that authoritative glare into each one of us.

When it landed on me and Finn, it softened — just marginally, enough for his true feelings to slip through the façade.

Disappointment.

Again.

It was the final rock on the pile of rubble, and suddenly I wasn't just struggling to breathe.

I was crushed.

"What the hell is going on here?" he asked, voice booming as he tore his gaze from us and back to the crew still gathered at the foot of the bed.

"Pretty easy to see, isn't it, Cap?" Gisella fired back, throwing her arms toward me and Finn. "That's our chef and chief stew — also known as my boyfriend and roommate."

I squeezed my eyes shut, wishing this was a nightmare I was going to shake awake from any second. I didn't miss the frustrated flare of Finn's nostrils at Gisella's accusation.

They weren't together anymore, but no one knew that except the three of us.

No way was Gisella going to admit that now.

And if it was our word against hers, I had a pretty good feeling who everyone would believe.

"Right," Captain said, severe. "Everyone, get to work. We have charter guests in six hours and this boat is in shit shape. We'll talk about this when our guests are satisfied and gone, understand? And not a word of it until then. I expect professionalism."

"You're going to let them stay?!" Gisella gaped at Captain, but when he arched a brow into his hairline, her mouth snapped shut.

I knew she wanted to argue, but to her credit, she fought it. Because while Captain may have wanted to get more of this story before he made any decisions, we all knew he wouldn't stand for even one second of insubordination.

No one moved for a breath, but then slowly, everyone started to shuffle. Palmer released his grip on Cameron, who immediately ran off — I assumed to find Leah. Bernard smirked at me with a wink on his way out, like we were best buds and he approved of my scandal.

Lovely.

Palmer waited for Gisella, trying to usher her out of the room with a hand at the small of her back. But she jerked away from him, muttering something under her breath with a glare that had Palmer's lips flattening as he chased after her.

Captain Gary stayed behind, the tension left in the room once it was just the three of us so thick I could have choked on it.

He looked at us, expression unreadable. His voice, when it came, was low and cold.

"You two. Get yourselves together and meet me in the bridge. Ten minutes."

He turned without another word, and I dropped my head into my hands.

My ribs ached with the struggle of my lungs trying to fill, my chest on fire like I was having a heart attack. My hands and feet went numb. My vision darkened at the edges.

Distantly, I was aware that Finn was trying to talk to me, that his hands were framing my face, his concerned eyes searching mine.

But his voice was muted, muffled by the ringing in my ears and the thrumming of my racing heart.

There was movement behind him, a camera duo adjusting to better see my face.

And that was it.

Like a caged animal who realized someone had forgotten to latch the door, I threw the covers off me, shoved Finn away, threw on my pajamas, and bolted.

I didn't know where I was going — just that I had to move.

I rushed through the hall, bare feet slapping against the stairs as I flew down them toward the crew quarters. I nearly ran into Palmer and Gisella on the way down. I heard Gisella scoff, heard someone call my name — maybe Finn, maybe Leah, maybe a producer — but I didn't stop. Didn't look back.

I took the corner too fast and slammed into a wall. Pain bloomed in my shoulder, but I kept going, sucking in oxygen like I was drowning and clinging to each sip of air I could catch when a wave receded. My cabin door was cracked open, and I all but dove inside, slamming it behind me and twisting the lock with shaking fingers.

Then I collapsed onto the bed, gasping.

Oh my God.

Oh my God.

Oh my God.

It's over.

It's all over.

Everything I'd worked for. Everything I'd dreamed of. Everything I'd sacrificed — all gone.

Because I'd let myself get lost in a moment of desire.

I cringed at the reality, shame washing over me at the same time I felt fists beating on my chest from the inside. I almost heard the voice screaming over the rattling of my breath, a distant cry that I shouldn't be ashamed, that I loved Finn and what happened between us wasn't wrong.

But I snuffed out that voice with a cold splash of reality.

I'd lost the respect of my crew. I'd lost their friendship. My third stew couldn't even look at me, and I couldn't blame her. I'd hurt her. Betrayed her. Betrayed them all for something selfish and stupid.

You don't believe that. What you have with Finn isn't stupid.

Again, I ignored that voice.

It was easier to latch onto the panic slowly taking me under. And when I remembered everything that had just happened was on camera, I started sinking faster.

A knock came at the door, followed by a muffled voice. "Ember? We'd love to get a quick interview while emotions are still fresh."

I raked my hands through my hair, face-planting into my pillow and screaming into it.

This cannot be happening.

But it was.

And there was nowhere to run, nowhere to hide.

Another knock. Another producer. "We're rolling, Ember. Just one minute. That's all we need. We have your mic here, if you don't mind putting this back on for us."

I curled tighter, shaking my head like I could will it all away. My skin was on fire. My mind was running so fast I couldn't hold onto a single thought. There was a commotion of noise and voices outside my door, and then another knock, this one louder.

"Em, it's me."

Finn.

My pulse answered his like it always had.

I wanted to run to him and fling myself into his arms as much as I wanted to throw him overboard. My skin was still warm from his, my soul still bound to him.

"Let me in, Firefly."

I shook my head even though he couldn't see me. I couldn't let him in — not right now, not when I only had minutes to get myself together enough to face our captain with him.

Captain Gary.

My heart flipped, bile rising in my throat as I imagined what he'd say. What he'd do. Would he fire me? Strip me of the role I'd worked years to earn? Blacklist me in the industry?

Would he even have to?

Once people saw the show, they'd be able to make up their own mind. No glowing letter of recommendation could overshadow what I'd just let the whole world bear witness to.

And then the worst thought of all slammed into me like an anvil falling from a skyscraper.

My father.

He was going to see this.

He was going to see all of it.

Every shameful second. The crew piling into the cabin. Me in bed with a man everyone thinks is still dating my roommate. Me choosing a thoughtless act of desire with Finn over everything I'd built. The fallout. The chaos. The scandal.

He wouldn't need to say a single word for me to know how he felt.

I could already hear his voice in my head.

I had one shot to prove to him that what I did mattered, that my career was valuable, that *I* was worth something.

Instead, I'd only proved to be the disappointment he'd bet on.

Tears burst from me like a dam breaking. I sobbed into my pillow, choking on the weight of it all — the failure, the humiliation, the sheer horror of being exposed in front of the entire world.

I'd once believed surviving the storm of my breakup with Finn would be the toughest thing I'd ever face, that if I could survive that, I could survive anything.

But there was no surviving this.

Chapter Twenty-Seven

POST-PRODUCTION CONFESSIONAL
CLOSE QUARTERS

SEASON 4

LEAH BROOKS: THIRD STEWARDESS

PRODUCER
Looking back now, did you know, walking into charter
eight, that it was going to be a disaster?

LEAH
I didn't know for sure, but I felt it. We all did.
It was like the wind picking up or the smell of
rain before a storm moves in. After what happened,
everyone was just… raw. Wound up. Looking for fights
rather than solutions.

PRODUCER
Do you blame Finn and Ember for the way the season
ended?

LEAH
They weren't the only guilty ones.

Finn was at my side as I rapped my knuckles on the door frame
leading to the bridge. He'd been there as soon as I opened my
cabin door, but he hadn't pushed me to talk, hadn't invaded
my space. He'd simply handed me my mic to strap back on, his

presence letting me know without words that he was there.

He knew what I needed right now, and I'd never been more thankful for that.

My ears were still ringing, heart still pounding like a jackhammer in my throat. The whole morning felt like a nightmare I couldn't wake up from, and yet it was all right on the heels of a dream I wished I could relive again and again.

It didn't make sense to me, how so many emotions could exist inside me at one time. How could I feel devastated for hurting our crew, guilty for betraying Eli and Leah and Gisella, but also elated from my reunion with Finn? My soul was on fire, body begging for me to seek comfort in his arms, and yet I felt sick at the thought of giving in to those desires.

It was too much to hold at once, and I wondered if Captain Gary could see the teetering tower of fragile dishes I was struggling to balance as he waved us into the bridge.

"Have a seat," he said, gesturing to the bench along the back of the bridge. A beautiful Mediterranean day sprawled out behind him, the water shockingly blue and little white puffs of clouds floating in the sky. It was such a contrast to the storm wrecking me inside.

Captain leaned a hip against the helm, folding his arms and staring at the floor for a moment before he lifted his gaze to meet mine and then Finn's.

There was no warmth in his eyes.

Captain Gary had always been firm, but fair. Blunt, but with a side of humor. But this... this wasn't the man who gave nicknames or winked when we nailed service. This wasn't the man who cheered on a cheeky dance during crew night out or tossed out jokes mid-docking to cut the tension.

This was the captain of a fifty-five-meter vessel.

And he looked ready to sink us both.

"I'm not gonna waste time sugarcoating it," he started, his voice low and clipped. "What happened this morning was a disaster. You know that. The crew knows that. The cameras sure as hell know that."

He paused, letting the weight of those words hang in the air, and I swore I could hear my heartbeat echoing inside the silence that followed. Said cameras were aimed right at us, capturing our lashing for everyone to see.

I didn't have the ability to be embarrassed anymore, not after this morning. I'd already sealed my fate with the viewing public. Now, all I could think about was my career and how the hell I could save it.

Okay, so that wasn't entirely true.

I was thinking of my career, yes, but I was also thinking of Finn, of the words we whispered to one another in the dark last night, the promises made, the confessions kissed against skin.

I chanced a glance at him, and though he didn't reach out for my hand or meet my stare, his hand twitched in his lap — a subtle sign that he was still with me.

But could we be together?

My heart crashed into my stomach at the thought that we couldn't, that there was no way for us to weather this without splitting. The right thing would be for us to stay apart, to do our jobs — if we even still had them anymore — and try to earn back the trust of the people we hurt.

But I couldn't stand the thought of losing him again after knowing what it felt like to have him back.

Could we possibly have both?

My gut churned like a stormy sea, those thoughts warring inside my head as I tried to focus on Captain Gary.

"I brought you two on as department heads," he said. "Leaders. People the rest of the crew could look to for guidance, for professionalism. And what I got this morning..." He shook his head. "Was a complete breakdown in trust."

My lungs burned, but I couldn't seem to pull a full breath in. Finn was still beside me, his forearms resting on his knees now, fingers interlaced so tight his knuckles had gone white.

Captain's voice hardened. "The moment you lost the respect of this crew, you lost the ability to lead them. And without leadership? Everything falls apart. Service. Deck. Galley. Interior. Doesn't matter how good the food is or how well the table's set if everyone's too busy watching the damn fallout to do their jobs."

I swallowed hard, vision stinging.

He was right.

This wasn't the type of job where coworkers could hate each other and still somehow make the final product shine. We had to be a united team or the guests would notice. Service would suffer — and so would our tip. It could get even worse than that. It could be so bad that the guests demanded their money back altogether — and this wasn't just a fifty-dollar dinner tab. This was a six-figure refund no one wanted to make.

Memories of the morning shocked me in rhythmic flashes of light, and I wondered how the hell we would work together seamlessly again after all that went down.

"I don't care what your reasons were. I don't care if it was love or lust or a bloody lapse in judgment. This—" Captain pointed toward the door like he could still see the explosion we'd left in our wake "—is drama. And I don't want it interfering with these last two charters. We've got guests flying in from halfway across the world, paying astronomical amounts for the experience of a lifetime. They didn't sign up for a soap opera."

He pushed off the helm then, standing tall.

"I'm not firing you. Yet."

My heart thudded with hope I didn't dare name.

"There are only two charters left, and frankly, I don't have the time or the resources to replace you. And technically, you haven't committed a fireable offense. But make no mistake — if things don't change, if the tension continues, if the crew keeps turning on each other because of the two of you?"

He stepped forward, eyes sharp as broken glass.

"I won't hesitate."

Finn nodded beside me, stiff. I did the same, forcing my head to move even though my entire body felt frozen.

"Keep your heads down. Do your jobs. Make amends with who you can, and lead. Together." He looked between us, that word heavy with expectation. "You don't have to like each other, you don't have to speak outside of what's necessary. But I expect the interior to function like a well-oiled machine. I expect dinner service to run without a hiccup. I expect you both to act like the professionals I hired."

The silence that followed his statement was heavy with that expectation.

"I don't want to fire anyone," Captain Gary said again, softer this time — but somehow even more dangerous. "But that doesn't mean I won't."

We both nodded once more. My mouth was dry as sand, but I managed to croak out my biggest fear.

"What about after the season?"

His gaze snapped to mine.

I hadn't meant for it to sound as broken as it did. But he knew what I was asking. Would this ruin me? Was I done? Captain had taken a chance on me this season. He'd given me my shot as chief stew.

Had I ruined it?

Captain's jaw ticced, his lips pressing into a flat, unreadable line. "We'll cross that bridge when we get to it."

He held my gaze, and something in his eyes flickered — not kindness, exactly. Maybe pity. Maybe frustration. Maybe a mix of the two.

"You're both damn good at what you do. But professionalism is half the battle, if not more, in this career. And I'm not sure a glowing recommendation from me can overshadow drama that makes a whole crew melt down."

I bit the inside of my cheek hard against the emotion threatening to overtake me from that little truth bomb. I knew he was right, but I'd hoped he could somehow reassure me that it would all be fine.

I hoped, somehow, this could all be fixed with the wave of a magical Captain wand.

"Dismissed," he said, turning back to the helm. "Get to work."

For a beat, Finn and I just sat there, like the lecture had stripped us of the ability to move, like our limbs no longer took commands from our brains.

Finn broke the spell first. He stood, slow and heavy, then waited for me to do the same.

We stepped out of the bridge, and the second we made it to the end of the hallway and paused at the stairs leading down to the crew quarters, my lungs turned to concrete.

It was a foreign sensation — and yet familiar all at once.

I'd been here before, this edge-of-a-cliff feeling. The moment when your body starts reacting before your brain can even label what's happening. My pulse was a war drum, thudding in my ears, in my throat, in my wrists. My chest tightened like a vise, ribs constricting, lungs shrinking, the air around me too thick to breathe.

I couldn't get a full breath. No matter how hard I tried, it wasn't enough.

It felt like drowning.

My fingers tingled, then went numb. My knees threatened to buckle. My skin went cold, clammy, a sheen of sweat blooming across my back even though I was shivering. Every sound was muffled except the rush of my own blood roaring in my ears.

Too much. Too fast.

Can't fix this. Can't breathe.

My thoughts splintered. Logic left the room. All that was left was panic, clawing up my throat like a scream with no exit.

My feet carried me down the stairs like they belonged to someone else, like they were just trying to outrun whatever explosion was building inside me. Every breath came too fast, too shallow, scraping down my throat like I was breathing in broken glass.

The words kept echoing.

I don't want to fire anyone. But that doesn't mean I won't.

Not sure a glowing recommendation can overshadow drama.

You've lost the trust of the crew.

I'd worked so hard.

I'd given everything to this job. Every late night, every impossible party theme, every tear I'd cried in a guest cabin while scrubbing a toilet — none of it mattered. I'd erased it all with a stupid, careless surrender to desire.

I felt so... human.

All of it — all the years of effort and sacrifice — were hanging by a thread now and fraying fast.

Because I couldn't stay away from him, even when I knew this was a possibility.

I nearly laughed at our stupidity. *I'll set an alarm. We can sneak back to our cabins.*

And then what?

What did we actually think would happen?

We didn't think. That was the problem.

"Ember," Finn said softly behind me.

I kept descending the stairs, not stopping when my feet hit the bottom. Eli was in the mess making himself a quick breakfast. His eyes shot to us before he tore them away, only muttering an, *"Excuse me,"* as he shuffled past us and up the stairs.

He could barely look at us.

"Em..." Finn said again.

His voice chased me down the hall to my cabin, but my head was roaring. Blood pulsed in my ears like the crashing of waves in a storm, and my heart was beating so hard I thought I might black out. My hands shook at my sides. My eyes burned.

No.

No, no, no.

This couldn't be it. This couldn't be how it ended — all of it, everything I'd worked for. It wasn't just the crew or the tip or the next charter. It was my future. It was my name. I could see it already, hear it in the whispers between captains, in the silence from potential employers.

Unprofessional. Unstable. Emotional.

"Ember, stop."

I didn't.

I couldn't.

I reached my cabin but walked past it, even though I knew I had nowhere to go but the end of the hall. I just hoped if I kept moving, the feelings would lose their grip. But they only got louder.

My father's voice joined Captain Gary's in my head. Cold. Clipped. Full of disappointment.

So this is the so-called job you've been so adamant about wasting your time on?

This is what you wanted me to take seriously?

This is what I was supposed to see as a valuable, stable, impressive career choice?

"Ember," Finn said again, more firmly now, catching up, stepping into my path. He blocked the end of the hall like I had anywhere to go even if I did shove past him. "Em, look at me."

His words nearly broke me.

"I can't," I gasped, voice cracking. "I can't— I can't fix this. I can't—"

"Hey. Breathe. Just breathe, alright? You're having a panic attack."

Panic attack.

The words made sense as soon as he said them, but my insides still bucked against that truth like it was a death sentence.

Finn stepped closer, slow, hands raised like he was approaching a wild animal.

Because I was. Inside, I was thrashing. Screaming. Splintering in a thousand directions, sharp and spinning and dangerous.

Finn's voice softened. "Can I just hug you?"

I blinked, like the words were a switch that finally cut through the ringing in my ears.

"Please," he said. "Just… one hug. One moment."

I was panting. I was so dizzy I felt like I could topple at any moment.

I think I nodded. I must have, because Finn gently reached for me, pulling me into him and slowly wrapping his arms all the way around me. He held me firmly, but not too tightly. He was supportive without suffocating me.

And as soon as he had me firmly in his grip, the moment I felt the permission to let him hold some of the weight…

I broke.

All the strength I'd been clinging to crumbled. My arms looped around his neck as I sagged into him, sobs bursting from me before I could stop them. I cried like I hadn't in years, cried until I couldn't see, until I couldn't breathe, until all I knew was the feel of him — the steady thump of his heart, the warmth of his arms, the way his hand cradled the back of my head like I might fall apart if he let go.

He didn't say anything. He just held me, rock steady and solid. And I didn't need a single word.

Because in his arms, I wasn't the chief stew. I wasn't the failure. I wasn't the drama.

I was just me.

And even if it was just for a stolen moment, I felt safe.

He shifted just enough to lean his cheek against my temple,

his voice barely a whisper against my skin.

"I know you need a moment," he said. "I'll give you that. But please, Firefly…" He pulled back just enough to see my face, his hand sliding up to tuck my hair behind my ear, fingers brushing tenderly along my jaw. "Don't push me away on this. Not now."

My eyes fluttered shut, breath shaking, but he kept going.

"I'm not sorry. I don't regret it. I don't regret us." His thumb swiped beneath my eye, catching a tear before it could fall. "It's just a show. It's cameras and chaos and carefully edited moments. But what's between us?" His voice dropped, low and sure. "That's real."

I pushed against his chest — reflexively, defensively. The words came out of me before I could stop them, raw and sharp. "We can't, Finn. This can't work." I shook my head even as more tears pooled in my eyes. "They'll keep coming for us. The crew. The producers. The guests—"

Finn didn't let me finish.

His arms stayed around me, grounding me, and his words cut through the spiral with a steady conviction.

"I don't fecking care, Em, and I'll be right here with you until you don't care either. Maybe we didn't find the right way back to each other," he said. "But we found a way. That's got to mean something. Hell, maybe it's the universe yelling at us this time instead of whispering the way it did two years ago."

I blinked up at him, lip trembling.

"We wasted so much time," he croaked, his voice heavy with regret. "Christ, I hate meself for that. We can't go back in time and change it, but for some reason, whether it was easy or not, we got our second chance. Don't let them tear us apart again. Not when we just found our way back. Not when it finally feels like we're home again."

My breath caught, chest still tight, but something shifted in it — like the panic didn't own me anymore. It was like when the downpour turns to a drizzle and then to a drip, like when the sun makes a rainbow before breaking up the clouds altogether

Finn was making space for something softer to grow in its place.

He touched my hair gently, threading his fingers through the strands. "They've already made up their minds about us, Firefly. Let 'em. Let them call us the villains. Let them talk. But we know the truth."

His eyes searched mine, burning with something that made my knees weak all over again. I clung to him instinctively — my lifeline, my home.

"We don't have to play into their narrative. We don't have to fight back or prove anything. We just keep our heads down, do our jobs, and be together. Quietly. Steadily. All in."

He kissed my forehead, soft and reverent.

"Don't you want that?" he whispered. "Because I swear to God, Em... it's all I want. *You* are all I want."

And somehow, that wrecked me more than the lecture had.

Because I wanted it, too.

I wanted it so badly the thought of not having it was enough pressure to crack a rib.

I nodded, over and over, and when Finn realized I was with him, his eyes shot open wide.

"Yeah?"

"Yes," I whispered.

And then I kissed him.

My fingers wove into his hair, holding tight as he wrapped me up in his arms and held me to him. Our kisses were frenzied and wild — just like our love.

I didn't know what came next.

I had no fucking idea how we would survive the next two charters, how we'd keep our teams working together when they all seemed ready to tear each other and the two of us apart. I couldn't control what story the production crew would tell, but I had a good feeling whatever was spun wouldn't reflect me or Finn in a good light.

It seemed impossible to stay afloat, and yet we were. We would. Together.

So, I kissed him with the cameras watching and the whole world judging.

And I buckled in for what I didn't know would be the wildest charter of my life.

Chapter Twenty-Eight

CHARTER CONFESSIONAL
CLOSE QUARTERS

SEASON 4, EPISODE 12
IN BETWEEN CHARTERS 7 AND 8

PALMER HUGHES: BOSUN

PRODUCER
Well, this morning was… something. How are you
feeling after the madness?

Palmer blows out a breath.

PALMER
Nervous. We've got a high-profile group of guests
coming aboard and everyone is at each other's
throats. Hard to work together as a crew when every
ounce of trust has been obliterated.

PRODUCER
So, what's your game plan to make it through the
charter?

PALMER
Keep my focus on the deck team and making sure they're
successful — but that sounds easier than it will be.
Eli's feeling foolish after that shit with Ember.
Cameron is sick over Leah shutting him out. Gisella
is…

Palmer swallows.

PALMER
No one is at their best right now. My job is to
make sure the guests can't tell. We need a perfect
departure, a smooth anchoring, water toys galore, and
a clean, safe deck. If we can pull that off, it'll
feel like a normal charter to the ones holding our
tip.

PRODUCER
And interior?

Palmer shrugs.

PALMER
Not my problem.

The dockside breeze carried the scent of sunscreen and saltwater, the sun peeking out between puffy white clouds on what should have been a perfect day. It was warm but not too hot, the water was smooth, the wind pleasant without being enough to make it an uncomfortable cruise.

I felt like a zombie.

I stood with my tray of Veuve, white blouse crisp and smile polished within an inch of its life, as the latest guests boarded *Sinking Sun*. They called themselves "The Successful Six" — a self-proclaimed name I'd only learned a few hours ago, thanks to the four-page preference sheet that read more like a *Forbes* feature and less like a hospitality request.

The tension had been thick at the table in the crew mess as Captain Gary read over everything, not a smile in sight. Palmer wouldn't look at either Finn or me, content to talk to Captain like we didn't exist. Finn and I chose to stay quiet for most of the meeting, chiming in only when necessary to give our opinion on something with service or food.

It *seemed* like a straightforward charter — a group of old

friends reuniting for a vacation with very little demands. There were a couple of food allergies, nothing Finn couldn't handle, and their one interior request was to have a "high school reunion" themed dinner and party where they got to give out superlatives to one another.

Even for the deck team, it was an easy setup: water slide, jet skis, requests to snorkel.

With the crew as wound up as we were, we *needed* an easy charter.

I crossed my fingers that this one would actually fall into that category in the end.

My head pounded as the guests made their way up the passerelle, each of them stepping out of their shoes at the bottom and placing them in the basket Eli was holding out for them. I was exhausted, both from the lack of sleep and the abundance of tears I'd shed in Finn's arms. I felt more hungover than ever, and I hadn't had an ounce to drink last night.

The guilt swirling in my gut didn't help, especially any time Eli would catch my gaze. He couldn't mask the anger and hurt there, and gone was the big goofy dude I'd come to adore all season.

He was shut off now, tight-lipped and sharp-jawed. And he made it very clear that he wanted nothing to do with me.

I owed him an apology, and very much wanted to give him one. But I knew now was not the time.

Tammy was our primary and the first guest to come aboard. Her hair was platinum blonde, her skin impossibly tan, and she was dripping in diamonds that probably weighed more than she did. She was in high-end real estate and made sure to mention it in nearly every sentence of her preference sheet. Her husband,

Russell, followed close behind, one arm slung around her waist, the other balancing an espresso martini he'd brought with him from the beach club. He was paler than she was, with jet black hair and a carefully trimmed beard. A rockstar in hedge funds, he wore no-show socks and mirrored sunglasses, and had the confidence of someone who once cheated on the SATs and got away with it.

Jacob was next, the very successful, very tortured artist. With warm brown skin and his lips in a flat, assessing sort of smile, he was all flowy linen and manicured fingernails. The bright silver jewelry he wore clinked like wind chimes as he shook hands with the crew.

Maria came after him, the stunningly gorgeous heiress-turned-jewelry mogul. Her waist-length black hair shined like silk in the sun, her smile blinding against her light brown skin. She seemed pleased as punch to be here, her grin the widest, though I could already sense the distaste of her so-called "friends."

Then there was Benny, the fashion designer who practically glowed with theatrical energy, followed by Katie — the quietest of the group and, incidentally, the bestselling author of psychological thrillers currently topping charts in both the US and UK. She gave me a tight smile that didn't quite reach her eyes. Benny was the tallest of the group, his skin a deep, dark brown and his black hair gathered in thick, gorgeous braids. Katie was his polar opposite, it seemed — petite and pale white, shrinking in on herself where Benny stood tall like he was used to being on a stage.

Tammy and Russell were married, but one look at Russell and Maria finding their way next to each other had my infidelity alarm blasting. Tammy couldn't hide her disdain for Maria, either. I wondered if it was because, in her eyes, Maria didn't fit with her inheritance being her success story, or if she knew what I already assumed about her husband's affection for the girl. Jacob and Katie had already let little snide remarks clip about the other, something about what constituted as art and literature. And with Benny, it seemed like he was here against his will, like these people *used* to be his friends but he felt like he was above them now in every way possible.

I could smell the drama from a mile away.

No doubt the producers had to, which was exactly why this group was here.

"Welcome aboard!" I greeted as brightly as I could muster after Captain's welcome speech, offering each of them a glass of champagne.

"This boat is just... stunning," Tammy drawled, turning a full circle with her designer skirt flaring in the wind. "Ugh, this is going to be the best Successful Six vacation ever."

I faked my smile so hard I was pretty sure I looked constipated. "We're so happy to have you. I'll give you a quick tour while the deck crew gets your bags stowed and we prep for departure."

It was dizzying, walking our new guests through the yacht and pretending like everything was peachy when there were ticking time bombs walking all around us. Not only was I anxious from the crew, but I was also spinning from my night with Finn. I was glad we talked a little last night, but we hadn't had time to really decompress from any of it. We hadn't had time to make a game plan or discuss how we were going to face the rest of this season. I longed for a stolen moment with him, for us to be able to curl up in bed together and sort through the knotted mess we'd found ourselves in.

But we were heads of department on a superyacht, leading a crew being filmed for a television show.

There was no time to stop, no time to plan.

And now, I was a fish out of water on a boat that should have felt like home.

By the time the Successful Six had unpacked their designer duffels and started requesting drones, floaties, and freshly muddled cocktails, the interior I was desperately trying to hold together was already slipping.

It all snapped when Leah mixed up a drink order. A gin fizz instead of a gin and tonic. A simple, harmless mistake — but it was one I knew I needed to catch before she took the drinks to the guests, especially because I had zero doubts that they'd know the difference and be sure to complain about it.

But I knew there was no way to give feedback and it go well in this moment.

"Leah," I said gently as I corrected the glass on the tray, "he actually asked for tonic, not fizz."

She froze, blinking at the drink and then at where she was making the next one. She didn't look at me. "Right. Got it."

Leah threw the shaker into the sink with such force it clattered loudly, and then she was angrily twisting the top off a bottle of tequila to work on the next cocktail.

"It's okay," I offered, reaching for her arm. "There's a lot happening—"

"I said I got it."

The words landed like a slap against my cheek. My nerves were shot from the morning, and even though I knew it would be pointless to try to talk to her about everything now, it was difficult not to. I wanted to explain myself, to make her hear me out, to prove to her that I valued our friendship, and I would have told her if I knew everything I knew now. I also wanted to comfort her, not from the pain I'd caused, but from that which I knew Cameron had. Leah's emotions were more complex than just feeling betrayed by a friend.

She had been lied to by a man she was considering moving across the world for.

I just wanted to hug her, to tell her it would all be okay — somehow, some day.

Instead, I stood there with my hand still reaching for hers and not a word in my mind that I felt would make anything better.

Leah ignored me, moving on to the martini request. When she poured entirely too much dry vermouth in, I grimaced.

"Hey," I said, lowering my voice. "If you need a break—"

"Why would I need a break?" she snapped, finally turning to face me. "You think I can't handle this?"

"No," I said quickly. "I... I just can see you might be a little shaken from the morning, which is understandable."

"Nothing shaken but this martini, and I'm only doing that because Russell thinks he's James Bond."

She clamped the lid on the shaker hard and got to work, the ice rattling, her arms tense.

"I'm trying to help," I whispered when she started pouring the drink. I knew just by looking at it that Russell would send it back.

"Right," she scoffed. "Now you care."

Bernard, who had joined us from where he'd been steaming a few clothing items for the guests down in laundry, finally spoke up then. "Alright, my darlings. Let's have a little perspective, yeah? It's barely midday — bit early to be drawing blood."

"Oh, now you care about the crew?" Leah's voice was sharp enough to cut bone. "Sorry, find that hard to believe after watching you stir the pot so much, I'm surprised you don't have tendinitis."

Bernard barely flinched. "Love, if you need a punching bag, may I suggest the gym? Or perhaps the Scot who has been telling you pretty lies. I warned both of you not to get caught up together." He pinned me with a glare next. "Guess I should have been handing out those warnings more liberally."

"We were *fine* until *you* pulled that shit in the hot tub," Leah said, poking Bernard hard in the chest with the *you*.

"Hey," I warned. "That's enough."

Bernard smiled at Leah. "I didn't poke holes in that boat, my darling. I just poured water in and made them harder to hide."

In the worst possible timing known to man, Gisella swung through the sliding glass doors from the deck, rapping her knuckles on the bar. "Guests are asking about their drinks. Need a hand?"

"Don't you think you've had your hands in enough places they don't belong lately?" Leah shot at her.

Bernard stifled a laugh.

"Okay, I think everyone is just a little frustrated," I said, hands on Bernard's arms as I turned him toward the deck. "Leah's got this. Bernard, why don't you go talk to the guests about lunch. Gisella, if you don't mind—"

"I mind," she spat before I could finish, and then she whipped around and stormed out of the salon, muttering something in Spanish under her breath. I didn't need to speak the language to know it was nothing nice.

I ground my teeth just as Leah sent more barware clattering.

"I don't need you coming to my rescue," she seethed, spinning toward me with fury in her eyes. "I don't need your support. I don't need your fake kindness or your *hands-on* management style or whatever the hell you're trying to do here."

"I'm not trying to do anything other than help," I defended, my professionalism slipping. "We're friends, Leah, and I can tell that—"

"Friends don't keep secrets," she said, cutting me off. "You didn't tell me the truth about Finn, not any of the times I tried to be there for you, and meanwhile, I told you *everything* about Cameron." She sniffed, her eyes welling. "And now, I'd bet my tip that you knew more happened with him and Gisella that night and didn't tell me."

My jaw hinged open. "Leah, I didn't. I swear. I—"

"Yeah, well, your word doesn't count for shit."

She lifted the tray of drinks then, not giving me so much as another glance as she side-stepped where Bernard and I still stood. She was out the door in the next breath, and a long, slow one deflated out of me.

Bernard's mouth twisted to the side. "Sorry, Em."

I swallowed, shaking my head. "It's fine. We just need to get back to work. Are you good?"

"Better than her," he said, tipping his head toward where Leah had stormed out.

I nodded. "She'll be okay. She's hurt, and rightfully so. Hopefully it'll blow over soon. Until then, I need you on your game. These guests will chew her up and spit her out if we don't back her up."

"Way ahead of you," he said, jumping behind the bar.

"What are you doing?

"Re-making that martini. God knows Russell isn't going to like whatever cloudy mess she's about to serve him."

I didn't know why, but my nose stung as I watched him get to work. "Thank you," I whispered.

He nodded, his eyes briefly catching mine before he focused on what he was doing. "And I'm sorry everything went down the way it did today. You and Finn don't deserve that." He paused. "Even if you are cheating little foxes."

I somehow managed a chuckle. "Would you believe me if I told you he and Gisella broke up days ago?"

"Yes," he answered, surprising me. "But I don't think I'm the one you need to prove anything to."

That twist in my gut was back in full force, and then my radio crackled.

"Interior — can I get a head's up on the lunch service timing?"

Finn's voice was a lifeline I didn't know I needed.

I cleared my throat. "On my way."

The galley smelled like garlic, roasted tomatoes, and something spicy I couldn't name. The second I walked in, it was like crossing into another universe — a quieter, less hostile one.

Finn was plating. Focused. Intentional. He heard me enter and was all business. "We still good for three o'clock? I'm on time, but I haven't heard from you. If I need to adjust, I can—" His voice cut off when he looked up and saw me. "What happened?"

"Nothing," I said quickly. Too quickly. "We're fine. Everything's... fine."

He studied me for one second too long before he stepped away from the cutting board. "Come here."

"I don't—"

"Have time?" He opened his arms, waving me toward him.

"Me either. But I'll make some for this. For you."

I exhaled and crossed to him, still holding tension like it might slip out and kill someone if I let go. Finn looked around — just a quick glance to confirm we were alone, aside from the cameras we couldn't escape — then reached for my waist.

One breath and his hands were on me, and the next, he was lowering his lips to mine.

It was unexpected, that soft, demanding kiss. I'd gone in for a hug and been met with something so much deeper. It wasn't rushed or hungry like last night.

It was an anchor.

My eyes fluttered closed. My hands twisted in his apron. I melted into him like honey over warm bread.

And for the first time all day, I breathed.

When he pulled back, his forehead rested against mine.

"We can do this," he whispered. "Two more charters. That's it. You're a leader, Em. You know what you're doing. You can handle this."

I tried to laugh, but it broke halfway out. "I can handle a crew that hates me?"

He pulled back just far enough to meet my eyes.

"You can handle anything. Because you're Ember Fecking Reed."

Another broken laugh from me.

"Because you're chief stew," he added, thumbing my jaw. "And you earned that title."

I stared at him for a long beat, those words rooting deep, loosening something heavy inside me. I nodded once. Then again. A little stronger.

"Okay," I whispered.

Finn kissed my forehead, warm and lingering.

"Now," he said, reluctantly breaking away and rounding the island back to the plates. "Talk to me. Are we good on timing for these?" He checked the clock on the wall. "Guests seated in thirty?"

I snapped back to the present, looking up at the same clock. It was two thirty.

"Yes. I'll go double-check with the guests now, but Tammy seemed adamant that they wanted food as soon as possible after anchoring."

"Brilliant. Go get 'em, Firefly."

He winked at me, and I felt a little lighter as I swept out of the galley and made my way to the sundeck.

I almost believed he was right, that I could do this, that it would all be okay.

Almost.

Chapter Twenty-Nine

PRE-PRODUCTION CONFESSIONAL
CLOSE QUARTERS

SEASON 4

GARY PARKS: CAPTAIN

PRODUCER
So, part of your stipulation before signing your contract for the show was that we require a mandatory day of safety training for each crew member.

CAPTAIN
That's right.

PRODUCER
Can you tell us more about that decision?

CAPTAIN
They should all already have a training or two under their belt, but I'm not taking any chances. It's stressful enough running a boat this size with demanding charter guests. Add the chaos of a reality show on top and, well — let's just say we're tempting fate. If something goes pear-shaped, I need to know my crew's not gonna freeze.

PRODUCER
What could go wrong?

Captain Gary laughs.

CAPTAIN
You're kidding, yeah? Anything. Everything. Guest could get hurt, there could be a fire, someone's off their face and making dumb choices, putting themselves or someone else in danger. Happens quicker than you think.

PRODUCER
What about man overboard? I see here that was something you specifically required in the safety training. Is that one that happens often?

CAPTAIN
Not often, but it happens. And it's bloody dangerous.

PRODUCER
Why's that?

CAPTAIN
If we're anchored and it's daylight, no worries. Warm water, good visibility - we're in and out, guest back on deck with a towel and a drink.

Captain swallows, pauses.

CAPTAIN
But you throw in a few variables - nighttime, choppy swell, vessel's underway - it's a different ballgame. You'd be surprised how fast you can lose someone in the water.

PRODUCER
Well, let's hope nothing like that happens.

CAPTAIN
From your lips to God's ears, mate.

We managed to survive day one of the charter, but as the sun set on day two, I swore I saw the smoke before the fire.

The light turned gold and soft across the water, casting long shadows over the teak deck. It should have been a moment of peace — the Successful Six dressed for dinner, cocktails in hand, laughing and seemingly enjoying each other's company. But the wind had picked up slightly, threatening to dismantle the carefully curated tablescape Bernard and I had worked so hard on.

And I felt that wind like the warning it was.

Bernard nodded his head at where Russell was leaning in close to Maria by the bar, his face pinched in concern as Maria confessed something in soft whispers. "Think there's anything between those two?" he asked.

I'd picked up on the oddities of our guests over the last day and a half, and though no one was outright saying it, I knew there were plenty of stories in this group. One thing I knew for sure was that I had been right about the general feeling around Maria — that she didn't belong.

Well, at least not to anyone but Russell.

He was married to our primary, but just like right now, I'd seen him spending more of his time with Maria than anyone else.

Fortunately for him, his wife was busy the whole charter trying to get the approval of her fashion designer friend. She begged to see his latest designs before showing him the houses she had closed on recently. It was easy to see by his flat lips that he was not impressed in the slightest.

I had no idea why anyone would want to spend time with people who clearly didn't care for them. It made me feel a bit sad for the rich and famous. From what I'd seen of them, it was damn near impossible to have real friends.

"Whatever it is, Tammy has been oblivious to it," I muttered back.

Just then, Tammy glanced over at her husband mid-laugh. The moment she saw who he was cuddled up with, her smile slid into a frown, her neck turning red.

Bernard ticced a brow. "Perhaps not."

The wind blew in a strong gust, and Bernard and I sprang into action, hands flying to cover the cards we had at each table setting. It was the high school reunion night theme they'd asked for, and we had cards printed per Tammy's request where they could vote for their favorites, everything from Most Likely to Shamelessly Brag to Most Likely to Die Alone.

Seemed a bit harsh to me, but she was delighted about the whole thing.

The wind died down again, and I was adjusting the ribbon around a menu when I heard the first shout.

It was indistinguishable at first, but my head whipped toward the sound just in time to see Russell flip the tray of drinks Leah had in her hands. It clattered to the deck.

Glass shattered everywhere.

"How many fucking times do I have to tell you to shake my goddamn martini?!"

Maria backed away from Russell just as Tammy came rushing over. "What in God's name is going on?"

"This genius can't make a cocktail to save her life, which is sad, considering it's the whole fucking point of her job."

I rushed over, trying to calmly, but firmly, contain the situation. I gently squeezed Leah's shoulder when I realized she was trembling. But the second I touched her, she shrugged away, dropping to the deck to put her focus on picking up glass.

"If I could have all of you step over here away from the glass, that would be best for safety reasons," I said, trying to usher the group toward the table. "Dinner will be ready soon, and—"

"Shit!"

We all turned toward Leah, who was sitting back on her heels now, her hand held up as she inspected it.

Blood dripped from a nasty cut on her middle finger.

"Serves her right," Russell muttered.

That did it for me.

"Sir, I understand you're upset about your drink. Bernard will rectify that immediately." Bernard jumped into action as I said the words, dashing inside to make a new martini. "But I need you to know that we will not tolerate any abuse toward our crew, verbal or otherwise."

"Abuse?" He laughed. "You Gen-Z kids are so fucking sensitive."

"Russ," Tammy chastised, yanking him toward the railing. "You will not ruin this trip for me." She smiled back at me over her shoulder, mouthing, *"I got him."*

I gave her a weary look that I wasn't so sure, but there was no time to dwell on it. Instead, I raced for the first-aid kit just inside the sliding glass doors and then right back to Leah.

"Let me see," I said, digging through the kit for tweezers.

"I'm fine."

"You're bleeding."

"I'm *fine*," she shot at me again, and then I felt a hand squeezing my shoulder. I looked up to find Eli with a sympathetic, but strained, smile. He bent down to join us, then nodded his head toward the waiting guests.

It was my cue to leave.

Reluctantly, I stood, backing up when Palmer swept in to finish cleaning up the mess. I had a dinner service to prepare for, so I was thankful for everyone's help.

But it didn't make the judgment in their eyes any easier to stomach.

I checked in on Russell and the other guests, making sure

no one had caught a rogue glass shard. By some miraculous feat, Bernard had Russell laughing by the time we sat them at the table, and Leah didn't need stitches.

I thought we'd made it out unscathed.

The guests' asses had barely hit the chairs when Finn's voice cut in over the crew radio.

"Ember, Ember, Finn. Can you come to the galley as soon as possible?" His voice had an edge to it that made the hair on my arms raise.

"Copy, on my way."

I bolted for the galley with a short instruction for Bernard to get wine service started, and when I slid into Finn's domain, I paled.

The galley was filled with smoke.

"What the hell happened?!"

I picked up the nearest dishtowel and started waving it in the air, trying to disperse the smoke before an alarm went off. Captain Gary ran in next, cursing before he was on the radio telling engineering to get ready to cut the alarms.

"No idea," Finn said. "The oven shorted, I think. Something electrical? The whole unit is out — burners, too."

"Engineering is on the way," Captain said.

"Are you okay?" I asked Finn, registering that he was running his hand under the faucet.

"Just a little burn," he promised. "I thought I'd be a hero and save dinner, but the lamb is toast. Literally. And I've got no heat on the second course. No mains, no sides. Nothing. Unless you want to serve them raw fennel and vibes."

"Would have worked for our first charter guests, wouldn't it?" Captain Gary tried to joke. I couldn't find the humor. "It's alright, team. We can handle this. Take a breath and think."

"We... can serve salads. And we have the griddle," I said. "It's high school reunion, right? What if we did old cafeteria staples — elevated grilled cheese, maybe some sloppy joes. We can use the microwave for that, can't we? Grill up some meat?"

Finn looked unsure, shaking his head, but he sighed in agreement that we had to do *something*. "I'll pivot, but I need someone to run interference out there."

I nodded. "I'm on it."

I swung out of the galley, eyes landing on where Eli was finishing up the bandage on Leah as I smoothed my hands over my black dress and tried to troubleshoot what the hell I was going to do to save this dinner.

I was intercepted before I made it to the deck.

"Ember." The name came from Brittany, one of the producers, who stepped right in my path. "Can we get a quick reaction shot from you?"

I stopped, blinking rapidly, sure I'd misheard her. "Now?"

"It's a perfect moment. Things are kind of blowing up and we'd like to capture the raw thoughts going on inside your head at the moment."

I stared at them.

"Are you out of your mind?" I shoved past her, noticing some commotion on the deck behind her.

"Just one question."

"I said no."

The sliding glass doors slid open for me to join the guests on deck — right as another scream rang out.

"Fuck! My ankle!"

The commotion I'd been witnessing from inside was Benny and Jacob nearly fighting. Apparently, one of our camera operators had tried to intervene before things got too serious.

And paid the price for it.

Luke was sprawled on the deck now, clutching his ankle and grimacing at the sight of the expensive camera gear he'd lost control of in the process of the fall. Brittany gave up hassling me and focused on making sure the equipment was okay while Eli grabbed the first-aid kit we had yet to even have time to put away, his focus on Luke now.

"Jesus Christ," I breathed.

Then the wind picked up again.

A heavy gust slammed through the sundeck, flipping over menus, superlative cards, half the centerpiece Bernard and I had assembled with painstaking care. Linen napkins the guests had taken out of the metal rings were whipped over the railing. I scrambled after what I could, heart pounding.

My radio crackled again.

"Interior — Finn. I figured dinner out. I need ten minutes and an extra set of hands."

"On my way," Leah responded, and I knew from the crack in her voice that she'd been crying.

My chest tightened, but before I could think too much on it, Palmer appeared on the deck, his expression tight.

"Hey. I just spotted a vessel drifting." He pointed off the starboard side. "Pretty sure they pulled anchor. They're coming toward us." He picked up his radio and barked into it, my skin prickled. A drifting vessel could cause a big bill for our owners — or worse, an injury for one of us on board. "Captain, this is Palmer on the bow. We've got a vessel adrift. Heading our way."

"Good eye. I'll try to radio them now. Grab as many fenders as you can and prepare for a collision," Captain said back, his voice calm and even despite the possible disaster.

And that's when I heard it.

A splash.

Distant, but distinct.

Every nerve in my body froze.

All the voices from the guests and the radio muted as I turned and ran for the swim platform, scanning wildly. My eyesight was twenty-twenty, but that didn't mean shit now that the sun had set. I peered through the dusky night, and by some sort of miracle, I saw her.

Maria was in the water.

"Oh, God." Panic sliced through me, and when I turned, I realized Captain had ordered the anchor up. Cameron was already working on it, probably so Captain could maneuver around the drifting vessel Palmer had spotted.

But if we started moving, we'd lose Maria. The wind was up, which meant the swell was, too.

No one had noticed — not the guests, not the producers, not a single member of our crew, who were all pulled in other directions handling chaos.

And Maria was drifting. Head dipping.

I didn't have time to wait for someone else to help me.

"Guest in the water!" I screamed, and then picked up my radio. "Man overboard! Man overboard!"

I barely got the words out before my shoes were off, radio dropped, mic stripped. I somehow remembered my training enough to throw the life preserver in; though I knew even as I did it that it would be pointless with the swell carrying her so quickly.

And then I dove in.

The world was muffled for the brief moment I was underwater, and then I emerged to the sounds of screaming from the boat and screaming from Maria, who was at least twenty meters away from me. I swam as hard as I could, thankful for the years of lessons I took and the rigorous training I went through before I ever worked on a boat.

Every time you trained for a situation like this, you prayed it would never happen. For many, it never would.

I didn't have such luck.

Saltwater slapped against my face as I struggled to time my breath with the waves I was fighting against. My muscles screamed, the current strong, the light fading more and more as we rotated farther from the sun.

All I could do was keep my focus on Maria. She did her best to swim toward me while I swam toward her. It was easier for me, the waves carrying me out, but they tried to do the same to her. She fought hard.

And then she disappeared beneath the water.

My adrenaline spiked, legs kicking harder, arms swinging. I dove when I thought I was close to her, the saltwater stinging my eyes as I opened them underwater and searched for her.

She was kicking toward the surface, and I swam with all my might until I reached her.

The moment my hand reached her, hope trickled in.

We both emerged, just in time for another swell to cover us. But we spit the water out, and Maria was gasping, clinging to me, threatening to sink us both if she didn't calm down.

I looped an arm around her chest and kicked hard for the boat. "You're okay," I told her, not even sure she could hear me. "I've got you."

The tender reached us just as my arms began to give out.

I heard the low whir of the motor over the crashing waves and nearly sobbed in relief when I spotted Palmer at the helm, eyes wide and frantic as the boat bounced toward us. Behind him, Eli crouched at the bow, arms braced and ready.

"Ember!" Palmer shouted over the wind. "We've got you!"

I nodded, barely able to lift one arm in response, and then Eli reached for Maria first, hoisting her up into the tender.

As soon as she was safe, those strong arms were hauling me up and over the side of the tender like I weighed nothing. I collapsed against the cool vinyl bench, chest heaving, heart hammering against my ribs.

Eli dropped beside me, his hand on my back, breathing hard. "You alright?"

I nodded, but I was already looking for Maria.

She was curled in on herself, shivering so violently her teeth chattered. Palmer called our safety in over the radio, saying we were en route to the yacht. Captain radio'd back that the drifting vessel had responded and were no longer a threat. Anchor had been dropped again.

I held Maria's hand and tried to comfort her while I felt my own shock settling in.

By the time we reached the swim platform, a crowd was waiting.

Captain Gary stood at the stern, expression grim as he helped pull Maria up into Cameron's waiting arms. Cameron wrapped her in a big blanket immediately. Cameras were rolling. Producers were whispering furiously behind them. Tammy made a dramatic scene upon Maria's return, crushing her in a hug that the rest of the guests side-eyed, cocktails in hand.

"What happened?!" she asked. "We were so scared!"

Maria was shivering, her eyes flicking to me. "I just slipped. I... I was looking over the edge... I thought I saw dolphins. I climbed onto the railing a bit to get a picture on my phone and..."

Tammy wrapped her in another dramatic hug, wailing.

I blinked when Palmer extended a hand for mine. He helped me climb onto the swim platform, but I was too exhausted to move past that.

"Medics are on their way," Captain said, his voice tight. "I

need to make sure the guest is okay. You need to get warm, too."
He snapped his fingers at someone. "Blankets. Hot tea. Check for
injuries."

I barely heard him, but managed a nod to let him know I was
okay.

"You saved her life, Ember," Captain said. Then he turned to
tend to Maria.

And Finn was there.

He shouldered past everyone the moment Captain no longer
needed me, eyes blazing as he dropped to his knees at the edge of
the platform.

"Jesus, Ember—" He grabbed my face in his hands, cradling
it while he looked me over like he might find a shark bite. "Are you
hurt? Are you—fuck—you're so pale. I thought—I thought—"

I couldn't speak. Couldn't form a single word with how my
throat burned and my limbs shook. I just nodded, eyes stinging
as I leaned into him.

"I thought you were gone," he whispered, pressing his
forehead to mine. "I thought the swells—Christ, I..."

His words trailed off as he kissed me — hard, desperate, not
caring who was watching. I clung to him like a life raft.

"I'm okay," I murmured, my voice barely audible. "I'm okay."

Finn broke the kiss with a ragged breath, scanning me,
searching again. Then he was up, helping me to my feet and
wrapping an arm around my waist.

"Let's get you warm. Blankets! Now!" he barked at no one in
particular, voice hoarse but commanding.

Someone shoved two into his arms — Bernard, I thought —
and he wrapped one around my shoulders, tugging me close again
as he led me inside. My legs felt like Jell-O, and I leaned into him

fully, too weak to fight the comfort of his touch.

And it was the only comfort I'd find, too.

Because not a single other member of the crew checked on me.

The medics came. Maria was cleared first and then me. Finn's dinner was abandoned, Captain Gary calling in a big order of pizza and fielding the guest complaints for us. Fortunately, they were a little too busy fighting over who had been voted what in their little superlative game to care too much. I was sure the fact that Leah kept the drinks coming didn't hurt, either.

I felt bad for Maria. Her so-called friends were content to get right back to their vacation, no one other than Russell showing much more than a blip of concern. Tammy stopped her fake dramatics as soon as the cameras moved their attention back to the crew, and even Russell was subdued in his concern — likely to not raise any flags with his wife.

Other than Captain Gary and Finn, no one really asked about me, either. Palmer and Eli had checked in briefly, but it was the kind of check-in you do when protocol requires it. Once the med team cleared me, it was as if I'd vanished — like I hadn't just jumped into open water on a moving boat to pull a charter guest from the sea.

I didn't expect a hero's welcome. But I thought... I don't know. I thought maybe Leah would've stopped by. Just to say hey. Just to make sure I was okay.

Instead, I sat alone at the bow, wind in my hair and hot tea clutched in my hands. Finn held me without a word, solid and warm beside me even though I knew he had a galley to clean and a half-finished dinner to salvage. The boat hummed around us, the occasional burst of laughter from the guests floating down from the upper deck like it was a different world entirely. They were playing some game, or maybe still bickering over superlatives. I didn't know. I didn't care.

I stared out into the endless black of the sea, moonlight glinting off the waves like shattered glass. Everything was calm now — too calm. Like the ocean itself was trying to pretend it hadn't almost swallowed one of us whole.

But I remembered. My lungs still burned. My arms still ached. My heart still hadn't found its normal rhythm.

"I don't know if I can do this," I whispered.

The words tasted like failure, like salt and shame and the thousand things I'd been too afraid to admit out loud. It had been the longest, hardest day of my life, and as much as I wanted to be strong, I didn't feel it.

I was letting down the version of myself who used to be so sure. But tonight had cracked something wide open. I wasn't invincible. I wasn't immune to fear. And I wasn't sure I could keep pretending I was.

Finn held me, silent but steady.

"I know how they'll cut it," I said, voice low, bitter. "I can see the edit already, how they'll make it seem like I'm unstable. Unhinged. Reckless. They'll make it look like I jumped for attention, like I was trying to be the hero for applause than just doing the right thing. And I won't be able to defend myself. I'll just be the girl who lost it on camera."

I shook my head, the salt of the sea and my own frustration stinging behind my eyes.

"No matter what I do, I can't win."

My voice cracked, the words catching in my throat.

"What was it all for?"

Finn's arm tightened slightly around me, but he didn't speak. I appreciated that he was giving me the space to feel through everything without trying to fix it. He just let me sit in the sadness of it all, letting me know I wasn't alone.

"I really... I really don't know what the point is anymore."

He exhaled slowly beside me, rubbing my back. "Then we walk away," he said. "Screw the cameras. Screw the job. Let's leave. You and me. Tonight. We'll pack a bag and go."

I turned to look at him, and there was nothing but sincerity in his eyes.

And for a moment, *God*, I wanted to say yes. I wanted to take his hand and fly down the stairs to the crew quarters, pack our shit, and be off the boat in the next thirty minutes. I imagined us hiding away in a hotel somewhere in Naples, getting lost in each other and pretending like the rest of the world didn't exist.

But there was this part of me still burning despite the waves that had tried to douse every flame. It may have only been embers, but by my namesake — that was enough.

I shook my head. "No."

Finn's brow furrowed, but he didn't push. He just waited — silent, patient.

I sat up straighter, setting the half-empty mug of hot tea to the side.

"I'm not ready to give this up," I said, and the admission cracked my heart wide open. "I love this job. I love what I do. I've worked too damn hard to let a production team or a mean crew or some bored internet trolls take it from me."

I took a shaky breath, the wind whipping at my frizzed ponytail, the stars overhead like a thousand tiny witnesses.

"I don't need them to see me. I don't need the crew to like me. I don't need the audience to follow me online or my dad to say he's proud. I know what I did today. I know who I am. And I'm a damn good chief stew."

The corner of Finn's lips tilted up, his eyes beaming as they flicked between mine. "Fecking right, you are."

"I deserve to be on this boat. I deserve this career. I deserve this dream. And I'm not walking away, even if they wish I would. *Especially* because they wish I would."

The fire that had dimmed in me since the moment I surfaced with Maria in my arms sparked again, small but sure. Those embers were hot and alive and just waiting to catch.

Finn watched me for a long moment, then he wrapped me up tighter, his lips on my temple.

"That's my girl," he murmured, the words carrying on the wind.

Warmth found me for the first time since I dove into the water, and I burrowed into Finn, into the comfort he provided. I was almost shocked by the fact that I meant what I said.

I really didn't care what my father thought anymore — or anyone else.

Maybe all it took for me to drop the weight of their expectations was to realize this was *my* life, to live the way *I* wanted to.

I didn't have the power to make everyone in the world understand me, but I did have the power to give myself the approval I'd been wishing for.

I pulled in a deep breath, the sea air sharp and clean in my lungs, and let it anchor me.

Let them edit me into a villain. Let the crew whisper behind my back. Let my father never see the value in what I've built.

I know what I'm worth.

"Finn."

"Mm?"

I lifted my chin, eyes finding his in the dark. "Take me somewhere?"

Our shift wasn't over. We had so much we still needed to do — clean the galley, prep food for tomorrow, clean up dinner service, make sure the guests were okay.

But for the moment, the rest of the crew had it handled. I didn't know how long they'd give us this pass so I could regain composure, but I knew I didn't want to waste what time we had just sitting here.

I needed him.

Finn swallowed, the motion thick in his throat before he helped me stand. I thought I saw a hint of a smile. "Trying to get us in trouble, Firefly?"

"Won't be any trouble if we're not caught."

That had his eyes lighting, his fingers dragging the length of my arm until he took my hand in his.

"I know a place."

Chapter Thirty

CHARTER CONFESSIONAL
CLOSE QUARTERS

SEASON 4, EPISODE 13
CHARTER 8

GISELLA DÍAZ: DECKHAND/STEWARDESS

PRODUCER
Are you okay after all the craziness last night?

GISELLA
It wasn't that crazy. Deck team had a pretty great day, I think. It was the interior going off the rails.

PRODUCER
You aren't shaken up by the fight between the guests or Maria going overboard?

GISELLA
I'm not shaken by much these days.

PRODUCER
What did you think of Ember jumping in to save—

GISELLA
Oh, *por favor*. Are we really going to make this a thing? She saw someone go overboard so she jumped in. Any one of us would have done the same, it's really not the big heroic act she's trying to make it out to be.

PRODUCER
So, you didn't see Maria go overboard?

Gisella pauses.

GISELLA
Of course not. Why, did someone say I did? I was
helping Palmer with the drifting vessel situation. He
can vouch for me.

PRODUCER
No one said anything.

GISELLA
Oh. Okay, good. Because I didn't see.

PRODUCER
But you don't think what Ember did was brave?

GISELLA
¿Crees que la voy a aplaudir? I'm not giving any kind
of praise to the girl who pretended to be my friend
while she was hooking up with my boyfriend.

PRODUCER
Finn claims you two broke up before he and Ember
reconnected.

Gisella crosses legs, uncrosses them, stands.

GISELLA
Well, we didn't.

PRODUCER
He also said you—

GISELLA
Haven't you learned by now that everything out of
that man's mouth is a lie? I have to get to work.

Gisella exits.

Finn didn't waste a second.

The blanket abandoned on deck, he grabbed my hand and
tugged me toward the aft companionway, ducking low to avoid

the mounted camera fixed to the overhead beam. I barely stifled a laugh as I followed, breath catching when we passed the bar — where Bernard's voice floated out in a lazy hum, just a few steps away from spotting us.

Finn pressed his finger to his lips, then grinned like a kid up to no good as we crept past, shoulders brushing, our footsteps featherlight on the teak flooring.

We slipped through the service corridor, navigating narrow passageways that twisted around guest cabins and crew storage closets. When we crept down a second set of stairs that was steeper and narrower, a shortcut used mostly by engineers, my stomach cartwheeled.

Every step we took felt like peeling away another layer of logic.

The air grew warmer the deeper we went, thicker — charged with the scent of grease and diesel, mechanical heat and metal.

When we reached the heavy, steel door marked ENGINE ROOM – AUTHORIZED PERSONNEL ONLY, I was panting.

"Finn, we can't," I said on a laugh, glancing at the warning sticker plastered below the handle. But my body buzzed in anticipation.

And I knew Finn was wordlessly refuting my argument when he smirked and twisted the handle, pulling me inside.

The door clanged shut behind us.

Instantly, we were engulfed in a low, bone-deep rumble — the hum of the engines reverberating through the floor and walls. Everything vibrated, the sensation embedding itself in my chest and ears. It mirrored the way I felt inside, and as if the room provided cover for it, my desire ramped up, need coursing through me like wildfire.

The space was tight but not cramped. Pipes lined the walls like tangled veins, wrapped in insulation and marked with colored tape to signify their purpose — fuel, coolant, seawater. Massive engines sat in the center of the room like sleeping beasts, humming with restrained power, their housing gleaming with silver bolts and oil-slicked shadows. Overhead, fluorescent lights flickered against metal grates and hanging tool racks, casting hard-edged shadows along the bulkheads.

A rolling mechanic's stool rested beside a workbench cluttered with rags and wrenches. A fire extinguisher was strapped into its holster near the back wall, beside a metal locker used for spare parts. The air was stifling — warm, stale, metallic.

Heat was already sticking to me like humid night air, and it only fueled me more.

I turned to Finn, half-laughing, half-scolding, "You've got to be kidding me."

He grinned, tapping his ear. *Can't hear you*, that motion said.

I rolled my eyes, laughing louder this time, confident that the sound would be drowned out by the machines. My blacks still clung to my skin, the fabric damp from my time overboard, and I watched Finn's gaze heat as he dragged it along every curve my wet dress hugged.

His nostrils flared, igniting the flame inside me more.

His apron was half-discarded, the neck strap undone, and the fabric slung low across his hips. His chef's jacket was unbuttoned just enough to expose the gleam of sweat at his collarbone, the rise and fall of his chest mirroring my own labored breathing.

His sleeves were shoved up to his elbows, forearms corded with tension, hands flexing like he wasn't sure what to do with them now that he had me alone.

There was something devastating about the way he wore the aftermath — sweat slick on his brow, flour smudged across his chest, his bandaged hand a reminder of the way this night had burned us both. Somehow, the mess only made him hotter.

He took a tentative step and then another, time slowing as his hands reached for me. He framed my face, thumbs hooking at my jaw as his fingers curled into my damp hair. One tilt of his hands and my neck was arched for him. One flick of his tongue wetting his lips and then his mouth covered mine.

I inhaled the kiss, the steam, the tantalizing feeling that we could get caught at any moment. Finn pulled at my hair tie, gently unfastening it until my hair fell in a damp mess of frizzy waves. Then, his fingertips were on my scalp, hands fisting my hair as he let out a guttural groan.

Those hands were rough and certain, that mouth confident and sure. There was no hesitation, even though we were breaking every rule in the book. The heat of him, of the room, of *everything* had me struggling to catch my breath as I melted into him.

When I started unfastening the buttons of his chef's jacket, he broke the kiss to watch me, his mouth curling. He leaned in, lips brushing the shell of my ear.

"No cameras here," he said, his voice barely audible over the engine's growl. "No crew. Just us."

I didn't have time to react before I felt him gather the hem of my dress, hiking the wet fabric up with determined hands. Goosebumps paraded over my thighs as I hooked my arms around his neck.

"We have to be quick," I warned, panting, my palms braced

against his chest.

He grinned, and when he bit down gently on my neck, just below my jaw, I let out a moan just because I knew I could.

"Challenge accepted."

There was no use trying to talk after that. We could barely hear each other, anyway, and we didn't have time to whisper sweet nothings. In that moment, I needed him — on me, around me, inside me. Any centimeter of distance was too much, and I climbed him with a yearning that didn't need words to translate.

My grip fastened around his neck, one leg hiking up as he backed me into a machine humming with lights and switches. A glass case covered those switches, serving as our headboard as Finn pressed into me and kissed me harder.

One of his hands held my ass firmly as the other fought with his belt. I reached between us and tugged my thong to the side, enough to give him access. And there I was, torn again between the desire to slow down and savor every taste of him and the need to satisfy the ache between my legs immediately, to claw at his back until he gave me what I wanted.

But we were playing a risky game, sneaking away during shift and while the charter guests were still awake. Everyone might assume I was taking a break to gather myself, but that break would only be allowed for so long before Captain Gary would expect me to get back to work — and so would my team.

So as soon as Finn wrenched down his zipper, I helped him maneuver his briefs, both of us groaning when I wrapped my hand around his cock and pulled him free. I spat on my hand, smoothed it over him, and lined him up at my entrance. I was already wet. It was so fucking hot, the desperate need we couldn't control, the way we were playing with fire and risking it all because we couldn't stand one more second of not being together.

Finn moved my hand out of the way once his crown was notched inside me, and then his hands found my waist and he slammed it home. I arched off the glass and dug my nails into his neck, his back, crying out as he withdrew and slid in again — just as hard, just as deep.

It was a wild frenzy of hands and mouths, of gasps and groans, the hum of the engines drowning out the sound and somehow amplifying it, too. I stretched to accommodate him more and more with each thrust, and Finn kept the pressure of his body against mine, rocking my hips so my clit found the perfect friction.

Last night, I'd been suspended in disbelief. I couldn't wrap my head around how I'd ended up in bed with Finn after everything that had happened between us, after months of whatever games we'd been playing.

But tonight, all I felt was how inevitable we were.

He was mine. I was his. Every flex inside me reminded me how my heart and body and mind and soul belonged to him.

There was every reason for us to stop this before it even had the chance to start when it all went to hell this morning. I could have run away. I *tried* to, but Finn wouldn't let me. He saw how afraid I was and how I wanted to hide away before I even realized what it was, and he held me through it.

He didn't walk away from me, even though that would have been the easiest thing to do.

He chose me even when he knew the whole world would judge him for it.

And I chose him, too.

Cameras, production team, crew, and world be damned.

Our skin was sweat-slicked and hot, Finn's forehead pressed to mine as he pushed inside me again and again. His hand wrapped around my neck and held me to him, his mouth bruising mine as his grip tightened just enough to make me sigh and whimper and beg for more.

It was all encompassing, the buzzing of the room and the electricity coursing through Finn straight into me. Every nerve in my body was tuned into where he touched me and kissed me and fucked me. Nothing else mattered. There was no past and no future.

It was just us, right here, right now, forever, unending.

I came in a slow build of shocking numbness, fire licking at my ribs until I combusted. I let myself cry out Finn's name, let him swallow that sound with a punishing kiss as he groaned out his own release. But he didn't stop. We both moaned at the feel of him sliding in and out with ease now, knowing it was his cum providing that extra lubrication.

And that spawned us right into round two.

Finn gripped my ass in his hands, my legs wrapping around him as he carried us over to the rolling engineer stool. He sank down in it with me in his lap, and then his fingertips ran through the line of my ass and dipped to where we were still connected.

"Fuck." I saw his mouth form the word more than I heard it, and my eyelids fluttered at the sensation of him rubbing the wetness between us, coating his shaft with it before he'd fill me again. He held his slick fingers out for me to taste, a moan rumbling through him when I sucked them clean.

And then his hands were on my ass and helping me ride.

I tilted my hips forward, catching that pressure against my clit with every rock. I was already so sensitive from my first release that I was a trembling, whimpering mess. Finn let me set the pace, content to enjoy the show, his gaze devouring every twitch of my muscles, every pant that left my lips. His hands roamed up my back, then down again, thumbs tracing reverent circles over the curve of my ass before gliding inward, gripping my hips to guide me deeper.

I rocked harder, then softer, chasing that edge but not quite tumbling over it. Something shifted between us — the urgency still there, still pulsing like electricity beneath our skin, but the desperation gave way to something deeper.

I swore I felt his heartbeat mirroring mine as Finn leaned in, brushing a strand of damp hair behind my ear before cupping my face in both hands. His thumbs stroked my cheeks as I moved on top of him, our foreheads pressed together, breath mingling in the heat between us.

His kiss came softer this time — no bite, no hunger. Just slow, aching devotion. That kiss was an impenetrable steel beam in a storm. It was an anchor grounding us to the moment.

"I've got you, Firefly," he mouthed against my lips, too quiet to hear over the engines but I felt every syllable. "I always will."

I winced, not because the words hurt, but because I couldn't articulate what it meant to hear them. I sat fully on him before grinding in a slow circle, shivering when his forehead fell to my shoulder. Then his lips were on me, kissing and climbing until I grabbed his face in my hands and forced him to look at me.

I didn't need him to say more. I saw it in the shadow and light playing on his skin, felt it in the way he held me like I was something worth fighting for. The world outside this engine room didn't matter. Not the cameras, the whispers, the reputation I'd be handing over when this aired. Not my past. Not his.

We had one more charter to survive and then we could walk away from all of this and build something new.

Together.

I moved again — slower, deeper — and he breathed my name like a vow.

There was still sweat between us, still tension, still friction and heat and the ache of release building again. But now, those sensations surrendered to the deeper emotions within.

Trust.

Forgiveness.

Love.

And I knew, from that moment on, it was us against the world.

Chapter Thirty-One

POST-PRODUCTION CONFESSIONAL
CLOSE QUARTERS

SEASON 4

EMBER REED: CHIEF STEW

PRODUCER
Well, I think that's all we need for now, Ember. We want to thank you again for coming in for some bonus footage and commentary. We know the season wasn't what you expected. We appreciate you being so open.

Ember laughs, stands.

EMBER
I don't think I had a choice with that whole *open* part.

PRODUCER
Is there anything else you want to say before you take your mic off for the last time? Anything you really want the viewers to know about you?

Ember pauses, smiles.

EMBER
There's nothing I can say to make them change their minds about me, and that's okay. Because I know who I am. I know my intentions. I know my truth. And that's enough for me.

PRODUCER
What about your father?

Ember looks directly into camera.

EMBER
I love you, Dad. You raised me to be a strong,
independent, intelligent woman. Thank you for
instilling bravery in me, for always reminding me I
can do hard things, and for passing on a little of
your stubbornness, too.

PRODUCER
That's it?

Ember smiles, begins removing microphone.

EMBER
What else is there to say?

Four days later, I laid in my bunk with Finn, covers kicked to our feet and limbs tangled into a pretzel. Gisella was already on deck for the early shift — not that I would have cared much at this point — and we had a few minutes before Finn needed to get started on breakfast for the guests and I'd go help Leah with service. I didn't care that the stationary camera in the corner of my cabin was catching our every move on film, either.

It was the last day of our last charter.

We'd fucking made it.

The Successful Six had left with big smiles, a big thank you for all we'd done, and a big tip — not from Tammy, but from Maria. Tammy had left less than twenty percent, despite the fact that we did all in our power to give her group everything they wanted. But she was upset about the chaotic night and how it detracted from her vibes. She was particularly pissed that the wind swept away her Hermès scarf.

Damn us for not controlling the wind.

But after Tammy and the rest of the guests disembarked, Maria handed Captain Gary another envelope with a soft smile. He tried to assure her it wasn't necessary, but she'd insisted. Then, she'd grabbed both of my hands in hers and thanked me, sincerely.

And I hadn't been able to help myself.

"These people are not your friends," I'd said as quietly as I could, though I knew Leah heard me. She was right next to me, and I noticed her tense a little at my next words. "Life is too short to spend it with people who treat you poorly, especially when you've done nothing to deserve it."

Maria had squeezed my hands. "I know you're right. It's just... hard to let go of the group I always wanted to fit in with."

"Maybe you were born to stand out."

She'd winked at that, giving me one last hug before she was gone.

Then, the final charter had been rowdy but otherwise uneventful — a bachelor party for a Texas paper mill owner getting married for the fifth time. The guys drank more than a fraternity, and poor Leah was likely scarred from cleaning their cabins, but they ate what we gave them with pure delight and didn't ask for any frills with their events. They just wanted to party in Italy, smoke cigars, drink a gallon of whiskey each per day, and bake in the sun.

Now, I laid with my head on Finn's chest, smiling a little against the warm skin as I traced the firefly tattoo on his ribs. By one, the guests would be gone. By eight, the boat would be clean. And by this time tomorrow morning, we'd both have our bags packed and be the first ones off this damn boat.

We had one more crew night out obligation and then we were free.

And unlike two years ago when we were ending a yacht season, there wasn't an ounce of fear or anger in me this time.

There was no confusion, no concern for what the future might hold.

Because I knew we were in it together.

"What was the restaurant like?"

Finn inhaled, his chest rising and falling with my head on it while he rubbed my shoulder. "What do you mean?"

"I mean, what was it like? How was it decorated, what was the food, what was the ambiance? What was your favorite thing about it?"

"A very layered question, I see."

I leaned up, balancing my chin on my hands where they splayed his chest. "I want to know."

Finn stared up at the bottom of Gisella's bunk for a long moment, his brows pinched in concentration. "It was warm," he finally said. "Cozy. Like stepping into a small pub in your hometown while the snow is coming down."

I smiled. "That sounds nice."

"It was all wood and candles and low-lit chandeliers. Everything was repurposed or thrifted, so none of the tables or chairs matched. But it worked somehow." The corner of his lips lifted. "Reminded me of Gran's."

"Well, that was the point, wasn't it?"

He nodded, his brows folding together again. "Breaks me heart, the way I trusted that bastard who killed me in the end. Gutted, I was. It hurt more than I can say, to put all that work into the restaurant that honored my gran only to have it stolen from me."

"That's his karma," I said. "Not yours, okay? And maybe it was a sign from the universe. Maybe there's an even better place out there. Maybe your gran knew something you didn't and was... I don't know, pulling strings from above."

I laughed a little as I said it, not sure what I believed when it came to what happened to us after death. But Finn smiled at the story I'd painted.

"Maybe she knew, somehow, that leaving would be what brought me back to you."

I bent down and kissed him for that one. "What was your favorite dish on the menu?"

"Easy. The beef and Guinness stew with colcannon." Finn groaned and rubbed his stomach. "My sous helped me perfect the recipe. I brought in what I had from Gran, of course, but he added in some unexpected ingredients — gruyere cheese melted on top of the stew, roasted bits of pear in the potatoes. It shouldn't have made sense, but it did. Felt like home in a dish."

My eyes searched his, stomach tightening. "I wish I could have seen it, Finn. I wish I would have been there."

"You're here now," he said, his lips finding mine. "You get to watch me stumble into the next disaster."

I laughed. "Do you know what that will be?"

"Not quite," he confessed. "But... I've a notion."

"Care to share?"

"Not yet."

I pouted, but he dug his fingers into my ribs until I laughed and squealed and rolled onto my back. Then, it was him over me, his hand brushing my hair out of my face as he looked down in reverence. "I'm sad I missed out on these two years of your life, too, you know."

I shrugged. "Didn't miss much. Just more of this." My hands swept out toward the boat.

"You've been building your dream," he countered. "I saw it the first day we were on board. You were a great stew two years ago, but now?" He shook his head. "I can see it, Ember. I understand why you love it so much. It... it just seems effortless from the outside. It seems like you're really in your element."

My chest squeezed. "It means a lot to me that you see it the way I do, that you don't think I'm... I don't know. Wasting my intelligence by serving others."

"It takes an incredible human being to provide hospitality with a smile the way you do. It's not just service; though, you're excellent at that." He paused. "It's an art form. Truly. Cabins, interior, experience, service. It's like this meticulous dance, and you move with such grace that it looks easy when I know for a fact that it is not."

"Are you trying to get laid?" I asked, fingers tangling in his hair and pulling his mouth to mine. "Because it's working."

He laughed against my lips. "No time for that now, love."

"The engine room would beg to differ."

"Aye, well, I'll not be rushing things the next time I get to touch you." He spanked the side of my ass, checking the time on his watch before his eyes found me again. "What about you?"

"What about me?"

"What do you want after we leave this show behind us?"

I let out a heavy sigh. "If you would have asked me that even two weeks ago, I would have said all I wanted was for my father to watch the show and realize I'm making something of myself, that I'm a daughter he can be proud of. But now?" I shook my head. "I think I've realized that approval will never come, and I'm okay with that. Because this season has shown me that I'm enough for *myself*. It's my life to live — not my father's. I love this career. I love traveling and meeting interesting people and living the yacht life. At least for now," I added with a shrug. "Who knows what the future will hold. Maybe I'll end up running a chic restaurant with the best chef in the world."

I said that last part jokingly, but a part of me tingled with excitement at the thought. It was no secret that I loved dinner service — it was by far my favorite part of running a yacht as chief stew. Part of me wondered if I'd enjoy crafting the experience of a restaurant with Finn, if he'd ever see me as a partner.

What could we build together, now that we weren't being young and stupid?

The clink of silverware against porcelain was the only sound in the quiet restaurant that night as Captain Gary stood at the head of the long table, champagne flute raised. A slow smile pulled at his sun-wrinkled face as he swept his gaze over the crew — each of us in our civilian clothes, relaxed and glowing under the warm twinkle of string lights overhead.

"Well," Captain said, voice thick with humor and fatigue. "I can't say this was the easiest season I've ever done. Not by a long shot." Laughter rippled through the group, a shared acknowledgment of the chaos we'd barely survived. Everyone outside of me and Finn were back to a unified group.

We were the outsiders.

But we were content in that, Finn's hand holding tight to mine under the table. It didn't bother us that only Captain Gary included us in the group conversation over dinner. Once he left, we knew we'd be ignored.

That was fine by us.

"I will say, despite the hurdles — and there were plenty — you lot kept the guests happy, kept that old bucket afloat, and put on one hell of a show, whether you meant to or not." Captain's grin widened. "I'm proud of you. All of you. Thanks for not making me fire any of your asses." He lifted his glass higher. "Cheers to surviving the *Sinking Sun*."

"Cheers!" we echoed, lifting our glasses high before we drank the crisp bubbles down.

The words landed heavy and sweet in my chest. All day long,

I'd been floating in a kind of haze, the way I imagined someone might feel after completing an Ironman race. I felt accomplished and depleted at the same time, proud and exhausted, so high off adrenaline I could fight a tank, and also so bone-deep tired I could sleep for the rest of my life.

We'd made it.

Somehow, some way — bruised, battered, and a little broken — we'd made it.

Captain Gary stood, shaking hands with Palmer first before he turned to me as I pushed my chair out. It wasn't goodbye officially yet, we'd say our final farewells in the morning, but Cap seemed to be leaving a little piece of something with each of us tonight.

"Ember," he said, his grin wide and warm as he took me into an embrace. He held me tight, giving me a little pat on the back as he released me. He looked around before lowering his voice. "This was a tough one, aye? But listen, it isn't over for you. Not if you don't want it to be. I think you handled these last two charters with absolute poise. And at the risk of sounding like a broken record, I'm proud of you. You have my respect — and my recommendation. No matter what you choose to do next."

"Thank you, Captain," I said, offering a small smile. "That means a lot to me."

He nodded, squeezing my shoulder, and then he moved on to Finn while I took my seat again.

There was a deep pit in the middle of my stomach once Captain Gary was gone. I longed to talk to Leah, but knew it was no use. I wished for a moment to explain myself to Eli, but felt I didn't deserve his forgiveness even if he'd give it to me. I even found myself wanting to make amends with Gisella, but the way she glared at me as soon as Captain left and then flicked her hair over her shoulder and turned her back on us to effectively cut us from the group, I knew I didn't stand a chance.

I was still lost in my wishful thoughts when Finn stood up.

His chair scraped back loud against the stone, pulling everyone's attention. My brows furrowed as he placed both hands flat on the table, his shoulders squared.

He looked like he was going into battle, and my hackles rose like I was his second in command.

"I'd like to say something," Finn said, voice calm but carrying weight.

"Cool," Gisella said flatly. "No one cares."

She turned back around, but Bernard sucked his teeth and waved her off. "Pipe down, Gisella. Let the man have his go."

"He can speak all he wants. I won't be listening," she said, crossing her arms defiantly.

Bernard rolled his eyes and then smiled politely at Finn. "Go on, love."

"I know there's been a lot of speculation this season. About me. About Ember. About Gisella," Finn started, his eyes scanning everyone at the table. "And I know we didn't exactly do a good job of controlling the rumors or the optics."

A ripple of unease passed through the crew. It was the ugly beast we'd all been ignoring since the morning everyone found me and Finn in the guest cabin. We'd shoved the thing into a closet and latched the door, acting like there was nothing more to discuss even when we all knew there was.

But now, there were not guests on board to tend to, no charters to run, no jobs to do.

And Finn was apparently done holding his tongue.

"Before the reunion happens — before you all hear it from producers or see it edited and twisted into something it's not — I want you to hear the truth from me." Finn's gaze flicked to me, warm and steady. "From us."

My heart slammed against my ribs. He looked so confident and sure, but I was near positive he was barking up the wrong tree with this crew. They wouldn't listen. They wouldn't *want* to listen.

"I'm sorry for the way we hurt you," Finn said, addressing the table. "It wasn't our intention to have things blow up the way they did, to make a mess of a crew that had become friends. Believe us or not, that night was the first between us, and we intended to tell all of you that next day. We just never got the chance."

Gisella scoffed, her arms folded, body rigid at the other end of the table. Finn addressed her directly next.

"I'm especially sorry to you, G."

That made her tight expression slip.

"I know it must have been painful, finding us the way you did, and you shouldn't have had to experience that."

Gisella was quiet as Finn looked back to the crew, that apology weighing heavy in the air.

"But I want to be clear about one thing." His voice sharpened slightly. "When I crossed the line with Ember, it was after I ended things with Gisella. Not before. I owed her honesty — and I gave it, before anything happened."

The table erupted in whispers, eyes snapping to Gisella.

"Is that true?" Bernard asked bluntly, leaning forward with interest.

All heads turned to her.

Gisella's face flushed a dark red, her mouth opening and closing without a sound. She finally shrugged, tossing her hair over her shoulder. "Depends on how you define 'ended.'"

"That's not fair, G," Finn said, his tone still even but firmer now. "I was clear. You knew where we stood — probably well before I put words to it, if we're being honest. I hadn't touched you all season. We hadn't shared more than a public kiss that I know *you* knew was performed on my part."

Gisella's jaw clenched.

"There was also a note that I left for Ember explaining all of that," Finn added. "I slipped it under her door after the crew beach day, but for some reason, it never made it to her."

Gisella shrugged again. "I don't know why you're looking at me when you say that. I couldn't care less about the stupid love notes you wrote to my roommate."

I sighed. There was no way she was ever going to admit she'd taken it — even though we all knew she had.

"Look, I'm sorry for the way it all unfolded," Finn said, his voice softening. He shifted, pinning Gisella with a look full of regret. "While I didn't cheat on you, I did let things continue between us for far too long when I knew my heart wasn't in it. I was trying to do the right thing — whatever that is. I was trying to untangle the messiest knot of all time, but I shouldn't have made you believe I still had feelings for you when I knew I didn't. I'm sorry I hurt you. Truly, I am." He looked at everyone else then. "I'm sorry I bollocksed the energy we had on board. We were a family, and I regret that I ruined that."

And then, without hesitation, he turned to me.

"But I'm not sorry for this."

He grabbed my hand — bold and sure — and lifted it to his mouth, pressing a kiss to my knuckles with a reverence that stole my breath.

"I love her," he said simply. No drama. No theatrics. Just the truth that had been burning between us since the first day we boarded the *Sinking Sun*.

My heart split wide open.

The table was silent, stunned into a stillness that felt

deafening. Finn rubbed his thumb over my knuckles, his eyes never leaving mine.

"And maybe the thing I'm most sorry for is not realizing that sooner."

My eyes welled, pulse thrumming in my veins. I wanted to kiss his face off.

Before I could say *fuck it* and do just that, Gisella let out a sharp, incredulous laugh.

"Oh, sure," she snapped. "What a romantic story you've spun. Star-crossed lovers against the big, bad reality TV show. But even if you did call it quits with me before you shagged her, you obviously had feelings before that. Don't act like you're innocent."

Palmer snorted.

That had all the heads spinning to him, Gisella most of all, her brows furrowed in offense. Palmer shook his head at first, like he wasn't going to elaborate on that reaction.

But then, he laughed and said, "You know what? Fuck it." He leaned forward, pressing his finger to the table with his eyes on Gisella. "Are you really going to sit there and pretend like I wasn't in your bed that same night?"

My jaw hit the floor, along with half the table. Bernard was the only one seemingly not shocked. He sat back with his hands threaded behind his head and a giant grin. "Here we go."

"What?" Leah gasped, her hand covering her mouth.

Cameron let out a low whistle. "So that whole thing when you kissed me in the hot tub — that wasn't to piss Finn off, was it? You were trying to make Palmer jealous."

Gisella paled, her façade cracking under the weight of the accusation.

"Wow," Leah breathed. "So Cameron wasn't enough? What, did you plan to hook up with *every* guy on the boat and just pick which one suited you best?" She shot a glare at Eli. "Have something to tell us, too?"

Eli threw his hands up. "Don't look at me, bru. I was all in for Em." His expression was hard when it met mine. "What a chop."

"I'm sorry, Eli," I croaked. "You didn't deserve that."

"Damn right, I didn't."

Bernard picked up his drink and gave it a swirl. "Bloody hell. Someone pass the popcorn."

I tried to hold Eli's gaze as arguments erupted around the table, but he shook his head and looked away, not giving me the time of day.

And he didn't owe me that. He didn't owe me anything.

The only person who *did* look at me as Gisella and Cameron and Palmer screamed at each other was Leah. She didn't say a word, but there was a softness in her gaze. I knew it wasn't the time, but something about the way she looked at me told me she had room for forgiveness in her heart for me.

Not now. But one day.

Finn caught my eye in the chaos, his demeanor calm and steady. He jerked his head slightly toward the exit.

Let's go.

Without a word, I slid out of my chair, following him through the crowded restaurant and out into the quiet night. I barely registered Luke and Lexi trailing us with their cameras until we hit the curb, Finn throwing a hand up for a cab.

When we were finally tucked inside, the doors closing out the noise, I let out a long, shuddering breath. "Well, that was unexpected," I said with a laugh, leaning into Finn as he put his arm around my shoulders. "You know this isn't going to change anything, right? Not their perception of us, not the world's either."

Finn rubbed my shoulder with a sigh of his own, kissing my hair. "Maybe not. But I spoke our truth."

"I hate that we hurt them so much," I said, voice low with the aching honesty. "I shouldn't have used Eli to make you jealous."

"I should have told Gisella I didn't feel the same way she did — not just when we got here, but well before." He scrubbed a hand over his jaw. "I think I wanted to believe it, that I was moving on. I wanted to be all in with her. But I knew I wasn't even before I saw you again. And once I did…"

"I know," I said. "You fucked me up bad, too."

He laughed at that, turning those ocean eyes down to me. "Should I apologize to you as well, then?"

"I think we've had enough apologies between us to last a lifetime."

"Hopefully, we won't add any more."

"I'm sure we will," I said. "Love is messy. We're human. We're not meant to be perfect."

"I don't know. You're pretty close."

I rolled my eyes, kissing his jaw. "I'm sure I'll screw up again. You probably will, too. But we'll figure it out." I hummed. "In fact, I will be apologizing to you in the morning."

"For?"

I trailed my fingers over the buttons of his shirt. "Ruining this when I tear it off you."

Finn tipped his head back in a loud laugh, his profile outlined by the glow of passing streetlights. When he settled, his eyes were on me, heated and satisfied and so full of love it made me weak.

"So… what's next, Chef?" I whispered.

His hand found my jaw, lining it softly before he used his knuckles to tilt my chin.

"No idea, Firefly," he said, his mouth on track for mine. "But as long as I'm with you?"

A kiss, strong and sure and sweet.

"I'm happy."

Chapter Thirty-Two

CHARTER CONFESSIONAL
CLOSE QUARTERS

SEASON 4, EPISODE 15
CHARTER 9/SEASON END

FINN PEARSON: HEAD CHEF

PRODUCER
That was some speech you gave at the table last night.

FINN
I guess. I was just speaking my truth, since I doubt you lot will tell it.

PRODUCER
We just show the footage we have- hey, wait, we're not done yet.

Finn unwraps mic.

PRODUCER
Wait. Finn, please, just one more moment of your time.

Finn stands, places mic on chair.

AUDIO SWITCHED TO BOOM MIC

FINN
Listen, my friend — I said goodbye to Cap. Ember has already filmed her last shot and she's waiting for me on the deck. You've had your pound of flesh.

Finn stands.

FINN
But I get to take control of the story now, and your time in it is over.

PRODUCER
You're contractually obligated to attend the reunion.

FINN
Then you can feck off until then, can't you?

Finn exits.

The lights above were hot and relentless, washing out every feature, every flaw, and somehow still highlighting them all at once. I swore the makeup artist had caked on a full jar of foundation, but even that wasn't enough to hide the months of stress that lined my face.

I was wishing an ill-timed wedgie was still the worst of my problems, but alas, it was this damn reunion.

The cameras were already rolling in the backstage holding area, mostly phones held up capturing exclusive live content for social media. Nothing was sacred. I knew better than to pull up the stream on my own phone and read the comments rolling in.

No doubt, more than half of them would be shitting on me and Finn.

Speaking of the handsome Irish devil, where I was trembling, he was solid, standing beside me like an old oak tree with roots too deep for even the strongest storm to disturb. He was sexy as ever, his golden-brown hair tussled, the navy-blue suit he wore bringing out the deep aqua of his eyes. His stubble was a well-grown beard now, trimmed short and tight to his jaw but thick and purposeful. He had one hand stuffed into his pocket, the other linked tightly with mine.

He hadn't let go since we arrived.

In fact, he'd rarely let me go since the day we left the *Sinking Sun*.

For the first two months, we worked. We found a gig together on a yacht in Greece, for old time's sake, and threw ourselves into doing what we do best. Fortunately for us, we were with an older, more experienced crew — and there wasn't a single ounce of drama.

Which was great, because we'd had enough of that to last our entire lifetime.

When it was getting close to the show airing, we holed up together at my apartment in South Florida, laying as low as we possibly could. We would watch the episodes when they aired, but Finn kept me from spiraling when I saw what I already knew would happen.

The production crew made us look awful.

Not that we were innocent — we were far from it. But the show had attacked not only our character, but our professional abilities, too. They somehow twisted the footage to make me look like a micromanaging perfectionist who was putting all the work on Bernard and Leah as opposed to taking it on myself. I wanted to cry when I saw the post-production interviews where Leah and Bernard were weaseled into saying *just enough* that the production team could use it against me.

Bernard had texted me when the third episode aired, apologizing profusely and promising me they'd twisted his words. I believed him, of course — but the damage was already done. Still, it was nice to have at least one member of the crew reaching out to us, and Bernard even came over to watch an episode with us when he was in the States for a tour the show had set up for him. Turned out he'd made quite the splash and had fans demanding more of him.

Bernard was happy to oblige.

The show wasn't nice to Finn, either. They highlighted the *smallest* comments from the guests about something they didn't like about his food rather than the mountain of compliments he received all season. It didn't even make sense. We wouldn't have had as big of tips as we had if the food sucked. My team wouldn't have run so smoothly until the very end if I was a bitch.

But it was good television, and the viewing public ate it right up.

The episode we watched when Bernard visited was the one where Finn had his one weak moment of the season and broke down in the galley. But of course, they'd edited out anything soft and sincere between us. Instead, it was all about Finn throwing a fit and then painted to seem as if it was the rest of the crew who saved dinner while Finn and I sat on the floor and did nothing.

Bernard had cringed, shaking his head where he sat next to me on our couch. He had made us strong martinis, and they were all that was getting us through the carnage.

"That was brutal," he said. Then he smiled, shimmying. "But hey — my arse looks *fantastic*, dunnit?"

Whenever it got to be too much, Finn would wordlessly turn the TV off and grab for my hand. He'd ground me back in the present moment, in what was real, in who knew me best.

Those were some of my favorite months.

We worked local jobs — Finn at a Michelin-Star restaurant as a sous, and me on whatever charters needed help — and then we'd come home to each other and get lost in the world we were creating. We stayed off social media. We let the rumors fly.

We made our own peace.

But there was no running from the reunion.

It was part of our contracts, the *last* part we had to uphold. The second half of our payment to be on the show would hit our bank accounts within a week, and then we could wipe our hands of this forever.

The buzz of the crowd filtered through the black curtain just ahead of us — muffled cheers and chatter from fans who had waited all season to find out what happened to everyone once the cameras stopped rolling. I'd done my best to stay completely offline, but there were times, in my weakness, that I'd log on just to see what the comments were.

I always regretted it.

The people waiting in that audience, the people watching at home? They wanted my head on a stake.

There were some who loved us, some who cheered us on from the beginning. Maybe they saw what the cameras and production crew tried to hide — that we were in love, that we didn't mean to hurt anyone, that Gisella wasn't innocent in all this.

It was easy to say *who cares*, but it was harder to watch a lie play out about you and be powerless to stop it.

Knowing my father was part of that viewing audience had been the hardest part of the equation. Fortunately, he'd lost interest after episode three — or so he told me. I had a feeling he knew what was coming even before I did.

He hadn't said a bad word about it to me, though I knew he

had plenty to say. There was no way he hadn't heard about the scandal. *Someone* close to him would know. We just chose to ignore it whenever we spoke, and I was fine with that.

There was a roar of applause mixed with a very loud symphony of jeers, and I blinked back to the present, my hand sweating where Finn held it tight.

He gave me a squeeze. "Ready?"

"Absolutely not."

The corner of Finn's lips tilted up, and he leaned in for a quick kiss on my cheek.

"You and me against the world, remember?"

"Quite literally in this moment," I mumbled.

He chuckled, gave my hand another tight embrace, and then the showrunners were ushering us through the curtain.

We stepped out onto the soundstage to a cacophony of noise that quickly turned to a ringing in my ears. I tuned out any jeers, focusing on putting one foot in front of the other.

The reunion set was the same as every other season: sleek white couches, nautical theme, giant *Close Quarters* logo projected behind the host's seat. Overhead, cameras slid on their tracks like vultures waiting for the moment we'd finally crack.

I hoped I wouldn't give them that satisfaction.

Finn and I sat side by side on the left couch, the rest of the crew already in place on the opposite side. Leah caught my eye first, then Bernard. Gisella was dressed like she was walking the runway in a crimson red dress, her nails filed into pointed stilettos so sharp they could draw blood. Who knew. Maybe they would by the night's end.

Eli offered me a tight smile. Cameron didn't look at me at all.

Captain Gary was the only one who really beamed at us, and

when he saw my expression, he nodded, his brows folding in. It was like he was silently dismissing any worry I might have, telling me I had this.

Glad one of us was confident.

The host was Graham Lavender. Tanned, toothy, and as practiced as any politician, he'd been steering these reunions since season one. And while he was good at his job, I knew better than to believe he'd tell our story the way it actually happened.

I didn't trust a damn person here except Finn, of course.

"Welcome back to the *Close Quarters* reunion!" he said, his voice booming. "We're here with the full Season 4 crew, now — welcome to Finn and Ember — and... we've got a lot to talk about."

Cue the salacious grin from him, the laughter and mumbled agreement from the crowd, and the somersault of my gut.

Finn's thumb traced a slow, steady rhythm against my knuckles. He was my grounding force — always.

Without wasting any time, Graham sat back in his chair, crossing one ankle over the opposite knee and tapping his notecards on the sole of his polished dress shoe.

"Ember. Finn." He shook his head, laughing a little at the audience before he turned back to us. "Where do we even start?"

"How about from the part where my chief stew and *roommate* faked nice to my face before *BLEEP* my boyfriend behind my back?"

That from Gisella, who was now smiling victoriously as she got the reaction she wanted from the crowd. I was sure the production crew advised her to really play into the dramatics, and she looked all-too pleased to oblige.

I opened my mouth to say... something, though I wasn't sure

what. But Finn beat me to the punch.

"I wasn't your boyfriend," he said — calmly, no bite in his tone whatsoever. "You know that, whether or not the production crew chose to show it or not."

And they hadn't.

When the last few episodes had aired, I'd been physically ill. They'd edited out *all* the footage of Finn breaking up with Gisella, Finn telling *me* he'd broken up with Gisella, and of course, the final dinner with the crew when everything hit the fan.

Instead, they'd chopped it up to look like we left when Captain Gary did. They then showed a few clips of the crew taking shots and cheersing their drinks and laughing it up that I knew was filmed *before* dinner.

It didn't make sense to me. If anything, I thought the whole story made for *better* TV. But I guessed the production team had their story mapped out, and our truth was too innocent for their liking.

There were murmurs from the crowd at Finn's words, but Graham didn't play into them. He pointed the attention right back at us. "You were both fan favorites early on. But by mid-season, the narrative shifted. Viewers were shocked. Hurt. Some called it betrayal. Others, true love. How did it feel watching it back?"

Finn's jaw tightened along with his grip on me. "Hard."

That one word carried so much weight.

"We knew we'd face backlash," I added. "But we didn't know how far the producers would go to make us the villains."

"*Make you*," Gisella spat. "I'm pretty sure you did that yourselves."

I noted the way Palmer's nostrils flared and he shook his head, and I wondered if he'd been told to keep his mouth shut about it all.

Bernard, on the other hand, was grinning like the Cheshire cat, watching me like he knew something I didn't.

That scared me more than Gisella.

"I think we knew going into it that it wouldn't be pretty, but we hoped there would be more truth than what there was. Still, we watched every episode together," Finn continued, voice steady as he dutifully ignored Gisella. "And we talked through it all. Laughed at the edits, cringed at some things, sure. But we never let it change how we saw each other."

"Did you ever consider breaking up?"

"Not for a second," Finn said instantly. "We already wasted too much time apart because we were young and stubborn, full of pride." He looked at me then. "Once we made our way back to each other?" A shrug. "There was no tearing us apart, no matter how the world has tried to."

Graham tried to drive the wedge deeper. "Finn, do you regret it? What happened with Gisella, the crew tension, the fallout?"

"I regret hurting people," he said, and then his eyes found mine. "But I'll never regret loving her."

The room fell quiet, the audience was waiting for the big, dramatic moment while Graham tried to create it. But we weren't biting.

Then, Graham shocked us all when he said, "Well, that's very sweet. But it's quite a shortened version of the speech you gave that last dinner out with the crew, isn't it?"

The crowd began to murmur. Gisella's eyes popped wide. Cameron and Eli shared a look of annoyance while Palmer looked a bit smug holding back a grin.

"Let's roll that footage!" Graham declared with a smile.

And they did.

Finally, after months of hell, the truth played out on a screen in the studio and on televisions all over the world. Emotion surged in my chest as I watched it play out, as I watched everyone react to it in real time. Gisella was throwing a fit, threatening to leave if they didn't stop playing it. When the part played where Palmer called her out for her infidelity, she stormed off stage.

The room was buzzing when the clip stopped, and Graham cocked a brow at me, as if to say, *See? I'm not so bad.*

I still didn't trust him.

"Bernard," he said, whipping his head toward my stew. "Care to tell us the dirty details about that night?"

Bernard looked like a kid in a candy store as he regaled the crowd with his version of it all. I mostly blocked it out, ready to be done and out of here. More questions were tossed around to the rest of the crew while I stayed silent except to answer with brief statements when necessary.

When we were nearing the end of the show, Graham went around and asked everyone if there was anything they wished to say.

I used my time to apologize to Eli as sincerely as I could. I told him I didn't expect nor deserve his forgiveness, but I wanted him to know I was sorry for leading him on and using him as a pawn in a game he didn't sign up to play. I'd expected him to tell me to go fuck myself, but he'd surprised me with an, "Ag, don't fret, Em. It's all good." And then he'd hugged me to the crowd cheering, and a piece of my broken heart was mended.

Palmer told his side of the whole Gisella situation. Cameron expressed his regrets with Leah. Captain Gary kept it professional, saying that he was still proud of us as a crew despite the drama.

When it came to Leah, I was surprised to find her already crying, sniffling as she dabbed at the corner of her eyes with a tissue. Her eyes slammed into mine, and she cried harder.

"I'm so sorry for how harshly I judged you, Em," she said, shaking her head. "I was hurt, but not just by you. I was... I wasn't myself. And I just wished you'd have told me, but I understand now why that might have been hard to do. And you would have told me, had things not gone down the way they did."

"I would have told you that *morning*, I swear," I told her.

"I know," she nodded. "I know. I'm sorry I was such a *BLEEP*."

"I deserved it."

"No," she said, standing and shaking her head. "You didn't. You didn't deserve any of it. Can I have a hug?"

I met her in the middle of the stage, squeezing her tight as the crowd *aww*'d. I whispered a promise to her that we'd catch up soon, and she nodded, squeezing my arm before she went back to her seat.

Then, it was Finn's turn.

And the surprises kept coming.

"I wasn't sure if I'd announce this here," he said, standing and slipping one hand into the inside pocket of his jacket. It was the first time he'd released the grip on my hand all night. "But it feels right."

He pulled out a glossy photo and handed it to me first, his eyes locked on mine. The moment our fingers brushed, my pulse kicked up, time slowing around the two of us. The photo felt heavier than paper should — like it was weighted with meaning I hadn't yet uncovered.

"What is it?" I asked, even as I stared down at the image.

It looked like a print from a real estate listing — a small storefront tucked between a Pilates studio and a bakery. The windows were covered in newspaper, but there was something charming about the white brick and abandoned flower beds framing the door.

"It's my new restaurant," Finn said.

I blinked up at him, heart thudding as Graham motioned for me to pass the photo down the line.

And then Finn had my hand in his again, his eyes searching mine.

"I thought the first one was it for me," he said, voice steady but full of emotion. "I built it in Dublin with everything I had. But the truth is… I wasn't ready. Not the way I thought I was. And maybe that failure wasn't the end of my dream — maybe it was the beginning of something better. I think we both know now that the universe had other plans."

His lips quirked up, and my eyes watered, my heart so full I could burst.

"I think maybe my Gran knew I couldn't do it without you."

I pressed my lips together, trying not to cry as the audience collectively melted.

"This time, I've got the right people. The right investors. The right team. A new menu I'm already testing with my future staff. A fresh start — in South Florida, where I can be with you." He smiled. "And a name."

I expected Graham to make a joke, but he was quiet, all attention on Finn.

"It's called *Pygo*," he said. "Short for *pygolampída*."

I quirked a brow. "Am I supposed to know what that means?"

"It's Greek," Finn said. "For firefly."

That was it.

Whatever emotional dam was holding me together broke in an instant. Greece — the place we met, the place we fell in love, the place he called me *Firefly* for the first time.

"This is too much," I whispered, breath catching on a laugh as my thumb brushed his knuckles. "Are you sure about the name?"

"I've never felt surer of anything in me life," he said, voice thick now. "About who I am. About what I'm doing. And I know it's because I have you by my side. I want you to keep chasing what lights you up, Ember. So I'm making me home in Fort Lauderdale, because that's where you shine. This way, you don't have to give up anything. And I don't have to do this without you."

I couldn't see him through the tears bubbling in my eyes now. My heart was a mess. I was smiling so big my cheeks hurt.

"Well," I said, voice shaky but sure, "speaking of chasing dreams…"

It was Finn's turn to cock a brow.

"I've accepted a new position," I said. "Chief stew on a private yacht for a family."

His mouth parted. "You're kidding."

"I was going to tell you right after this," I said on a laugh. "It's an interior twice the size of the *Sinking Sun*. Full creative control. A path to purser, if I want it."

Gasps and applause rippled through the room, but I barely heard it. All I could see was the way Finn looked at me.

Like he'd known I could do it all along.

"So," I said, teasing, "we're both out here living our dreams, huh?"

He reached for me, cupping my cheek, and pulled me in for a kiss. "Life is a dream with you."

The crowd lost it.

Even Graham laughed. "Okay, okay, you two — get a room."

Everyone chuckled as the cameras panned out, Graham delivering his final address and telling everyone to tune in for bonus content on the website. Crew members were already beginning their wrap-up shuffle, the show winding down.

But I stayed there with Finn, heart pounding, his arm around my shoulder, the weight of everything we'd survived finally lifting.

And though I was bursting with excitement for my new job, I found that pesky thought swirling in my head again...

What would it be like to run a restaurant with Finn?

Not just as the girlfriend of the chef, but as a partner. To design the service, the experience. To run dinner every night beside him. To create something together, something that felt like us.

My stomach fluttered, those same butterflies I'd felt when we first locked eyes on that hot, impossible day in Greece tickling my belly with their wings.

And just like that, I knew the answer.

Chapter Thirty-Three

The second the hotel room door clicked shut, I kicked off my heels and groaned. My earrings hit the nightstand next, then my necklace, my rings. I was ready to scrub off the mound of makeup on my face, too, but decided I'd wait until after Finn fucked my brains out.

Because that was definitely happening tonight.

Finn let out a heavy exhale as he tossed his suit jacket over the back of a chair. He loosened his tie, popped the top button of his shirt, and collapsed onto the bed with a dramatic flop.

"Well," he said, rubbing his face. "That went about as well as it possibly could."

I smiled, padding over to him. "I mean, we didn't get booed off the stage, so I'd call it a win."

His phone buzzed once. Then again. Then three more times.

Finn groaned and pulled it from his pocket. His brows lifted almost immediately. "Whoa."

I raised a brow. "What?"

"Apparently, whatever we said... or whatever the producers decided to show... changed some minds. Look."

He handed me the phone. I scrolled, stunned as post after post flashed across the screen:

> **@closeqbaby:** Okay… I get it now. That
> firefly line?? Someone write the damn
> movie.

> **@crewteaqueen:** Still not over the Gisella
> drama, but gotta admit Ember and Finn
> feel like the real deal.

> **@saltyandsweet:** Gisella talking about
> betrayal like she didn't bed-hop her way
> across the Med lmaoooo be so for real girl.

> **@teamfirefly:** Listen, they weren't perfect,
> but they owned it. And that's love. Real,
> messy, worth-it love.

"That's… new," I said.

The hate was still there though, fewer and farther between, but there.

> **@yachtwatchdog:** They're still shady AF
> for how they went about it. No amount of
> Greek poetry changes that.

I scrolled a few more times, eyes bulging when I saw the most recent post from the show. "Um… apparently they're releasing all this bonus footage." I pressed play, and Finn leaned up to watch with me as the screen revealed the two of us outside on that second crew night out when Finn confessed everything about the restaurant and his gran.

The views ticked higher as we watched, the comments pouring in.

But this time, they were positive, demanding to see more of us, to know more of our story.

I knew without question that the showrunners would eat this

up and take every opportunity to get more out of the audience before they let the season really die.

Before I could fall too far into the spiral, I shook my head, setting the phone face down on the nightstand. "Who cares. I'm just glad it's over."

Finn rolled to face me. "I'm proud of you."

"I'm proud of *you*. Pygo? You're really doing it. You're getting back on the horse."

"I was so nervous to tell you."

"Why?"

He gave me a look. "The last time I tried to talk to you about opening a restaurant..."

I laughed, cringing. "Yeah, okay. Fair. But I think we've learned a few things since then."

"Apparently so."

"I really am proud of you," I whispered, eyes on his mouth.

"Thank you," he said, kissing me once. Then again, a little slower. His fingers started bunching the silk fabric of my dress, hiking it up my leg inch by inch. "But now I'd like to talk less about pride and more about you in this feckin' dress..."

I let out a breathy laugh as he tugged me into his lap, rolling until I was on top of him, and he could properly tug that fabric up over my hips.

"I'm excited about the new position," I said, breath hitching as he kissed down my neck.

"Being on top?"

"Chief stew," I exhaled on a laugh. "But... I've been thinking about maybe another job opportunity."

He was still focused on undressing me, the zipper along my spine expertly unfastened by those master chef hands of his.

"Oh?"

I was panting more now from what I was about to say than his touch. "Would you think I'm crazy if I said... I might want to be a part of the restaurant?"

His whole body stilled as soon as he peeled my dress over my head. Then I was naked, save for my panties, sitting in his lap after having said the last thing he expected.

"What?"

Fuck.

The look on his face was either confusion, like he didn't hear me right, or it was horror. Here he was about to chase his dream, and I just invited myself to crash it.

"No, never mind," I rushed, cheeks heating. "It's a bad idea. I don't know why I said that, I—"

He cut me off with a kiss — urgent, possessive, smiling against my mouth.

"Are you fecking joking?" he said, pulling back just enough to speak. "Be a part of it. Run it. Own it the way you own me, Em. It would be my honor to do this with you."

"Really?" I whispered.

"Yes, you beautiful eejit."

I grinned, breathless. "I just... I got so excited thinking about crafting the experience with you. Making this thing ours. The interior design, the menus, the lighting, the uniforms. Every little touch. I want to be in it with you."

"I'm in," he said instantly. "But what about purser?"

I paused, feeling the weight of the decision settle in... and then lift.

"I don't know if it was the show souring my outlook, or if everything just played out for me, but... I think maybe this whole chapter was a phase. One that led me to the next part of the journey," I said. "Kind of like what you said about the restaurant in Dublin. I love my job as chief stew, I do. But when I think about building a Michelin-Star restaurant with you—"

"Whoa, whoa," he laughed, sliding his hands up my thighs. "Getting ahead of ourselves, are we? That's hard to do."

"We'll do it," I said, no hesitation.

Finn's eyes darkened as his hands found my hips, his mouth catching mine again — this time with fire. "Fine. We'll do it. Now, let me do *you*."

I barked out a laugh into his next kiss, but then I matched his frantic energy, the two of us shedding clothes as fast as we could.

Just like that, the rest of the world faded.

The cameras, the crew, the audience, the drama — it was all behind us now. We were all that remained. Our time on the *Sinking Sun* was over.

A new dawn was rising.

I had a feeling it'd be the brightest day yet.

Epilogue

Two Years Later

The kitchen buzzed with a low hum of life — pans clattered in the sink, someone was laughing in the back, and the sharp scent of citrus and fire lingered in the air, long after the last dessert had been torched.

It was just past midnight at Pygo.

We'd closed an hour ago. The guests were gone, the lights in the dining room dimmed to that soft golden hue we always said made everyone look ten percent hotter and twenty percent richer. And back here in the kitchen — this was our sanctuary. The pulse of the restaurant.

Finn moved behind the line like it was still mid-service, sleeves rolled up, apron smudged and messy, hair mussed from the rush. I leaned on the bar across from him, sipping a glass of red, watching him. Admiring him.

Over the last two years, I'd had the privilege of watching him grow Pygo into something more magical than I ever could have dreamed. I knew he was a brilliant chef. I knew his food was special. But I didn't know what it was like when he was set completely free, when there were no guests telling him what they wanted or what they couldn't have, when it was just his creativity leading the way.

What started with him and his sous chefs playing in the kitchen as I designed and decorated the front of house slowly transformed into what we had today: a sensory-rich culinary experience. From the time the customers secured their reservation on our website all the way until they were escorted out of the restaurant, they were taken on an adventure.

It was mesmerizing to behold.

As I watched him now, I found my chest a little tight with longing. I was so thankful I got to be a part of this journey with him, but I still longed to know what he'd been like at the restaurant in Dublin. I wondered if this one was different somehow, or just a more polished version of what he'd already created there.

But those years we were separated allowed us both to grow. We endured heartache and pain, but we found our way back.

And that was where my focus would be: on the here and now.

Two years had flown by in a blur of designing and planning and dreaming. If I'd thought being a chief stew was rewarding, it was nothing compared to how it felt to build Pygo with Finn. Just like he had full control of the menu, *I* had full control of the experience — the mood, the atmosphere, the way every detail worked together to make someone *feel* as they ate.

From the forest green velvet booths and the mosaic of broken wine bottles and sea glass to the rustic light fixtures and local art, I put thoughtful care into every inch of space. I curated the playlist, pored over fonts and linen textures for the menus, and selected each dish and glass like a stylist would choose everything to make up a red-carpet look.

Everything guests saw, touched, or felt — I touched first. I thought it through. I made sure it said what we wanted it to say.

Every service was a performance.

And Pygo was the stage I built.

If I were the set designer, then Finn was the main actor, the man everyone came to see. Our team of chefs and waitstaff were supporting actors of the highest caliber, but it was *he* who made the tickets sell.

"You seriously just made a duck confit croquette after a

fourteen-hour shift?" Tobias asked Finn, blinking at the plate like it personally offended him.

Finn shrugged, flicking sea salt over the top like it was fairy dust. "If it's wrong to decompress with luxury, I don't want to be right."

"It's excessive," Tobias muttered.

"Everything good is."

I smirked into my wine glass.

Tobias turned to me. "You enabled this, didn't you?"

"I'm his wife in everything but paperwork," I said. "You'll have to be more specific about which crimes I've enabled."

I didn't miss how the word *wife* made Finn's ocean eyes flick to mine. The corner of his mouth curled, the heat in his gaze enough to make me want to notch the A/C down a degree or two. We'd been living together ever since the show ended, working side by side day in and day out, sharing every ounce of our lives with one another.

And somehow, I'd only fallen more in love with him. Maybe it was because our love was born in tight quarters, but it never bothered me, the fact that we were nearly always together. We thrived when we were connected.

Of course, Leah wouldn't stand for letting me spend *all* my time with Finn and the restaurant. Blessedly, she'd moved her offseason home to Fort Lauderdale, and whenever she wasn't on charter, she was dragging me out with her or kicking Finn out so we could rot on my couch.

After the reunion, we'd reconnected, both of us profusely apologizing and lamenting that we'd missed so much time together already. She was my best friend now — with Bernard edging his way in to be our third wheel whenever he was in the States — and I couldn't imagine my life without her.

She and Cameron had never recovered from the chaos at the end of the season, but I knew she'd find her person one day. When she was ready.

Right now, she was more focused on her first charter as chief stew coming up.

I knew she would blow them all away.

"I've seen drug cartels operate with less chaos than the two of you," Tobias said, still assessing Finn's creation.

"Speaking of crimes—" I set down my glass. "Show him the picture, Finn. The foie bao with the candied figs."

Tobias winced. "God, the gold leaf—"

"Show. Him."

Finn pulled out his phone, still grimacing as Tobias rubbed his hands together. "No way. Cheffy embarrassed about a dish he made? This ought to be good."

"You have to promise not to—" The words died on Finn's tongue, his brows pinching in. He glanced at me and then brought the phone to his ear.

"What is it?" I asked.

He didn't answer.

His body went still, the kind of still that always made my stomach flip. His eyes locked on the floor, mouth slightly parted.

"Finn?" I took a step forward. "What?"

He looked up at me, pale.

"We got a star."

Time froze.

All movement in the kitchen stopped, from where the dishwashers were scrubbing away in the back corner to where the chefs were prepping for tomorrow. All noise died, save for the playlist that hummed quietly through the speaker. We never heard it back here in the kitchen. It was always too loud.

But it was silent now.

Until everyone lost their damn minds.

"WHAT?!"

"No way. No fucking way."

"We got a star?!"

"You're talking about *the* star?!"

"PLAY THE VOICEMAIL!"

Finn, still in shock, fumbled to put it on speaker. And then we all heard it — the smooth, unmistakable voice of a Michelin Guide rep, congratulating Chef Finn Pearson of Pygo on receiving his first star. Official. Verified. Real.

Tobias screamed. Casey, one of our hostesses, started sobbing. Chefs were hugging, dirty cutlery and half-prepped dishes abandoned as everyone ran around like wild animals let out of a zoo. Someone screamed that they were grabbing the most expensive bottle of champagne in our cellar as I blinked and smiled and tried to wrap my head around it.

A star.

"I'm calling my mom!" Tobias yelled.

"I'm calling my ex just to rub it in!" Casey called out.

And Finn — my brilliant, reckless, maddening, passionate Finn — just stood there, blinking, staring at his phone like he wasn't sure if it was a bomb or a gold brick. The eye of the beautiful storm.

My wine glass abandoned, I ran to him, sliding across the cleared part of the stainless-steel island until I collided with that gorgeous man. He laughed in surprise, his phone dropping to the floor, but I didn't give him the chance to reach for it again.

I wrapped my arms around his neck and pulled him into me, my lips caressing his with all the words I knew could never convey what I felt for him in this moment.

Finn inhaled the kiss, his hands finding my hair, the chaos around us muted as we leaned into that touch, into each other.

"You did it," I whispered, tears stinging the corners of my eyes as we pressed our foreheads together. "I told you. I *knew* you would."

"They called when we were prepping for dinner service," he murmured, dazed. "I... I missed it. I missed the call."

"You got the voicemail," I said on a laugh. "And it's real, babe.

Somewhere in Los Angeles, they're having a party and announcing your star. By tomorrow morning, the news will be in all the papers." I shook my head, pressing another long kiss to his perfect lips. "You did it."

"*We* did it," he quickly corrected, his hands locking on either side of my face as his eyes searched mine. "I fecking love you."

"I love you, too."

And then we were torn apart, the team dragging Finn outside before I was hoisted up in the air to follow.

We tumbled into the street outside Pygo, where the light from the windows spilled across the sidewalk and the champagne became a weapon. Finn was soaked with it in under thirty seconds, laughing in a way I'd never seen — wild and free, like something had cracked open inside him and let the light pour in.

This was what it looked like to witness a dream come true.

Through it all, his eyes kept finding mine.

Like no matter how bright the spotlight, he could still only ever see me.

One Week Later

The restaurant looked like a fever dream.

Sunlight spilled in through the floor-to-ceiling windows, catching on gold accents and flickering across velvet booths. The floor was a mosaic of tile — chaotic, colorful, magical. Hanging plants dipped from the ceiling. The lighting fixtures were warm and strange and beautiful — all curves and antique brass, casting shadows on the lacquered walls.

I took it all in slowly while I could, the quiet of pre-service something this restaurant rarely experienced. One fingertip skimmed the smooth marble of the host stand, the soft wood of the bar, the mismatched antique mirrors on the wall that made every corner feel infinite as I tried to grasp what we'd created, the recognition we'd earned.

It felt like so much more than just an award at a job, so much bigger than any *atta girl* I'd been given on a yacht. Pygo wasn't just a themed tablescape and party or a seven-course tasting menu gone right.

It was a piece of us, a visual and culinary expression of our story.

Finn walked in from the back, holding a glorious red box.

My heart caught at the sight. "Is that—"

He opened the lid, revealing the plaque. Our Michelin Star. Engraved and glowing.

We just stared at it, quiet for a moment.

"We should hang it right above the urinal in the men's room," Finn said. "That's what you do with one of these, right?"

"I was thinking next to the garbage in the kitchen. You know — the one that always overflows before one of us takes it out?"

"Brilliant."

We shared a smile that was both teasing and reverent, and I felt my skin heat in the way it always did when I knew my chef wanted to touch me. He was giving me *that look*, and I checked the time on my watch, doing the math to see if we could sneak away before the rest of the staff trickled in.

But before I could make a decision, my phone rang.

It was my father's name and photo that filled the screen.

My stomach dropped. "It's my dad."

I blinked up at Finn, who frowned but nodded for me to answer it. I knew it was hard for him to understand my relationship with my father, especially after our time on the show. My father had grown more distant than ever when it all went down. He was pleasant enough when I called, or when Mom invited me and Finn over for dinner, but over time, we'd grown more and more apart.

It was a boundary I needed, to live my life without him casting his opinions over my choices. But I still missed him. My father may have been demanding of me. He may have been stubborn. He may have been loud with his judgment.

But I knew he loved me.

I knew he enforced control because that was what made him feel like he was keeping me safe.

"Hi, Dad."

"There's my girl," he greeted, his voice warm even despite the discomfort I sensed. My heart squeezed like always, the greeting as confusing as ever. "I hear there's a shiny new star in town, and it belongs to my daughter and an ornery Irish chef who stole her heart."

"Hi, Mr. Reed," Finn sang, and then he kissed my cheek on a grin before nodding toward the kitchen, letting me know he was going to leave me alone.

I reached out and squeezed his hand just as my father's voice rang through again. "Congratulations, Ember. That is quite the accomplishment."

"Thank you, Dad."

I appreciated his congratulations. I knew this meant something to him because a Michelin Star was something he could quantify. It was a reliable source, a standard way of measuring success. He never would have given the same greeting for something I earned in yachting.

But that was okay.

He didn't need to understand what I did or what made me happy. I didn't need anyone's approval to live.

He was quiet again, and I thought maybe that was it. A courtesy call. But then his voice came again, softer this time.

"Not just for the restaurant. For... everything. For surviving."

That had my brows pinching together. "What do you mean?"

"I watched the show. The whole show."

Well, shit.

I stayed silent, not sure what to say to that. Was he ready to lay into me for all the drama, for the way I'd portrayed myself to the public? *Close Quarters* had released countless "bonus footage" since the reunion, so much so that the reality TV lovers now regarded me and Finn as one of their favorite couples. The truth had come out — all of it — and though neither of us needed anyone else to know the truth but us, it was nice to not be painted as the bad guys any longer.

And while we chose not to share much of ourselves on social media, both of us fed up with our time living under public scrutiny, we were also thankful to the show and the audience it had brought us. They'd been the first to sell out our reservations when we opened Pygo, and we knew we wouldn't have had such a jumpstart on success without them.

Strange, isn't it, how sometimes the very things that try to break us are just the final test before the breakthrough. How the moments that bring us to our knees — the ones that make us question everything, that leave us gutted and breathless and bruised — are often the last hurdle before we rise.

"I know what you went through," Dad said. "Well, I guess I don't *really* know — but I can imagine. And I know if my personal life had been aired for public consumption, I wouldn't have handled it with half the grace you did."

I exhaled shakily. "Thanks, Dad."

"You know your mother and I are college sweethearts," he continued. "But what you don't know is that she was dating my best friend when we met."

My jaw hinged open. "What?"

"I'm not proud of it. But when I met her, I knew. I just... knew she was it for me. It wasn't clean. It wasn't easy. But love rarely is."

I sat down slowly on the edge of a barstool, the world shifting under my feet.

"I'm not saying what I did was right," he finished. "Or that what you and Finn did was, either. But what I am saying is that I'm sorry for not taking you or your career choice seriously. I'm sorry I wasn't there for you at a time when you needed to know that I'm on your side — always. Me and your mother, both."

My eyes welled. "That means a lot to me."

"I see you now, and I get it. I understand. What you did in the yachting world, what you did on that show, and what you've done now, with Pygo?" There was a long pause. "I'm damn proud of you."

I pressed my palm to my chest, squeezing my eyes shut against the emotion threatening to strangle me just as Finn crept back into the room. He wordlessly took me into his embrace, holding me as the tears stained my cheeks.

"You don't need my approval," Dad said. "You never did. But damn if you haven't earned my respect, Ember."

I tried to think of something to say, but I was breaking, the emotion too strong. Finally, I managed, "I love you."

"I love you, too," my father echoed.

There were a few more pleasantries exchanged, as well as a promise that we'd come over for a dinner soon on one of Finn's off nights to celebrate, and then the call ended.

I was still blinking through the tears when Finn swept my hair from my face, a knowing smile on his. "Can you help me with something in the back?"

I followed him through the kitchen, wiping my face and shaking out my shoulders so I could get right for the evening. My father's words still sang in my head as we pushed through the doors into the kitchen.

I slid to a stop then, my eyes on a beautiful scene on the middle island.

One perfect stack of banana pancakes was framed like a centerpiece, candles flickering around it. Flower petals were scattered across the stainless steel and one simple fork and knife lay on a perfectly folded linen napkin.

I laughed, breath catching in my chest. "Well, if I'd known you were doing all this, I wouldn't have eaten lunch."

I turned back to Finn — and promptly froze.

He was on one knee.

In his trembling hand was a ring — delicate, stunning, the marquise-cut diamond resting in a setting made of two entwined bands of yellow gold.

"I used Gran's ring," he said, voice a little hoarse. "Melted the gold down. You know how I clung to that ring after Gran passed." He swallowed. "But I've found me peace in you, Firefly. You're my home. And that's what I want you to wear — something with history. Something that has my heart — just like you always will."

"Damn it, I really didn't want to cry more before service," I whispered, and then we both laughed as tears spilled over the apples of my cheeks.

I shook my head, staring at where he was on his knee like it was all a dream.

"You made a comment to Tobias last week that you were my wife in all but paperwork, but I think it's time we changed that." Finn reached for my hand, holding the ring an inch from my finger. "Let me make you banana pancakes 'til me hands are mangled and useless. Give me the chance to love you with everything that I am until I cease to exist." He grazed my finger with the gold, waiting. "Allow me the pleasure of being your husband, Ember Reed, and I promise I will cherish every second we have. Until the lights go out. Until the doors are locked for good. Until we climb into bed old and gray and hold each other close and let the night take us, I will cherish you."

My throat was impossibly tight as he slid the ring just over my nail.

"Marry me, Firefly."

"Yes," I whispered.

It was the only word I could find, the only word that mattered as Finn grinned and slid the ring the rest of the way on. I didn't even stop to admire it. I just yanked him up off the floor and kissed him with my heart bursting out of my chest.

He held me like he never wanted to let go — and I clung to him knowing I never would again.

How had we gotten here?

How had one crew placement, one unexpected reunion, one chaotic, cameras-everywhere summer unraveled and rewoven our entire lives?

We met on a boat. Lost each other. Broke and bled and clawed our way through heartbreak and hell, only to crash right back into each other. It was like we'd been in a boxing ring with the universe, and it had tapped out, sweating and exhausted from our fight as it whispered, "*Fine. You win.*"

And now, here we were — in a kitchen we'd built from nothing, sharing a ring made in the past, on the cusp of a future so bright and bold, the universe must have been shaking in its boots again.

"You know..." Finn murmured, thumb tracing the edge of my mouth, "we've got at least thirty minutes before staff starts rolling in."

A slow smile curled my lips. "Oh, do we?"

He wrapped me in his arms, walking me backward, steps steady, kisses messy and eager until we hit the walk-in freezer.

He reached for the door handle with a wicked grin. "Care to christen this ice box with me, *wife*?"

"Fiancée," I corrected even as I let him tug me inside.

"Semantics," he breathed, and then I was pressed against the icy door, my breath shuttering out of me in a gasp at the cold. "Been dreamin' of takin' you against this feckin' door for two long years."

"Holy shit, that's cold," I said on a pant, but still I clung to him, not protesting so much as pointing out the truth. "I'm going to have frost bite on my ass."

He laughed, hand already sliding up my thigh. "You want heat?" My dress hitched up around his traveling wrist. "I'll give you heat, Mrs. Pearson."

"I think you're confused on how marriage works."

"And I think you're going to need a new pair of tights," he said, and that was the only warning I got before his fingers curled into the sheer fabric lining my inner thigh and tore.

Riiip.

A laugh tumbled from my lips as his mouth claimed mine, warm and hungry, all tongue and teeth and breathless urgency. I fumbled with the buttons of his chef's jacket, hands trembling as they found purchase against his chest.

One finger slid inside me as his tongue massaged mine, both of us moaning the second we were connected. I broke our kiss to let my head fall back, stars prickling the edges of my vision already as he moved his finger inside me with expert care. He knew everything about me, all the ways to touch and tease. On a lazy Sunday morning in our bed, he'd take his time, that touch lingering in all the soft places before he'd finally let me come apart.

But right now, he was on a mission, the palm of his hand rubbing me right where I needed as he clamped his teeth down on my neck enough to elicit another gasp.

I savored the feel of his hands on me, relishing in each kiss and groan as he got me wet and ready. Then I shoved against his chest until he released me and I could turn, pulling my ripped tights down along with my thong. I flipped up the hem of my skirt next, hands on the cold door of the walk-in, ass out, back arched, body primed and ready.

I glanced over my shoulder just in time to watch Finn bite his lip, one hand hooked at the crease where my thigh met my hip as the other smoothed over my ass cheek with appreciation. He reared back for a spank with just enough bite to make me moan, and then his hands left me long enough to make quick work of his pants.

He unbuckled his belt, sliding the button of his pants through the slit before the sound of his zipper sent a delicious chill down my spine. He freed himself with a quick pull of fabric and then he was at my entrance, the slick head of his cock pressing between my lips as I arched more to give him the space he needed.

"Christ, this perfect little cunt was made for me," he groaned, sliding his tip through the wetness he'd created before he notched himself inside me.

I moaned as he pressed in, all the way, filling me as I gasped and scrambled for purchase against the door and hissed at the burning pleasure. His lips were on the back of my neck next, kissing the ink there as he flexed and moved. His cock hit so deep my legs quaked, but he held me steady, rocking into me with one hand snaking around to rub against my clit.

"Finn," I cried.

"That's it, Firefly. Fuck my hand. Squeeze my cock with that tight cunt. Come for me, *wife*."

I didn't even argue this time. The sound of that word rolling off his tongue in that gruff, lilted accent of his had my toes curling, blood rushing to where his hand circled expertly.

I came with fire licking at my bones, and even with the risk of a staff member being on the other side of the door, I let myself cry out his name, let him hear how much I wanted him — how I always had.

Finn picked up his speed at the sound of my ecstasy, and then he was gripping me tight, slamming it home, his orgasm chasing mine. That only spawned mine to last longer, and when he found his release, it was with me reaching back to grip his hair and his teeth dug into my neck, both of us clinging to each other for dear life.

And that was who we were.

What we were.

All-encompassing. Passionate. Unruly and messy and wild.

Not just an ember — but a raging fire.

One that created rather than destroyed.

We burned through the rules, through the wreckage, through every line that tried to tie us down. And what was left in our wake wasn't ash — it was new life.

Love.

Legacy.

Nowhere near perfect, but perfectly *ours*.

There wouldn't be cameras rolling to capture the rest of it — no edits, no soundtracks, no curated version of the truth.

Just us.

Unfiltered. Unscripted.

Real love.

Now *that* was a show worth watching.

Read on for bonus content,
exclusive to this paperback edition!

Episode 10 Airing Night

FOUR MONTHS AFTER FILMING WRAPPED

Ember

"I swear to God, if I see one more TikTok theorizing that I worked with Giselle on a boat in the past and have some vendetta against her, I'm deleting the app."

Finn didn't even glance up from the bowl of popcorn in his lap. "You already deleted it. Twice."

"And I'll do it again."

"Anything new about me?" He leaned over, pretending to be interested as I locked my screen and rolled my eyes at him.

"Like you care."

"Ah, some of the shite they come up with is pure entertainment."

"Don't worry. You've still got the thirst comments to keep your ego inflated."

"'Finn can butter my baguette anytime,'" he quoted in a terrible American accent. "That was a real one, by the way."

I snorted.

We were holed up in my apartment in Fort Lauderdale, where we'd hidden away ever since the show started airing. Other than our mandatory public appearances required at the end of the show, we were allowed to do whatever we wanted while the show aired.

And where Bernard, Cameron, and Eli were posting on social media after every episode, asking for fan interaction on their posts and sharing behind-the-scenes photos, Finn and I were completely silent.

There was no use trying to argue our way out of how the show had painted us, anyway.

"I still don't think we should watch this one." I tugged the blanket higher on my lap, eyes on the screen as I prepared for the shit show to unfold. "Episode ten was peak character assassination."

Finn tossed a piece of popcorn in the air and caught it with his mouth, casting me a wink with the feat like he was an Olympian.

I hated that it turned me on.

Everything he did turned me on.

"Aye, but I love watchin' you get feckin' righteous when they cut you dirty. It's like foreplay."

I shot him a look, but it fizzled the second he grinned. Beautiful bastard.

"I just don't think I'm ready to be the villain I know they're about to make me," I said on a sigh.

"Hey," Finn said, reaching over to squeeze my thigh. He set the popcorn aside and pulled me into his lap. "We don't know what they've done yet."

"Judging by the way the rest of the show has been framed, I can damn well guess."

"They didn't even get our kiss on camera. Remember? We were alone."

"Or so we think. We also thought they hadn't caught you with your hand under my bikini top in episode nine, but we were sadly mistaken."

"Well, only one way to find out how bad this gets," Finn said, and then he hit play on the latest episode.

I curled into his side, letting him hold me like he could save me from what the producers had done.

But he couldn't.

And I was right about all of it.

The episode played, picking up from where episode nine had left off with us barely surviving the terrible rainy charter. I was sick just remembering how stressful that whole mess was — especially after the night with Finn on the beach.

"You look fit for someone who got drowned in rain for two days straight," Finn said when it was the scene of me, Leah, and Bernard on screen trying to figure out what to do with casino night.

"I was a wreck inside," I said, unable to even joke back as I folded my arms over my stomach. "All I could think about was the beach night with you."

"And we were thinking two completely different things." Finn shook his head, swallowing as he watched the screen. "I thought you'd received the note I slid under the door explaining that I'd already called everything off with Gi. I thought we were just being professional until the guests were gone."

"You were so fucking happy, it drove me nuts," I said. "Now I know why. You thought we were fine. Meanwhile, I was two seconds away from a breakdown thinking you'd kissed Giselle right after playing with my tits on the beach."

"Sounds like a delightful cocktail, doesn't it?" he teased, pulling me under his arm again and kissing my nose. "Tits on the Beach."

I laughed and burrowed into his side, thankful we were past the shit show even if we had to relive it playing out in half-truths on television.

I bit my lip as the stairwell scene started. There I was, cheeks flushed, voice sharp, calling him "Chef" like it was an insult. There he was, eyes locked on mine, looking like he wanted to eat me alive or fall at my feet and beg for my love.

"God, we were feral," I whispered.

"Speak for yourself. I was calm and professional."

"You slammed the call button on my phone and chased me down the stairs."

"Professional concern."

"Mm-hmm." I reached over him for the bowl of popcorn just so I could throw a piece at him. "Keep lying and I'll feed into all those threads with the hashtag TEAMEMBERLI."

Finn narrowed his gaze before digging his fingers into my ribs, tickling me until I was squealing and begging for relief.

We watched the whole date with me and Eli play out with Finn stiff at my side. And when it came to the bar scene, when I kissed Eli knowing Finn was watching, my stomach did a nosedive.

"Here we go," I said, holding my breath as the cameras showed me and Leah on our way to the bathroom. I didn't miss in the background of the shot what I'd missed in real time — Giselle clinging to Palmer in the back, pulling him somewhere.

I snapped upright. "Hey! Did you see that!"

"I did," Finn said. "But it doesn't look like that's the story the showrunners went with."

He said it just as the cameras went from showing the dance floor chaos to an out-of-focus shot of me and Finn.

In the alley.

"Goddamnit," I said on a sigh, covering my face with the blanket. "I fucking knew it."

"We did have mics on," Finn said.

"Yeah, and you were all *I don't care, let them make me the bad guy.* Now look at us."

"Having regrets?"

I let out my longest sigh yet, screaming into the blanket before I dropped it and turned to face him. "No," I said confidently. "I love you. I'm glad we're here, even if we had to go through hell to make it. I just..."

"It's not fair," he said, pulling me in for a kiss. "I know, Firefly. But just remember that you know who you are. It doesn't matter what picture they paint or what story the public lets the show feed them. None of those people are a part of our lives."

I nodded, leaning into his side.

It still hurt to watch them capture the kiss without any of the nuance, to make it seem like Finn and Gisella were still together, and he was a cheating sack of shit and I was a home-wrecking bitch.

I didn't have to log onto any social media to know those were likely the exact words being used, too.

I barely made it through the end of the episode before I reached for the remote and clicked the television off, rubbing slow circles on my temples to relieve the pressure building in my head.

"Well, that was painful," I said. "But the next episode..."

"It'll be a doozy," Finn said, but he took my hands and squeezed them with assurance I only wish I felt. "But I'll be here with you. I'll be here to remind you of the truth. They can chop and cut and rearrange all they want. People'll believe what they want to believe. But I know you. And so do you." He brushed a thumb along my cheek. "You were never just a storyline to me, Firefly."

My throat tightened.

"Look at me," he requested, waiting until I lifted my eyes to his. "I need you to tell me you understand. Tell me we're okay."

He swallowed. "I already lost you once. I'll be damned if I let some production team edit me out of your life a second time."

I shook my head, already surging forward to wrap my arms around his neck and pull him to me. "They never could."

"Promise me."

"I'm with you."

I kissed him hard, sealing that intention.

"It sucks, I won't lie about that. I don't love what they're doing to us. But I believe just like you do that we know who we are in the end, and that's all that matters."

"It's almost over," Finn said, brushing my hair back. "A few more episodes and a reunion and then we can walk away."

"Start over."

"Write a show of our own."

"God, can we not? In fact, I think I'd like to throw this TV off our balcony at the end of it all and never watch another thing in my life."

Finn chuckled against my next kiss, and then that kiss deepened, his hands gripping me tighter and pulling me back into his lap.

I didn't know where the kiss ended and the need began.

One second we were laughing through the remnants of pain, and the next I was straddling his lap, his mouth warm and familiar and promising against mine. The weight of the episode still lingered in the room — in the way our brows knit when we paused, in the way my hands trembled where they threaded into his hair — but Finn kissed me like he could exorcise it all. Like his lips were an antidote.

My sweatshirt slid over my head and hit the floor in a lazy thud.

"Fuckin' hell," he muttered, eyes dragging over my exposed skin. "You're just... always this bonnie, aren't you?"

I smiled against his neck as I leaned in, kissing the stubble along his jaw. I knew what he meant. It was one thing to undress one another when we were first starting out, horny as hell and desperate for each other. Different again when we reunited, and every touch felt urgent.

But now, we lived together. We woke in the same bed, ate breakfast side by side, brushed our teeth before we crawled back in together later at night.

I reveled in the fact that I got to see him so comfortable, and I found him sexier than ever.

He was already shirtless — had been since halfway through the episode, his hoodie abandoned when the tension got high. I raked my nails down his chest now, mapping out old territory, reacquainting myself with the muscles that always twitched under my touch. His sweatpants did nothing to hide the effect I had on him.

I kissed him again — slow, drugging, tongues sliding with the kind of languid, knowing friction that came from years of history. This wasn't the desperate, wild reunion in the primary suite. This was the slow-perusing tease of two lovers who didn't have to hide anymore.

"I want to taste you," I whispered against his lips.

Finn's exhale was jagged. "Christ, Firefly."

I slid off his lap and tugged at the waistband of his sweats. He helped shimmy them off, then kicked them free with a lazy, open-mouthed kiss to my collarbone. He was already thick and heavy against his stomach, flushed dark and pulsing with need.

But before I could go for him, Finn caught my wrist and tugged me back up.

"You want me to feck that beautiful throat of yours? I will," he said, pulling me down to the floor with him. "But I know that gets you going, love, and I want to taste what I do to you."

I bit my lip as he guided me down with him, rolling onto his back and commanding me to strip for him before he was pulling me up to straddle his chest.

I hovered above him, teasing him with a wiggle of my hips as I bent low enough to press a featherlight kiss to his shaft. It jumped a bit at the touch, and I smiled, peeking over my shoulder at him.

Finn's hands slid up the backs of my thighs to my ass, and he spanked me with just the right force to have me gasp and moan.

"You told me on the boat that I'd never touch you again," he mused, and then the first lash of his tongue had me arching my back, eyes rolling up to the ceiling. "Mmm... so lovely to watch you eat those words now."

"Eat *me*," I shot back.

Finn barked out a laugh, and then granted my wish, his fingers digging into the soft swells of my ass as he pulled my hips down and began to feast.

He licked a slow stripe up my center, then circled his tongue with deliberate pressure, teasing the edges before giving me the full weight of him. I gasped, grinding gently against his face as his arms wrapped around my thighs, locking me in place.

I let myself enjoy the pleasure for a while before I lazily began to return the favor, kissing along his shaft again before I ran my tongue from the base to his tip. I used my hand next, spitting on him and coating him in the wetness. Slowly. Up and down. A little squeeze before I'd release and tease him with the lightest pressure.

He groaned, jerking beneath me, hips flexing up. I knew he wanted more, so I slowed it even farther, ghosting my mouth over him with my fist just barely adding pressure.

Finn was losing himself in the way I touched him. I knew by the way he slowed in his own perusal; in the way his tongue was lazy and his breaths were coming hot and labored against my cunt.

"You alright down there?" I teased, waving my ass in his face.

He smacked it harder than last time. "Sassy wee thing."

Then he redoubled his efforts.

It was a slow, winding build — both of us taking our time, using every trick we'd learned from years of knowing each other's bodies. I flattened my tongue along the top of his cock and hollowed my cheeks, taking him deeper as his groan rattled against my clit.

"Fuck, you're gonna kill me," he muttered into me.

I moaned around him in response, and that almost broke him. He bucked into my mouth, hands gripping my thighs tight enough to bruise. I could feel the tension in his legs, the way his body began to shudder — the quiet surrender that told me he was close.

I wasn't far behind.

He sucked me with slow, precise pulls of his mouth, circling his tongue just right, then flicking it hard and fast until my thighs were trembling. I fought to stay focused, to keep taking him in, but then he hummed low in his throat, and I shattered.

My orgasm crashed over me in waves — a slick, breathless quake that had me crying out around a full mouth of his beautiful cock, hips bucking as he kept licking me through it. And as soon as I came down, he slipped a hand under my belly, tugged me back, and flipped me onto my back in one swift move.

I released his cock with a pop and a pout.

"You didn't finish," I panted.

"I'm about to."

He slid inside me in one smooth, perfect stroke, both of us groaning at the stretch and the aftershocks of pleasure. Finn didn't pound into me. He moved slow — deep, steady rolls of his hips, eyes locked on mine.

It was a claiming. A reassurance. A vow.

"You and me," he whispered.

I nodded, threading my hands around his neck. "You and me."

We moved together like waves in the tide, gentle and relentless, his forehead pressed to mine, and our breath mingled between kisses as he chased his release. I wrapped my legs around him and begged him to fall with me again.

And when he came — low, guttural, buried deep inside me — I held him through it, both of us tangled and spent on the living room floor.

I couldn't help myself.

I rolled onto my side, hand on his chest as we both panted and tried to catch our breaths. "So... think that'll make the highlight reel at the reunion?"

Finn frowned — until I nodded to my phone at the edge of the couch. I'd set it up to record us when he was busy teasing my pussy with that expert tongue of his.

"You didn't just feckin' record that, did ya?"

I nodded, biting my lip.

"Jaysus..." He pulled me into him, shaking his head as he tickled me again. "That's fecking hot, Firefly."

"Think the Internet will agree?"

"Aye, the Internet will not be having a say, because no one will ever watch that video but me."

"And me."

"Maybe together."

"Maybe right now?"

"I'll get the popcorn," Finn said, and then we both laughed as he swatted my ass and I grabbed my phone for the playback.

Read on for a sneak peek of The Wrong Game –
Kandi Steiner's hilarious enemies-to-lovers romance.
Available in bookstores now!

Prologue

GEMMA

This is not the conversation we were supposed to have.

On the drive home, I saw every word that would form. I saw how they would be born, first in my mind and then in my mouth, each one standing strong and brave as it slipped from my lips and landed on his ears.

I knew what I'd say. I knew what he'd say. I had a *plan*.

My particular brand of anxiety was having an ungodly amount of stress over that which I could not control. It'd been this way since I was a young girl, and it'd only worsened with age. I made lists, and plans, and deadlines. I gave myself goals, and when I met them, I celebrated only long enough for me to decide what I would tackle next on the list.

It was all about being in control.

So, unlike a normal woman discovering her husband's infidelity, I did not cry or scream or throw objects across the room when I learned the truth. No, instead, when I found the first sign of his indiscretions, I made a check list. And I checked items off that list with a mixture of both dread and satisfaction.

Perfume that wasn't mine staining his shirt? Check.

Text messages from an unknown number, slipping through the cracks of my husband's technology-ignorant fingers onto our shared computer, but missing from his phone? Check.

Hotel rooms booked on a card I shouldn't have known about, one I only discovered by receiving the statement in our teal mailbox? Check.

We painted that mailbox together, by the way. It was one of the first things on the list I'd made when we bought our house. We'd both been covered in that teal paint — the color I loved so much in the store, but actually rather hated once it was splashed on our mailbox.

But it didn't matter the day we painted that mailbox.

On that day, my husband kissed my paint-splattered lips and told me I was the only woman he would ever love.

And I believed him.

My husband was the kind of man who looked at me so adoringly, who said the sweetest things, that I was *certain* I could have tossed him into a pit of gorgeous super models and he wouldn't have so much as even looked at them, let alone touch them. In fact, he'd be searching for me, calling out my name, seeking me out.

My entire relationship with him, I'd believed every word he'd said — perhaps blindly, it would seem. I believed him when he cried the day he asked me to marry him, and when he told me over breakfast one morning that no one in this world made me happier than him. There was never any reason to suspect him. There was never any reason to not feel safe.

And yet...

The last little box on the list I made when I first suspected my husband was cheating on me was visual proof. I had the clues, the emails and texts, and late nights with no alibi. But it wasn't until I followed him, until I saw with my own eyes that his hands could hold another woman the way he held me, that his mouth could kiss hers, that his smile could beam for someone other than me.

And when that box was checked, I still didn't cry. Or scream. Or throw anything, though I did debate shoving my heel down on the gas pedal of my car and leaving it there as I drove toward where they stood, kissing and laughing, pulling luggage out of my husband's car.

No, instead of letting emotion rule me, I did what I do best. Just like with the rest of my life, I made a plan.

I focused on what I could control.

I could control me, what I would say, what I would do. I could control who I told, how our families would find out, how we would go about the divorce. I could control who got what, how assets were split, and where we each would stay as the signatures were scrawled against cold, lifeless pieces of paper that would end our young marriage.

I could control how I would tell him that I knew, and could temper my emotions as I told him.

Perhaps all of this was why, sitting across the table from my husband, my heart was beating rapidly, loud and thunderous in my ears as it threatened to bang right out of my ribcage. It could have been why my breath was shallow, my eyes dry from not blinking, my mouth clamped shut without a single word to offer, though I had so many planned in my head.

I had a plan. I knew how this conversation would go. I had everything in control.

I know about her. I know what you've done. I'm leaving. We're done.

But my uncanny sense of control and my ability to make a checklist didn't matter once I actually sat down at our kitchen table across from the man who'd lied to me for years.

Because he spoke first.

And everything changed.

"Gem," he rasped, his voice broken under the weight of his words. "Gemma, did you hear me?"

"I heard you," I managed.

My own voice mirrored his, broken and raspy, laced with dread. Of course, he assumed it was because of the blow he'd delivered. My sad-eyed, exhausted husband thought he'd broken my heart with his news. But the truth was my dread was born of a different source. It was simply me mourning the absolute conviction with which I'd believed in my plan and its certain success.

Now, I had no plan.

Now, my cheating husband and his secret lover were not the center of this conversation.

Now, my cheating husband had cancer.

The kind that couldn't be fought.

The kind that would end his life.

Soon.

It's okay, I tried to assure myself, pressing a hand to my chest so I could feel how fast my heart was beating beneath my ribcage. *Just make a new plan.*

But, as it went with my special brand of anxiety, my plans not working out the way I envisioned them often left me grappling. Suddenly, everything I thought I had on a leash was running wild, and no matter how I tried to talk myself down, I couldn't. Every time that happened — every time my plan went wrong — my emotions would win, all logic gone, all sense of what should be done lost like a whisper on a breeze.

"Please," he whispered, grabbing the legs of my chair and pulling me toward him. The wood made a terrible noise as it rubbed against our kitchen floor, sparking a wave of chills from my ankles to the top of my spine. "Don't cry, my sweet gem. It will be okay. We'll be okay."

He wrapped his arm around me, one hand cradling my head into his chest as the other caressed my back. Those hands had touched another woman, and they were now touching me, and I wanted to pull away just as much as I wanted to stay there forever.

He was going to leave me. He was going to leave this world.

My tears felt like they belonged to someone else as they soaked his sweater, and I tried to decipher where they came from. It didn't take long for me to realize they weren't born from one, singular source, but rather from all of them — like a waterfall made of glaciers melting all at once in the first warm wave of spring.

My husband was cheating on me.

He loved another woman — one who did not bear my name.

I would be alone, because I would lose him.

Only now, it wouldn't be because of his infidelity. The choice to be alone would not be made by me standing tall, demanding more, not accepting his affair.

Instead, he would fade from the Earth and I would remain, mourning him along with his other lover.

Maybe I cried because, though I had a plan, I secretly prayed he would thwart it. Perhaps I half-envisioned me leaving him, chin held high as I walked away, and half-envisioned him begging me to stay, promising to relinquish his love affair, for our marriage meant more to him than she ever could.

Regardless, it didn't matter now.

Now, I had a cheating husband who would never learn my knowledge of his infidelity.

Because now, I would never tell him I knew.

What would be the objective? With a blow as hard as terminal cancer, was there really any point to leaving him now, to letting him fight the final weeks of his life alone? Was there any point to telling him I knew about the other woman he touched, other than satisfying *my* need to feel in control, to shove my proof in his face and say *Ha! I know what you did!*?

Death has a funny way of putting life into perspective for us. And what had once been so important to me — that need for vindication I held so tightly on my drive home — didn't seem to matter now. There was really only *one* thing that did.

I loved him.

That emotion was easy to pin down.

And because it was the only thing I could truly grasp, I held onto it tightly, knuckles white and aching. Carlo Mancini was my husband, and I, his wife. He was my everything — and that was still true, regardless of who else he'd shared a bed with.

So, I pulled back from his embrace, and kissed his lips — lips I always thought would be *only* mine to kiss — and I told him I loved him. I told him I was there. I held his hand and told him that, come what may, he had me by his side.

And by his side I stayed, until the very day he died.

Somewhere in that warped, whirling span of time, I think a part of me died, too.

I watched cancer wither my strong, commanding husband into nothing but skin and bones. I watched his eyes grow hollow, his lips ashen, his hands weaken where I held them in mine. Every day that I looked in the mirror, I watched my own eyes change, a hardness settling in. I watched a twenty-nine-year-old girl become an old woman in just weeks — weeks that felt like years, but flew by like days.

And on the day of his funeral, I watched a girl younger and prettier than me mourn him from the back row of our church.

She cried the same tears that I did, though I swore her heart was in more pain than mine. Because she had the satisfaction of being the other woman, of being the one he couldn't live without — so much so that he was willing to risk his marriage, his reputation, his life that he had built. She knew without a doubt that she had been his world, that she had been the last face in his mind before the light was extinguished and he faded off into nothing.

I didn't have that same comfort.

I had casseroles from neighbors and life insurance policies from lawyers and a house full of things that smelled like him. I had a down payment on a condo downtown that I'd secured, thinking I would be walking away from him, away from his infidelity. I had an empty hole in my chest where a young heart used to beat, where love used to grow like flowers, now turned to weeds.

I had a secret to keep, one that would eat me alive every second it dwelled in the dark, unspoken depths of my mind.

And I had a plan.

To preserve control over my future, over my heart, my soul, my well-being, over the life I would lead *after* my husband — I had to eliminate the factors that were uncontrollable. It was just that simple.

And right there, in that first-row pew, with my dead, cheating husband's mother's hand in mine, I made one simple plan, with one simple rule.

Never fall in love again.

It was more than just a plan, more than just a goal. It was a promise.

And it was one I vowed to keep.

More From Kandi Steiner

A Love Letter to Whiskey

Some love stories aren't meant to be easy. They're meant to break you, rebuild you, and burn in your soul forever. This fan-favorite by bestselling author Kandi Steiner is a raw, addictive, and deeply relatable tale of unrequited love, bad timing, and the kind of connection that never fades. It's heartbreakingly honest, utterly intoxicating, and impossible to forget.

The Wrong Game

Gemma's plan is simple: invite a new guy to each home game using her season tickets for her favorite team. But after Zach gets his chance to be her practice round, he decides one game just isn't enough. A sexy, fun sports romance.

The Right Player

She's avoiding love at all costs. He wants nothing more than to lock her down. Sexy, hilarious and swoon-worthy, The Right Player is the perfect read for sports romance lovers.

Acknowledgements

First and foremost, I want to thank my agent, Ariele Fredman, as well as Christine Bendorf and the entire team at Arndell for believing in this story and in me. After eleven years of self-publishing, this is the first time my book will release widely into bookstores everywhere at the same time the eBook releases. It is an absolute dream come true and I am forever grateful for the team who made it happen.

To my husband, Jack – thank you for your constant love and support through this one. Writing this book while also navigating becoming a new mom would have been impossible to do were it not for you. I love you more than all the stars in the sky.

And to Rosie, my sweet baby girl who amazes me daily. It has been an honor being your mother in this first year of your life, and I hope one day you will feel as inspired by me as I am by you.

As always, I must send the warmest thank you to my momma, LaVon Allen. From the time I picked up a pen with a dream to write at the age of nine, you have always cheered me on. And now, as a mother myself, I understand more than ever the sacrifices you made for me. I can never thank you enough, but I'll continue trying. I love you.

To "the weird babes," my ride or die group who always believed I'd be in bookstores everywhere one day even when I wasn't so sure... I love you. Thank you.

A gigantic thank you to my dear friend and executive assistant: Tina Stokes. The Kandi Steiner brand would not function without you and, honestly, neither would I. You are a one of a kind gemstone and I'm so fortunate to have you in my life.

There were many women in this industry who helped me push through the toughest parts of writing Love Overboard. Laura Pavlov, Lena Hendrix, Catherine Cowles, and Staci Hart – thank you for the tough love and encouragement along the way.

Thank you to the crew at OSYS Studios for bringing this book to life in audio and to Hannah Chiclana and Walker Williams for your incredible voice acting.

To my team of beta readers: WOW. You really outdid yourselves with this one, providing thoughtful and instrumental feedback that truly helped make this book shine in the end. A huge and heartfelt thanks to Frances O'Brien, Elizabeth Turner, Allison Cheshire, Kellee Fabre, Janett Corona, Jayce Cruz, Ana López, Carly Wilson, Nicole Westmoreland, Diana Daniel, and Kellie Clarke. I am so happy to have you all on my team.

To the team of readers who came on board from all over the world to help me with character language choice and dialect, thank you for helping me write an authentic representation of these characters who mean so much to me. My sincerest gratitude to Celia Rodriguez, Abigail Pendlebury, London Tunilla, Corinne Mazille, and Ryleigh Sloan.

To the team who helps bring my vision to life: Elaine York with Allusion Graphics, Nicole McCurdy with Emerald Edits, Nina Grinstead, Kim Cermak, the whole team at Valentine PR, Shaye Lefkowitz and Lindsey Romero with Good Girls PR, Isabella Bauer – THANK YOU. From editing and formatting to social media and promotion, it truly takes a village. I'm so thankful for each and every one of you.

Thank you to Ethan, Paloma, and Laurie-Maude with UTA for all you do for me, from foreign deals to administrative support.

And finally, to YOU, the reader. Thank you for picking up my book out of the millions you could have. I am constantly blown away by how you show up for me and by the opportunities you have afforded me. Because of you, I get to write what I love and share it with the world. I will never take that for granted. Thank you for diving into my stories, for sharing them on social media, for leaving reviews, and for championing romance books. Let's connect on your favorite social platform — I'd love to be friends.

About the Author

Kandi Steiner is a USA Today and #1 Amazon Bestselling Author living in Tennessee. Best known for writing "emotional rollercoaster" stories, she loves bringing flawed characters to life and writing about real, raw romance — in all its forms. No two Kandi Steiner books are the same, and if you're a lover of angsty, emotional, and inspirational reads, she's your gal.

An alumna of the University of Central Florida, Kandi graduated with a double major in Creative Writing and Advertising/PR with a minor in Women's Studies. Her love for writing started at the ripe age of 10, and in 6th grade, she wrote and edited her own newspaper and distributed to her classmates. Eventually, the principal caught on and the newspaper was quickly halted, though Kandi tried fighting for her "freedom of press."

She took particular interest in writing romance after college, as she has always been a hopeless romantic and found herself bursting at the seams with love stories she was eager to tell.

When Kandi isn't writing, you can find her reading books of all kinds, planning her next adventure, or pole dancing (yes, you read that right). She enjoys live music, traveling, hiking, yoga, spending quality time with her family (fur babies included) and soaking up the sweetness of life.

Connect With Kandi

✉ NEWSLETTER: geni.us/kandisteinernews

𝐟 FACEBOOK: @kandisteiner

⚓ FACEBOOK READER GROUP (Kandiland):

facebook.com/groups/kandilandks

📷 INSTAGRAM: @kandisteiner

◉ THREADS: @kandisteiner

♪ TIKTOK: @authorkandisteiner

🌐 WEBSITE: kandisteiner.com

Kandi Steiner may be coming to a city near you!

Check out her "events" tab on her website to see all

the signings she's attending in the near future.

Arndell

Connect with Arndell

Love this book? Discover your next romance book obsession and stay up to date with the latest releases, exclusive content, and behind-the-scenes news!

Explore More Books

Visit our homepage: keeperton.com/arndell

Follow Us on Social Media

Instagram: @arndellbooks
Facebook: Arndell
TikTok: @arndellbooks

Stay in the Loop

Join our newsletter: keeperton.com/subscribe

Join the Conversation

Use **#Arndell** or **#ArndellBooks** to share your thoughts and connect with fellow romance readers! Thank you for being part of our book-loving community. We can't wait to share more unforgettable stories with you!